"Sandfor
gut-level

"When i
no peer."

The Republicans are coming to St. Paul for their convention, but crashing the hotel party is a crew of professional thieves looking to take advantage of a weak security system. Lucas Davenport doesn't need this kind of distraction, not when he's about to be hit with something far worse . . .

A while back, a stray bullet put pimp Randy Whitcomb in a wheelchair. Ever since, he's nursed his grudge into a full head of psychotic steam. He blames Davenport, and revenge is going to be sweet. Because Whitcomb has his eye on Davenport's pretty fourteen-year-old daughter.

"[An] amped-up, ultraviolent . . . thriller. A slam-bang shoot-out climax proves that Davenport still has what it takes when it comes to guts and gunplay." —*Publishers Weekly*

"A . . . wham-bam tale." —*St. Louis Post-Dispatch*

"Sandford expertly dramatizes a tug-of-war complicated by two wildcards: Oklahoma neo-Nazi sharpshooter Justice Shafer, who claims he's just passing through, and cranked-up paraplegic Randy Whitcomb, a sociopath determined to wreak vengeance against Lucas . . . Sandford keeps stepping up the pressure." —*Kirkus Reviews*

"*Wicked Prey* . . . never slows down. The story line is fast-paced and filled with plenty of action. John Sandford provides a tense thriller." —*Midwest Book Review*

continued . . .

Praise for John Sandford's Prey Novels

"Relentlessly swift . . . genuinely suspenseful . . . excellent."
—*Los Angeles Times*

"Sandford is a writer in control of his craft."
—*Chicago Sun-Times*

"Excellent . . . compelling . . . everything works."
—*USA Today*

"Grip-you-by-the-throat thrills . . . a hell of a ride."
—*Houston Chronicle*

"Crackling, page-turning tension . . . great scary fun."
—*New York Daily News*

"Enough pulse-pounding, page-turning excitement to keep you up way past bedtime." —*Minneapolis Star Tribune*

"One of the most engaging characters in contemporary fiction." —*The Detroit News*

"Positively chilling." —*St. Petersburg Times*

"Just right for fans of *The Silence of the Lambs*."
—*Booklist*

"One of the most horrible villains this side of Hannibal."
—*Richmond Times-Dispatch*

"Ice-pick chills . . . excruciatingly tense . . . a double-pumped roundhouse of a thriller." —*Kirkus Reviews*

TITLES BY JOHN SANDFORD

Rules of Prey
Shadow Prey
Eyes of Prey
Silent Prey
Winter Prey
Night Prey
Mind Prey
Sudden Prey
Secret Prey
Certain Prey
Easy Prey
Chosen Prey
Mortal Prey
Naked Prey
Hidden Prey
Broken Prey
Invisible Prey
Phantom Prey
Wicked Prey

The Night Crew
Dead Watch

KIDD NOVELS

The Fool's Run
The Empress File
The Devil's Code
The Hanged Man's Song

VIRGIL FLOWERS NOVELS

Dark of the Moon
Heat Lightning

WICKED PREY

John Sandford

BERKLEY BOOKS, NEW YORK

THE BERKLEY PUBLISHING GROUP
Published by the Penguin Group
Penguin Group (USA) Inc.
375 Hudson Street, New York, New York 10014, USA
Penguin Group (Canada), 90 Eglinton Avenue East, Suite 700, Toronto, Ontario M4P 2Y3, Canada
(a division of Pearson Penguin Canada Inc.)
Penguin Books Ltd., 80 Strand, London WC2R 0RL, England
Penguin Group Ireland, 25 St. Stephen's Green, Dublin 2, Ireland (a division of Penguin Books Ltd.)
Penguin Group (Australia), 250 Camberwell Road, Camberwell, Victoria 3124, Australia
(a division of Pearson Australia Group Pty. Ltd.)
Penguin Books India Pvt. Ltd., 11 Community Centre, Panchsheel Park, New Delhi—110 017, India
Penguin Group (NZ), 67 Apollo Drive, Rosedale, North Shore 0632, New Zealand
(a division of Pearson New Zealand Ltd.)
Penguin Books (South Africa) (Pty.) Ltd., 24 Sturdee Avenue, Rosebank, Johannesburg 2196,
South Africa

Penguin Books Ltd., Registered Offices: 80 Strand, London WC2R 0RL, England

WICKED PREY

A Berkley Book / published by arrangement with the author

PRINTING HISTORY
G. P. Putnam's Sons hardcover edition / May 2009
Berkley international edition / May 2010

For information, address: The Berkley Publishing Group,
a division of Penguin Group (USA) Inc.,
375 Hudson Street, New York, New York 10014.

ISBN: 978-0-425-23533-1

BERKLEY®
Berkley Books are published by The Berkley Publishing Group,
a division of Penguin Group (USA) Inc.,
375 Hudson Street, New York, New York 10014.
BERKLEY® is a registered trademark of Penguin Group (USA) Inc.
The "B" design is a trademark of Penguin Group (USA) Inc.

PRINTED IN THE UNITED STATES OF AMERICA

10 9 8 7 6 5 4 3 2 1

To Mom

1

RANDY WHITCOMB WAS a human stinkpot, a red-haired cripple with a permanent cloud over his head; a gap-toothed, pock-faced, paraplegic crank freak, six weeks out of the Lino Lakes medium-security prison. He hurtled past the luggage carousels at Minneapolis–St. Paul International Airport, pumping the wheels of his cheap nonmotorized state-bought wheelchair, his coarse red hair a wild halo around his head.

"Get out of the way, you little motherfucker," he snarled at a blond child of three or four years. He zipped past the gawking mother and tired travelers and nearly across the elegant cordovan shoe tips of a tall bearded man. "Out of the way, fuckhead," and he was through the door, the anger streaming behind him like coal smoke from a power plant.

The bearded man with the elegant cordovan shoes, which came from a shop on Jermyn Street in London, leaned close to his companion, a dark-haired woman who wore blue jeans and a black blouse, running shoes, and cheap oversized sunglasses with unfashionable plastic rims. He said, quietly, in a cool Alabama accent, "If we see yon bugger again, remind me to crack his skinny handicapped neck."

The woman smiled and said, "Yon bugger? You were in England *way* too long."

Brutus Cohn, traveling under the passport name of John Lamb, tracked the wheelchair down the sidewalk. There was no humor in his cold blue eyes. "Aye, I was that," he said. "But now I'm back."

Cohn and the woman, who called herself Rosie Cruz, walked underground to the short-term parking structure, trailing Cohn's single piece of wheeled luggage. As they went out the door, the heat hit them like a hand in the face. Not as bad as Alabama heat, but dense, and sticky, smelling of burned transmission fluid, spoiled fruit, and bubble gum. Cruz pushed the trunk button on the remote key and the taillights blinked on a beige Toyota Camry.

"Ugly car," he said, as he lifted the suitcase into the trunk. Cohn disliked ugly cars, ugly clothes, ugly houses.

"The best-selling car in America, in the least attention-getting color," Cruz said. She was a good-looking woman of no particularly identifiable age, who'd taken care to make herself mousy. She wore no makeup, had done nothing with her hair.

Cohn had once seen her in Dallas, where women dressed up, and she'd astonished him with her authentic Texas vibe: moderately big hair, modestly big lipstick, two-inch heels, stockings with seams down the back; her twice-great-grand-uncle might have died at the Alamo. Cruz, when working, dressed for invisibility. She fit in Dallas, she fit in Minnesota, she fit wherever they worked—she was wallpaper, she was background. She took the driver's side, and he sat on the passenger side, fiddling with the seat controls to push it all the way back. At six-foot-six, he needed the legroom.

"Give me your passport and documents," Cruz said, when the air conditioning was going.

He took a wallet out of his breast pocket and handed it

over. Inside were a hundred pounds, fifty euros, fifty dollars, an American passport, a New York State driver's license, two credit cards, a building security card with a magnetic strip, and a variety of wallet detritus.

The whole lot, except for the passport and currency, had been taken from the home of the real John Lamb by his building superintendent, who was a crook. Since the credit cards would never be used, no one would be the wiser. The passport had been more complicated, but not too—a stand-in had applied by mail, submitting a photograph of Cohn, and when it came to Lamb's apartment, it had been stolen from the mailbox. As long as the real Lamb didn't apply for another one, they were good.

Cruz took out the currency and handed it back to Cohn, tucked the wallet under the car seat and handed over another one, thick with cash. "William Joseph Wakefield—Billy Joe. Everything's real, except the picture on the driver's license. Don't use the credit cards unless it's an emergency."

"Billy Joe." Cohn thumbed through the cash. "Two thousand dollars. Three nights at a decent hotel."

"We're not staying at a decent hotel," Cruz said. She reached into the backseat, picked up a baseball cap with a Minnesota Twins logo, and said, "Put this on and pull it down over your eyes."

He did, and with his careful British suit, it made him look a bit foolish. She wouldn't have given it to him without a reason, so he put it on, and asked, "Where're we set up?"

She backed carefully out of the parking space and turned for the exit. "At the HomTel in Hudson, Wisconsin, just across the state line from here. Thirty miles. Two hundred and twenty dollars a night, for two rooms for you, adjoining, which is twice as much as they're worth, but with the convention in town, you get what you can. I'm upstairs and on the other side of the motel."

"Where're the boys?"

"Jesse's across the street at the Windmill, Tate is at the Cross Motel, Jack is at a mom-and-pop called Wakefield

Inn, all in Hudson. All within easy walking distance from the HomTel." Multiple nearby rooms in different hotels made it easier to get together, and also easier to find an emergency hideout if the cops made one or another of them. They could be off the street in minutes, in a motel where they'd never been seen by the management.

Standard operating procedure, worked out and talked over in prisons across the country. Cohn nodded and said, "Okay."

"I almost went home when you invited Jack back in," Cruz said, threading her way through the concrete pillars of the parking ramp.

"Better to have him inside the tent pissin' out than outside the tent pissin' in," Cohn said.

"I don't know what that means," she said.

"It means that when he gets picked up—and I do mean *when*, it's only a matter of time—he'll try to cut a deal," Cohn said. "We're one of the things he's got. I need to talk to him."

"He'd cut a deal whatever we do."

"No. Not really. I've thought on that," he said, in an accent that spoke of the deep southern part of Yorkshire. "There are circumstances in which he would not cut a deal, no matter what the coppers might have offered to him."

"You've got to lose that bullshit British syntax, right *now*," Cruz said. "You're Billy Joe Wakefield from Birmingham, Alabama. You need khakis and golf shirts."

"Give me two minutes listening to country music," Cohn said. "That'll get 'er done."

"Anyway, about *Jack* . . ."

"Let it go," he said. "I'll take care of Jack."

"Okay," she said. "Put your sunglasses on."

At seven o'clock, the sky was still bright. Cohn took a pair of wraparound sunglasses from his jacket pocket and slipped them on. At the pay booth, Cruz dropped the window and handed ten dollars to a Somali woman in a shawl. Cruz got the change from the ten, and a receipt, rolled the window back up, pulled away from the booth, and handed the receipt to Cohn.

"Check it out," she said.

He looked at the receipt, said, "Huh. The tag number's on it."

"There's a scanning camera at the entrance," Cruz said. "I'm wondering if it might digitize faces at the same time that it picks up the license plates—hook them together, then run them through a facial recognition program."

"Would that be a problem?"

"Not as long as somebody doesn't put your face in the car with your face in the FBI files," she said. "That's not a question with me, of course."

"Got the beard, now," he said. "And the hat and glasses. I cut the beard off square to give my chin a different line. I was wondering about the baseball hat . . ."

They rode along for a minute or two, as she got off the airport and headed into St. Paul, past the confluence of the Minnesota and Mississippi rivers. Even in the middle of a big urban area, the river valleys had a wildness that reminded him of home in Alabama. In Britain, even the wild areas had a groomed look.

"Jack, I can't get him off my mind. I'm sorry . . ."

"Never mind Jack." He was looking out the window. "You almost went home, huh? That'd be . . . Zihuatanejo?"

"Never been to Mexico in my life, Brute," she said with a grin. "Give it up."

"With a name like Cruz, you gotta have been in Mexico."

Her eyes flicked to him. "Why would you think my name is Cruz?"

He laughed and said, "Okay." But she looked like a Cruz.

She clicked on the radio, dialed around, found a country station. "Instead of worrying about where I'm from, see if you can get the Alabama accent going."

The first song up was Sawyer Brown singing "Some

Girls Do," and Cohn sang along with it, all the way to the end, and then shouted, "Jesus Christ, it's good to be back in the States. The United Kingdom of Great Britain and North Ireland can go fuck itself."

RANDY WHITCOMB, JULIET Briar, and a man whose real name might have been Dick, but who called himself Ranch, lived in a rotting wooden house on the east side of St. Paul that sat above a large hole in the ground called Swede Hollow; once full of houses full of Swedes, the hole was now a neglected public park.

Whitcomb was a pimp. He'd become a pimp as soon as he could, after his parents had thrown him out of the house twelve years earlier. He liked the idea of being a pimp, and he liked TV shows that featured pimps and pimp-wannabes, and his finest dream was to own a Mercedes-Benz R-Class pimpmobile in emerald green. He enjoyed the infliction of pain, as long as he wasn't the object of it.

Briar was his only employee.

She was a heavy young woman in a shapeless gray dress, her hair the sad tatters of a curly perm gone old. She sat half-crouched over the steering wheel of Whitcomb's handicapped van, and alternately chirped brightly about the sights on the street and sobbed, pressing her knuckles to her teeth, fearing for what was coming. What was coming, she thought, would be a whipping from Whitcomb, with his whipping stick.

He'd broken the stick out of a lilac hedge a block from their house. A sucker, looking for light, the branch had grown long and leggy, an inch thick at the butt, tapering to an eighth of an inch at the tip. Whitcomb had stripped the bark off with a penknife; the switch sat, white and naked, spotted here and there with blood, in the corner of the room next to his La-Z-Boy chair.

He'd beaten her with it three times over the summer, when her performance had sagged below his standards.

He liked the work. He couldn't stand up, so he made her drop on the floor like a dog, on her hands and knees, while he sat on his chair and whipped her with the switch. The thing was limber enough that it didn't break bone—he wouldn't have cared, except that broken bones would have kept her from waiting on him—but it did maul her skin. So she laughed and chirped and pointed and giggled and then sobbed, the fear rising in her throat as they got closer to the house.

They couldn't afford a van equipped for handicapped drivers, and Whitcomb hadn't been trained on one anyway. They did get one with a hydraulic ramp, bought used and cheap through CurbCut, a St. Paul charity. At the house, Briar parked next to a wooden ramp built by Make a House a Home, and Whitcomb dropped the ramp and rolled out of the van, used the remote to retract the ramp and close the van door. He hadn't spoken a word since the airport, but his breath was coming in fast chuffs.

Whitcomb was getting himself excited, though, of course, nothing would come of it. He'd taken the bullet low in the spine, and he'd not have another erection in this life.

Now he spoke: "Inside."

"The light's on," Briar said. She stopped. She was sure she'd turned the lights off as they left. "I turned them off."

She was stalling, Whitcomb thought. "Ranch must be up."

"Ranch is *not* up."

Stalling. The crazy bitch had got the flight wrong, and now a pharmaceutical salesman was wondering why he couldn't find his sample case, and somebody else was wondering why a green nylon bag was going round and round on a baggage carousel somewhere else. Eventually they'd look in it, and find the sample case, and put two and two together, and the whole goddamn racket could come down around their ears. She was stalling.

"In the house," he said.

"The light . . ."

He shouted at her now: "Get in the fuckin' house . . ."

She turned and climbed the ramp, unlocked the door and pushed inside, holding the door for him, and he bumped over the doorjamb and turned toward the living room and accelerated. Moving too fast to turn back. And there were the Pollish twins, Dubuque and Moline, sitting on the couch, big bulky black men with cornrowed hair, drop-crotch jeans, and wife-beater shirts.

Ranch was lying in a corner on a futon, facedown, mouth open, a white stain under his chin, breathing heavily.

Moline had one of Whitcomb's beers in one hand and a piece-of-shit .22 in the other. The twins were managers in the sexual entertainment industry, and were known around the St. Paul railroad tracks as Shit and Shinola, because stupid people found them hard to tell apart. The cops and the smarter street people knew that Dubuque had lost part of his left ear in a leveraged buyout on University Avenue. Moline pointed the gun at Whitcomb's head and said, "Tell me why I shouldn't shoot you in the motherfuckin' head."

"What are you talking about?" Whitcomb asked. "What are you doing in my house?" He rolled across the room to Ranch and jammed the foot-plate on the wheelchair hard into Ranch's ribs: "You alive?"

Ranch groaned, twitched away from the pain. The door slammed in the kitchen. Dubuque jumped and asked, "What was that?"

"Woman runnin' for the cops," Whitcomb said. "She knows who you are. You're fucked."

Moline looked at the front door, then asked, "Why you running Jasmine down my street?"

"Jasmine?" Whitcomb sneered at him. "I ain't seen her in two weeks. She's running with Jorgenson."

"Jorgenson? You pullin' my dick," Moline said.

"Am not," Whitcomb said. "Juliet's all I got left. Jasmine got pissed because I whacked her lazy ass with my stick, and she snuck out of here with her clothes. The next thing

I hear, she's working for Jorgenson. If I find her, she's gonna have a new set of lips up her cheek."

Dubuque said to Moline, casually, "He lying to us."

"Juliet knows us, though," Moline said. He was the thinker of the two.

"I'm not lying," Whitcomb said.

Moline stood up, pulled up his shirt, stuck the .22 under his belt and said, "Get the door, bro."

Whitcomb figured he was good: "The next time you motherfuckers come back here . . ."

Dubuque was at the front door, which led out to the front porch, which Whitcomb never used because of the six steps down to the front lawn.

"We come back here again, they gonna find your brains all over the wall," Moline said, and with two big steps, he'd walked around Whitcomb's chair, and Moline was a large man, and he grabbed the handles on the back and started running before Whitcomb could react, and Dubuque held the door and Whitcomb banged across the front porch and went screaming down the steps, his bones banging around like silverware in a wooden box.

The whole crash actually took a second or two, and he wildly tried to control it, but the wheels were spinning too fast, and there was never any hope, and he pitched forward and skidded face-first down the sidewalk, his legs slack behind him like a couple of extra-long socks.

Moline bent over him. "Next time, we ain't playing no patty-cake."

Juliet showed up three or four minutes later, crying, "Oh, God, oh, God. Are you all right, honey? Are you all right? The cops are coming . . ."

Whitcomb had managed to roll onto his back. Most of the skin was gone from his nose, and he was bleeding from scrapes on his hands and forearms and belly.

He started to weep, slapping at his legs. He couldn't help himself, and it added to the humiliation. "Davenport did this to me," he said. "That fuckin' Davenport . . ."

BRUTUS COHN DIDN'T have much to unload. He tossed his suitcase on the motel bed and said, "I need to take a walk—haven't been able to walk since I got on the train in York. You get the guys together. See you in a half hour."

Cruz nodded and picked up a pen from the nightstand and handed it to him: "Write my room number in your palm. Remember it."

Cohn wrote the number in his palm and Cruz led the way out, and he said, "See you in a bit, babe," and gave her a little pat on the ass. She didn't mind, because that was just Cohn being Cohn, no offense meant.

So Cohn took a walk, looking up and down the street. They'd gotten off at Exit 2 in Wisconsin, a major fast-food and franchise intersection outside the built-up part of the metro area.

From the front of the motel, straight ahead, he could see a Taco Bell, which made his mouth water, and a McDonald's, both a block or two away. Closer, an Arby's, a Country Kitchen, a Burger King, and a Denny's. To his right, across the main street off the interstate, a Buffalo Wings, a Starbucks, a Chipotle, and a couple of stores. To his left, a supermarket, a liquor store, some clothing stores, a buffet restaurant. Behind the hotel, to the left, a Home Depot.

Excellent. He needed fuel, liquor, and a hardware store, and here it all was.

He hit the Taco Bell first and got a Grilled Stuft Burrito with chicken; while he ate, he read the *Star Tribune* about the Republican convention. The paper was just short of hysterical, which was good. The more confusion, the more cops doing street security, the better. Besides, he was a political conservative and wished John McCain well. He liked the thought of a bunch of little anarchist assholes getting beat up by the cops.

Out of the Taco Bell, he stopped at the supermarket, got

some apples, one doughnut, and three Pepsis. He picked up a bottle of George Dickel at the liquor store, then carried the whole load down to Home Depot, where he bought a box of contractor's clean-up bags and a crescent wrench, the biggest one he could find.

"Big wrench," said the cute little blonde at the checkout.

He gave her a twinkle: "I gotta big nut to deal with," he said.

She giggled, seeing in the comment a double entendre of some kind, which may or may not have existed, Cohn thought, as he walked back to the motel with his bags.

SO THE GANG was back in town.

Jesse Lane was a white man with dirty-blond hair that fell on his shoulders, a thick face with eyes too closely spaced, a bony nose marked by enlarged pores, and thin, pale-pink lips. A handmade silver earring, big as a wedding ring, hung from his left earlobe. Fifteen years earlier he'd done time in an Alabama prison, for armed robbery, where he picked up the weight-lifting habit. He was still a lifter, and showed it in the width of his shoulders and his narrow, tapered waist.

Lane owned a farm in Tennessee, on the 'Bama border, where he grew soybeans and worked on cars in a shop in the barn. His specialty was turning run-of-the-mill family vehicles into machines that could flat outrun the highway patrol—not for crooks, but just the everyday *Dukes of Hazzard* wannabes.

Tate McCall was a black version of Jesse Lane. He'd done a total of ten years in California, both sets for robbery, but had been clean for eight years. Like Lane, he'd been a lifter, but where Lane was square, McCall was tall and rangy, like a wide receiver, with hands the size of dinner plates. McCall owned a piece of a diner on Main Street in Ocean Park, a neighborhood in Santa Monica.

Jack Spitzer was from Austin, Texas. He looked like a big-nosed French bicycle racer, or a runner, mid-height but greyhound-thin, his thinning black hair slicked back on his small head. His nose had been broken sometime in the past. He was mostly unemployed.

Lane was sitting at the computer desk, McCall was draped over an easy chair, Spitzer sat on a bed, more or less facing the other two. Lane and McCall were wearing golf shirts and slacks, while Spitzer wore a short-sleeved dress shirt and a black sport coat, because, all the others thought, he was carrying a pistol in the small of his back, the dumb shit.

Rosie Cruz came through the door that connected Cohn's two rooms and said, "He's coming."

"Nothing around here to see but chain restaurants," McCall said.

"How'd you know?" Cruz asked.

"I looked," McCall said. "While you were pickin' up Brute."

"And that's what Brute's doing—looking," she said. "You know what he's like."

"We gotta get this shit straightened out," McCall said, looking at Spitzer.

Spitzer said, defensively, "I'll do whatever Brute says."

"Goddamn right," Lane said.

THEY ALL SAT, waiting, the television on but muted, a CNN chick soundlessly running her mouth with a forest fire on a screen behind her head. A minute or two, then a key rattled in the door lock, and Cohn came in. He was wearing tan golf slacks, a red golf shirt, and a blue blazer, carrying a grocery bag and a plastic sack. He looked like a city manager on his day off.

He saw them and flashed his smile, genuinely happy to see them, and they knew it. He shut the door and said, "Boys. Damned good to see you. Jesse. Tate. Jack . . ." He stepped through the room, shaking hands, slapping shoulders. Cruz was leaning in the doorway to the second room, watching.

Lane said, "Man, you're looking good. I like that beard."

"Yeah, yeah," Cohn said, scratching at the beard. "Let me run down the hall and get some ice."

He picked up the ice bucket, went out, and was back in a minute with a bucket of ice cubes.

"Got some Dickel," he said. "I been drinking nothing but scotch and gin, and it's good, but it ain't bourbon."

McCall said, "We got some shit to figure out." He looked at Spitzer.

"All right," Cohn said. "Let's get it out." He found a glass, scooped some ice into it, and poured in a couple of ounces of bourbon. "I think we agree that Jack sorta screwed the pooch the last time out." He took a sip of the drink and closed his eyes and smiled: "That's smooth."

"Screwed the pooch? He signed us up for death row," Lane said. "Wasn't no point in shooting those boys."

"Accident," Spitzer said. "Goddamn one in a million. I thought he was coming for me. What the fuck was I supposed to do? Once he was down, I had to do the other one."

"They were cops," McCall said.

"Jack's right, though. After the first one went down, he had to do the second," Cohn said. He was standing next to Spitzer, one hand on his shoulder, drink in the other hand.

McCall said, "Brute, you know I like working with you. You got a class act. But this asshole . . ."

Spitzer turned his head toward McCall and away from Cohn. When he did that, Cohn put the drink down, pulled the eighteen-inch-long crescent wrench from his back pocket, cocked his wrist, and slammed it into the back of Spitzer's head. Spitzer jerked forward, his face suddenly blank, eyes wide, and fell on the floor.

Cruz said, urgently, "No, no, Brute . . ."

"Go in that other room," Cohn said.

"Brute . . ." She didn't move.

Cohn ignored her, went to a closet alcove with a dozen wire coat hangers on a rod. He'd already unwrapped one of them and he took it down, carried it back to Spitzer's body. Spitzer was out, and maybe dying, but making low growling sounds. Cohn bent the coat hanger around Spitzer's neck, put his knee down hard on the unconscious man's spine, and pulled up on the wire until it cut halfway through his neck. His teeth bared with the effort, he did a quick twist of the wire, turning it around itself. Spitzer stopped making any sound, though a minute later, his feet began to tremble and run as his brain died.

Cohn looked at McCall and Lane and said, "Sooner or later, he'd have given us up. He didn't have a job, like you boys. He was on the street. Sooner or later, he was going to get caught, and then he was gonna cut a deal. We were nothing but money in the bank, to him."

They all looked at the body for a minute, then Cruz said, "You should have told me what you were going to do."

"Didn't know how you'd react," Cohn said, in apology. "I'm sorry if this offends you."

"That's not what I meant," Cruz said. "What I mean was, if you'd told me, I'd have figured out a better place to do it. He's bleeding, ah, for Christ's sakes, if they find blood in the carpet . . ."

She took three long steps to the closet niche, snatched a HomTel plastic laundry bag off a hanger, and as the men watched, bent over Spitzer's body, lifted his head by the hair on the back of his skull, and pulled the bag over his head. Then she tugged the head to one side and said, "The carpet's okay. Goddamnit, Brute, try thinking about consequences once in a while."

Cohn was embarrassed and shrugged, and said, "Sorry, babe."

"Go wash that wrench. We'll throw it out the car window somewhere," she said. "And don't call me babe."

McCall looked at Lane, who shrugged. "Be good if nobody found out about this for a while."

"We'll take him out in the woods and bury his ass," Cohn said. "When I was buying the wrench, I bought some garbage bags at Home Depot. We can pick up a shovel on the way out."

They looked down at the body, and Cruz said, finally, "Four guys would have been better."

Cohn grinned at her: "You'll just have to carry a gun yourself, darling."

She shook her head. "I need to be outside. If I'm not outside, I can't manage the radios and all the other stuff. Three is okay, four would be better. I don't know how many people we'll be handling."

Cohn looked at Lane. "How about your brother?"

Lane shook his head. "We can't go on the same job. You know, so there'll be somebody to take care of the families, if something happens."

McCall asked, "You remember Bob Mortenson from Fresno?"

Cohn nodded.

"He had a wheelman named Steve Sargent, he was in Chino until last year. He got caught on a jewelry deal that broke down in L.A. after Mortenson quit. I know him, some, he's careful, he can keep his mouth shut. If we needed him . . ."

"We'll talk about it," Cohn said. "But I'd rather not work with someone new. Look what happened when we brought in this piece of shit." He prodded Spitzer's body with the toe of his shoe. "We'll work it with Rosie, see if we can do it with three. What happened with Mortenson? I haven't heard about him in years."

"He retired. He's in Hawaii," McCall said. "Got a place there. Goes fishing a lot. Plays golf."

"That's what we're talking about," Cohn said, the enthusiasm lighting his eyes. "That's what this job'll do for us.

Rosie says this should be large: we pull this off, we're all done."

Lane levered himself to his feet. "In the meantime, we gotta get rid of Jack," he said.

"You're the farm boy," McCall said. "You know about the woods. I'm city, man. I'm scared of them bears and shit. Wolves."

A bad smell was coming from the body—flatulence, emptying lungs, or maybe death itself. Cruz said, "We need to get some air freshener. Some pine scent, that's what the motel uses."

Lane said to Cohn, "You know, even if we weren't here for a job, Jack would have been worth doing. I feel a hundred percent safer already."

McCall said to Cohn, "If you got that garbage bag . . ."

But then Lane asked Cruz, "What're we gonna hit, anyway? You never said."

"Not one hit," she said. "Maybe six or eight."

Lane and McCall stared at her for a second, and Cohn said, "She'll tell you all about it—but let's get rid of Jack and she can lay it all out."

"Just give me one minute of it, right now," Lane said. "Not the details, just the outline."

Cruz said, "There are two parts to the deal, but they're not really connected. The Republican convention is starting, and the people who run the party down at the street level are here, as delegates and spectators. So these big lobby guys come in with suitcases full of cash, and pass it out, expense money. They call it street money, hire guys to put up signs and all that, off the books. Everybody knows about it, nobody tells. Can't tell, because it's illegal. I've got the names and hotel rooms for seven of them. They could have anywhere from a quarter-million to a million dollars, each. We hit them until we feel nervous. We'll have to feel it out as we go, but three or four guys anyway. Five, maybe? We'll see. Look for reaction on TV, watch the targets, see if they get bodyguards, whatever."

"Who watches them?" Lane asked.

"I do, basically. I've got a file on each of them," Cruz said. "They're schmoozers, they want to make sure they get the credit for the cash they're handing out, they'll be hooking up with people all the time."

"You're going into the convention?" McCall asked.

"No. Neither will these guys. The security is super-tight and they don't want to get caught with a hundred thousand in small bills," Cruz said. "So they do the business at the hotels. Two of the guys are thirty seconds apart in the same hotel; we can do them both at the same time—and they're two of the biggest money guys. The third guy and the fourth guy we'll have to check. If we see any reaction from the cops, we quit and go on to the second part."

"Which is?" Lane asked.

"A hotel job. The night McCain gets nominated there's a big ball at the St. Andrews Hotel downtown. We hit the strong room afterwards. Three in the morning. I'm thinking twenty million in jewelry, maybe a million or two in cash."

"You got a guy inside?" McCall asked.

"Had one. A guy in Washington. Worked for the committee that sets up room assignments."

"What about at the hotel?"

"I couldn't find anybody there that I could risk recruiting," Cruz said. "The Secret Service is all over the place. I stayed there a couple of times, a week at a time, did a lot of scouting . . . put my stuff in a safe-deposit box. I've been in and out of the strong room a half dozen times. I know the hotel, top to bottom."

"Lot of people coming and going in a hotel," Lane said.

"That can be handled," Cruz said. "There's no more risk than an armored car or a bank. And I'm working a little thing that'll keep the cops occupied while we're inside."

Nobody said anything for a moment, and she added, "Guys, this is it: this is one where we all get out. If we get two million from the political guys and a million from the hotel and twenty million in diamonds, that'd be another seven or eight in cash—and we'll get at least that, I swear to God—we can quit. Shake hands and walk."

They'd worked with her on a dozen jobs and she'd never been wrong. And they'd talked about quitting. Lane had a family, McCall had a longtime lover, Cohn was getting old, Cruz was getting nervous. Past time to quit. Lane and McCall glanced at each other again, McCall tipped his head and said, "All right; we can get the details later. Right now, we need those white-trash bags."

RANDY WHITCOMB, STRAPPED into the back of the van, with Juliet Briar at the wheel, Ranch sitting in a fog layer in the passenger seat, rolled past Lucas Davenport's house every few minutes, until they saw the girl getting out of a private car. She waved at the driver and headed up the driveway to Davenport's house. She was a rangy blond teenager, dressed conservatively in dark slacks, a white blouse, and sandals.

"Maybe a babysitter," Ranch said.

"She's got a key," Briar pointed out. "They don't give keys to babysitters."

"Then it's gotta be his daughter," Whitcomb said. "Too young for him to be fuckin'. Daughter'd be good."

"Never done anything to us," Juliet said doubtfully.

"*Davenport* did *this* to me," Whitcomb said, whacking his inert legs. "Set it up. Started it all."

"The girl didn't . . ."

"Davenport set me up," Whitcomb said. He watched the girl disappear into the house. "I'm gonna get him back. No fun just shootin' *him*. I want to do him good, and I want him to *know* what I done, and who done it. Motherfucker."

"Motherfucker," Ranch said, and the word made him giggle, and then he couldn't stop giggling, even when Whitcomb started screaming, "Shut up, shut up, you fuckin' scrote." He didn't mention it, but he was also frightened of Davenport, who he thought was crazy.

They went back to the house, Ranch trying to suppress the urge to laugh, but cloudbursts of giggles broke through anyway.

Because Ranch *was* crazy.

2

LUCAS DAVENPORT ROLLED in his Porsche through the August countryside, green and tan, corn and beans, the blue oat fields falling in front of the John Deeres, weeping willows hanging over the banks of black-water ponds, yellow coneflowers climbing the sides of the road-cuts, Wisconsin farms with U-Pick signs hung out on the driveways, Dutch Belted cows and golden horses and red barns, Lucas's arms prickling from sunburn . . .

One of the finest summers of his life.

His wife, Weather, dozed beside him, despite the gravelly ride of the car. She'd tuned to a public radio station before she'd gone to sleep, and it was playing something by Mozart or one of those big guys, and the sound floated around them like the soundtrack in a chick flick.

Weather's nose was burned and would be peeling; so were her stomach and her thighs. Twenty minutes, she said, only twenty minutes, lying back in a two-piece bathing suit, on the front deck of Lucas's boat. She'd known better, but she'd done it anyway.

Twenty minutes was all it took. Lucas grinned at the thought of it: she was cooked. Because she was almost constitutionally unable to admit error, she wouldn't even be able to complain about it.

He idled through Hammond, up the hill past the golf course, down the hill past the high school, the small-town boys out on the football field, turning at the burble of the car's exhaust to look at the Porsche; and then on down County T to I-94, where he made the turn toward the Cities in the evening's dying light.

They'd spent two days at their lake cabin outside Hayward, hiding out. Two weeks before, one of Lucas's agents, Virgil Flowers, had arrested two Homeland Security officials for conspiracy to commit murder.

The shit hit the fan with all the expected velocity. The governor and his chief weasel were handling it—had asked for it. The arrest was as political as legal, although the big newspapers, the New York and L.A. and even the London *Times*, the *Washington Post*, the *Boston Globe*, said the legal looked fairly strong. Of course, it was hard to tell whether the papers were serious, or just fucking with George Bush.

The governor was definitely fucking with George Bush, since the Republican National Convention was in town the next week.

In any case, Lucas took two days at the lake to avoid the growing siege of phone calls, while Virgil went fishing in northern Minnesota, and the governor continued to make the rounds of the Washington talk shows. They'd watched him on satellite and Weather had been delighted. She'd once had a favored pair of manicure scissors seized by the TSA, and as far as she was concerned, this was payback time.

Now Weather woke up and groaned and said, "Ah, God, where are we?"

"I-94. Six miles from the river," Lucas said.

"Mmm." She fumbled around for her purse, took out her BlackBerry and punched it up, stared at the screen for a moment, then put it back in her purse. "Nothing from anybody . . . I can't believe you're listening to Chopin."

"Well, no phone calls means that everything's okay," Lucas said. Weather hadn't wanted to leave Sam, their son, though he was almost two, and they had a live-in housekeeper who was like a second mother to the kid. Still, she was anxious about it: she'd never been away from him for more than eight or ten hours, and wanted to get back.

"You feeling a little pink?" Lucas asked.

"What?"

"Sunburned?"

"Oh, not really," she said. "It's nothing."

He laughed and said, "Bullshit—you're toast."

She said, "Check your phone. See if Ellen called."

Ellen was the housekeeper. He fished out the phone, opened it, turned it on: three messages, all from the same guy. "Dan Jacobs," he said. "Nothing from Ellen."

"Too late to call him tonight," Weather said.

"He called three times . . . last time was twenty minutes ago . . . he'll be working twenty-four hours a day now."

He punched redial and waited. Jacobs ran the convention-security coordination committee for Minneapolis and St. Paul. A woman's voice, tired: "Jacobs committee, Sondra speaking."

"This is Lucas Davenport, returning a call from Dan."

"Just a minute, Lucas, I'll switch you in."

After a snatch of country and western music, Jacobs came up: "Lucas—we've got a problem. I'm going to send you a file on a man named Justice Shafer. We need to get our hands on him. I'd appreciate it if you could coordinate with your opposite number in Wisconsin."

"Who is he?"

"A nutcake. Sells copies of *Rogue Warrior* at gun shows . . . you know *Rogue Warrior*?"

"Yeah, sort of." Guerrilla war fantasies set in a future America somehow taken over by Islamic revolutionaries, except for those parts run by the Jewish bankers. "Something more specific?"

"Well, we never heard of him, tell you the truth," Jacobs

said. "Then some guy who goes to gun shows ran into him at a quarry over in Wisconsin, in Barron County, where he was sighting in a .50 cal. The guy talked to him and said Shafer got going on Jews and jihad and how the politicians were selling out America, you know . . . and he had this .50 cal, and the guy who saw him said he was knocking over metal plates at seven hundred and forty-five yards."

"Unusual distance," Lucas said.

"Which has us worried. For one thing, Shafer lives in Oklahoma, and we've got no idea what he's doing up here. He's poor as a church mouse and he runs around in a rattrap Ford pickup—but he's got this shiny new rifle with a thousand-dollar scope and a Nikon rangefinder, and he's shooting at this specific distance . . . seven hundred and forty-five yards. Like he had the distance in mind. He's got an FBI file: he tried to join the marines and then the army, years ago, but they didn't want him, said he was a little shaky on his feet. He may have hooked up with some of the extremist white gangs—he's got a skinhead brother who did some time. The feds think he might have painted some swastikas on a synagogue in Norman, tipped over some Jewish tombstones . . . Got 'eighty-eight' tattooed on his chest. Like that."

"We'll get on it," Lucas said. "The file's on the way?"

"I'm pushing the button on it. ATF is working it, too, and the FBI's interested, so you may be bumping into some of them."

"I'll warn everybody," Lucas said.

LUCAS DAVENPORT WAS a tall, tough, dark-haired man, heavily tanned at the end of the Minnesota summer. The tan emphasized his blue eyes, his hawkish nose, and his facial scars: a long thin one down through his eyebrow, like a piece of white fishing line, another circular one on his throat, with a vertical line through it, like the Greek letter *phi*—the remnants of a .22 wound, followed by the tracheotomy that kept him alive. The tracheotomy had been done by Weather, with a jackknife.

"So?" Weather asked.

"Some redneck with a .50-caliber sniper rifle, up here from Oklahoma," Lucas said. "One of the eighty-eights. They're worried, but not too worried."

"What's an eighty-eight?"

"You know—H is the eighth letter in the alphabet, so eighty-eight is HH. Heil Hitler," Lucas said. "You got guys who get it tattooed on their scalps."

"Then I'd be worried, if I were Dan Jacobs," she said.

"Yeah . . . The ATF guys are out looking for him, and probably the Secret Service," Lucas said. "They want me to call our Wisconsin contacts, and people around the metro, see if we can spot him. I'll make some calls tonight, get some deputies looking around."

"Good luck with that," she said. The longer they'd lived together, the more skeptical she'd become of the concept of sharp-eyed cops picking the bad guys out of a crowd. She'd moved toward Lucas's view, as regarded cops and robbers: it was all chaos, accident, stupidity, insanity, and coincidence.

He'd cited as evidence the case of the doper who'd gotten out of Stillwater prison on Wednesday, who'd promptly gotten drunk with his release money, had fallen asleep at midnight in a filling station parking lot, had woken at three o'clock in the morning, out of money, only to spot the Coke machine right there, with a brick sitting next to it, had smashed open the machine with the brick, and was still scooping up the coins when the cops arrived. On Friday, he was back in Stillwater for the remaining three years of his original term.

Yowza.

They crossed the St. Croix River into Minnesota and twenty-five minutes later were home. There were lights all over the house, and from the garage, they could hear Letty, their ward, shrieking with laughter. Inside, they found Letty and Sam playing a kind of volleyball using a sponge batted over a string.

Sam quit the moment he saw Weather and Lucas, and Letty called, "Quitter," which he understood, and he said, "No-no-no-no," one of his few dozen words, and ran to Weather.

Perfect, Lucas thought. Just perfect. The kid was obviously brilliant, as well as athletically gifted, and probably the best-looking toddler in the Minneapolis–St. Paul metropolitan area. And Letty was growing up into something interesting. Her mother had been murdered in a case broken by Lucas; and he'd been so taken with the child that he'd brought her home to Weather.

Now she was growing up, and Lucas and Weather were back in court, with her consent, to formally adopt her, to make her Letty Davenport. She feigned nonchalance, but once or twice a week she'd ask, "So, how's things with the court?"

LUCAS BROUGHT IN a fabric cooler full of beer with a slab of walleye fillets—the only cooler he'd found that would fit in the Porsche—and Weather's overnight case. He gave Letty a hug, Sam a head-rub, got a piece of blueberry pie from Ellen, and went off to the den and brought up the computer.

The file on Justice Shafer was sitting in the e-mail at his office, at the Bureau of Criminal Apprehension. He pulled it out, opened it, and read it as he ate the pie.

Shafer was one of the border-state bad boys who looked like an antique photo of Cole Younger or Jesse James: hair like straw, freckles, pale eyes, bones in his face; like he hadn't had enough to eat as a kid, like he'd never had baby fat. In the photograph, he was standing next to the back of a pickup truck, a pump .22 in his hands, a pile of dead squirrels on the tailgate. His tongue was tucked in one corner of his mouth, the tip protruding, and it made him look both stupid and crazy, the kind of guy who couldn't keep his tongue out of the cold.

His file was full of the small details that spelled trouble: never made it out of high school; juvenile record for theft; failed the psychological tests for both the marines and the army. Might have robbed a couple of gas stations, but hadn't gotten caught at it. Hung out with the Clan, a mid-continent neo-Nazi motorcycle club that mostly got in fights with other neo-Nazi groups and Chicano gangs.

All right. Lucas did some editing on the file, then called the duty man at the BCA and told him to circulate the file to sheriffs' departments in Minnesota and western Wisconsin.

Kicked back, and thought about the Republican convention.

In the months leading up to the main event, the nomination of John McCain for the presidency, he'd argued that the Twin Cities weren't prepared to deal with it. He'd made the argument hard enough, and loud enough—he had excellent contacts with the local TV stations and the two major newspapers—that the local agencies finally got some intelligence work under way, and contracted with police agencies around the country to bring in more cops. In doing that, he'd made himself unpopular enough that he'd been disinvited from the party.

Well, what the hell. He didn't want to go anyway.

Glanced at his watch, called a pal in the Ramsey County sheriff's office. "Surprised you're home," he said, when the guy came up. "I thought you'd be out violating the rights of the protesters."

"I would be, but my kid's leaving for Madison this weekend. I'm packing a trailer," the guy said.

"Not bad," Lucas said. "I always liked that place. When I was at the U, we'd go down there and try to get laid."

"Glad to hear that, since it's my daughter I'm taking down," the guy said.

Oops. "Mmm. Anyway, you got things under control?"

"I think so. We're going out tomorrow night, hit some of the assholes," the guy said. "Preempt them. They think they're hiding in Minneapolis, but we've got a couple of guys with them."

"Ah, jeez . . ."

"You're welcome to come along and watch."

Lucas was tempted, but it would be a bit humiliating, standing there, rubbernecking, while the other guys got the action. "Ah, you know. I pissed off too many people. But . . . glad to know you got it covered."

They talked a few more minutes, then he went out and hung with Letty and Sam, and started an Alan Furst novel, and eventually went to bed and slept the sleep of the righteous.

FRIDAY MORNING, ANOTHER gorgeous day, driving north up Cretin Avenue.

Anti-Semites were milling around the corner at Summit Avenue, with signs about Palestine; on up to I-94, then blowing the doors off the chain of Camrys and Priuses as he merged into traffic. Made him smile, made him feel happy, as though there were possibilities in the world. He hustled across town, up I-35E, off on Maryland, down the road to the headquarters of the Bureau of Criminal Apprehension . . . past the filling station where a madwoman once tried to shoot him to death.

He parked in the BCA lot and walked up to his office, peeling off his jacket to show the .45 he carried under his armpit. Pulled off the shoulder rig, stuck the whole apparatus in a file cabinet. His secretary, Carol, trailed him into his office.

"You've got a call, sounds like it might be important," she said.

"The security committee? I got that . . ."

Carol looked at a piece of paper. "From New York. You know a woman named Lily Rothenburg? Says she's a captain with the NYPD?"

"Absolutely," Lucas said.

"She wants you to give her a call," Carol said. "She says it's semi-urgent."

"Ring her up and transfer it in," Lucas said. "Dig up a phone number for Dan Coates over in Wisconsin—it's the Special Assignments Bureau in their Justice Department. I need to talk to him right after Lily."

"Gotcha." She hesitated in the doorway. "One more thing. You got a nut call: the guy says, 'Is this Davenport's office?' I say, 'Yes.' He says, 'Tell that motherfucker that I'm coming for him.'"

Lucas laughed. "Did he say who it was?"

"There was a caller ID. Do you know an Achmed Mansoor?"

Lucas shook his head. "Nope. Did he say anything about Allah?"

"No . . . and this guy sounded like an American. Ghetto accent. I did a reverse directory and came up with a Middle Eastern sandwich shop in Dinkytown."

"Gimme the address: I'll look into it."

DEL CAPSLOCK HAD come through the door while they were talking, and said to Carol, "You sweet thing."

Carol, feigning propriety: "How's the pregnant wife?"

"She's fine. She's great," Del said. "She looks like a goddamn rosebud. Doc says she's starting to dilate, but she's still a while out. She's got me running around like a Shriner parade."

Lucas asked, "Do they still have those?"

"They must, somewhere," Del said. "They still got Shriners." He eased into one of the visitors' chairs and put his boots on Lucas's desktop. "So what's this about a sandwich shop in Dinkytown?"

Carol explained and Del said, "I'll go over and have a chat with the guy."

"I'm not doing much," Lucas said.

"Yeah, but you go walking in the door, maybe he pulls

out a shotgun and kills you," Del said. "Me, he doesn't know from Adam."

"As far as you know."

"Whatever." Del yawned then added, "I never heard of a cop getting killed by somebody who called ahead."

"Probably happened somewhere," Lucas said.

"Everything's happened somewhere."

DEL WAS A battered man in his late forties, in jeans and a Pennzoil T-shirt with grease spots on it, rough-side-out Red Wing work boots, and an old, unfashionable nylon fanny pack, worn in front. He had a cell-phone-sized digital camera hung on a string around his neck and a .38 revolver in the fanny pack. He'd been working the streets around the convention center.

"So what's happening?" Lucas asked.

"Ah, you know: kids and old people. There are some assholes out there, but most of them are hobbyists. They seem like my mom . . . you know, old. They've got these recycled chants from the sixties. 'Hey, hey, John McCain, how many children have you slain?' Like that."

"With a few assholes."

"A few," Del said. "Vandals. Red-and-black flags. Slingshots. Guys who want to wreck the place for the pure pleasure of it. I could point out twenty people, if we picked them up and put them in the basement for a few days, the convention would be a sea of peace."

"Ramsey County sheriff is setting up a raid tonight, tomorrow night, pick some of those guys up," Lucas said. "Or so I'm told."

"Here?"

"No, over in Minneapolis," Lucas said. "They're pulling in some Minneapolis cops."

They talked about that for a while, and Lucas told Del about the guy with the sniper rifle, and Del shook his head and said, "That's all we need."

"You having a good time?" Lucas asked.

"Yeah, I am," Del said. "I like talking to them; pretty good folks, for the most part. Even the assholes are interesting."

"I'd like to get out there; just to see it, you know?" Lucas said.

Del was doubtful. "You look too much like a cop—or even a Republican."

"Not *that*."

"Well—you got that vibe. You'd have to tone it down," Del said. "Like, borrow clothes from me."

Lucas shuddered. "Maybe not."

He was, in fact, a clotheshorse, this morning wearing a light checked sport coat over an icy-blue long-sleeved dress shirt, black summer-weight woolen slacks hand-knit by an Italian virgin, and square-toed English-made loafers.

CAROL SHOUTED: "LILY Rothenburg on two."

Lucas said to Del, "I got a call coming here."

Del said, "Pick it up. I ain't going anywhere, if it's Lily calling."

"Fuck you," Lucas said. He and Lily had once been a passing fashion, including a geometrical insanity in an earlier Porsche. Del knew all about it: Lucas shook his head and picked up the phone. "Lily?"

"Lucas Davenport," she said, "how's every little thing?"

"Well, we got a lot going on, so . . . pretty good," Lucas said. "How about you? How's the kid? If you're divorced, I can offer you space in my garage."

She laughed and said, "From what I hear about Weather, it'd be more like the backyard. But, the kid's fine and I'm not divorced."

"Del's here, he says hi . . ."

They caught up for a few minutes, then she said, "Look. We've got a problem—or, maybe, you've got a problem. We had an armored car robbery here two and a half years ago, and two guards were killed. They were off-duty cops. The robbery crew got away with a half-million dollars."

"Not that big, for an armored car," Lucas said.

"Well, there was more inside, but the thing went bad. Most of the money was behind a locked barrier inside the truck," Lily said. "The idea was, if trouble started, the guards would put the keys in a solid-steel lockbox inside the back, which they didn't have keys to, and then nobody could get at the money . . . that's what they did. But somebody got pissed, we think, and started shooting, and all the shooters got were the receipts from a couple of big-box stores that hadn't been put behind the barrier yet."

"How does that get to us?"

"We think the leader of the crew was a guy named Brutus Cohn," Lily said. "We got an anonymous tip. A male caller, deep southern accent, calling from Kennedy. He said that he'd seen Cohn getting on a plane at Heathrow, in England, yesterday, going to Los Angeles. He said he knew him from Alabama, and Cohn is from Alabama. He said Cohn had grown a red beard, and Cohn is a redhead."

"So he sounds good," Lucas said.

"Yes. Anyway, this guy said he was waiting to get on his plane when he saw Cohn. He didn't want to call from London, because he was afraid we'd identify him, and he's afraid of Cohn. So he got way back and watched Cohn going into a gate for a flight to Los Angeles. By the time we got to the L.A. cops, Cohn's flight was an hour out. They met the plane, and there was no Brutus Cohn. There was no way to get back to the original source, so we checked with Heathrow. Everything was right: there was the Kennedy gate, and down the way, the L.A. gate. But the gate was a joint gate—and the next gate down, where Cohn could also have been headed . . ."

". . . came here."

"Right. The Minneapolis plane was on the ground for three hours before we got it straight. Our people talked to the flight crew, and there was a man in first class who probably was Cohn. He almost certainly was the guy that the source saw, and the source said he knew Cohn pretty well. The crew said he was very tall, fairly thin, muscular, red hair, and charming with the flight crew. The girls liked him, and that's Cohn, from what we hear."

"What's he doing?" Lucas asked.

"Don't know. It's possible he moved right on through the Cities, changed planes, and is gone. But it's also possible that he's up to something," Lily said. "He's a serious, ultra-violent holdup man who needs a big score so he can bury himself somewhere. He mostly worked in the south, down to Florida, north to Atlanta, west to New Mexico. Maybe California. Maybe one job in Mexico. The FBI isn't sure about all of that, but if they've got him right, there have been at least five dead in thirty to forty robberies, and one survivor shot through the chest who should've died. He's the guy who eventually identified Cohn for the FBI, from prison photographs. So. We've been looking, and waiting, and here he is. You've got that convention going on . . . lots of cash there. A boatload of cash."

Lucas said, "Let me ask you this—how'd the caller know you were looking for Cohn?"

"We didn't make any secret about it," she said. "We put out posters, we sent some guys to Birmingham to look up his old acquaintances, his relatives, dear old Mom. They got some TV time, it was sort of a thing, you know, a modern Jesse James. Got some attention down there."

"You want him pretty bad," Lucas said.

"Yes, we do."

"Send me what you got," Lucas said. "I'll spread it around to the TV stations."

"Ah—don't do that," Lily said. "He's very careful. You could almost call that his MO. If he suspected we were on to him, he'd be gone in a minute."

The problem, she said, was that New York really had no

solid proof that he'd been involved in the armored car robbery. They had DNA that they believed had come out of the struggle between the cops and the shooter, but they didn't know whether it was Cohn's DNA, or DNA from somebody else in the gang.

"Cohn would have done the killing, if he thought he needed to, but we don't know that he was the shooter. He was there, but maybe didn't pull the trigger. Then, we think we found the place where they got together before the robbery, a motel out in Queens, but they burned it down, so we got nothing. No DNA, nothing."

"Burned it down?"

"Yeah. Fire guys say somebody doused the place with a mix of gasoline and motor oil, and torched it," Lily said. "Fire kills DNA . . ."

"I know. But it seems kind of extreme," Lucas said.

"That's Cohn. He's Mr. Extreme. He did three years in prison in Alabama, a newbie, but he was running the place by the time he left."

"So if you don't want us to spread his face around, what do you want?" Lucas asked.

"We want to send you a bunch of photos," Lily said. "They're twelve years old, but we Photoshopped them to age him, and we added the beard. We thought some of your guys could walk them around to the local hotels and motels, see if you can spot him. And then . . . see what he's doing."

"You mean, let him take a shot at another armored car?"

"You wouldn't have to wait until the last second," she said, but her tone was rich with suggestion.

"But they'd have to be making a move . . ."

"Yeah, well. Life in the big city, huh?" Lily said. "The thing is, if he knows he put some DNA on somebody, here in New York, he'll try to shoot his way free."

"You want us to kill him," Lucas said.

"I didn't say that. I said, he killed two of our guys, and probably three more people, along the way," Lily said.

Lucas thought about it for a moment, then said, "Send the stuff. I'll get it to the people who need it."

"Lucas . . . thank you. And stay in touch."

"INTERESTING LITTLE CONVERSATION," Del said.

CAROL ROUTED THROUGH a call from Dan Coates, his opposite number in Wisconsin. Lucas filled him in on Justice Shafer. "We sent the file across the river, to the sheriffs' departments between us and Eau Claire, but it'd help if you goosed them along a little. You know, so you can deflect the blame when something goes wrong."

"Who'd point the finger at us? If something went wrong?" Coates asked. He was crunching on something like a carrot or a celery stick.

"Listen, if something goes wrong at the convention, with a seven-hundred-and-fifty-yard shot from a .50-cal, everybody will point the finger at you. And at me, and every other local cop. Think about it."

"I'll call everybody," Coates said. "How much you want to put on the Vikings?"

"Screw the Vikings. They're a bunch of criminals," Lucas said. "Not that Green Bay won't stink the place up."

"Let me tell you . . ."

They were discussing the possibilities when Del yawned and stood up and said, "I'm gonna go see that Arab dude in the sandwich shop."

Lucas took the phone away from his mouth. "Careful."

"Think about a disguise," Del said. "If you go out on the street."

From the outer office, Carol called, "Why don't you drive the Oscar Mayer Wienermobile? Nobody would suspect."

Lucas said, "Del . . . shut the door on the way out, okay?"

DEL DIDN'T SHUT the door. Carol propped herself in it, and when Lucas got off the phone, asked, "Are you serious about going out there?"

"Yeah. There are about a million people wandering around out there, and I'd like to go out and see it," Lucas said.

She nodded: "Listen, I was looking at *National Geographic* . . ."

"Didn't know you were an intellectual . . ."

". . . and one of the guys in it, one of the photographers, this war photographer, looked like you. Attitudinally, if you know what I mean. If you got some Levi's and gym shoes and, like, a long-sleeved shirt and rolled the sleeves way up over your elbows, and messed up your hair, and put some convention credentials around your neck, and borrowed a camera bag from Dan Jackson and a couple of cameras—you could make it as a photographer."

Lucas shook his head. "Pretending that you're a reporter tends to piss people off."

"Don't. Wear your official ID," Carol said. "Who looks at it? They just see the tags."

"I'll think about it," Lucas said.

She shrugged. "Do what you want—but you could look like a photographer."

HE THOUGHT ABOUT Lily for a while, and the Cohn gang, and then he went on the Internet and looked at pictures of war photographers. Carol was right, he decided; he could be a photographer. Maybe. He called Jackson, said he was coming down for wardrobe and makeup.

On the way out of the office, he told Carol to print the

pictures of Justice Shafer, and of Brutus Cohn, when they came in. "Call Minneapolis and St. Paul and Bloomington and get a list of firearms dealers who might be dealing dirty. Big enough so that their names would be around: somebody that a bad guy could find if he blew into town."

"You want them rated by their dirt quotient," she suggested.

"Yeah. I'll go chat with them. Give me something to do," he said.

LUCAS HAD A small Nikon single-lens reflex digital camera, given to him for Christmas by Weather, along with a couple of zoom lenses. He used it to take pictures of the kids. When Jackson backed out of the equipment closet with two Nikon cameras, and an old Domke cloth camera bag and three lenses, he knew more or less how they worked.

"What we're gonna do," Jackson said, peeling a strip of black gaffer tape off a roll, "is we're gonna tape out the Nikon and the D2X logos, which some war guys do to reduce visibility, you know? Then, not many people will know that you're shooting older cameras."

"I'm not going to be shooting them much," Lucas said.

"Gotta look like it, though," Jackson said. "Do take a few shots, you might like it. The other thing is, make your shirt kinda military. Black, or olive green, with the sleeves rolled up. Military's sort of photo-trendy."

"What do I do if somebody asks me who I'm with?" Lucas asked.

"I just keep moving and say, 'BCA,' and they'll nod like they know who it is," Jackson said. "Sounds sort of like BBC, NBC, CBS, ABC."

"Maybe I oughta wear white socks," Lucas suggested.

"Maybe you oughta take it seriously," Jackson said. "You could get your ass kicked, if somebody took you the wrong way."

"Lots of cops around . . ."

Jackson looked up. "You know, one way you'd be safe is, wear a police uniform. Nobody'll fuck with you. Nobody'll talk to you, either, other than to say hello."

"This is better," Lucas said, peering through the camera's viewfinder. "I'm looking pretty good here."

"Your hair is way too combed," Jackson said. "You gotta get some Brylcreem or something, get some hair spiked up. Wear jeans. And you gotta scuff them up—you're way too neat. *Way* too neat. You gotta look like you slept in the jeans. Every time I see you in jeans . . . What do you do? Do you *dry-clean* your jeans?"

"No, I don't dry-clean my jeans," Lucas said.

"Then you iron them," Jackson said.

"The housekeeper irons them, sometimes," Lucas admitted.

"*Irons* your jeans?" He was appalled.

"Hey . . ."

"Sorry . . ."

"You're sorta getting into this," Lucas said.

"Well, you know, it's interesting," Jackson said. "Carol was right: you do sorta look like a conflict photographer. So: let me show you how to handle the camera. It's like shooting on the range, very similar to a gun . . ."

Del called during the lecture, from the Middle East sandwich shop, and talking around a gyro, said, "They got a phone on the counter here, no long distance company, so they let anybody use it. They got no idea who called you, but they say they remembered one guy yelling into it, and Carol told me the guy who left the message was yelling, but this yelling guy was in a wheelchair."

"That's a relief," Lucas said. He hung up and asked Jackson, "You got any lighter lenses? This lens is big as my dick."

"You wish."

3

JENKINS AND SHRAKE were chipping golf balls at a cup in a corner of the atrium, using an old MacGregor eight iron that had been in the evidence room since sometime in the eighties. Shortly after the turn of the millennium, somebody had gotten tired of looking at it and had thrown it away, and Jenkins rescued it from a trash can.

When they hit the ball, it would go "chock," and then "chink" if it hit the glass at all, or "tock" if it hit the wall's baseboard.

Lucas watched for a minute, then said, "I need an assistant."

Shrake, without looking up from the ball, said, "Take Jenkins. He's a born assistant." He chipped it and the ball clinked off the side of the glass.

"Take both of them," said a dark-haired woman from the DNA lab. She was sitting at a table with a *New York Times* and an egg-salad sandwich. "That clinking sound is driving me crazy. It's like water dripping on my forehead."

Shrake said to Lucas, "I've got a date. If I go out with you, God only knows when we'll get back. Jenkins ain't doing shit."

"Not entirely true," Jenkins said.

Shrake said to Jenkins, "I'll cancel your debt on this game, today's game, if you go with him."

Lucas asked Shrake, "You're not still dating Shirley Knox?"

"Yeah, he is," Jenkins said. "He's in love."

"Aw, for Christ's sakes, Shrake, she's in the Mafia," Lucas said.

Shrake chipped again, but this time missed the cup entirely, and the ball tocked against the baseboard. "You made me jerk at the ball," he said.

"Honest to God, it's driving me nuts," the woman said. "I can't stand that sound."

"She's not in the Mafia," Shrake said. "I asked her. She said no, she wasn't, and I believe her."

Lucas said to Jenkins, "He's lost his grip. She's in the fuckin' Mafia."

"His grip was never that good in the first place," Jenkins said.

"Have you tried talking to him about it?" Lucas asked.

"I did. I says, 'Shrake, the chick is in the Mafia,' but then he says the woman could suck a golf ball through a water hose. So—how do I answer that?"

"Aw, for Christ's sakes," the DNA woman said, "I heard that. Am I invisible or something?"

Jenkins turned to her and said, "Shut up." Then to Shrake, "Cancel today's debt and half of the rest and I'll go with Davenport."

"Done," Shrake said, and Jenkins asked Lucas, "Where're we going?"

"See some gun guys," Lucas said.

"Thank God," said the woman with the egg-salad sandwich.

THEY TOOK JENKINS'S new Ford CVPI, for which he'd had to get a special authorization from the head of the agency. "I can't believe you bought another one of these things. It's like riding in a Boston Whaler. You'd lose a drag race to a John Deere," Lucas said.

"Not once I get this baby rolling," Jenkins said, and, "You won't see anybody doing moonshiner turns with one of those cheap-ass front-wheel drives. The tranny would be all over the street. This baby . . ." He patted the dashboard. "Which way we going?"

THE FIRST STOP was a shop on Arcade at East Seventh, a hole-in-the-wall with a hand-painted steel sign that read, "Terry's Sports." Inside the front window, behind a steel mesh screen, was a pump twelve-gauge shotgun with the butt cut down to a pistol grip.

"Seven-Eleven special," Jenkins said, as they walked past it.

"I could never figure out why it's a federal crime to saw the barrel off a shotgun, but it's okay to cut off the butt," Lucas said. "Same effect—you can carry it under your jacket."

"Lawyers," Jenkins said. "They make laws, they got no idea."

THEY RATTLED THE door and the owner buzzed them in; the shop smelled of cigarette smoke and gun-cleaning solvent. Terry was a nervous, dried-out man of fifty, the fingers of his right hand stained amber with nicotine. He nodded when they came in, recognized them as cops, and said, "Officers."

"How much you want for the cop killer in the window?" Jenkins asked, getting the interview off on the right foot.

"Self-defense gun," Terry said with a placating smile, showing teeth as yellow as his fingers. "Sell them mostly to women."

"Right," Lucas said. He took the photos of Justice Shafer

and Brutus Cohn out of his pocket, unfolded them, with Cohn's picture on top. "You seen this guy?"

Terry looked at the picture for a long five seconds, then shook his head. "Can't say as I have."

"How about this guy?" Lucas shuffled the papers, and put the Shafer head shot on top.

Terry looked at it for a couple of seconds, then an extra wrinkle appeared among the set on his forehead. "What'd he do?"

"Never mind that," Jenkins said. "You seen him?"

"I did," Terry admitted. "About a week ago. He was here maybe twenty minutes. I didn't think he was gonna buy anything, and he didn't."

"Was he looking for anything in particular?" Lucas asked.

"He was looking for some .50-cal rounds in bronze," Terry said. "I told him I could get it, good lathe-cut stuff. He asked how much, and I said, 'Eighty bucks for ten rounds,' and he said that was a little high. Then he looked at a Bushmaster M4, and went on his way. Haven't seen him since."

"Didn't buy any ammo?" Lucas asked.

"Nope. Didn't buy a thing," Terry said.

Lucas said, "We're local guys, and I gotta tell you, you'd be better off dealing with us if you're not telling the truth. The Secret Service and the ATF are chasing all over looking for this guy. With the convention in town, I don't have to tell you why. You don't want to be the one who sold him some ammo and then get caught lying about it."

"Didn't sell him anything, with Jesus as my witness," Terry said, holding up his right hand as though taking an oath. He looked satisfactorily worried.

Lucas nodded. "All right. Gonna have to talk to the ATF though, so you'll probably be hearing from them. Maybe the Secret Service."

"How much you want for the cop killer in the window?" Jenkins asked again.

"Six hundred dollars," Terry said. "Lot of handwork in a self-defense gun. There *is* a police discount."

OUT ON THE street, Jenkins said, "Ten percent. I'd almost be willing to do it, to get the piece off the streets, but the little cockroach would make another one."

"First stop, and Justice Shafer is right there," Lucas said. "That's a hell of a coincidence."

"That happened to me one time," Jenkins said. "One-stop shopping."

"When did it happen to you?" Lucas asked.

"Well, it didn't exactly happen to *me*, but it happened to a guy I knew," Jenkins said.

"Never happened to me," Lucas said.

Back in the car, he got on the phone to Dan Jacobs at the security committee. "I don't want to yank your weenie when everybody else is, but I've got some news about your pal Justice Shafer."

Lucas told him about Terry's, and Jacobs said, "That's pretty interesting. The Secret Service and the ATF are doing research on him, down in Oklahoma, and they're getting worried. Some of these gang guys say Shafer's never been accepted because he's sort of a pussy—never proved himself."

"Uh-oh."

"I'll call them with this. They'll send a guy around to talk to . . . Terry?"

THEIR SECOND STOP was a two-man weapons outlet in a warehouse district in Eagan, south of the Twin Cities core, a concrete-block building filled with hunting knives, compound bows, crossbows, samurai and fantasy swords, a barrel half-full of Louisville Slugger baseball bats, a shelf of lead-weighted fish-whackers, and a rack of used guns; but mostly knives. To one side, a customer in camo cargo pants was methodically pounding a six-inch target with carbon-fiber arrows, on a four-lane archery range.

The two owners, who were brothers, named Jenkins—they agreed with Jenkins that they weren't related—both checked the photographs, and swore they'd never seen either man. Lucas asked, "What's the advantage of the crossbow over the compound bow?"

The customer, who was shooting a compound bow, said over his shoulder, "You don't have to know nothing to shoot a crossbow."

Jenkins asked one of the Jenkins brothers, "If I were to ask you where I could get a switchblade, you wouldn't know, would you?"

The Jenkins brother looked puzzled: "Well, sure. Right here. What do you want?" He walked down the counter and tapped the top of a case. Inside, a half dozen switchblades nestled on red velvet.

Jenkins was taken aback: "Switchblades are legal?"

"Well, sure, in Minnesota," Jenkins said. "You can order them on the Internet."

"I didn't know that," Jenkins said. "Is there a police discount?"

THE FOURTH AND fifth dealers hadn't seen either Cohn or Shafer, but the sixth one, their last stop of the day, had seen Shafer. The dealer, Bob Harper, worked out of his house. "He said he'd heard of me down in Oklahoma, a boy named Dan Oaks outa Norman. He thought maybe I'd have some premium .50-cal, but I didn't. Wouldn't have sold it to him anyway."

"Why not?" Lucas asked. He wrote "Dan Oaks" and "Norman" in his notebook.

Harper was a thin man gone old, but still hard, with shiny cheekbones and killer eyes, two dry wattles hanging under his chin. "'Cause I'm not stupid. Some skinhead from Oklahoma shows up on my doorstep looking for .50-cal, the week before the Republican convention? I don't need *that* kind of publicity."

IN THE CAR, Lucas called Jacobs again, gave him Harper's name, and the name of the Oklahoma dealer. "I don't know what Shafer's doing, but he sure as hell isn't hiding out," Lucas said.

"Okay—hey, thanks for the time, Lucas. This has been a help. Could you keep spreading those photos around? We need to talk to this guy."

"No problem."

"ALL DONE?" JENKINS asked. He pushed the button on his new switchblade, and the blade jumped out and snapped into place.

"All done," Lucas said. "You know, you're gonna reach in your pocket for your cell phone and you're gonna hit that button, and the blade's gonna jump out and cut your nuts off."

"I'll give it to Shrake," Jenkins said. "If it cuts *his* nuts off, maybe he'll stop dating Shirley."

"We really ought to do something about that relationship," Lucas said. "I mean, if he won't give it up, maybe put a legal notice in the newspaper, so nobody could accuse us of covering it up."

JENKINS DROPPED HIM at the office. Carol had gone home, and Lucas looked at all the paper that she'd printed out from New York, on Cohn, looked at Cohn's picture for a while—this was a different personality than Justice Shafer; this was a serious guy—and then slipped it into a file and walked out to his car.

Great late summer day. He trolled once through St. Paul,

looking at all the cops around, saw shoulder patches from Virginia and Illinois. Like a big storm coming in, he thought, everybody watchful and hoping for the best.

He got home, kissed Sam, kissed Letty, kissed Weather, got a banana from the housekeeper, and Weather asked, "Whatever happened to the assassin?"

He told her about his day, and she said, "Well, you're done with that, anyway. One less thing to worry about."

4

CRUZ AND COHN spent Saturday morning cruising the Lyman High Hat, a boutique hotel on Loring Park in Minneapolis, a place that featured forty-dollar cheeseburgers and fifty-dollar-a-glass house champagne.

Cohn, in a baby-blue golf shirt and tan slacks, walked through the front doors, past the desk to the restaurant, past the maitre d', took a quick look around, as though checking for friends, and then walked back out to the car. He'd already surveyed the nearby streets, and the park, stopping now and then to look at a printout of a Google satellite view of the area. He'd seen both McCall and Lane, walking separately, McCall in a neat blazer and pressed slacks, with an Obama button, Lane improbably in cargo shorts and a golf shirt, his hard, knobby legs looking as though they'd been carved from hickory.

"Let's see the door again," Cohn said to Cruz, when he got back in the car.

"There's a light and a video camera covering the loading dock; they both record and live-monitor," Cruz said. She was flipping through a notebook with handwritten notes. "The only people who look at the monitors are the desk crew, and they don't have time for it. You won't be breaking in, so even if they see you, they'll think you're staff. You'll wear hats, keep your heads down. You go in, the staff stairway is to your left. No cameras in the stairwell. There are cameras in the hallways, but they're direct-recorders and aren't live anywhere."

"So if we come out of the stairwell with masks . . ."

"You're good. They'll look at you afterwards, but by then, it's too late."

"Where did you get the uniform?" An idle question: he didn't really care. The talk was his way of nailing down the terrain.

"Macy's. It's a tuxedo jacket and pants with a red dress shirt," she said. "Now, when you're in the hallway, you'll see the cameras hanging down from the ceiling—they're smoked-glass bubbles, about six inches across. You get to the door, then McCall turns his back, takes off his mask, knocks . . . If they look through the peephole, they'll see a black guy with the room-service uniform. If they open the door on a chain, you kick it and go in, and McCall pulls the mask back on. If they open it, you go in."

"What if we meet somebody in the hallway?" Cohn asked.

"Well, you peek first, see if there's anybody there. We're doing it right during all the big meetings and parties, so there shouldn't be a lot of traffic. There's a big party in the Mississippi Ballroom, so you may get somebody coming up to pee. If you do, well, you take them into the room with you. Holding them would not be a problem: you'll only be inside for five minutes."

They were headed around the block, and Cohn looked back at the hotel. "Two rooms."

"Two rooms." Cruz nodded. "After you take five-oh-five, Lane stays with the people there, freezes them. You and McCall go down to four-thirty-one. We do the lower floor second, so if anything goes wrong, we'll get out that much quicker. And four-thirty-one is closer to the staff stairwell.

When you finish four-thirty-one, you call Lane on the cell and you all walk."

They were easing through the tangle of streets between the park and the downtown. Cruz pointed at a parking garage.

"Two blocks, around two corners," Cruz said. "If we have to ditch the car or if somebody gets caught on foot, we'll have one emergency car here, another one on the street down from the park. We'll have to position that one just before we hit. Everything like we've always done it: keys are with the car, magnetic box under the rear left bumper. Each car has a two-gallon plastic gas can in the back, half gas, half oil. If you have to ditch a car, try to burn it."

Cohn nodded: of course there'd be emergency cars. And, of course there'd be gas cans. There always were, on his jobs. He adopted any advantage, or possible advantage. That was why he'd survived, and why he worked with Cruz: they saw eye-to-eye on advantages, and survival.

"I want to see that layout again—we have to know which way to go however we get out, even if we have to throw a chair through a window," Cohn said.

"Yes," she said.

"Feels strange," he said, looking back at the hotel, busy, well-dressed people flowing around it. "That much cash, with no protection. You're sure about the money?"

"Ninety percent. That's as good as I can get it. Not as good as with a duck, but pretty damn good," Cruz said. The group had its own slang, and referred to armored cars as "ducks," as in "sitting ducks." She added, "The thing that sold me was, it's so soft."

They stopped at the mouth of a short alley and she pointed down the alley to a loading dock. "That's the door, off to the left. I checked the key last week. If they changed the lock last night, well, you walk away."

Cohn looked at the door for a long five seconds, then said, "Back to Hudson." He glanced at his watch, leaned back in the passenger seat, laced his fingers across his chest and closed his eyes. "Check the layout one last time. I want to see the emergency car. Then, do it."

"You know what worries me the most?" Cruz asked. "What worries me is that the guy might not be there—you know, he goes out for a drink or something. Then you'll have to make some decisions right on the spot. Whether to wait or go, and if you go, whether to come back."

"You said there's always somebody with the money," Cohn said.

"That's what I was told," Cruz said. "There's always somebody with the money, until it's gone."

THEY CALLED LANE and McCall, got them started back. At the motel in Hudson, Cohn got a cup of coffee, and then they began working over the drawings of the hotel's interior. "Don't want to meet a busboy carrying food up there," McCall said.

Cruz said, tapping the drawing, "They use the staff elevator, over around the corner, here. That stairway is mostly a fire escape. I walked it up and down, there's concrete dust on the treads, like it hardly gets used at all."

"Two weeks ago," Lane said.

"Nothing's perfect," Cruz snapped.

"Just sayin'," McCall said.

THEY TALKED ABOUT the uncertainties. As a unit, they'd always focused on scheduled money deliveries—ATM restockings, armored cars, credit unions in southern auto-factory towns, which carried heavy cash on paydays.

Of them all, they liked the armored cars the best, because they offered a choice of attack points, and if you found the right armored car, at the right spot, you were guaranteed a major payoff and a slow reaction by the cops. None of them had ever gone after individuals, for the simple reason that individuals didn't carry enough cash. If you're looking at the possibility of years in prison, then the payoff should be worth the risk, they all agreed.

With the earlier targets, the certainties were large. If the armored car wasn't at point X, and if the local cop cruiser wasn't at point Y, then you rescheduled. Credit unions didn't move, and they always opened at the same time and closed at the same time. If the factory passed out the checks at 10 A.M., then the first guys wouldn't sneak out to cash them before 10:05. Therefore, you had the hour between 9 A.M. and 10:05 to hit the place . . .

With this job, they weren't even certain that the money would be there. Cruz said it would be—ninety percent, anyway—but still: with this job, the uncertainties were larger than usual.

"THE FIRST GUY, John Wilson, he's a little guy, but he's got a temper," Cruz told them. "He could give you some trouble. That's the way it is. There may be one or two other guys in the room with him. If there isn't anyone else there, handle it however you want. If there is, you crush him. McCall—use your pistol. Beat him up, get him on the floor, kick his head, kick his balls. Don't kill him, but hurt him. The thing is, downstream, the word is going to start getting out about these guys. If the later targets hear about it, they'll get worried. We need them scared. We need them backing away from us. Makes everything easier."

"What if they get security?"

"They won't. They can't have anyone else around when they're passing out the cash. What they're doing is a crime."

"But . . ."

"If they *do* get a guy with a gun, you'll have to deal with it. But they won't: that's the beauty of the whole thing. The cops finding out what they're doing is worse than getting beat up and robbed. Now, the room. I couldn't get into all the rooms, but I got into a few. I believe he'll have a sitting room with a bedroom off to your right as you go in . . ."

CRUZ WAS ABOUT to go on, but there was a knock at the door. She froze. There was a "Do Not Disturb" sign on the doorknob.

"They're not using a key to knock," she blurted. "It's not the hotel."

"Answer the door," Cohn told Lane. He'd been lying on the bed, now was on his feet.

Lane went to the door, opened it just a crack, said, "Shoot," and opened it wide. A young blond woman carrying an old-style hard makeup case stepped through, spotted Cohn, cried, "Brutus," and threw herself at him. He picked her up, her legs wrapped around his waist. Cruz shouted at him, as Lane closed the door, "You fucker. You fucker, Brute. Goddamn you . . ."

"How are you, Lindy?" Lane asked, and to McCall, he said, "It's Lindy."

"I'm outa here," Cruz said.

"Rosie, calm down, okay?" Cohn said, over Lindy's shoulder.

Lindy said, "Yeah, calm down, Rosie. Jesus Christ."

"Lindy's just visiting. I'll put her on the plane home in a few days," Cohn said.

Cruz put her hands, in fists, on her hips, her face a hard clutch of anger: "Why the hell . . ."

"Because I couldn't wait," Cohn said. "That's why."

"Brute . . ."

"Y'all get out of here, back in an hour," Cohn said, "or we're all gonna be pretty embarrassed."

They shuffled out, Cruz running her hands through her short hair in exasperation, and Cohn said, "Better make it two hours."

SATURDAY ON THE sloping front lawn of the state Capitol, in St. Paul.

Letty strolled through the crowd, protesters, rubberneckers, street people, vendors, cops, taking it all in. She was a teenager, one toe in senior high, but for two years she'd worked unofficially for Channel Three, an unpaid intern. She was sponsored there by one of Lucas's ex-girlfriends—a girlfriend with whom he'd had a daughter, who now lived with her mother and her mother's new family.

Letty occasionally thought about how tangled it all was—women having children with two different men, men having children with several different women, and she was about to become the official daughter of the only husband and wife who'd ever behaved like parents with her . . .

Letty had been born in the bleakest part of northwest Minnesota, the daughter of an alcoholic mother; her father took off when she was a child, and she hadn't seen him since. They'd lived in an old farmhouse outside a small country town, so she hadn't even had the benefit of close-by neighbors. They had no satellite TV, so there'd been only two weak over-the-air TV channels, and she'd grown up as a county library patron, and a reader.

When she got into school, she'd encountered a man who made his living wandering through the local marshlands in the late fall and winter, trapping fur. He'd taught her how to do it—not much to learn, you could get most of it in a few days of observation—and she'd become a trapper, taking muskrats out of the marshes and raccoons out of the county landfill. That had gone on for most of her elementary school days; she'd taught herself to drive at the same time, and how to avoid the local highway patrolmen. The money from the trapping had become the family's main source of income.

A tough kid.

A series of murders had torn up her life: had resulted in her mother's death, and had brought Lucas Davenport and Del Capslock into town. She and Lucas had hit it off almost immediately, and he'd brought her home as his legal ward.

Cinderella.

Her job with Channel Three was more than decorative. Lucas's cop pals kept her well-stocked with tips, and since they were always reported by other producers and reporters, her favored reporters did *very* well with her.

A woman with a baby, sitting outside a tiny orange nylon tent, smiled at her, and Letty smiled back and said, "Hello, there."

"You can't really be a TV person," the woman said, looking at the credential tags around Letty's neck.

"But I am," Letty said happily.

Across the park, in the street, a white van cruised by, the side door open, and a man in a wheelchair looking out at the park—and at *her*, Letty thought. Just a spark, an impression, their eyes clicking, and then he was gone.

"How old are you?" the woman asked.

"Almost fifteen."

"And you work for a TV station?" She was both amused and skeptical.

"I've got an in," Letty said. "See, my dad had a baby with this woman . . ."

LUCAS WORE FADED jeans and a khaki military-style shirt rolled up to the elbows. He had a plastic credentials case strung around his neck like a baggage tag, one side with a yellow Session 1 Limited Access tag, the other side with a BCA identification card. Though he was still self-conscious about the camera resting against his chest, and the second one hanging off his shoulder, and the beat-up Domke bag, nobody was giving him a second look. He took a couple of crowd shots, trying to look bored.

And he *was* bored. The convention was the biggest single cop-action in Twin Cities' history, and he was out of it, part of the crowd, and the crowd wasn't doing much. Letty was supposed to be around here somewhere . . .

"HEY, DAD! DAD!"

Letty was there, under a spreading elm tree, waving. He smiled and headed over. She had a couple of credentials hung on an elastic string around her neck, like his. She was standing next to an orange nylon tent, where a young woman in a tired blue blouse and blue-jean shorts sat on a blanket next to a baby in a papoose sling.

The woman went straight for his liver: "Are you a cop?"

He tried for a wry smile. "Do I look like a cop?"

"Yup." She wrinkled her nose, being funny about it, but the question was serious. Letty broke it up with, "Did you see John and Jeff? They were going to give me a ride over to the convention center."

"What are they doing here?" Lucas asked.

"Just looking around. They got a car . . ."

"Letty . . ."

"I know, I know. They're okay," she said.

"I know *exactly* what they're like, because they're exactly like I was," Lucas said.

"Dad, I can handle them, all right?" Fists on her hips.

"All right. Be careful," he said. He looked around. "Wasn't a march supposed to go off five minutes ago? I need some street stuff."

The woman with the baby had now bought the cameras. She said, "Nothing is on time. These people couldn't organize a phone call. My husband said he'd be back in five minutes and he's been gone two hours."

"Yeah? He's a marcher?" Lucas asked.

"Anarchist," she said. "Or anti-Christ. One of the two. I can't keep them straight."

Letty laughed and said, "I gotta get a camera in here . . . Hey, there they are." She waved across the hillside at two gangling teenage boys, brothers, both with braces on their teeth. One of them, the older one, was a wicked street basketball player, and had nearly taken it to Lucas at the hoop mounted on Lucas's own garage. Lucas generally approved of them, but they were *looking*. He knew it, and they knew he knew it, and so were careful. "Take it easy," he said.

"Yeah . . . could I get ten dollars?" Letty asked.

"I suppose . . ."

She said quickly, "Twenty would be better."

He gave her a twenty and she was gone.

"Nice girl," said the woman with the baby.

"That sun is nasty," Lucas said. "Is the kid okay?"

"The kid's fine, but he's sucking the life out of me," she said. "I desperately need a cheeseburger, and Mark's got the money."

"I could float you a cheeseburger loan," Lucas offered.

She stood up and dusted off the seat of her shorts: "I accept. I'm really starving. Who do you shoot for . . . ?"

"BCA," he said, and she nodded, and Lucas asked, "Too quiet. I'd like to see a little life in the crowd."

"Too hot," she said. Speaking as an old riot professional: "Basic rule of riots: you don't have riots when it's too hot. People get all pukey. Gotta wait until the evening, when things cool off. The best riots are when you have a long summer day, with a long evening where it cools off a little."

"I don't know all that technical stuff," Lucas said with a smile.

They stepped around legs and bikes and clumps of people with signs and got to a street grill—the woman and the kid were convenient cover—and he bought her a cheeseburger and fries and a Coke, and got a Diet Coke for himself, and twiddled his fingers at the baby, and then took the baby while the woman, whose name was Lucy, ate the cheeseburger and they walked back to the tent. The baby had quiet blue eyes, observant and contained, and seemed interested in Lucas's nose.

A passing stoner, with a sun-bleached ponytail, hazy blue eyes, and a lute in his hand, looked at Lucy, and then Lucas and the baby, and said, "Got that May and December shit going, huh? Good one."

Lucy said, "Well, the sex is terrific."

Lucas said, "More like May and August."

The stoner tapped Lucas on the chest and said, "Good one, man. I mean, you know? Keep it going, you know? Long as you can."

"It's hard, man, you know, sometimes, with a woman like this," Lucas said. "They want too much, sometimes."

The stoner bobbed his head: "I know that for sure, man. Life is hard, and then you fuckin', you know . . . die." Sobered by the thought, he wandered away.

"WE'RE GONNA BUILD a new egalitarian culture, *man,*" Lucy said to Lucas as she sat down on her blanket, chewing on the cheeseburger. "To each, according to his needs, from each, according to his ability. Which means that the insurance agents can keep on selling insurance for sixty hours a week and that stoner can keep getting wrecked every day."

"Just a guy," Lucas said. "A lost soul."

"I'm getting tired of it," Lucy said. She squinted up through the tree leaves, and the sun sliding down to the west. Equinox coming in three weeks, and then winter. "Think I'm going home to Massachusetts. Get my dad to send me to grad school."

"Think he'll do it?"

"My dad will do anything I want him to," she said. "Like you and your daughter."

Lucas nodded. "Yeah . . . What about your husband?"

"Why wasn't he here to buy me a cheeseburger when I needed it?" she asked. She took a few fries. "Fuck the revolution."

A group of ten protesters in black began a chant: "No War but the Class War! No War but the Class War!" and people in the park began drifting that way, and a couple of cops idled along with them.

Lucas and Lucy chatted for a while—Lucy had been

living in Iowa, where she and her husband were summer visitors at a drama commune, which gave revolutionary plays to local farm communities, and her husband was working on a screenplay—and then Lucas got up to leave. "Say hi when you see me around," he said.

"Thanks for the food," she said. "I was starting to hurt."

BACK IN THE HomTel, Lindy screeched, in a high-climbing soprano, "Goddamnittttttt . . . Brutus . . ."

Brutus had turned her every way but loose, faceup, face-down, upside down, and when he was all done, he lay sweating and naked and red on the bed, and said, worn out, "You really are the best piece of ass on the North American continent."

"Not including Europe?" She was sitting on a towel, because she didn't want to leak on the bed. She must be in her mid-thirties, now, Cohn thought, and still had small curved breasts with pink nipples and freckles.

"I don't know about Europe," Cohn said. "You hear stories about the French women. But hell, they're in France. It's like that song: 'She ain't Rose, but Rose ain't here.'"

Lindy pouted: "I'm better than anybody in France."

"Probably," Cohn agreed. "I sorta haven't tested those waters."

"Better not, either," she said.

"You fuck anybody while I was gone?" he asked.

"Well, sure, a couple," she said. "It was two years, Brute. What was I supposed to do, scratch?"

"I hope to hell you didn't catch anything," he said.

She slapped his leg: "I didn't. I'm careful. They were married men—I was saving my good stuff for you."

"They pay you?"

"They bought me some stuff," she admitted.

"Expensive stuff?"

"Well, Richard, there was this guy Richard Blanding in Birmingham, he paid my rent and bought me a car."

"That's something," Cohn said.

"A Pontiac Solstice. Bright yellow. Not exactly a Ferrari."

Cohn closed his eyes and sighed, and sank into the softness of the memory foam, and let all his bones relax. She started to hum, like she did when she was getting bored. He thought, Fuck her.

He'd lied to her about being the best piece of ass in North America. Lindy was a good old country girl, but more the Pontiac Solstice of pussy, rather than the Ferrari. Richard Blanding, whoever he was, had known precisely what he was getting.

LINDY, FOR HER part, humming, rubbing at the polish on her toenails, thinking that she needed another pedicure, took a long careful look at the naked man beside her. She'd met him when she was sixteen, and he was in his mid-twenties. He'd been a wild one, who liked it all: money, women, gambling, cocaine and reefer and Saturday night fights in the gravel parking lots outside country roadhouses, with the frogs croaking from the roadside ditches and the fireflies blinking out over the farm fields.

He'd grown up with a middle-class family, and if he'd done what they'd wanted him to do, he'd have gone to college and might have had his own construction business now, building out the suburbs of Atlanta or Birmingham. Might even be rich, but he wouldn't have had any fun.

His fun—the women, gambling, cocaine and reefer—took cash money, and didn't leave much time for actual work. The solution to the problem was obvious: take the money from people who already had it. He did it for a few years, finally got caught and sent to prison, where he got his graduate education and had time to think it all over.

He'd decided not to go straight, but simply to get better at his job.

He had.

That's when they met, Cohn flush after an armored

car holdup, and now here they were, almost twenty years later, in another motel. Cohn's face had developed some harsh lines on both sides of his mouth—smile lines, but frown lines, too—and crow's feet at the corners of his eyes. His hair was still thick and curly, and he had the great teeth. Still thin and tough, but getting older. Gray in his chest hair . . .

Getting older, like she was, she thought. Not many more years when she could count on being taken care of because she was nice to somebody . . .

COHN REACHED OVER and stroked her leg: "Can't tell you how much I like seeing you," he said.

"Me too," she said.

RANDY WHITCOMB HAD red hair precisely the same shade as Cohn's, but never had Cohn's potential. Whitcomb had been caught up in the early days of gangsta music, riveted to MTV when he should have been in school. Unlike most people, he believed the words. And though he lived in a ticky-tacky St. Paul white-bread suburb where the biggest public facility was a hockey arena, Whitcomb was naturally a gangsta, even with his bony white face and improbable thatch of hair. When he finally got kicked out of high school, he moved to north Minneapolis, a modest but occasionally violent black ghetto, where he picked up the language and sold dope on the street and eventually started running two or three whores that nobody else wanted.

Those were the big days of the crack wars, when everybody was buying the stores out of baking soda and everybody was cooking up the crack in the kitchen, twelve-year-olds were walking the streets with nines and bad attitudes. The cops were going crazy, and nobody really paid much attention to a small-time white guy living off marijuana and a short chain of low-rent women.

But Whitcomb was living the gangsta life, with paisley shirts and wide-wale corduroy pants and green-dyed lizard-skin cowboy boots. Then one day he found out that one of his whores was talking to a cop about who was doing what, who was selling what, who might be getting what package from El Paso through UPS or FedEx, or what guy might be coming in from Chicago with a big suitcase, riding in on the 'dog . . . well, Whitcomb, with one too many gangsta musicals banging in his head, went for the pimp punishment: found her and cut her face up with a church key.

The thing is, she'd been talking to Davenport.

Davenport got him in the back of a bar and beat him like a big bass drum.

Later Whitcomb had accidentally gotten involved with a guy who was a serial killer—really was an accident, in that street way, where all kinds of people bump into each other—had gotten involved in a shootout, and was left paralyzed from the waist down. That ended his sex life, but hadn't changed his head that much. Davenport had been responsible for the shootout, in Whitcomb's eyes; had been responsible for everything that had gone wrong in his life, including two stretches behind bars . . .

He sat in the van and watched the cops and the protesters streaming up and down the hill, another guy in a wheelchair, one of those happy dildos you see around who don't even seem to realize how fucked-up they are, and he tracked Letty through the park, as she talked to a woman at a tent, and then to a tall guy who looked like Davenport, but didn't dress right, and then hooked up with two kids, boys, the kind whom Whitcomb hated, good-looking athletes who probably got good grades and had money and ate peanut butter sandwiches with Mom and Wally and the Beav . . .

Briar sat behind the wheel, watching the crowd, until Whitcomb said, "There she goes. They're going someplace. Get going that way . . . that way, dummy. Hurry . . ."

LETTY LEFT LUCAS in the park and went off with John and Jeff, taking the front passenger seat in John's car. John would have to concentrate on his driving—he'd only had his license for a month—and Jeff was safely stuffed in the back. No hands to deal with.

She was going to have to start thinking about sex pretty soon, she knew, but now was too soon. When she really got back to school, maybe. A friend of hers, a month younger than she was, was already being thoroughly mauled by her boyfriend, bra up, pants down, and though there hadn't yet been any actual intercourse, that wasn't far off. She'd be giving it up during football season, unless something happened to the relationship, Letty thought. The girl was in love and that made it all a lot more complicated.

Still, the whole thing made her uneasy. She'd get around to it, but . . . later. Not with John. He was too old, a senior. Jeff was in her grade, and had a shot, when he got rid of the braces. And she was still a little flat-chested. That bothered her a bit, that a boy might go in looking for a mountain and find a molehill.

Weather had told her not to worry: "I know you can't *not* worry about it—but, don't worry about it. You're not the big-boobed kind, and believe me, that's better. The boys are going to like you fine. More than fine. You're going to have to fight them off with a baseball bat."

Letty rode around with John and Jeff for a while, looking at the political freaks, and then John said, "You get any money off your old man?"

"Yup. A twenty."

"You gonna treat?"

THEY WENT TO the McDonald's on West Seventh Street, down from the Xcel Center where the convention was being held. The guys got supersized and Letty went for a Quarter Pounder, no cheese, a small fries, and a Diet Coke, and they sat there and talked about the school year coming up, and who was going with whom, and who might like who else, and what they'd heard Harry was doing with Sally, and that Frank had made enough money working two summer jobs to buy a dork-mobile, meaning a Camaro, ten years old, which they made fun of, although John was driving his mother's Camry, which nobody mentioned; and they watched the convention people come and go.

Then Randy Whitcomb rolled through the door in his wheelchair, trailed by Briar. Letty recognized him as soon as he came in, and caught Whitcomb's eyes when they flicked toward her. She said nothing, but looked down at her fries. Whitcomb and Briar got their food and rolled back to the table next to Letty and the boys. Whitcomb cocked his head when they got close, looked at Letty, and smiled and asked, "Don't I know you?"

She smiled and shook her head. "I don't think so."

"Lucas Davenport's girl? I think I met you when you were smaller."

She bobbed her head. "I guess. Lucas Davenport's my dad."

"I thought so," Whitcomb said. He stuck out his hand and Letty gave it a little shake. "Nice to meet you. My name's Carl Rice, and this is my friend."

"Nice to meet you," she said.

The boys wanted to talk to Letty, and Whitcomb's presence annoyed them; Whitcomb was trying to be friendly but gave off the stink of the hustler, the shyster, the guy who leans on young women. But they were polite, so they chatted, and then John said, "We better get home. My mom's gonna need the car."

"Mom's car, huh?" Whitcomb said, still friendly, but they all felt the hook of the put-down.

"Yeah . . ." John was embarrassed, but they got out of there, and in the parking lot, on the way to the car, John said, "He's a fuckin' creep."

"He's a crippled guy," Jeff said.

Letty asked, "Could you do me a favor?"

They were in the car, buckling up, and John said, "Sure. What?"

"Drive around the block and come back and park over there. I want to see what car he gets into," she said.

"Sure. Why?"

"Because I think he was looking at me today, at the Capitol," Letty said. "It's like he followed me or something."

"I told you he's a creep," John said.

They went around the block and parked for fifteen seconds, and then Whitcomb and the woman came out and got into a white van, using a ramp that folded down from the side. They watched as the woman did something with straps to hold Whitcomb's chair in place, and then got into the driver's seat.

"That's him," Letty said. "That's the guy I saw. Could you guys do me one more favor?"

"Sure."

"Get up close enough behind him that you can read the license number. Not too close. Jeff and I can get down, so if his girlfriend looks in the mirror, she'll only see one guy."

And that's what they did.

WHITCOMB NEVER KNEW.

He said to Briar, "Gonna give her to Ranch. Gonna let Ranch fuck her. Gonna whip her with my stick until she looks like a skinned rabbit."

Briar said, "I don't know."

"You're not supposed to know, dummy. I'm supposed to know. So shut the fuck up and drive."

5

SATURDAY NIGHT, AND Rosie Cruz was driving west on I-494 on the Bloomington strip near the Mall of America and Minneapolis–St. Paul International, a digital police radio on the floor of her car, the illegal software picking up police calls from the major dispatching centers in the metro area. The sun was down and the lights were up, and people were ricocheting through the bars and motels along the strip, putting cocaine up their noses and Wild Turkey down their throats, and Rosie said into her cell phone, "The radios are hot, but they're all in St. Paul. There's some kind of cop rehearsal going on. If you're ready—do it."

"See you back at the motel," Cohn said.

Cruz dropped off 494, up the ramp and across the highway to the south, down the side streets to the Wayfarer Motel, thinking about Cohn and Lane and McCall going into the High Hat with masks and guns.

Nothing she could do about it now. They were ninety-five percent good, five percent in trouble; but *she* wasn't in trouble. If Cohn and McCall and Lane went down, well, there were more where they came from.

SHE PARKED OUTSIDE the Wayfarer Motel, walked down the side of the first floor, past all the doors, climbed the concrete stairs to the second floor, knocked on 214. The door popped open, and Justice Shafer was there in all his flat-eyed, underfed shitkicker glory. He stepped back and asked, "Anything?"

"Not a thing," she said. "You all sighted in?"

"Ready to go, if we need it." His tongue touched his dry bottom lip. "I'm running low on cash."

She nodded and took an envelope from her pocket, ripped the end off, and thrust the naked stack of bills at him, holding on to the envelope. He pulled the bills free—fifties—thumbed them, and nodded. "How's Bill?"

"Bill's lying low," she said. "There are about a million cops out here." She checked the time on her cell phone. "He's moving around, but he said he'll call you at eight-thirty, or thereabout, if he can get to a clean phone. The last time I talked to him, he was in some roadhouse over in Wisconsin."

Shafer turned to look at the bedside clock: 8:13. "I'll hang around here."

Cruz stepped back to the door. "You keep down, Justice. There's a big chance that nothing'll happen and you can go on your way, no harm done. But you gotta stay sober. If this thing does pop, and the anarchists head in toward the Capitol, we're gonna need every man we can get. Gonna need to take out the leadership."

"I'm ready," Shafer said. He squared his shoulders. "How long should I wait for Bill to call?"

"I'd wait until nine—after that, I doubt that he will. Like I said, things are getting tense. One of these anarchist guys put out the word that he wants Bill's head. They put a hundred thousand on it."

"Ah, man, a hundred grand?" Shafer was amazed by the

amounts they threw around. He'd never made more than twelve dollars an hour, except when he was holding up gas stations.

"Stay tight," Cruz said, and she was out the door.

Shafer was a moron, and he was undoubtedly sitting on the bed staring at the phone, but once down in the parking lot, she sat five minutes and watched the door to his room. She'd made a big point about his policing up his brass at the quarry where he sighted the gun in . . .

Five minutes gone, she pulled on a hairnet and gloves and walked over to his truck and took the key out of her pocket and popped the back hatch on his topper, crawled inside and pulled it down. He'd thrown a plastic sheet over the gear inside, and she pulled it back, spotted the olive drab army-surplus ammo boxes. There were three of them, and she popped the lid on the lightest one and found it half-full of empty .50-caliber shells. She took four, crawled back out of the truck, locked it, and went back to her car.

Looked up at the room: the dummy was still sitting there, she thought, staring at the phone, waiting for Bill. But Bill wasn't making any phone calls to hotels in Minnesota: Bill was in jail in Portland, Oregon.

COHN, LANE, AND McCall had each driven separately to the hotel, positioning the cars for trouble. If the cops got a call about three guys doing a stickup, and saw a car with three guys in it, they might pull a traffic stop to take a peek. If there was no trouble, and they all left separately, they had an extra inch of safety.

The night was warm and starlit, quiet in Hudson, but with traffic building into Minneapolis. At the hotel, Cohn circled the block a half dozen times, saw Lane's car ahead of him, saw Lane spot a car backing out of its parking place, circled a couple more times, saw a movement, pulled in smoothly, got the space. McCall would have gone to the parking ramp, the other emergency car. The scene was just as Cruz said it would be: people coming and going around the hotel. He walked a block back, could hear cheering in the distance—some political thing in Loring Park, he thought—and turned down the alley toward the hotel's loading dock. McCall was already crossing the dock, Lane behind him. Cohn took a last look around.

This was a danger point—if, for some reason, a cop car went past the mouth of the alley, saw him, and the cop got curious, Cohn would be there with a mask and a gun, and that would be hard to explain.

So he'd kill the cop. He'd killed a cop in Houston one time, and never thought about it anymore. Bad luck, for him and especially for the cop. No animus involved. Some black guy went to death row for the killing—more bad luck for the black guy.

Lane and McCall were inside. There were five concrete steps up to the dock, nothing on the dock but a metal Dumpster, two steel doors where deliveries would go in, and a steel door to the left, open just an inch. He walked through it and found Lane and McCall at the bottom of the stairs, their masks in their hands.

"Ready?" He pulled his mask out, slipped it over his head.

McCall said, "All set," but there was tension in his voice. He tended to get more and more stressed until the action began, and then he was fine. He added, "Car's right where we planned: back of the third floor."

Pulled on the latex gloves. Adrenaline starting to flow with all of them now, Cohn could hear them breathing in the enclosed concrete stairwell, as if they'd already climbed the stairs. McCall was wearing the tux and red shirt, his mask rolled on top of his head like a watch cap, an empty FedEx envelope in his hand.

"Ready," McCall said. Lane nodded.

They were fast going up the stairs, their footfalls echoing off the multiple concrete walls that went up nine stories, the smell of raw cement pushing through their masks. They stopped at the door with the red-painted "5" on it, listening. McCall stepped out into the hallway, one hand to his face, like he had a headache. The hall was empty and he pulled the mask most of the way down. He could see the smoked-glass camera dome halfway down the hall. Film only, Cruz had said; no live monitoring.

She'd better be right. But of course she was.

Room 505 was nearly at the front of the hotel and they had to move a long way down the hallway, not quite at a run; found it, knocked with a car key. Felt a vibration from inside.

"Somebody's coming," McCall muttered. Cohn stood between McCall and the camera, and McCall rolled up his mask. From inside, "Yes?"

"FedEx," McCall said. He held up the envelope, so it could be seen through the peephole.

"Just a minute." The door rattled and popped open and McCall turned his face away as a short bald guy in suit pants and a blue dress shirt opened the door, and Cohn was on top of him, flashing the gun, hit him squarely in the center of the chest with his good right hand and the short guy went down and the door banged shut and a young woman in a burgundy dress, sitting on a couch with a carton of chocolate milk, yelped and looked like she was about to scream and she lifted her feet off the floor and Lane was there and he batted the milk away from her like a T-ball, and it splattered across her face and across the curtains and McCall landed on the short man's chest, and hit him once in the face with his fist, breaking the short man's nose, and the woman yelped again and screeched, "Don't do that." Lane put his face six inches from hers and yelled, "Shut the fuck up, bitch," and she shut up, but whimpered, and he swatted her in the face and she went down on the couch, bounced, and rolled off on the floor, losing her shoes.

The short man was stunned and crying and holding the heels of both hands to his nose, and Cohn put the gun three inches from his forehead and asked, "Where's the money?"

and before the short man could answer, he started counting down seconds: "Five, four," and he pulled the hammer back on the pistol.

The woman blurted, "Behind the bed." McCall went to look behind the bed, but she said, "Not that bed—in the next room," and she began weeping. There was a connecting door and McCall peeked through, and then went through, and a minute later he was back with a suitcase.

Lane was inches from the woman, who was supine on the floor, her side against the front of the couch, and he laughed and said, "Boys, if we got time, I'd like to get a piece of this one," and he reached out and ripped down the front of her dress. She cowered away and Cohn said, almost absently, "Don't have time for a fuck," and Lane said, "She could suck it while we wait . . ." He pressed the muzzle of his gun against her head and said, "Bet you sucked a little dick in your time, huh, honey?"

McCall was unzipping the suitcase and he said, "Don't have time for that. We could take her with us, though. Get back to the crib, get her airtight, and when we're done, we could rent her pussy out. Make even more money."

The short guy said, "Please don't hurt her," and Cohn snapped and kicked him in the ribs and said, "Say what, fool? Say what? You talking to us? We wanna fuck this bitch up every hole she's got, that's what we'll do, fool."

The short guy groaned and rolled away and Cohn kicked him twice more, and McCall looked in the suitcase and said, "Holy shit," because he'd pulled out two shirts and had found layers and layers of fifty-dollar bills, bound together with rubber bands.

Cohn said, "Let's go. Jim, we'll be five minutes. You wanna stick your dick in her mouth, you better get off in five minutes, because we're outa here in five."

Then Cohn and McCall were in the hallway and as the door closed, they heard Lane say, "You got a pretty little mouth, missus," and Cohn said as they were going down the hall, "The dumb shit got that out of that hillbilly movie."

McCall said, "I felt a little sorry for her. She looked nice."

Cohn nodded and said, "You do what you gotta do, and she's gotta be scared to death."

McCall said, "One thing: Rosie's information was right on."

Cohn chuckled. "Good thing for us."

THEY WENT DOWN a flight to 431 and did it all over: but when they kicked the door, a fifty-something, tubby, pasty-faced man with a beard staggered back across the room, and before Cohn could get to him, lifted his hands over his head and said, "Ah, shit. It's behind the bed."

Cohn stopped dead, then reached out and patted the man on the face. "Smart guy."

McCall fished another suitcase from behind the bed, looked into it, and said, "Better and better."

"I knew this was gonna happen someday," the bearded man said. "I told them."

Cohn had been pointing a gun at the man's head, but the fat man, seeming unconcerned, carefully sidled away, and reached out and picked up a glass of scotch.

Cohn said, "Don't call for help for a couple of minutes. If the cops come down on top of us, and I've got to run, I'll call my brother on my cell phone and read him your name and address and he'll come to your house and cut the heads off anybody he finds there. You understand that?"

"They won't find anybody—I've been divorced so many times I rent the furniture," the man said. "Anyway, I don't want to get my head cut off. I'll give you five minutes."

"Even better," Cohn said.

"I told them it was going to happen. Too much money floating around," the man said.

Cohn was backing toward the door. "Five minutes."

The bearded guy said, "Take one of my business cards."

Cohn glanced at McCall, who shrugged. "What?"

"Take one of my business cards. Give me a call once in a while," he said. "You know, couple years from now. A few weeks before the midterm congressionals."

"Why would I do that?" Cohn asked.

The guy spread his hands, rattled the ice cubes in the scotch glass. "Because there's a lot more money than this going around. I know where it is and who's got it, from time to time. I'd want . . . a third?"

Cohn looked at him for a moment, then said, "Where's the business card?"

"On the table," the guy said.

Cohn stepped over, saw them in a desktop card dispenser. He took a couple, slipped them into his pocket. "I might call."

"I'll keep my eyes open," the guy said.

"You do that," Cohn said. To McCall: "How much money we got in there?"

"Shit, I can't tell. It's stuffed. Fifties and hundreds, just like the other one. All used."

Cohn nodded, then got on his cell phone and called Lane: "Go."

He put his phone away, stepped away from the bearded man, then lashed out, hitting the man on the cheekbone below his left eye. The man went down, and then crawled, on his elbows, saying, "Oh, Jesus. Oh, Jesus," and then rolled over and looked up, frightened now. The blow had cut open his cheek, and he was bleeding heavily.

Cohn went over to the bag, where he took out as many bundles of cash as he could span in one hand. He knelt next to the bearded man and said, "Sorry—it won't hurt for long. Need the verisimilitude, you know . . . There's gotta be fifty thousand in this little pile." He dropped it on the guy's chest. "It's yours. Give it to somebody you trust before you call the cops. Or hide it where they won't look. Maybe in two years, get a real payday, huh?"

He patted the man on the leg, and they left: down the hall, down the stairs, where they met Lane on the way down, out on the street, down to the cars.

As they walked along, Lane said, "I scared the shit out of them." He laughed, a low growl that went huh-huh-huh. "When you left, the little asshole started running his mouth, about how all the cops would be looking out for us, because of how important he is. I picked him up by his shirt and shook him like a baby."

"Didn't hurt him too bad?" Cohn asked.

"No, no. I was careful. He's bleeding, he's gonna have so many bruises he'll look like he's been in a car wreck, but he's not hurt."

"How about the Nazi signs?" McCall asked.

"The chick saw them—I saw her looking at them," Lane said. "Some poor sonofabitch cop is going to spend the next week with his nose in the tattoo files."

Cohn nodded. "Good." And it *was* good: he had a competent crew.

AT THE MOTEL, they were like ballplayers after a big win, knuckle-bumping each other and laughing, reliving it; even Cruz, when she showed up, got into it. Then they dumped the money on the bed and started counting: it was all fifties and hundreds, all used, nonsequential, and showed nothing under a black light. Counting took the best part of a half hour, with all of them at it, ten-thousand-dollar bundles, wrapped with rubber bands.

When they finished, Cohn counted the bundles: "One forty-one, one forty-two, one forty-three . . . and a half."

Cruz said, "One million, four hundred and thirty thousand, and a half."

"Good one," Lane said.

McCall gave Cruz a squeeze. "You da man."

6

IN THE YEARS they'd been married, the telephone rang in the bedroom once too often, so they finally took it out. At five o'clock Sunday morning, when the phone started ringing, Lucas had been asleep for four hours. Because of the convention, he got up and staggered out through the living room to the nearest portable and looked at the caller ID. Nothing but a number, but he recognized the number.

"Yeah."

"Can you come down to my office?"

"Right now?"

"That'd be good."

"Half hour?"

"Okay."

"WHO WAS THAT?" Weather asked. Sunday was her day to sleep in.

"Neil Mitford." Mitford was Governor Elmer Henderson's executive assistant, chief weasel, confidant, fixer, and maybe bagman. He'd been in Washington for the fight over the Homeland Security arrests.

"What'd he want?"

"Dunno," Lucas said.

She went back to sleep and Lucas stared in the bathroom mirror for a couple of minutes, trying to get his eyes open, then shaved, brushed his teeth, stood in the shower and let hot water beat on the back of his neck. Toweled off, he got dressed: jeans, a blue T-shirt, walking shoes, sport coat, Colt Gold Cup .45. On the way out, he remembered the convention credentials, got them off the dresser, slipped them into his pocket with his ID. The cameras were still in the car.

Feeling tired, but not bad; and the morning was perfect, cool, crisp. August was Minnesota's most perfect month, and this was the final day of it. September might be fine, too, but not perfect. Sometimes, they saw snowflakes in September.

He rolled the Porsche out of the garage, yawned, headed through the quiet city streets out to I-35E, the car's exhaust burbling along, north to the Capitol. When he got there, he took a lap around it, to see what was going on, if anything. A speaker's shell had been set up on the Capitol lawn, for an antiwar rally later in the day. A few people in message T-shirts were wandering around, two of them smoking, and a kid was going through a garbage can, looking for something to eat. He drove back up the hill, parked in the state garage behind the Capitol and walked down to the building, flashed his ID at a Capitol guard, and continued up to Mitford's broom-closet office. He knocked, tried the door, but it was locked, and he heard Mitford call, "Hang on."

"It's Lucas."

Mitford came to the door buttoning his pants, the belt undone. He was in a day-old undershirt and stocking feet, unshaven, beat up. He said, "Come on in," his voice creaking. He looked up and down the hall, then closed the door and locked it. A blanket lay on the floor next to the couch; he'd been asleep. "Got a big problem," he said.

Lucas nodded. "Yeah, I guess. It's not even six o'clock."

"I've been up all night . . ." Mitford walked around his desk and sprawled in his chair, pointed Lucas at the visitor's chair. "A hurricane is coming into New Orleans, probably going to flatten the place again. McCain may not come, the president and vice president have canceled, the whole thing is going up in smoke."

"Plus they're already pissed at your boss."

"There's that, but that's a good thing," Mitford said.

"So . . ."

"So three people got robbed at gunpoint in the High Hat last night," he said. "One of them's still in the hospital, one's a woman, she's still freaking out because the robbers threatened to take her with them, supposedly to gang-bang. The Minneapolis cops have all the information, but I want you to talk to them."

"How much did they get?" Lucas asked.

Mitford held up a finger. "They were violent, intimidating. Hats and masks and gloves. One white guy, one black, one undetermined—the white guy had swastikas tattooed on his wrists. In and out, and gone."

"How much . . . ?"

"Not much . . . a few hundred dollars . . . four-fifty, maybe."

Lucas waited for the rest of it. Mitford didn't call him in for a four-hundred-and-fifty-dollar armed robbery.

Mitford didn't get the reaction he expected, so he said, "Listen, you've been around. Political campaigns take all kinds of donations. Some of them, people don't want to know about. They tend to be in cash, for street-workers, canvassers . . ."

"Vote buyers . . ."

"Whatever," Mitford said. "But we don't really buy votes—it'd cost too much."

"How much?"

"I'm not sure exactly," he said. "I'd guess . . . a million-two? A million-five? Depending on how much they'd already moved."

"In cash?"

"Mmm . . ."

"Small, used, unmarked bills?" Lucas asked. Of course they would be.

"Mmm. In Philly, they call it street money."

"So what's the problem? Put the cops on it," Lucas said. "Hell, it's a bunch of Republicans. If the news leaks . . ."

"Nice thought, but I'm afraid that some of the people with, you know, this kind of cash, uh, might have been in Denver a couple weeks ago," Mitford said. The Democratic convention had been in Denver.

"Ah, man."

"And these guys can't really talk about it," Mitford said. He was all but wringing his hands. "Somebody, you know, could point out that moving this much money around might constitute some kind of infraction."

"Infraction? They'd be on their way to Club Fed if the word got out," Lucas said.

"Maybe. So they won't complain, they won't talk, they won't say anything to anybody they haven't been . . . reassured about," Mitford said. "They filed robbery reports to cover themselves with their bosses, so nobody would think they skipped with the cash. One of the guys really got the shit beat out of him. But they won't talk."

"So, if they won't complain . . . that's life," Lucas said.

"The problem is, there's probably twenty guys like this in town," Mitford said. "The robbers knew exactly where to hit, where to go . . . one of them was wearing a High Hat room-service uniform."

"You think they'll do more?"

"Why not? If you've got the information, it's easy pickings," Mitford said. "These guys are like accountants, pencil-necked geeks with sugar money, ethanol money, oil money, automobile money, union money . . . they don't know from robbery. They've got no security, because they can't afford to have other people know what they're doing. But these robbers, man—they're crazy. They must be coked up, cranked up, something. They beat the shit out of this one guy."

"Could be a technique," Lucas suggested.

"Yeah?" Mitford was interested.

"Get on top of people, intimidate them, scare them so bad that they won't resist," Lucas said. "Pro robbers'll do that, get on top and stay on top. Of course, some of them just like to hurt people."

"Can you take a look at it?"

Lucas shrugged. "Sure, I'll take a look. But I'm not going to jail. If somebody mentions big money, I'll make a note."

Mitford sighed and shook his head, turning, and looked at a blank wall, where, in most offices, there'd be a window. "When we went with you, there was an argument. We knew you were flexible, because you've always operated that way. But you've got so goddamn much money, the question was, were you flexible *enough*? Some guys, most guys, can't tell us to go fuck ourselves."

"I'm not telling you to go fuck yourself," Lucas said. "I can call you a confidential informant, that doesn't bother me. But I'm not a cover-up guy. There might come a time when I've got to go public with it. But not necessarily . . ."

"Not necessarily . . ." Mitford gnawed at a fingernail, spit a piece of nail at his wastebasket. "Well . . . take it easy. If you really get in a crack, and have to make a record, let me know ahead of time. Let me get a jump on the PR. But I'll tell you, I know for sure that none of these people will admit that they had the cash."

"So why do *anything*?" Lucas asked. "Why not call it a day and go home?"

"Because they're some of *us*," Mitford said. He patted himself on the chest. "Us political guys. We're like cops. Everybody hates us, so we've got to take care of each other. And I really don't want to see anybody get killed by these assholes."

"If I get them, if there's a trial . . ."

"I'll worry about that when I get to it," Mitford said. "Prosecutors are politicians—plea bargains are out there, things can be done. But right now, Lucas: stop them."

Lucas just looked at him for a moment.

Mitford pushed some paper across his desk. "Names, room numbers, cell phones. Please?"

"I'll take a look," he said.

"And . . . one more thing," Mitford said. "Keep it to yourself? Much as you can?"

LUCAS WENT BACK home, got undressed, crawled into bed, and went back to sleep. He woke again when Weather got up. She pulled a drape halfway back, and a shaft of sunlight cut across the room. "What are you doing here?" she asked.

"Need to talk," he said, rolling onto his back.

"Uh-oh. What happened?"

"Get cleaned up, then I'll come brush my teeth and we can get some coffee."

SEVEN O'CLOCK, AND quiet, though they'd all be up soon enough. Weather usually got up at five-fifteen on weekdays and was at the hospital by a little after six: sleeping to seven o'clock was a weekly treat. Lucas rarely got up before nine o'clock, rarely went back to bed before one-thirty or two o'clock. He got up with her on Sunday so they could get an hour together with a little quiet.

They got coffee going, and oatmeal, and some ready-made hot-cross buns from a can, and odors mixed pleasantly across the kitchen. When she sat down with the coffee, he told her about the robberies, about the no-tell cash.

"So Neil wants you to catch these people, or at least stop them, without telling anybody about the money," she said.

"That's about it," Lucas said.

"Why'd he tell *you* about the money? He could have asked you to look into it, without telling you about it," Weather said. "He could have told you that these people were important, or were political friends, and that would have kept you out of it, ethically . . ."

"He knew I'd find out," Lucas said. "He wanted to be able to predict what I'll do."

"All right."

"The thing is, I already have an idea who they might be. They might be some guys who killed a couple of cops in New York."

He told her about the Friday call from Lily Rothenburg. She'd heard a story from Del or Sloan about Lucas and Lily and the front seat of an earlier Porsche; she said now, "Old Bucket Seat."

Lucas rolled his eyes. "C'mon. It was years ago. She's married and has a family . . ."

"You never tried to get me in the Porsche . . ."

"At our age, we'd have to take a year of yoga first," Lucas said. "Anyway, she called to tell me that there's this heavy-duty stickup gang in town. They only go for large amounts of cash, and they're good at it—always work off a plan, bold, but very careful. This sounds like them."

"Then you've got a problem," Weather said. "You're going to have to bring some other people in on the deal. Other cops. You can't go up against them by yourself. Then you've got to tell the other guys."

"That can be handled," Lucas said. "Cohn might be down in Texas by now. On the other hand, he might have a list. If I can spot the gang, there'd be no problem bringing in a SWAT team to take them down. I mean, there're already two robberies on the table. Formal complaints, one guy in the hospital. It's more . . . You know, if I do this, I'm sort of one of them. The political guys."

"You already are," Weather said.

He wagged a finger at her. "No. I've taken assignments that had a political component, but the *assignments* were legit. You know, chasing down some asshole because Henderson owes some sheriff a favor. This is different—I know about a pretty serious crime. I'm going to have to ignore it. Probably."

"You've ignored crimes before," Weather said. "When we got Letty, all those nuns were bringing illegal drugs across the border. You knew about it and let it go."

"There was a certain morality involved, there," Lucas said. "I was on the right side of it. One of the women said, you know, they weren't smuggling illegal drugs—the drugs were legal both here and in Canada. What they were smuggling was illegal prices. They were doing right, even if it was against the law. These people, this money . . . you know, they're going to buy votes or something."

Weather said, "I can't help you on the morality thing. I can give you something to think about—whether or not there's all this money involved, you've got a lead on a gang that killed some cops. It's worth bringing them down no matter how much money might be involved."

"What do I tell the Minneapolis guys?"

"Tell them . . . something's going on. Something's going on, and that this gang sounds like the gang that Lily Bucket Seat was talking about."

Lucas thought about it: "Okay, you're right. If this is Lily's gang, they need to be taken down. But I've got to tell Minneapolis something—I can't send them up against Cohn without knowing."

She nodded: "There's gonna be some tap dancing, though. You won't get through this without your best Fred Astaire."

LETTY WANDERED INTO the kitchen, wrapped in a ratty blue terry-cloth robe, looking sleepy, rubbing one hand through her tangled blond hair. "Smells good," she said. "God, I need some caffeine."

Lucas grinned at her and said, "Long night?"

"I should have read it last month . . . Is there any Coke?" She opened the refrigerator and peered inside. She'd been assigned to read *To Kill a Mockingbird* over the summer, and to write a paper on it, and had let it go until the last minute.

"How much more do you have to read?" Weather asked.

"Eighty pages," she said, twisting the cap off a bottle of Coke. "But I've got to get over to the station. I'm getting a camera, I'm going to do a piece on the kids up at the Capitol. I mean, like, you know, people my age in politics."

Lucas dropped his eyelids and made a snoring sound, and Weather snapped: "Lucas!"

"Ah, he's right," Letty said. "Another thumb-sucker. But, I get the camera time. The kids at school freak out. Emily Grissom can't stand it. She thinks I'm sleeping with somebody over there."

"Ah, God," Weather said, outraged. "Letty, do you really have to do this stuff? You could be a surgeon, or—well, you probably wouldn't want to be a lawyer . . ."

Lucas stood up, kissed Weather on the forehead, and said, "Thanks," and "Counsel your daughter," and headed out the door.

As he went, he heard Letty ask, "Mom, could you give me a lift over to the station? I need to get there early . . ."

A MINNEAPOLIS COP named Rick Jones had caught the robberies. Lucas found him at the Dairy Delight, a downtown ice-cream stand modeled after a Dairy Queen, getting a chocolate-dipped vanilla cone. Jones was a tall, slender black man with a shaved head and a diamond earring. He not only *thought* he looked like a pro basketball player, but he actually *did*. He was wearing jeans, a loose gray army T-shirt, running shoes, and dark wraparound sunglasses.

"Lucas motherfucking Davenport," he said, as Lucas wandered up.

"That'd be *mister* motherfucking Davenport to the likes of you," Lucas said. He checked the menu behind the Dairy Delight window, ordered a small hot fudge sundae from the girl behind the counter, and said to Jones, "I was just over at the office. They say you caught those robberies at the High Hat."

"Yeah. I said to myself, 'RJ, there's something going on here that you don't know about.' And guess what—here comes Davenport."

"Well, you're right about that," Lucas said. "I got my ass jerked out of bed by a guy who works for the governor. These folks were here for the convention . . ."

"That's what they told me," Jones said.

". . . representing some big-time special interests. They get hit, they start making phone calls. I don't like it any better than you do, but they *did* get hit."

"They lied to me about it," Jones said. "I asked them how much was stolen, they said, you know, 'hundreds of dollars.' I was like, right—you're in a six-hundred-dollar-a-night hotel suite, and they got your money clip."

Lucas didn't try to deny it. "Anyway . . ."

Jones was crunching through the chocolate, dabbed his lips with a napkin, and said, "So they sent you along to put a wrench on my nuts."

"No, they sent me along to look into the robberies on my own. I talked to Danny"—Danny Lake was the head of robbery-homicide—"and he said I could sit in. The thing is . . ."

The counter girl passed Lucas his hot fudge and a plastic spoon, and Lucas paid and they ambled down the street. ". . . The thing is, it's possible that I got a line on these guys."

Jones's eyebrows went up. "How'd that happen?"

"An old friend called me from New York. Nothing to do

with politics, she just called out of the blue," Lucas said. He outlined what Lily Rothenburg had passed along, and mentioned the Photoshopped mug shots.

"You got these pictures?" Jones asked.

"Got them, but I haven't printed them," Lucas said. "Everybody's working this weekend, so I can get that done right away. I wanted to check with you first, so, you know—I don't step on your feet."

"I'll tell you what, I don't mind too much, you looking over my shoulder," Jones said, serious now. "Maybe some other time, I'd mind. But right now—everybody's used up. If we're gonna run these around to the hotels and motels, it's gonna be you and me. Everybody else is working the Republicans."

"I could probably get one guy to help out," Lucas said. "I can e-mail you the jpegs. You can pass them out on this side of the river, I'll take the other side."

"It's something. You wanna talk to the victims?" Jones asked.

"Yeah—but I wanted to talk to you first," Lucas said.

"I knew something was up with them," Jones said. "You got any idea how much these assholes really took?"

"Nobody talks about money—but these guys, Brutus Cohn, whoever, they don't steal four hundred dollars and an engagement ring," Lucas said. "They know what they're doing."

"Fuckin' Republicans," Jones said.

"Yeah, well—I was told that these guys were in Denver last week," Lucas said.

"Way of the world, baby," Jones said.

Lucas wadded up the hot fudge sundae cup and tossed it at a trash basket. Hit the rim and went in.

"Brick," Jones said.

"Brick my ass," Lucas said. "With my skills, looks, intelligence, and speed, and your tennis shoes, we coulda been in the NBA."

Jones laughed and said, "Well, maybe. If you could jump more than four inches off the ground. You wanna walk over to Hennepin? We could talk to Wilson again, if he's awake."

"Let's go. And fuck a bunch of jumping. With my skills, you don't need to jump."

7

HENNEPIN GENERAL WAS a rabbit warren, but Jones seemed to know where he was going. Lucas tagged along, stopping only to squirt a handful of alcohol foam onto his palms, because he liked the feel of it. When they got to John Wilson's room, Jones knocked on the door panel and Wilson waved them in, and said into his telephone, "I gotta go—the cops are back . . . Maybe, I haven't seen him yet. Conway called this morning . . . yeah."

A woman was sitting in the corner of the private room, on a rolling chair. She was conventionally pretty, dark-haired, brown-eyed, probably-not-yet-thirty, but tired, and Lucas could see forty in the wrinkles on her face. She had a bad bruise, as deep as a port-wine stain, on her left cheek.

Lucas watched Wilson as he talked on the phone. He was a small man with a button nose and tidy bow lips, dressed in a hospital gown. He had double black eyes, an aluminum brace on his nose, held in place with tape, a scrape on one cheek that might have been made by the heel of a shoe, and a bandaged ear. A lunch tray sat on a pull-out table, with a piece of white-bread sandwich crust, and a cup of brown stuff that might have been pudding.

Jones, not wanting to interrupt the phone conversation, leaned to Lucas and nodded at the woman and said quietly, "Miz Johnson."

Wilson said, "Yeah, yeah. Get back to ya on that. Talk to ya, man," and hung up and looked at Jones and asked, "You get them?"

"Not yet." Jones turned a hand to Lucas and said, "This is Lucas Davenport, he's an agent with the state Bureau of Criminal Apprehension. He's going to be working the case along with me."

Wilson said to Lucas, "You know Neil Mitford."

Lucas nodded: "Yeah."

"They told me you'd be coming along," Wilson said. "What do you think? Full-court press, or piss on the fire and go on home?"

"Well, *we're* going to push it," Lucas said.

"Lucas thinks we might have a line on the robbers," Jones said. "Not that we'll get back your four hundred dollars, but it'd be nice to get them off the street."

"You've *got* to get them off the street," the woman said. She hunched forward, her elbows on her thighs, her hands clasped, twisting. "They're *animals*."

"Lori's still pretty shook up," Wilson said.

"If they . . . if they . . ." she stuttered. "I mean, if they'd had me in a place . . ."

"The guy was pretty brutal, pretty . . . sexual," Wilson said.

"There's therapy . . ." Lucas began, but the woman waved him off.

"I'm scared. And appalled. What kind of place is this?" she asked.

"Pretty quiet, for the most part," Lucas said. "These guys weren't off the street: they came right at you. They had some intelligence, they had intelligence on the other man they hit . . ."

"Spellman," Wilson said.

Lucas nodded. "In any case, they weren't from here. They're from Alabama, we think."

"Weird thing, for four hundred dollars," Jones said, and Lucas looked at him and gave a tight shake of his head.

"Don't shake me off, man," Jones said irritably.

Wilson picked it up and said to Johnson, "Maybe head on home, when we get out of here."

"Everybody slow down," Lucas said. To Wilson: "I was told that one of the guys was black, another one was white, and the third you don't know."

"Yeah, but I couldn't identify any of them, and that's the truth," Wilson said. "I sorta saw the black guy from the peephole, when he was holding the FedEx envelope, but I mostly saw his uniform and the FedEx. When they kicked open the door, he already had his mask back on. I couldn't pick him out of a two-man lineup."

Lucas said, "And you only know about the white guy because you saw his arms."

"Just his wrists," Johnson said. "He had swastikas tattooed on his wrists, just where a watch would be. They were even tattooed to look like a watch. A swastika in a circle, with a little tattooed band going around his wrists."

"I didn't see that," Wilson said.

Jones said to Lucas, "We're going through all the tattoo registries, haven't found anything like that. Nothing at all."

"I saw what I saw," Johnson said.

"I believe you," Lucas said. "Though it's kind of weird, a Nazi guy with a black partner . . . what about the third guy?"

"I think the third guy was white, too," Wilson said. "I can't tell you why, he was completely covered up."

"I think so, too," Johnson said. "You couldn't see their eyes very well, but I think his might have been blue or green—light-colored."

"Tall," Lucas asked.

"Yes. Really tall, the guy we couldn't see. The other two

were big guys, over six feet, but the one guy was really tall."

Cohn, Lucas thought.

LUCAS WALKED THEM back through the entry and the robbery, the beating, the departure, with the unknown swastika man hanging on for five minutes, apparently while the other two robbed Spellman. "He just *hovered* over me," Johnson said. "I thought he might, you know, force himself on me."

"But all he did was talk?"

"He *ripped* my blouse off, almost!"

"But he didn't unzip himself or expose himself in any way?" Lucas asked.

"No, but . . . What are you saying?"

"He was intimidating you to keep you quiet," Lucas said. "There was never any intention of raping you."

"You weren't even there!" she blurted.

"I'm not saying that he wouldn't rape you, under other circumstances. Under *these* circumstances, he didn't have the time. He might have strangled you, or beaten you to death, but raping you would have taken too long and would have left DNA behind. These guys were too professional to do that—to leave the DNA. And Mr. Wilson, here, you say the attack was brutal, but here you are, sitting up and you just ate lunch. If they'd been serious about beating you, you'd be getting fed through a tube. They weren't taking any chances of actually killing you. If they'd killed you, then they would have gotten a lot of attention. As it is, a four-hundred-dollar robbery . . ." Lucas shrugged.

After a moment, Wilson said, "I sort of wondered about that. When they were beating me, I was scared, but it didn't hurt too bad, except for the nose. The nose hurt like hell—still does. I even thought about it at the time; it was like they were pulling their punches."

"Pretty interesting," Lucas said.

"If they weren't gonna hurt me, why even bother pretending?" Wilson asked.

"To intimidate you, so one guy could control you while the others went down to rob Spellman. Another thing—how many people have you told about this?"

"I don't know—a few."

"Those people probably told a few more, and all of those people probably told a few, so now it's all over the place that you got brutally beat up and robbed and Miz Johnson almost got raped," Lucas said. "If they're going after somebody else, somebody who might have heard about this, they've prepared the way."

"That's awful," Johnson said.

"Yeah, it is," Lucas said. "It's cold and calculated. On the bright side, you're both still alive and nobody got raped."

BART SPELLMAN WAS sitting in the High Hat bar, drinking a soda water with a slice of lemon, reading the Sunday funnies from the *Star Tribune*. He saw Jones coming and folded the paper and asked, "Get them?"

Jones said, "No," and "This is Lucas Davenport."

He made the introductions, and Lucas and Jones got Diet Pepsis because the High Hat didn't sell Coke products, and Spellman lifted a corner of the gauze pad on his eye. He had a black eye the size of a child's hand, with a nasty cut held together with a dozen stitches. Lucas winced and said, "Got whacked pretty good."

"Not like Wilson . . . bet old Jackie ran his mouth at them," Spellman said. "I fell on the floor and rolled around and moaned and let them see the blood and they left me alone."

"Been robbed before?" Lucas asked.

Spellman spit an ice cube back into his drink and nodded. "Once. In Washington. Beat the shit out of me, got three hundred dollars and my shoes."

"Your shoes," Jones said.

"Yeah. Alligator driving slippers from Italy. Last time I wore alligator shoes in Washington."

The attack on Spellman was virtually identical to the one on Wilson and Johnson: violent, fast, in-and-out. Hotel uniform and FedEx package. Spellman said that one man was black and one was white, but he had no further details. "I spent most of my time on the floor with my hands over my eyes," he said.

Lucas thanked him when they were done, and he and Jones walked back to their cars.

"Annoys the hell out of me that they won't tell us about the money," Jones said.

"Self-incrimination," Lucas said.

"I know. Still pisses me off. You gonna send those pictures to me?"

"Soon as I get back to the office."

LETTY.

The Channel Three newsroom was a long, narrow space divided into hip-high gray cubicles, each with a desk, file cabinet, and computer, some neat, some a garbage dump of notebooks and PR releases.

Letty didn't have her own desk, but Jennifer Carey, her mentor, not only had an office, but the office had a door, a sign of status. Carey wasn't in yet—there was hardly anybody around, early on a Sunday morning, even with the convention in town—so Letty sat at Carey's desk and typed in her password and went to the DMV site and entered the license-plate number she'd gotten from the van the afternoon before.

The owner was listed as Randy Whitcomb, and Whitcomb had an address on St. Paul's east side, off Seventh Street. She clicked off the DMV and ran the address through Google Maps, came up with an exact location, and printed it out. She didn't know the area, but it'd be easy enough to get to.

Then she switched to the Channel Three library and did a search, not expecting much. Whitcomb's name popped right up, and another name: Lucas Davenport.

Into it now, she started pulling up the archives, then went out to the *Star Tribune* library where she found much more: Lucas had once beaten Randy Whitcomb so badly that he'd been forced to resign from the Minneapolis police force. The beating came after Whitcomb had church-keyed one of Lucas's informants, and an editorial on the fight suggested that Lucas might even have been charged with a crime except that witnesses characterized the encounter as an attempted arrest and resisting-arrest, and because the church-keyed woman was black, and an "after" photograph had been circulated through Minneapolis's black areas by the police union.

So he'd walked, but had been out of law enforcement for a while—making a lot of money while he was out—until he slipped back in with a political appointment.

Letty went into the files for more on Whitcomb. After the beating by Davenport, Whitcomb had been sentenced to two years in prison for the church-key attack, but had gotten out in thirteen months. He'd been arrested once more for soliciting for prostitution, and fined; and then, a couple of years later, during an investigation of a serial killer, he'd been involved in a shootout that left him paralyzed. Lucas had been at the shootout but hadn't done any shooting.

In that case, Whitcomb had later gone to prison for perjury and obstruction of justice. He'd lied at a preliminary hearing, which resulted in the release on bond of the murder suspect, and *that* resulted in the suspect's murder. For the total sum of crime and effects, he'd drawn a six-year term. He'd lied, the *Star Tribune*'s report said, because he hated Lucas, and blamed Lucas for his paralysis.

The six-year term wasn't up, and why he was out, Letty couldn't discover in any of the newspaper records—probably paroled, or maybe because of some medically related problem, but whatever it was, he hadn't escaped. *That* would have been in the papers.

Letty kicked back from the desk and thought it over. Randy Whitcomb was a pimp, who apparently hated Lucas, and now was tracking her, and making nice. He had something on his mind.

The information was like a winter wind blowing on her face. She turned into the cold, and her nose quivered, like a hunter's.

LUCAS SENT THE New York photos to Jones, and told Carol, his secretary, who was pleased to be working her second straight day of overtime, to put together a list of hotels and motels and to figure out a distribution scheme, so he wouldn't have to hit all the hotels himself. Then he called Lily Rothenburg at her home in Manhattan.

"What'd you get?" she asked, when she picked up the phone.

"Something interesting. We had a couple of guys hit for large amounts of cash money last night . . ."

He told her the story, and when he was done, she said, "Lucas, that's them. The intelligence and the coordination are right. In the other jobs that the feds put them on, the intelligence was impeccable. They always hit at the moment when they'd get the most money and there was the least chance of getting caught. The coordination, the timing, the intimidation—it's all them. Damnit, I wish I could be out there."

"We're taking the photographs around to every hotel and motel in town. There's no reason for them to know we're coming, so we've got a chance," Lucas said.

"I hope they didn't pull out after last night—but I don't think that's enough money for Cohn. He needs to take out three or four million for himself, so he's probably got to take down ten, when you count the shares going to the gang. I don't think he'll leave any easy money on the table."

"Well, we could put him on CNN," Lucas suggested. "If we can't get him any other way."

"I think he's got a way out of the country. Something slick. Something we'd have a hard time stopping. After the killings here, he vanished," she said. "We don't want to lose him again. If you put him on CNN, he'll probably take off."

"All right. Last resort, only," Lucas said.

"Another thing: the Brits take pictures of everything, everywhere—kind of scares me, actually. It's like *1984* over there," Lily said. "Anyway, they backtracked him right out of Heathrow and across London to a train station, and then picked him up getting on the train in York."

"York?"

"Yeah. Like in New York. York. It's up north of London somewhere. Small place, a couple hundred thousand, I guess. He rented a house, told people that he was an American engineer named George Mason. He played golf, had a casual relationship with a woman who worked at a PR firm in another town. Harrogate. Mmm . . ." Lucas could hear her shuffling through papers. "That's about it. He cleared out at the end of his lease; the owner of the house was sorry to see him go. He was neat, he was quiet, the rent was always paid a few days early."

"How in the hell did he get to York?" Lucas asked.

"That's the thing that makes him so tricky—I think he chose the place at random. For no reason, except that people speak English. Oh, yeah. He took Spanish lessons while he was there, at a local university."

"Spanish lessons."

"He's headed for Mexico or Central America or Chile or Argentina," Lily said. "When he's gone this time, he's gone."

"What about the photography—the British photography?" Lucas asked. "The pictures might be better than the Photoshop stuff you sent me."

"They're not," Lily said. "The film was good enough to

track him, but it's kind of grainy black-and-white. I've seen it—our Photoshop stuff is better."

"Well, we'll push it," Lucas said. "I got yanked out of bed by one of the local political hotshots, and he wants this fixed. Quietly."

"I don't care how it's fixed, as long as Cohn's clock is fixed at the same time," she said.

CAROL CAME BACK with a list of hotels. "I talked to Jones. He'll take care of Hennepin County. I'll e-mail the Cohn photographs to Bloomington, and the sheriffs' departments in Dakota and Washington counties, and across the St. Croix to Hudson and River Falls and Prescott. So, you've got St. Paul."

"Do we actually have people walking them around, or are we dropping them into a black hole?" Lucas asked.

"I've got commitments," Carol said. "I'll call them every hour or so to get reports. Though, there are quite a few cops from the suburbs already here in St. Paul, working the convention."

"Hell, it's one guy walking the papers around . . ."

"That's what I told them," Carol said. "One guy, no problem. Trouble is, everybody's so short that it *is* a problem."

LETTY HAD BEGGED a ride to Channel Three from Weather, and Jennifer Carey was supposed to drive her home—but she had experience with local buses, and decided to head back to St. Paul. When she left, producers and cameramen were coming in, gearing up for convention coverage. Some kind of march was scheduled for St. Paul, and a couple of producers were talking about possible trouble in the streets.

She left a note for Carey and caught the 94 bus out of Minneapolis, transferred to the 84 at Midway Center, rode south down Snelling, then caught a 74, which took her to a couple blocks from the house. On the trip across the river, she mulled the problem. Randy Whitcomb had been feuding with Lucas for years, and now he was coming after her.

What did he want? Revenge, most likely. To hurt her, to get at Lucas.

She'd grown up out in the countryside, and had firsthand knowledge of the kind of focused dislike, hatred, disdain, that might lead to violence. Whitcomb blamed Lucas for a beating that put him in the hospital and in jail, and then for a shooting that crippled him.

So what kind of revenge would it be? Well, he'd cut up the face of one of his hookers with a beer-can opener; that seemed like a possibility. Maybe he'd torture and kill her—though how he'd go about that, she didn't know. He was crippled, and during the encounter at the McDonald's, he didn't look especially strong in his upper body; nor did the woman with him look especially competent. Rape? Could a crippled person rape somebody? She didn't know.

Probably planned to trick her somehow. Or maybe he'd have help. From what she'd read, he didn't seem to be a likeable sort, a leader, the kind of person who'd inspire any particular loyalty, in something as desperate as the kidnapping and murder of a cop's kid. Or almost kid, she thought. But, who knows? Maybe he'd met somebody in prison, somebody who also had a grudge against Lucas.

One thing, though, was clear in her mind—if Lucas heard about this, he'd kill Whitcomb. Not theoretically kill, but actually kill. He'd probably do it in a clever way that would be undetectable, unprovable. But there were always accidents. Lucas himself had told her that: that sometimes, the cleverest of crimes was foiled by an unforeseeable accident.

He would take the risk, she thought.

LETTY *NEEDED* A father, and a mother, and when her mother was murdered, Davenport and Weather had been there.

If there was any way she could prevent Lucas from taking the risk by acting against Whitcomb, she'd do it. She had, in fact, in the ugly denouement of the case on which she'd met Lucas, shot a cop—actually, she'd shot the same cop on two different occasions—and had never felt the slightest regret. She'd never had a problem being decisive.

She slipped the piece of paper out of her backpack, with Whitcomb's address on it, contemplated it.

All right, she thought. Take a look.

ELLEN, THE HOUSEKEEPER, was changing sheets when Letty walked through the door; Letty said hello, got a Coke from the refrigerator, put it in her backpack, and went quietly through the house and down the basement stairs. Lucas had a workbench in the basement, and a gun safe. She found the hidden key for the gun safe, unlocked it, dragged out a nylon bag of miscellaneous cop stuff, and took out the switchblade sheath. Lucas never used the knife, as far as she knew, and would never miss it. The sheath was made of black nylon with a safety buckle. She took the knife out of the sheath, put the sheath back, pressed the button on the knife, and felt the satisfying shock of the blade slamming out.

Good. Five inches of sharp steel, with a good point, and, halfway down the razor-sharp blade, two inches of serrations that would cut through the toughest nylon or Kevlar rope. The knife was flat and fairly thin, the handle made of a high-tech black plastic with a metal belt clip. She clipped it inside the waistband of her pants, where it would be handy.

THE DAY WAS gorgeous, warm, delightful biking.

She got her helmet and bike out of the garage, and headed north to Summit Avenue, then east, planning to cross St. Paul's downtown, only remembering about the convention detours when she got to St. Paul Cathedral and saw a band of protesters marching down the hill toward the downtown. They appeared to be towing a coffin. A veterans-for-peace march: she'd heard a couple of producers talking about it.

She sat at the top of the hill, in the shade of the cathedral, watching, drank a couple ounces of Coke, got out the map and figured out a detour down University Avenue behind the Capitol and Regions Hospital.

A little longer, but not much trouble, riding through an industrial area, across the railroad tracks, up behind Swede Hollow Park. From the map, it looked like Whitcomb's house was right on the edge of the park, but the other side from where she was, so she pedaled down to East Seventh and looked up the hill toward Metro State University.

All right. Here she was. Now what?

She had her hair up under her helmet, and was wearing sunglasses; that was enough of a disguise. Pedaling up the hill, she decided that she'd cruise Whitcomb's place on the downhill. If they spotted her, it'd be an easy run down to Seventh and into downtown, where there'd be lots of cops around as convention security.

She did that, climbing the hill, taking the left on Hope to Margaret, and paused there. She could see the trees from the park behind the houses on Greenbriar, but there must be, she thought, a huge hole behind the houses, because she was looking at treetops.

Needed more scouting; but the house was right there, or should be, about halfway down the street. She got up her guts, and pedaled on down. Before she could spot Whitcomb's number, she saw the van, sitting by the side of the house.

The house was old and decrepit, with peeling paint, a crumbling front porch, a sagging roof, and a front sidewalk of poured concrete slabs that were tilted this way and that. The grass on the postage-stamp lawn had rarely been cut, she thought; it lay flat, like the fescue grass in a cow pasture.

She rolled on by, saw nobody, looked to her left and saw the break in the line of houses. From a block over, she could look between two houses and see the front of Whitcomb's place. She'd heard Lucas and Del and Sloan and Virgil and all the others talk about the boredom of surveillance, and the sometimes spectacular payoffs.

She'd watch for a while, she decided. She could cruise the area around the park, and check the van every few minutes.

Get the lay of the land . . .

A BIKE PATH wound down through the park, as it turned out. The place was essentially a hole in the ground, but not just an ordinary hole: it was a huge, spectacular hole, almost like a quarry. She could see houses along the top rim, through breaks in the trees. As a park, there wasn't much, and what there was, was overgrown, weedy. A bum was wandering through, carrying a backpack, watching her curiously, as though she were a strange sight.

Maybe she was, she thought.

She pedaled out of the park, around the back, up the hill, and found a spot one block over from Whitcomb's place.

Got lucky. She'd sat there, with her bike, for ten minutes, when Whitcomb's door banged open, and Randy Whitcomb, followed by the woman, rolled down the wooden handicap ramp to the van. They were trailed by a third man, rail-thin, with a scruffy beard.

Whitcomb pointed a remote control at the van, and the side door rolled back, and a ramp unfolded onto the driveway. Whitcomb rolled himself up the ramp, and the woman strapped him in, the straps anchored to the floor. When she was done, the woman yanked on the straps, testing them, then walked around the van and got into the driver's seat, and the second man got in the passenger side.

The van backed out of the driveway, into the street, and

turned down the hill. Letty rode parallel, to Seventh Street, saw the van heading into town.

AS A YOUNG girl, she'd learned that if she decided to do something, it was best to do it immediately; otherwise, somebody would stop you from doing it, or you'd start thinking too much and chicken out. She'd taught herself to drive when she was eight, bumping around the field behind the house, and though the cops would get pissed when they caught her at it, she'd driven herself all over the county by the time she was eleven.

An old drunk would sometimes lend her his truck in return for a late-night pickup at the town bar; and when her mom got drunk, she'd provided the same service. In her driving years, she'd never had an accident.

Now, as the van dwindled in the distance, she looked back at the house. How quickly could they get back, anyway? With the snarl of traffic in town, with streets blocked by marches . . .

She turned around and pulled up the hill, pedaling hard, straight up the street to Whitcomb's place, down the side, turned the bike so it was facing out the drive.

The handicapped ramp ended in a newer-looking door with six small panes arranged in a square looking into a mudroom off a kitchen, just like the country farmhouse where she'd grown up. She knocked, loudly, heard nothing. Looked around. She could be seen from the street, but jeez, she was a young girl on a back porch.

Letty knew about burglary from Lucas and Del and Shrake and Jenkins and all the other cops who hung around with Lucas, and from the reporters and producers at the station. She knew you were allowed one loud noise, or two quiet ones . . .

She took the switchblade out of her waistband, flicked the blade out, took another quick look around, and shoved the blade through the glass next to the door lock. The glass dropped inside the door and she had to punch it again to get the last of it out. Then she reached through and flicked the turn-lock.

The house was quiet inside, smelled of rotten vegetables and dirty diapers and smoke. In fact, it was only half a house—an apartment. The front door led to the porch, but there was no way to get into the other side of the house.

She went back to the kitchen after the first look, got a dishrag off the sink, wiped the lock where she'd touched it, then moved through the house, looking for targets of interest. She found that there was almost nothing to see—a ratty old couch, two scarred tables, a couple of chairs, a broken-down bed in a room that may once have been a dining room, a new TV set with a cable connection. She found stairs going up to what might have originally been a bedroom, but the bedroom was empty, nothing but a half dozen Snickers candy-bar wrappers on the floor, and three or four cigarette butts.

Whitcomb had a lot of clothes, and so did the woman, most of them hung in a doorless closet, the others in a plastic-laminate chest of drawers. The woman wore cheap fashion jeans and low-cut blouses and black brassieres and thong underwear. Tucked in the rickety chest of drawers was a box of Reality female condoms. The woman, Letty understood, was a hooker.

She stopped to listen, heard nothing. Saw a flash of amber on a windowsill, checked it, found five empty pill containers. The names of the drugs meant nothing to her.

In the whole house, the only new thing was the high-def Sony television with an Xbox 360 game machine and a couple of controllers.

Then she found Randy's switch.

She knew what it was, because she'd known a man who'd beaten his children with a switch just like it, until one day, after whipping one of his daughters for some imagined moral infraction, his two older sons had taken him out into the side yard and had beaten him so badly that he hadn't been able to walk for the best part of a year.

Anyway, she knew what it was, and she took it out from behind the couch, handling it with the dishrag from the kitchen, and she looked at the blood spots. He's a pimp, she's a hooker, and he beats her with it. Letty considered breaking it into pieces, then thought, Huh, and put it back.

Took a last look around, and backed out of the house.

Pulled the door shut, got on her bike, and rode away, down the hill, toward town.

Things to think about.

8

LUCAS TALKED TO every manager, assistant manager, and bellman he could find, in all of St. Paul's hotels, got unanimous head shakes, and was headed out the door of his last stop when he saw Mitford walking toward the bar with a couple of other guys.

"Neil!"

Mitford turned, spotted him, walked over: "How's it going?"

"Slowly. I'm walking a picture around . . ." He showed Mitford the shot of Cohn, told him about the victim interviews, and about Jones's impatience with the victims.

"You told him about the money?" Mitford asked.

"He knew about the money. He knew there was something going on." Lucas shook his head. "There're going to be rumors, and when it gets out to the blogs, you'll have some damage control to do."

"It'll get swamped by all the other noise . . . Listen, come on over and meet these guys. They might have some ideas."

The guys were out-of-towners, professional handlers, Democrats in town to watch the Republicans do their stuff.

Ray Landy and Dick McCollum were talking about McCain and his vice-presidential pick, the unknown governor of Alaska, Sarah Palin. They couldn't stop talking about her, veering from amazement to ridicule, watching their BlackBerrys as commentary poured in from friends, reading the messages aloud. They got a table in the tiny bar, and Landy said to Lucas: "You're an outside guy. What do you outside guys think about Palin?"

Lucas said, "I'm mostly a Democrat, so . . . maybe I'm not the best judge."

"Oh, bullshit," Landy said. "What do you think?"

"I don't know anything about her. What bothers me is that it was a quick decision, I guess—that's what the papers all say," Lucas said. "They say that McCain is rolling the bones. I don't know about Palin, but I'm not sure I want to vote for a guy who'd roll the bones on a presidential election. Doesn't make him seem like a calm, rational decision-maker."

"Bless you," Landy said. "I hope everybody's thinking that way."

THE THREE POLS ordered Bloody Marys and Lucas got a Diet Coke. Mitford said, "Guys, Lucas is a big shot in our Bureau of Criminal Apprehension. He's looking into the robberies . . ."

McCollum was a pale-eyed man who fiddled with an unlit cigarette, twiddling it like a pencil between his nicotine-stained fingers: "You a cop?"

Lucas nodded. "Yup."

"He's handled things for the governor for a while—I asked him to look into these things," Mitford said.

The drinks came and they stopped talking until they'd all had a sip, and the waitress left, and McCollum said, "There are fifteen guys like them. Well, there were, anyway. Some of them might have taken off."

"You ever heard of anything like this before?" Lucas asked.

Both men shook their heads, and Landy said, "You hear about it at a lot lower level—but not at this level. You know, when the money gets down to the street, you'll have robberies, but they're random, small-time stuff. A few hundred here or there. That's what happens when you walk around in a bad area with your pockets full of twenty-dollar bills." He said "bad air-ee-a" in a way that suggested it was a cliché wherever he came from.

"I never quite understood where the money was going," Lucas said.

Landy looked at Mitford, who shrugged, and Landy said, "When you're running a campaign, you've got all these people down at the bottom who need walking-around money. They want to get lunch, or buy lunch for somebody, or catch a cab, or get somebody a cab, or pay for gas, or even get some lawn signs together. These are people who turn out the vote. You can't issue a check to all of them—and a lot of them don't have money to do it on their own. I mean, *any* money."

"Say you're working an area with gangs," McCollum said. "There might be somebody who is, like, an officer in a gang. He can turn out a certain vote—fifty people, seventy-five people, a hundred people, maybe even a few hundred people. He needs to get around for a few weeks. Somebody might toss him a few hundred dollars, depending on what he does . . ."

"A couple grand, maybe," Landy said.

"And the candidate might not want his name on a check going to a gang leader," McCollum said. "So, the cash is like oil. It greases the wheel."

"Seems like a lot of money," Lucas said. "A million bucks, more . . ."

"It *is* a lot, at this level, when it's in a suitcase. Once you get down to the street, it's pretty parceled out. You might put a couple of million in a big place like Philly, or Dade County, or Cleveland, but it's mostly in handfuls. Mostly, less than a grand. You know, you get two or three thousand people working informally, they need lunch and cab fare and so on . . . you can go through a mil pretty damn fast."

"Inflation," Mitford said.

"Damn right. Back in 'eighty-eight, I bet the dollar amounts were maybe a quarter of what you see now," Landy said. "Gas was cheap, food was cheap, everything was cheap. Now, it's more. Million doesn't go as far as it used to."

"If it's a million in Philly or Miami, what's it in Chicago or L.A.?" Lucas asked.

"Mmm, doesn't really work that way. Pennsylvania's in play, so's Florida," Landy said. "They could go either way, so getting out the street vote is critical. Illinois and California are pretty safe for us, so it's not that critical. Republicans won't spend much, either. There's going to be money, but . . . maybe not quite as intense."

WHILE LUCAS WAS sitting in the bar, sipping on his Coke, talking political money, Rosie Cruz was walking back toward her room from the Coke machine, and saw the cop in the lobby. The cop car was parked a few spaces down from the lobby door, and with a bad feeling, Cruz pushed through the lobby door and walked up beside the cop, a pudgy young blond guy, who was talking to a couple of desk clerks.

The cop was showing the clerks a badly colored Xerox printout of a photograph of Brutus Cohn. One of the clerks glanced at her and she asked, brightly, "What time is the shuttle to the airport?"

The clerk pointed at a sign, which said that the shuttle left every four hours starting at 7 A.M., and turned back to the cop. The other clerk was saying, "It sorta looks like a guy. But it sorta doesn't, too. Let me see, he's in a corner room, let me see . . ." And he hunched over a schematic of the hotel and the cop crooked his neck to look at it.

Cruz walked out the door and turned away from Cohn's room, and as soon as she was out of sight, called Cohn on her cell. Cohn's phone rang four times before he answered, and he said, "Yeah?"

"Get out of there. There's a cop in the lobby with a picture of you and he's coming down to your room. Get out, get out . . ."

"How many?"

"One, here, but he could call in more," she said. "Get out."

THEN COHN WAS gone and she snapped the phone shut and walked up a flight of stairs to an exposed walkway where she could see the parking lot. A minute or two later, she saw the cop, one hand on his gun, walking down the parking lot toward Cohn's room. She punched the speed dial and Cohn came up: "Yeah?"

"He's walking toward your room. He's alone. He'll be there in one minute," she said.

And he was gone again.

BRUTUS COHN WAS buck-ass naked, in bed with Lindy, when Cruz called with the warning. He jumped up, looked around: normally neat, he was with Lindy, now, and she was a walking hurricane. Clothes were strewn all over the room, shoes, papers, everything.

"Get dressed," he snapped.

They had a picture of him. They had fingerprints, too, but they'd never taken a DNA sample, because they didn't do DNA samples the last time he was in jail. Now his prints and his DNA were all over the place . . .

"What's going on?" But she'd been a criminal's girlfriend long enough not to ask too many questions, and she was already pulling up her underpants and the phone rang again and he said, "Yeah?" listened and snapped it shut.

"Take your pants off," he said.

"What?"

"Take your fuckin' pants off. A cop is coming down here, he'll be here in ten seconds and I want you to answer the door."

"Naked?" Now she sounded interested.

"Yeah, goddamned right, naked. Get your goddamned pants off . . ."

He looked around, picked up an end table by the legs, and smashed it against the floor. The legs broke, but didn't come completely free, and he flipped the table and wrenched one loose. It was half the length of a pool cue, but shaped like a ball bat.

"When he knocks, say, 'Just a minute,' and then pull the door all the way open and step back. Just let it swing. I'll be right behind it. Goddamnit, wake up . . ."

CHARLES DEE ("CALL me Charles") was about ninety-eight percent sure that the whole thing was the weekly windup by the guys back at the shop: send Dee around with a Xerox of some weird-looking guy with a red beard—the beard looked like it was painted on—to ask who'd seen him. This was a request, they said, from fuckin' Minnesota. Just about ninety-eight percent sure that somebody was about to hit him with an air horn or some other joke . . .

The fact was, Hudson was too big a town for him. He wasn't a metro cop, he was a small-town guy. He needed to be on a five-man force somewhere where the people *liked* you. Where everybody knew your name . . .

He got down to 120, looked around, sighed, wondered what was behind the door, and knocked. A woman called out, "Just a minute," and he thought, Here it comes . . .

LINDY PULLED OPEN the door, and stood there in all her big-boobed and bikini-shaved glory. Dee had time to take a breath and notice how *crispy* her pubic hair looked, when a big naked guy reached out from behind the door, grabbed him by the shirt and yanked him inside.

Dee had learned to handle himself in the Hudson bars, the Friday-night fights, but he was off-balance and falling into the room and turning and trying to look and he saw the club coming right at his eyes and he never even had time to yell.

COHN WHIPPED THE club through a tight arc and smashed the cop right across the bridge of the nose and he spun as he fell onto his face. Cohn clubbed him at the base of his skull and the cop went flat and Cohn hit him twice more and then tossed the club in the corner and said, "Get dressed."

"What about him?" Lindy asked, looking at the cop.

"What about him?"

"He saw us," she said.

"He's dead," Cohn said. "Get dressed. Pick up everything. Get the sheets off the bed."

"He's dead . . . ?" She was stunned. Her brother was a small-town cop, and she didn't like the look of this. Dead?

"He's dead," Cohn said. He was half-dressed. "Come on: move."

SHE STARTED CRYING but Cohn kept her moving. They stuffed everything into their suitcases, dressed, Cohn stripped the sheets off the bed, threw all the blankets in them, tied them tight, called Cruz.

"Take a walk on the walkway. See if anybody's looking at us," he told her.

"I'm up there now. I don't see anybody," she said.

"Let's go," Cohn said. He let Lindy lead the way through the door, propped the door open with the chair leg, walked down to the car, threw everything in the trunk, took out the two-gallon plastic jug of gasoline, said, "Start the car," and walked back to the room.

Inside, he gave the jug a shake, threw all the dry towels from the bathroom in a heap, soaked them with a half gallon of gas, threw one of the towels on the shower drain, poured the rest of the gas around the two rooms, including the beds, and backed out in a cloud of fumes.

Two gallons of gas is condensed energy: enough energy to drive a Ford F150 thirty miles or so. The rooms would burn. He picked up the club he'd used to kill Dee, wiped it, just in case, tossed it inside, shook his head: this was bad.

He trailed the last bit of gas onto the concrete walk, tossed the container into the room, dropped a match on the gas and hurried to the car.

The flame just sat on the gas patch for a moment, then crept over the door sill and then with a loud, attention-grabbing *Whump!* blew through the motel rooms.

They rolled down the parking lot, around the corner on the back, down a street, and headed back to the I-94 entrance ramp, passing the motel, and saw black smoke boiling from the room and a man running toward the motel office.

They ran down onto I-94 and saw even more smoke, and Lindy said, "The whole place must be burning down," and then, "What if he wasn't dead?"

"He was dead," Cohn said, and then they were coming down on the St. Croix River and the bridge to Minnesota and they never heard a fire engine.

LUCAS GOT A phone call, saw it was from Carol, pulled his cell and asked, "What?"

She said, "Something awful happened in Hudson."

THE FIRE WAS gone by the time Lucas got there. An angry Hudson cop lost his temper when he saw the Porsche nosing into the parking lot, past the warning tape, and did a fat man's arm-swinging red-faced tap dance until Lucas stuck his ID out the car window, and then the cop pointed Lucas into a far parking space and Lucas took it.

The parking lot was full of cop cars, with two fire trucks and two ambulances butted up to the soaking ruin at the corner of the motel. The fire had been intense, and anything wooden was charred, and anything cloth was burned to ash. The body-mound by the door, with the charred and cracking skin on the man's seared back, looked like a dirty roast hog.

Lucas found the police and fire chiefs, the mayor and a city councilman standing by one of the trucks looking at a couple of medical examiner's investigators, who were standing back away from the body. Lucas nodded at the chief, who asked, "Who're you?" and Lucas said, "Davenport, Minnesota BCA. We put out the request on the photos."

The chief nodded at the body. "Charles found him. We think."

"Was he by himself? You know what happened?"

"Yeah, he was by himself. Damn fool didn't call in," the chief said, and a tear trickled out of one eye and he wiped it away.

The fire chief said, "See the skinny kid up there?" He pointed toward the motel office, where a kid in an ill-fitting brown suit and necktie was looking down at them. "He's the last guy Charles talked to, if you want to know exactly what happened."

Lucas nodded and asked, "What about the fire? Was there an accelerant? How long did it take . . . ?"

The fire chief was nodding. "The arson guys are here, walking around. They say gasoline and oil, probably. Molotov cocktail. There's a melted two-gallon plastic gas container in there, by the end of the bed." The bed frame and box spring were a tangled mass of metal.

Lucas stepped over to the burnt-out front wall of the

room and looked through the hole that had been a window. Aside from the body, he could see nothing but motel equipment: beds, burned tables, telephones, lamps, television, a melted alarm clock, two burned picture frames.

"Doesn't look like they left much behind," Lucas said.

"They didn't—first thing the arson guys checked. They cleaned the place out."

"DON'T KNOW WHY this Cohn had to do *this*," the chief said. "He wasn't covering up anything. If he hadn't set it on fire, might have been longer before we found out about it."

"DNA," Lucas said. "Fire messes up the possibilities of pulling up DNA. If he'd been living there for a while, it'd be all over—body hair, skin, blood, semen, whatever. With this fire . . ."

"But you *know* who he is," the chief said.

"Can't prove it—but we do know it," Lucas said. "These guys killed a couple of cops in New York and pulled the same stunt. Burned the motel room. The NYPD got nothing out of it. No prints, no DNA, no nothing."

The chief's face stormed up. "New York? If he killed cops there, why in the hell weren't we warned? If we'd known he killed cops . . ."

"It was right on the photo," Lucas said. "With all the other personal information."

The chief looked down at a uniformed sergeant, a forty-ish sandy-haired man with a brush mustache and small round glasses, who looked away, shrugged, and said, "Nobody thought he'd find anything. I mean, the guys sent him up here because . . . you know."

Lucas said, "Because he was a fuckup?"

"Because they were busy with other stuff," the sergeant said, but his eyes said, Yeah, Charles was a fuckup.

"What was his last name?" Lucas said.

"Dee. His name was Charles Dee."

A HALF DOZEN motel employees clustered in the office and on the concrete slab outside, their voices buzzing with suppressed excitement, and Lucas pulled two of them, Joshua Martin and Kyle Wayne, into the stairway to the second floor. "Tell me exactly what Officer Dee said to you. Every word, from the minute he walked in the door."

The two looked at each other: Kyle had dim gray eyes, and Lucas suspected there wasn't much content behind them. Kyle shrugged and Joshua said to him, "Okay, you tell me if I go wrong, okay?"

Kyle bobbed his head: "Go."

"We were standing behind the desk . . ."

"Alone in the office," Lucas interjected.

Joshua nodded. "Yup. We were standing behind the desk, alone, and Kyle had come back from carrying some old lady's stuff up the stairs, she couldn't walk very good. I was counting out my change drawer, and we see this cop car pull through the lot and he parks. Then this guy comes in, Charles . . ."

"You knew him?"

Joshua shrugged. "We knew who he was. They sometimes put him on school patrol. Anyway, he comes in, and he's got this picture, and he says, 'You ever seen this guy?' We look at the picture, and Kyle says, 'Whoa, dude, he looks just like that big tall dude.'"

Kyle did a body-bob and said, "Yup."

"I don't know what he's talking about, but Kyle says this guy was down in one-twenty, which is the one that's burned, so I guess he was," Joshua said. "Charles asked Kyle if he was sure, and Kyle said, 'Dude, I don't know. Maybe not.'"

Kyle said, "I said, 'Maybe not. But maybe yes.' Not or yes, I said them both."

Joshua picked it up. "So, Charles went out of here, and Kyle went to watch him. I went to counting the money again."

"You watched him?" Lucas asked Kyle.

"Yeah, kinda. I didn't want him to see me, but I stuck my head out. He went down there and knocked on the door, and then he went inside. That's all I saw. I came back and got my plunger, 'cause we've got a bad toilet, some asshole woman stuck a whole roll of toilet paper down it . . . anyway, I came back, and we heard this . . . *Vooooommmm.* We ran outside and saw the fire and called nine-one-one."

"Didn't see anybody else?" Lucas asked.

"Not then," Kyle said. "But, there was this chick . . ."

He and Joshua exchanged glances again, and Joshua said, "She has, like, this amazing rack, you know? I mean, we're talking Hollywood, and she's showing them off. We think she went into that room, when we both saw her that once. We didn't see her go in, but she was headed that way, and she wasn't checked in here."

"You boys know a hooker when you see one?" Lucas asked.

Kyle did: he shook his head and said, "Not a hooker. Hookers always carry these big bags. She wasn't carrying anything. Maybe car keys. She was coming back from somewhere and I think she went in that room."

"Would you recognize her if you saw her again?" Lucas asked.

"Oh, yeah," Joshua said. "I'd recognize her."

Lucas took down the description: mid-thirties, blond, long hair, mid-height. Hollywood tits.

"Looked me right in the eyes for a long time," Joshua said. "Really sorta . . ." His voice trailed away.

". . . stroked your rod," Kyle finished.

Lucas was walking out of the office, then paused and turned back. "Kyle . . . you said you came in here to get your plunger, and then you heard the explosion. How much time between the time you came back in and the explosion?"

Kyle said, "Well . . ."

He walked over to the door, pushed it open, then stepped

back through and stomped around the desk and down a short hallway to a closet, opened it, got out a plunger, and walked back to the desk. "How long was that?"

Lucas said, "Thirty seconds."

"Then that's how long it was. Wasn't long."

"You didn't stop to chat or anything . . ."

"Nope. Went right back to the closet and got the plunger," he said.

"He did," Joshua said.

"When Officer Dee pulled into the parking lot, did he hang around outside, or did he come right in?"

"He came right in. You know, however long it takes to walk from his car to here."

Dee's car was thirty feet from the door. Fifteen seconds.

"And how long did you talk to him in here?" Lucas asked.

"Showed us the picture, Kyle said that thing about the corner room. We talked about it, and he walked out. Just, you know . . . not too long."

"No conversation . . ."

"Not really. Not long, anyway."

Lucas nodded, gave them business cards and said, "If you think of *anything* else, give me a call."

OUTSIDE AGAIN, LUCAS walked back to the crowd of cops, sorted out an arson guy.

"Is there any personal stuff in there? Anything left behind? Anything? Toothbrush?"

"Not that I've seen so far. But everything that wasn't nailed down, fell down, so there could be something under all the crap."

"Call me when you've worked through it; I need to know," Lucas said, and handed over a business card.

The arson guy nodded and stuck the card in his wallet. "What's up with that?"

"The kids up at the office say the fire started a couple of

minutes after Dee went through the door—probably less than five minutes. The question is, since they can't see the office from their room, how'd they know he was coming? They had to know, they had to start cleaning the place out before he got there. Dee pulled into the parking lot, talked to the kids, walked down there . . . they didn't have more than three or four minutes before he was knocking at their door. But they were ready for him, apparently, and got out within another minute or so."

"Yeah. Huh."

Lucas looked around at the range of buildings, at the motels farther down the strip. "They were warned. They've got a lookout. Might be looking at us right now."

The arson guy looked around, turned some more, and said, "Lotta windows."

9

LUCAS GOT THE Hudson cops crawling through the surrounding motels, looking for anyone who'd checked out of a room overlooking the corner room where Charles Dee had died. Somebody, he believed, had warned Cohn that the cop was coming; why Dee had gone inside the room, he didn't know, unless he'd been met at the door by Cohn, with a gun.

Nobody had heard a gunshot . . . There'd been a guest on the other side of Cohn's double room, and he'd been in the room at the time of the fire, asleep, but he should have heard a shot. He'd heard the gasoline explode, had gotten up to see what it was, but hadn't heard a shot.

Goddamned Hudson cops, he thought: they'd sent out one guy to look for a cop killer. And they knew it. They were tap dancing like crazy, but everybody else would know it, too, by the six o'clock news.

Which reminded him. He got on the phone to Carol and said, "Get those pictures of Cohn out to everybody. *Everybody.* Beg and plead if you have to, but get his face on the air. Get it to the newspapers, ask them if we can get it on the front."

"What're we doing?" she asked.

"Changing direction. He knows we're all over him, so if he's going to run, he's already on the way. See if we can get it on CNN and the networks, all the local TV, go out two tiers of states—down to Missouri, over to Indiana, out to Montana. Get it out to every airport police department in, say, six hundred miles. Border Patrol, Grand Portage, International Falls. Maybe we'll freeze him here in the Cities, so we'll get another shot at him. If he gets out to L.A. or down to Miami, he's going to be harder to spot. Beg for help."

"I'll get it started," she said. "But there was trouble downtown with one of the marches, a bunch of people are being arrested. Lot of them. That'll be the big story tomorrow . . ."

"Tell them about this cop getting killed," Lucas said. "Tell them . . . tell them he was left behind when they torched the motel. Tell them we don't know if the guy was dead. That'll catch them."

"Was he dead?"

"Yeah, probably. We really don't know," Lucas said. "We need to stress that, Carol—*we don't know*. Maybe he burned alive. We need the attention."

Lucas stayed until the reports came back from the adjoining hotels: nobody in any of the rooms in question had checked out.

"Nothing there," the chief said, as though Lucas had screwed up somehow.

"There's something there," Lucas said. "We just haven't found it yet."

"Yeah, well . . . any more ideas?" the chief asked.

"One," Lucas said.

COHN AND LINDY headed west on I-94 toward the Cities, and as soon as they were clear of Hudson, across the bridge in Minnesota, Cohn got on his cell phone and called Cruz.

"I talked to the boys and told them to stay put at least until tonight," Cruz said. "They're cleaning out their rooms, wiping everything down. Do you know where you're going?"

"I get off at the Sixth Street exit? Is that right? Then straight ahead to the parking structure."

"Do *not* take the elevator," Cruz said. "There's only one, and if there's anybody waiting for a ride, they'll see you, and we can't afford that anymore. You've got to keep out of sight until we can change your appearance. I'll get some hair dye, we'll give you black hair and a mustache, no beard. We can wipe down the condo tonight and get out of here."

"Okay. Maybe. When are you coming over?"

"I'll be a half hour behind you," she said. "I've got to get that dye."

"See you then."

While he was talking, Lindy had organized all the loose stuff into the two sheets, then flattened them and pushed them onto the floor of the backseat, and pulled their two suitcases over them. When she'd tidied up, she waited until Cohn had passed a semi-trailer, then squeezed over the seat back, into the front again. "I hope he was dead," she said. "I hope he didn't burn alive."

"Shut up. I'm sorry, but I've got to think." He thought for two minutes, then said, "Cruz said they had my picture. Where'd that come from? How'd they get it? How'd they know? Jesus Christ, how did that happen?"

"Somebody ratted you out," Lindy said.

Cohn turned his cool gaze on her, saw her sudden nervousness, then smiled: "Thank you, dear. That makes me think you weren't the one."

"If that jerk Spitzer was here, I'd say he's the one," Lindy said.

Cohn was silent for a moment, calculating, then said, "He was here."

"He was?" She was surprised. "Where is he?"

"He went away," Cohn said.

"But then, maybe he's pissed . . ."

"He went away," he said again. His voice had an icicle in it.

Ah. Now she had it. She looked straight ahead and said, "Good." Then, "Maybe before he went away."

"If he was going to do it, he could have told them exactly *where* we were at, and when we'd be there."

More silence, then Lindy said, "I can't believe it was the boys."

Cohn shook his head: "I can't either. For one thing, they helped us take down a couple of people already, and I can't believe they'd do that, if they were talking to the cops. Or if they did, we'd already have been busted. I mean, they were all there when Spitzer went away."

"Even Rosie, or whatever her name is," Lindy said.

"Yeah, even her." But he remembered Cruz's objection to the murder, and then her explanation, which now seemed less convincing.

Lindy said, "The thing about Rosie is, she might not just be ratting you out. You know what I mean?"

"I think so," Cohn said. "But say it."

"Maybe she's playing some other game that we can't see. She's really . . . complicated. Where does she get all this information? What is she really doing?"

"She's done a lot of jobs with us," Cohn said. "And three with Jerry, before Jerry's accident."

"Wonder whatever happened to the guy who got Jerry's heart?" Lindy asked.

"I don't know . . ." Cohn shook his head. "I have to think about Rosie. You're right, she wouldn't just give us up, because we could give *her* up. She sure as hell didn't tell them that she planned a robbery that ended in a couple of cop killings. Three cop killings, now. If she's the one, why'd she warn us? No—something else is happening."

Lindy pointed: "Exit's coming up."

"That's what I'm afraid of," Cohn said.

THE NEW SPOT was their disaster hole, a last-ditch hideout that Cruz had arranged, in a condominium building that was half-empty. When she rented the furnished model unit for a month, from the developer, she'd warned him that he couldn't show it: "I haven't shown a unit in three months," he said ruefully. "I got another model to show if I need to."

The developer was under the impression that Cruz worked with the Republicans, that the model would be used for secret meetings, and she didn't disabuse him. Cruz had had to buy sheets and a couple of blankets, towels and soap and toilet paper, but most everything else had been there, as part of the model.

Cohn pulled into the parking ramp and punched in the key-code, and went down through the ramp and around to their private parking spaces. Then they were out and climbing the interior stairs, five floors. They opened the lobby door and peeked, saw nobody moving—of the six condos on the floor, only two others were occupied—then hurried down to 402, unlocked it and went inside.

As soon as they were in, Cohn called Cruz, who was in her car, heading toward St. Paul.

"The motel looks like a cop convention back there," she said. "You did that guy?"

"I had to," Cohn said. He was looking out the window, over a small park, where a cluster of twenty or thirty peace demonstrators were wandering around, as if they'd lost something: peace, maybe, he thought. A young girl pushed a bike along the sidewalk, on the opposite side of the street, leaned it against a parking meter, walked over to a white van with *Channel 3* on the door, and knocked on the window. Cohn had gotten nothing but silence from Cruz, but he waited her out, and finally she said, "I'll see you in ten or fifteen minutes."

Across the street, whoever was in the TV van opened the door and the young girl got in.

FRANK AND LOIS were in the back of the van, eating pizza, and Frank said, "If you leave the bike like that, somebody's gonna run up and steal it."

"You think?" Letty asked.

"I think," he said. "Look at the crowd."

So Letty got back out and unwrapped the cable lock from around the seat tube, cinched it around the parking meter, got back in. Lois, a tall thin woman with spiky, close-cut black hair, said, "Mushroom and pepperoni."

Letty took a slice, realized that she was starving to death, took a bite, and turned to Frank. Frank had short curly hair and a round face and rimless glasses, a short fleshy nose, and thin, delicate pink lips in a rust-colored beard now going gray. Aside from being an excellent cameraman, he was somewhat famous for having gotten a blow job from a low-rent hooker on University Avenue. In his Sebring convertible. With the top down. At noon. He not only got caught, he got videotaped.

But that was water over the dam, at least until Letty, talking around the slice, asked, "If I wanted to find a low-rent hooker right now, on the street, where'd be the best place? Here in St. Paul."

Lois didn't move her face but her eyeballs clicked left, toward Frank, like a couple of marbles in a water glass. Frank carefully peeled a mushroom off his slice, dangled it for a moment over his upturned lips, sucked it in, chewed once, and then asked, "How old are you?"

"Never mind that. Where would I find her?" Letty asked. "I read that the St. Paul cops have cleared off University, but with this convention in town . . ."

"Why do you want to know?" Frank asked.

"A story," Letty said, and she half-believed it. An idea had been forming in the back of her head.

"You're too young to do a story about hookers," Lois said. "Forget it."

Letty looked at Frank. "Where?"

He whined, "If your dad even heard you asking the question . . ."

"Listen. I got a tip from a friend," Letty lied. "I'm the only one who could pull it off, and it'd be spectacular. One of my classmates is working the street—somewhere, and I'm sure it's got to be in St. Paul. Her boyfriend put her up to it, so they could get money for cocaine. If I can spot her . . . I mean, she's fourteen. All I want to do is find her, and talk to her. I mean, what a great story."

She was right about the story, if she'd been telling the truth. She went to one of the snottiest private schools in the Twin Cities, and if one of her classmates was out doing knobjobs on the Republicans, and *fourteen* . . . That would be a *story.*

Frank said, "If you can get Jennifer . . ." Jennifer Carey was Letty's mentor at the station.

Letty broke in: "I don't have time. I'll talk to her as soon as I can, but I think my friend Betsy, I think Betsy is out here right now. I need to know . . ."

Lois said, "I have nothing to do with this."

Frank sighed and said, "I suppose she'd be up on Wabasha, Fourth Street, Market . . . working that area between the Radisson and Rice Park . . . down St. Peter. That's where most of the convention people are, up there . . ."

"I owe you one," Letty said. "Thanks for the slice—and I'll talk to Jennifer the first minute I see her."

SHE LOCKED UP her bike a second time, now behind City Hall. The place was crawling with cops, wearing insignia that she'd never seen; cops from Illinois, the Dakotas, Virginia, Wisconsin. Cops from Cedar Rapids. Cops on horses—the horses had face shields—and cops in black armor carrying long wooden riot batons. They paid no attention to her as she walked over to the Radisson, wandered through the lobby, and then continued down Wabasha Street, looking for a wheelchair, for the heavy girl, not finding them. She walked around the block, through the St. Paul Hotel, in the back door, out the front, the doorman giving her the eye. As she went by, he asked, "Aren't you on Channel Three?"

"Yes, I am," she said. "Maybe you can help me. I'm looking for a woman, probably eighteen, a little heavy, dark clothes, kind of . . . sad-looking."

The doorman shrugged, and nodded at the sidewalk: "Look at this. There's ten thousand people an hour walking past here."

"Okay; well, thanks," she said. Across the street, in the park, a stage had been set up, red-white-and-blue bunting hung overhead, with the lights; cameras on three sides, and she could see people working in front of cameras: MSNBC. A crowd was watching, and she threaded through it, past the fountain with the bronze girl, and a guy, thirtysomething, geeky, wearing a McCain button, looked her over and said, "Hi there," and she kept going, around the park and down Fourth Street, against the stream of people walking toward the Xcel Center, where the convention was being held, and back to the Radisson.

And around again, and then off the loop, down St. Peter, to an open-air mall that ran between St. Peter and Wabasha, with people sitting outside, eating lunch, and watching the passersby; and she saw the wheelchair, at a bar called Juicy's.

Whitcomb was in it, talking to a man on a bench, and they were drinking beer. She watched for five minutes, staying back in the crowd, and never saw the girl.

She was out there, somewhere.

Would Letty be more likely to find her by walking the street, or by watching Whitcomb? Since the woman seemed to drive the car, she had to come back—but then she and Whitcomb might go somewhere else, and she had no way to stay with them. She thought it over, one eye on Whitcomb as she scanned the crowd, and decided that the best bet was to work along St. Peter Street, between the park at one end and the mall at the other, with occasional checks a block over on Wabasha.

She began working the loop. How long would it take, anyway, an appointment with a guy? When she was a kid, her mom would come home with men sometimes, and if they didn't stay over, they usually weren't more than a couple of hours . . . and sometimes only an hour or so. But her mom wasn't getting paid, so the guys probably felt like they ought to hang around for a while, and talk. Or whatever.

Not with Whitcomb's girl . . .

She worked the crowded streets for an hour before she saw her, and when she did, she was a hundred yards away and not more than a hundred feet from the corner of the mall, where Whitcomb was drinking. Letty hurried after her, moving fast, but there was no chance: the woman turned the corner. Whitcomb was farther down the mall, and she took the corner carefully, so she didn't blunder into them, if he'd moved—and threading through the crowd, saw him in the same place, saw the woman sit down next to him.

She was there fifteen minutes, Letty watching from fifty or sixty yards away, back in the doorway of a sandwich place. She thought they might be arguing, that the woman might be crying. Then the woman stood, heavily, as though she were old, and she started walking back toward Letty. Letty thought the sadness came off her like a morning fog, a sadness that you could almost touch.

LETTY CAUGHT HER two hundred yards down the sidewalk. She called, "Hey! Girl!"

Briar turned, her eyes uncertain. "Are you . . . Me?"

"Yes." Letty gave her a TV smile. "You're Randy's friend. We talked in a McDonald's. I was with a couple of friends."

"Oh . . . I didn't recognize you . . . here. What are you . . . ?"

"I'm with a TV crew. I report on young people. So what's up with you?"

Briar's eyes seemed to recede into her face: she was thinking about Randy, Letty thought, and what he might do about this conversation. She said quickly, "I won't tell Randy."

The woman's tongue flicked out: "Please."

"What's your name?" Letty asked.

"I shouldn't talk to you. Do you want to get Randy? He's right around the corner," Briar said.

"I know," Letty said. "I was watching you, but I don't want to see Randy, because Randy's a violent asshole and he beats you with a stick. Doesn't he?"

She looked at Letty without saying anything, then past her, checking for Randy, then said, "Tiara."

"What?"

"That's my name. Tiara."

"What's your real name?" Letty asked.

"That *is* my real name . . ." she began, but when she saw Letty's head shake, she said, after a couple more seconds, "Juliet. Briar."

"How are you, Juliet? I'm Letty. Did you know that? My name? Or just my dad's name?"

"You know?"

"Sure I know. Look at Randy. He's been trashed so many times that he's living in a wheelchair. He's not the brightest guy in the universe. Come on, I'll buy you a Coke."

Briar frowned: "Are you really with a TV crew? You don't act like it." She looked around. "If you're with TV, where's your TV stuff?"

"Down by Mears Park. Hang on." Letty flicked out her

phone and called Lois: "Are you guys still down by the park?"

"No. We're up at the Capitol, cruisin' for a bruisin'. Did you ever find your hooker?"

"Yes. Is there any possibility you could come down Wabasha? I'm at Fifth and Wabasha. She sorta doesn't believe me about TV and I need her to," Letty said.

"I thought you were schoolmates," Lois said.

"We're not close," Letty said, smiling into the phone. Whew.

"The cops have Wabasha blocked off, but we could come down Cedar," Lois said. "Meet you at Cedar and Fifth? Five minutes?"

"See you there," Letty said. She clicked the phone shut and said, "C'mon, ride around for a couple of minutes."

Briar, nervous: "If Randy finds out . . ."

"He won't find out," Letty said. "He can't get around, we're walking away from him. C'mon, girl, have some fun."

Briar bobbed her head, and Letty took her arm and started her across the street toward the hill down to Cedar. "So, how'd you get the name Tiara?"

"Randy gave it to me. He said, you know, I need a better show-business name than Juliet. He said Juliet was old-fashioned."

"Oh!" Letty put on some outrage. "Juliet is a *great* name. You know that song 'Romeo and Juliet'? My dad has it on his iPod, it's an old-timey band. Dire Straits, I think. You don't know it? Maybe I can get a copy for you . . ."

AS A CHILD in her time and place, with the mother she'd had, Letty had learned a number of things that would never leave her. She was exquisitely sensitive to social differences: who was rich and who was poor, who was smart and who was dumb, who was succeeding, who was failing. And she'd always kept an emotional distance from people that she'd had to deal with, an observational distance. Jennifer Carey carried the same space—and had told Letty, "You could be a hell of a reporter if you wanted to be. You're really smart, and I can see you watching."

Letty knew what she looked like, and what she looked like was a rich, popular, high school kid. She didn't have to look like that: she chose to, when she was doing her TV thing. She could also look like a smart kid, which was different, a little less put-together; she could look like a shlump, and sometimes, at home, she did that look, watching, watching, watching.

Today she was wearing jeans, but they were designer jeans, and her blouse came from a boutique, not from Macy's. Her sneakers were sleek and cool and olive green, with rust-colored laces; and her sunglasses were small and oval and glittery. She was slender with good cheekbones; she was put together, and she knew it. She could see the weight of it in Briar's face—the weight of being arm in arm with a rich, popular kid.

SHE GOT BRIAR talking about stage names, and then about clothes, and then about Randy—Briar didn't want to talk about Randy—and then the other girl, slowing, but not disentangling her arm from Letty's, asked, "Do you know what I do?"

Letty gave her another TV grin, one she'd practiced two thousand times. "Yup."

Now Briar disentangled herself and slowed. "Is that why you want to put me on TV?"

"Nope. I'm not going to put you on TV, because that would really mess you up," Letty said. "I just want to prove to you that I *am* on TV."

"Why?"

Letty went serious: "Because I'm worried about you. How old are you?"

"Sixteen. Almost seventeen."

Letty was surprised. Briar looked at least a couple of years older. "How long have you been doing this?"

"Four months."

"Ah, jeez." Letty let the sympathy out. "I'm *so* worried about you. I'm so worried about what Randy is up to. You know, if he hurt me . . . my father would kill him, maybe. And he'd find out. Randy is dumb, dumb, dumb."

"He's not that dumb," Briar said.

Letty shook her finger in Briar's face. "Yes, he is. If he was a smart guy, you think he'd be living in a shack? You think he'd have gone to jail four or five different times, and he's not hardly thirty yet?"

"He's twenty-four," Briar said.

Letty's eyebrows went up. "Juliet—he's not twenty-four. Look at his ID sometime, when he's not around. He's almost thirty. He lies about everything."

Briar glanced back up the hill, afraid again. She looked like a denizen of *1984*, caught talking about Big Brother. "He doesn't *always* lie . . ."

Letty said, seriously, "Yes, he does. He always lies. That's what he does for a living. He lies."

Briar looked down at the sidewalk: "Okay."

Letty studied her for a moment, then said, "Look, here comes the van."

"I really can't ride around," Juliet said, but there was a hint of curiosity in her eyes.

"You have to work?" Letty asked.

She looked away: "Yeah."

"How much do you get?"

"Hundred."

"A hundred? Always?"

"Not always, but that's what Randy wants. Sometimes, if I don't . . ."

"I saw the stick," Letty said. "I was in your house."

"What?"

"I saw the stick," Letty repeated. The van pulled up, and

Lois ran the window down. "What's up?" she asked, checking out Briar.

"We'd like to ride around for a few minutes, so I can show Juliet some of the equipment," Letty said. "And I need to borrow some money."

10

LUCAS HAD ONE idea, called Jones, the Minneapolis cop, and said, "I need to talk to the victims again. Soon as you can get them together. I hope none of them have checked out."

"They're still here. What's up?" Lucas told him about the murder of Charles Dee, and outlined the idea, and Jones said, "That could be something. Wilson's still in the hospital. We can meet there. As far as running around to these hotels—I got nothin'."

"That's 'cause they were in Hudson. How soon can we get these people together?"

"Soon as you can get here, I guess. That thing about Dee, man—I heard somebody was down, but nobody knew what happened. You sure it's our guys?"

"Ninety-five percent," Lucas said. "Like everything else, though, I couldn't prove it."

"Fucker's probably walking through Miami International right now, on his way to Brazil."

LUCAS ASKED THE Hudson chief to keep him updated, said good-bye, and headed west, fast; there was a regatta on the St. Croix, two dozen sailboats beating around in a gentle breeze, and then he was over the bridge and back in Minnesota and on his cell phone, calling Lily Rothenburg at her Manhattan apartment. Her husband answered, said, "Hang on," and went and got her.

"What?" she asked.

"We've got a cop down, dead. Cohn did it. Cohn himself, I think," Lucas said. "He set his room on fire and we've got no proof, except that two semi-stoner hotel clerks think they might have recognized him."

"Goddamnit."

"I put his face everywhere," Lucas said. "It'd help if you could do the same, out of New York. All the national feeds we can get. If he's running, we've got to make it hard. If he's still here, maybe we can freeze him, keep him off airplanes, trains, whatever."

"I can call some people," she said. "I can get it on *Today*, I think, tomorrow morning. Maybe—maybe—*Good Morning America*. CNN, I'd have to call somebody to call somebody . . ."

"Much as you can, it'd help," he said. "*USA Today*?"

"Don't know anybody there. Maybe . . . I might be able to get the mayor to call somebody."

"Whatever you can do, Lily."

HE FLASHED PAST the outlying shopping centers, slowed coming into St. Paul, worked back and forth through traffic, heading into Minneapolis. He was crossing the Mississippi when his cell phone jangled. He picked it up, looked at the face of it: Jennifer Carey; which meant that it could be Letty, since she used Carey's phone at Channel Three.

He flicked open the phone and said, "Yeah?"

Jennifer Carey said, "I've got something I've got to tell you. If you let on that I'm the one who told you, I'll kill you. I'm serious."

"If I have to go to court . . ."

"It's personal," Carey said. "Sort of."

"All right. What?"

"Letty took off this morning before I got here," Carey said. "So ten minutes ago I was talking to Lois Cline . . . you know Lois?"

"Vaguely. Looks like a pencil with a paintbrush on her head?"

"Yes. Lois said that Letty has been out trolling downtown St. Paul, looking for a hooker, who she said was a classmate," Carey said. "Lois wasn't really sure if she was telling the truth, but warned her not to mess around with any hookers."

"Aw . . ."

"That's not the good part, yet. An hour later, Letty flagged her down, and she's got the girl with her. Sure enough, this other kid's a hooker," Carey said. "Letty even got her talking about it. You know, the street. Letty's idea, apparently, is that she could interview an underage hooker about giving blow jobs to Republicans."

Lucas thought he felt a vein pop out in his temple. "Aw, for Christ's sakes."

"Hey. She's got the eye and she's got the balls," Carey said. "And she's apparently got the source."

"Aw, sweet bleedin' Jesus," Lucas said. "Where is she?"

"Downtown St. Paul, somewhere," Carey said. "You've got her cell phone?"

"Yeah. Have you tried it?"

"No, because then she'd know that I was the one who told you," Carey said. "I'd rather she didn't know that."

"Okay. Good-bye. Hey—thanks."

———

LETTY ANSWERED ON the third ring. "Hello, Dad?"

"Where are you?"

"Up at the Capitol," Letty said. "The big march is about to start, there are about a million people, I'm watching these black-flag guys . . ."

"Go home," Lucas said.

"What?"

"Go home. I'm going to call your mom to pick you up," Lucas said.

"I'm on my bike," Letty said. "But I can't go right now."

"Letty, go right now."

After a long silence, Letty asked, "Who told you? Lois?"

"Just go home, Letty," Lucas said.

"Bullshit. I'm going to march with my bike," she said. "I might not ever get to do this again for the rest of my life. Then I'll go home. I'm not with Juliet anymore."

"Letty, goddamnit . . ."

"I'm turning off my phone," she said, "since you can't seem to handle this in an adult manner." She was gone.

THE WOMEN IN Lucas's life reduced him to a chattering-chipmunk state about once a month. If not Letty, then Weather; if not Weather, then Jennifer Carey, mother of his other daughter; if not Carey, then Elle Kruger, a nun and lifelong friend; if not her, then Carol, his secretary. They were, he sometimes thought, when he had time to think about it, all crazier than a barrel of hair. All of them together, and also taken as individuals. But this, he thought, took the everlasting triple-decker chocolate-fudge cake.

He was already rolling into downtown Minneapolis, thinking about the best way to get turned around to head back to St. Paul, when it occurred to him that if he went back, he (a) wouldn't find her in the crowd, and (b) if he found her, what would he do with her bike? He was driving a Porsche, and (c) if he did find her, would he try to force her into the car? Knowing Letty, she'd probably start screaming for help.

Well, maybe not that. She'd just be . . . disappointed in him and she'd probably cry. That would break his heart.

Besides, she said she wasn't with the hooker anymore. She didn't usually lie to him, though she did sometimes. She was the toughest kid he'd ever met, and also the most levelheaded.

Still. He took a deep breath, relaxed his grip on the steering wheel. "Hell to pay when I get home," he muttered to himself. He stopped looking for a place to turn around, and headed into the Minneapolis loop.

JOHN WILSON WAS sitting upright in bed, his bludgeoned left eye unwrapped and looking like he'd been hit with an electric sander. He'd just gotten a strawberry shake when Lucas arrived, and was sucking a blob of whipped cream through a straw. Jones was leaning against the air conditioner and said, "Hey." Wilson's assistant, Lorelei Johnson, and Bart Spellman, the third victim, were propped in bedside chairs.

Lucas told the three of them about the murder of Charles Dee: "You guys were pretty lucky, in a way," Lucas said. "They banged you around a little, but now they've killed someone. We know it and they know we know it. The next people who run into them might not be so lucky."

"So Rick said you had an idea," Wilson said, nodding at Jones.

Lucas put a finger to his lower lip, thought a moment about how to lay it out, then said, "Okay. Somewhere back down the line—days ago, weeks ago—somebody gave Cohn information on where you'd be staying, when you'd be there, how much money you'd be carrying, and probably, how long you'd be carrying it."

Quick series of glances, but Lucas held up his hand and said, "Hold on . . . I'm not asking for a statement, I'm speculating on how this must have happened. Somebody knew those things and could point Cohn at you. The question is, who would have that information, on both of you? The details of where you'd be staying?"

Wilson and Spellman looked at each other, frowning, then Johnson suggested, "Travel agency?"

Wilson said to Spellman, "We use Dole," and Spellman shook his head. "I did mine online, direct with the hotel."

"How about the hotel?" Wilson asked.

Johnson frowned, shook her head: "How would they know about the money?"

"How about some kind of lobby group back in Washington?" Lucas asked, but Johnson waved him off.

"No, no, no, that wouldn't be it . . . You get all kinds of talk, who is *going* with who, who is *staying* with who, but you wouldn't get room numbers."

"People would tell people . . . you guys probably told people where you'd be staying," Lucas said.

"Yeah, but how would one person gather all the names up, *with* hotels?" Johnson asked.

Spellman said, "They've only got two. That's not a lot."

"Two for now—but I expect there'll be more," Lucas said. "The money's too easy. Plus, we think they need more money than they've gotten. The New York cops think Cohn's trying to retire, and the money gets cut up between several people."

Jones jumped in: "Do you remember anybody chatting you up, about where you were staying, and all that? Who was with who? Somebody unusual, who you might not normally have been talking to about it?"

They all shook their heads. Wilson said, "I didn't talk to anybody about it. I mean, people know about me and Lorelei . . ."

Johnson looked at Lucas and said, "I'm not entirely unmarried. Almost, but not quite, so we don't talk about traveling together."

Lucas nodded. "Okay."

Again, Spellman and Wilson looked at each other. Spellman finally said, "You know, there are a certain number of guys who know each other, like I know Johnny here. One of those guys could probably make you a list."

"If they had names, they could get room numbers—they could just do a social hack," Wilson said. To Lucas, "A social hack . . ."

"I know what it is," Lucas said.

Jones said, "So you think they got a list, and then they bullshitted people into giving them room numbers? Like bellmen or desk clerks or wives or whatever?"

Lucas: "No. Couldn't be that way. Had to be back in time. Days ago, or maybe weeks. Cohn flew in from England, where he'd been hiding out. And it was all planned—they were ready to go as soon as they got here. They had a guy in a room-service uniform that was specific to the High Hat. Their whole method of operation, the way they've done things in the past, and now this time, suggest it was all carefully planned. The hotel was scouted. They knew the route in and out. Then when we unexpectedly popped them at their motel, they had a can of gas on hand and burned it down."

"Jesus," Spellman said. "You're starting to scare me . . . But—they had to get the room numbers at the last minute. I didn't know what my room number was until I checked in, and I only checked in about six hours before they robbed me."

Johnson said to Spellman, "Not necessarily. Did you get a special rate through the hospitality guys?"

Spellman said, "Yeah, the standard."

"So did we," Wilson said.

Johnson said to Lucas, "The Republican hospitality committee would know where we were. They assigned rooms. They'd have a block of rooms, and a chart they'd fill in, depending, you know, on your status. What you do. If you're like us, you get a pretty nice room, but not right in with the delegates. Somebody on the committee had to know who was who . . ."

"You know that for sure?" Lucas asked.

"I used to *do* it, for car-sales association conventions," she said.

"Now we're getting somewhere," Lucas said. "*Now* we're getting somewhere . . ."

He pushed the three of them to come up with more organizations that might have the information, but they had no ideas. "I think . . . the hospitality committee. That's about it," Johnson said.

Jones said to Lucas, "Since they only hit people in the same hotel, it's possible that there's somebody inside the hotel. Maybe they got a reservations list, looked them up, marked down the people who worked for lobbyists, and went from there."

Lucas nodded. "You're right: that's a possibility. You chase that down, I'll run down the hospitality committee."

LUCAS CALLED DAN Jacobs at the convention security committee. Jacobs came on the line and said, "I was about to call you. We need you to go back and look for Justice Shafer again."

Lucas had virtually forgotten about Shafer, the guy with the .50-cal. "I got people looking for him all over two states and I can spread it out to Iowa, if you want. I won't be able to do much personally."

"We had something come up," Jacobs said. "Two hours ago, a Mexican guy—an illegal, God bless his soul for reporting it—was cutting a hedge behind one of those big houses up on Summit Avenue, right where the hill drops off. He trims it up once a month or so. So today he's cutting it, and he finds a couple of nice shiny .50-cal shells in the grass behind the hedge. He looks down the hill, sees the convention center . . . and calls his boss, who called us. The Mexicano says the shells weren't there when he cut the hedge last month. Said they were sitting right out in the open. Says he didn't touch them, and we can see some smudging, so we might get prints . . ."

"How far . . ."

"Seven hundred and fifty yards, more or less, from the hedge to the front of the convention center. Nice high angle, too. One more thing: the spot where the shells were, there's an old wall, probably going back to the nineteenth century. It's falling apart, but you never saw a better gun rest in your life. Put a beanbag on that, and *I* could snipe somebody at the convention center."

"Ah, shit."

"We've got the place staked out, and if our boy shows up, he's dead as a mackerel," Jacobs said. "But we'd like to find him sooner than that, if we could. The Secret Service is all over us."

"Yeah . . . Jesus. Now . . . Listen, there's another problem, and we've already got a dead cop."

"The guy in Hudson? I heard about it on the news. How's that tie in . . .?"

Lucas explained, and Jacobs said, "Man—the Secret Service is going to be pissing its collective pants. What do you need from us?"

"I need access to the hospitality committee. Like right now," Lucas said.

"Let me get you an address—you can talk to them as soon as you can get there," Jacobs said. "If you need an SS guy to add weight, I'll send one along."

"That might help," Lucas said. "Get me an asshole, if you got one."

Short, dry chuckle from Jacobs. "Okay. If I can find one," he said. "And, hey—Lucas. Talk to Iowa about looking for Shafer. Talk to everybody."

CRUZ HAD TAKEN two hours to dye Brutus Cohn's hair and beard. When he got out of the shower, after the final shampoo, he hardly recognized himself. In addition to the mop of black hair, he'd shaved off his beard, leaving behind a small trim mustache, also black. He put on his pants and trotted out to the condo's living room: "I look like a goddamned Irish cardsharp," he said.

"You looked like a goddamned Irish cardsharp when you had red hair," Lindy said.

Cruz nodded: "It's too even, too black, even with that little bit of color"—they'd isolated some of his natural hair with tinfoil, and let it fall back into the dyed hair—"but I wouldn't recognize you. Not walking down the street. Makes you look even taller."

Cohn went back and looked in the mirror again, and came back out.

"You're not still planning to leave?" Cohn asked Cruz.

"Damn right I am," she said. "It's time to go, Brute. We need to get in the cars and drive."

"But what if we do the guy tonight? Completely different situation," Cohn said.

"They may be watching everybody, now that there's a dead cop," she said.

"Can't watch everybody," Cohn said. "Especially not when these guys are dealing illegal money."

"Brute, they've got your number. You've got to get out of sight."

"I don't have enough money," he said. "I just don't have enough. I'm not going to be some old fucking guy, sitting on a dock in Costa Rica, pissing in his pants and eating cat food. It's not like I'm gonna have Social Security coming in. I need that hotel, Rosie. I need this guy tonight."

Cruz looked at him for a moment and then said, "I'm sure you've figured this out, but somebody pointed the cops at you. What we're doing now, there's no way that fits with your history. They knew something."

He looked at her for a moment, then grinned. "We've been talking about that," he said. "Our feeling—me and Lindy—was that you were the best candidate. My feeling, all alone, was that it was either you or . . . Lindy."

They both turned to look at Lindy, who, horrified, shouted, "Brute. Goddamnit. I would never, ever, ever do anything like that. You know I would never do that."

Cohn scratched his bare chin, thinking, then said, "One thing I know for sure. We killed a Wisconsin cop. They won't let anybody deal on that—or if you do get a deal, it'll be for thirty years, instead of no parole. So even if one of you is dealing, it'd be time to stop. Right now. Because if we go down, we'll take you down with us."

"I oughta get out of here," Cruz said. "I know I oughta get out of here."

"One easy hit on this third guy, and then the hotel, and we're set. I won't set foot out of this place until we're making a move," Cohn said. He looked around the sparsely furnished condo. "Let's get some beer in here, and settle in. Let's get the boys over." He grinned at Cruz—"Take a fuckin' aspirin, Rosie. We're gonna be good, and you're gonna be rich. Richer. Whatever . . ."

THE SECRET SERVICE agent's name was George Dickens. He met Lucas at the hospitality committee's office suite in a temp office in what had been an especially vacant stretch of the St. Paul skyway.

Lucas introduced himself and Dickens, a thin, hard, lank-haired man who looked like he could run down and arrest a greyhound, said, "My boss wanted me to ask you about the parameters of the alert on Justice Shafer."

"Which parameters?" Lucas asked.

"Who's looking?"

"Northern and Western Wisconsin and all Minnesota sheriffs have been contacted directly, with the full file on him, and they've all been asked to distribute the file to the local police forces in their jurisdictions," Lucas said. "We've also directly notified all the bigger police departments . . . like every town over about ten thousand or so—county seats, and all the towns here in the metro area. We're calling

Iowa now. They'll do Des Moines and the suburbs, the bigger towns and all the county sheriffs north of about I-80. Every place within about a short-day's drive from here."

"How many of them will take it seriously?" Dickens asked.

"Some won't—but most of them will post the pictures," Lucas said. "We've got the tag on his truck posted, too, and the highway patrol guys are looking for it."

Dickens nodded, then asked, "Why haven't we found him?"

"I'd say he's probably ditched himself," Lucas said. "He's here, or up in Duluth, or over in Eau Claire, watching TV and trying to get his guts up."

Again, Dickens nodded, as if Lucas confirmed what he thought, and said, "That's what I think, too. Damn hard to catch somebody who holes up, and when there's nobody to ask about him—no family. Shafer's mother hasn't seen him in eight years and nobody knows where his old man went, and that was twenty years ago."

They thought about that for a minute, then Dickens asked, "What do you want me to do in here?"

Lucas, who mostly dealt with the FBI, at the federal level, thought that was about the most modest and reasonable question he'd ever been asked by a fed. He smiled and said, "Do the unreasonable federal act: scare them."

THERE WEREN'T MANY people to scare the shit out of, as it turned out—three women in their forties or early fifties, all a little heavy, harried, confused about the questions.

Their leader, whose name was Helen Fumaro, who wore a large cluster of American Indian turquoise jewelry around her neck, said, Yes, they assigned blocks of rooms. Yes, if somebody had access to their computers, they could have figured out who was staying where, and when, and even the rate. Would they know who the lobbyist representatives were? Well, the billing addresses were right there in the computer . . . If you could get into the computers, and if you knew who you were looking for, you could find them.

"But *we* wouldn't know who they were looking for," Fumaro said, her hands fluttering in front of her, as though she were air-typing. "I don't know who any . . . moneymen are. I get a list of people who've been approved by our Washington office, and then we arrange the hotels depending on their numerical rating, one through ten."

"How does that work?" Lucas asked.

Fumaro said, "If you're a one—there aren't many—you get the best rooms in the best hotels. You get what you want. If you're a ten, well, we might have to tell you that, regretfully, the hotels are all booked up."

"I always wondered how that worked," Dickens said.

"So who'd have access to both lists?" Lucas asked. "Just you three?"

Fumaro scratched at her hair part with a Number Two pencil. "Well . . . everything we've got is mostly on our computers here . . ." She waved at three laptops. "We're networked and we're online, but . . . I mean, when we leave, we turn off the computers." She looked at the door to the skyway. "If somebody sneaked in here at night . . . but then they'd need the passwords . . ." She looked at the other two women. "Any ideas?"

They sat mute, shaking their heads.

"What about in Washington?" Dickens asked.

"You know, nobody in Washington cares, as long as the work gets done," Fumaro said.

Another one of the women, whose name was Cheryl Ann, said, "You know, really, what we do is clerical work. That's all. We get lists, we put them in a computer, and match them to available rooms. If we get a match, we send a confirmation. If it doesn't match, we call up people and see if we can figure out what to do. We put names in little squares. We don't know these people."

The third woman, whose name was Lucy, said, "You know . . . never mind."

Fumaro asked, "These people who were beaten up. What were their names?"

"John Wilson, Bart Spellman, Lorelei Johnson," Lucas said.

She scooted her office chair over to one of the laptops, called up a form and typed *John Wilson* into a blank. Another form blinked up, with Wilson's registration, showing the bare information of name, room assignment, billing address, and credit card guarantee. Lucas, looking over her shoulder with Dickens, said, "But that doesn't say who he worked for."

"That's on another input form," Fumaro said. She popped up another form, which showed Wilson's employer and a payment guarantee from a travel agency.

"But that doesn't have the room assignment," Dickens said. "You'd have to get both of these forms to put those together?"

They hashed that over, and decided that if you *knew* who you were looking for, you could find the room number; but you'd need the name first. Dickens said to Lucas, "Whoever did it had to have a fix on the targets. Then he could get the room assignments . . ."

"But he would have had to get them from these computers, or access to these computers," Lucas said. "In Washington, I think."

He told Dickens about the line of reasoning they'd worked out in Wilson's hospital room. "Cohn and the gang members had to have the names quite a long time ago."

"The logic is a little leaky," Dickens said. "But I see what you're saying."

Lucy, the third woman, asked Fumaro, "When was Wilson registered?"

Fumaro checked and said, "May seventeenth."

Lucy asked, "How about Spellman?"

Fumaro checked. "May ninth." To Lucas and Dickens:

"That was just before the big rush. The big rush started around the first of June. That's when everybody was getting set with their rooms."

"So they were before . . . Raphael," Lucy said.

The three women all looked at one another, and Lucas looked at the three of them looking at one another, and then he asked, "Who's Raphael?"

"Raphael is dead," Lucy said.

11

BETWEEN THE TIME Lucas got the call about Letty and the time he got home, he'd bumped and stumbled over what might be critical information about the Cohn gang. His initial dismay about Letty had dissipated; but it all came back as he got closer to home.

Her bicycle was in the driveway, so she was home, and by the time he went through the connecting door between the garage and the kitchen, he was steaming.

Weather, Sam, and Ellen the housekeeper were in the kitchen when he went through. He snapped, "Where's Letty?" and Weather looked at his face and asked, "What happened?" and Letty said from the living room, "I'm in here."

She'd been waiting. Her voice had a hard edge to it and Weather stood up and asked again, "What happened?" and Lucas started for the living room.

LETTY AND JULIET Briar had ridden around in the Channel Three van for a while, and Letty borrowed a hundred dollars, fifty each from Frank and Lois, promising to pay them back "as soon as I can steal it from Dad." She gave the money to Briar and said, "Now you're covered. You don't have to go around making dates."

Juliet said, uncertainly, "Randy might make me tell."

"You don't have to tell," Letty said. "You can make something up."

"What if he asks me what the guy was like?" Briar asked.

"Well . . . make something up. See that guy walking across the street?" Letty pointed through the windshield and they all looked at a guy wearing a blue seersucker suit with a white shirt and a red bow tie. "The bow-tie guy was your date."

"He has a southern accent," Lois said.

"He has a southern accent and he took you to a hotel room at the Radisson, on the twelfth floor, but he wouldn't let you look at the number, and then he took you back out and wouldn't let you look at the number when you were leaving," Frank said.

"Randy doesn't care about that," Briar said.

"But it's a good detail, and it makes it sound more real," Letty said.

"He only gave you seventy-five dollars," Lois said. "But he went in the bathroom and you stole the rest."

"You don't understand," Briar said. "Randy might *make* me tell the truth."

"*You* don't understand," Letty said. "You fib."

She was insistent, and Briar looked away and bobbed her head and said, "Okay."

Frank looked back from the driver's seat and said to Letty, "We need to get out and have a secret talk where Lois and Juliet can't hear us."

Letty frowned. "What?" He repeated himself and she asked, "Why?"

"Because." He pulled over to the curb, said to Lois, "I'll leave everything running, be back in a minute."

He got out and Letty followed, and they walked a way

down the street, where they could see a bunch of cops in riot gear, apparently waiting for something to happen that was out of sight. Two more cops, on horses, were riding slowly toward the riot cops.

"Listen, you know about the problem I had," Frank said. "Everybody in town does."

"I heard something about it," Letty admitted.

"I've known a few of these girls . . . sometimes, a lot of times, with the younger ones . . . they don't think for themselves. They're so . . . screwed up . . . that they think what they're told to think. When Juliet says that Randy will make her tell—she knows that if Randy pushes her, she'll tell the truth. Then, maybe, she gets beat up. I don't know. I don't know what kind of deal you got going . . ."

"But she's got the money," Letty protested. "All she has to do is tell a little lie . . ."

"She can't," Frank said. He looked desperately embarrassed. "She does exactly what people tell her, because when she doesn't, she's learned that she'll get beat up. So, back there in the car, you got a little sharp with her, and she agreed. Because you *made* her agree."

"I didn't . . ."

"Yes, you did," Frank said. "These people, sometimes, they can't resist a push. When she gets alone with Randy, if he smells a rat and pushes her, she'll tell the truth."

Letty scuffed along, then looked back at the truck. "Poop." She turned, and started back, and then said, "Frank, thank you. You're a great guy for telling me this. You know, after your problem."

Frank blushed and when they got back to the van, Letty popped the back door and said, "Juliet, let's walk."

THEY GOT OUT of the van and started walking up the hill and generally back toward the Radisson hotel. Juliet asked, "Do you want the money back?"

Letty, surprised, said, "No, of course not. That's your

money. You got it from a fat guy named Stan with a southern accent who was wearing a blue-striped suit and a red bow tie."

Briar's head bobbed and Letty continued: "Frank told me that you might have a little trouble lying to Randy."

Juliet looked away. "I can't do it. Or maybe, I can, if he doesn't find out. But if he guesses, he can *make* me tell."

Letty said, "How much trouble have you had with the cops?"

Briar shook her head. "I've never had any trouble."

"You've never been arrested?"

She shook her head and then smiled, proud to show off her expertise. "Randy told me how to do this. Taught me. It's not hard. You gotta watch out for the undercover, but the undercover usually operates up where all the whores hang out. I ask . . . guys on the street. I pick *them*. If somebody picks me, I'm supposed to get pissed . . . Keeps off the undercover. Randy, if Randy gets arrested for two more years, they'll put him back in prison."

"Okay. Well. I asked you because I've been in trouble with the cops," Letty said. "I even shot one. Twice. I mean, I shot him two different times, a couple days apart. I used to get busted by the highway patrol because I'd drive around when I was too young . . ."

Briar was looking at her openmouthed. "You shot a cop?"

"Yup. You can look it up on the Internet. My name is Letty West and you can look it up," she said.

"Okay," Briar said. "But we don't have an Internet."

Letty hooked her arm with Briar's. "Now. When I was in all that trouble, all the time, I had to tell a few fibs. Well, lots of fibs. The way I did this is, I made a little box in my mind, and I put the truth in that, and then I made the box small. So I knew what the truth was. But then, I imagined, you know, *another* truth. What might have happened. What people would rather have had happen. So, if the highway patrolman saw me downtown, and asked me if I was driving, and I was, I'd just say, 'No, my mom brought me.' That was a better truth for everybody, see? Then I didn't get in trouble, and he didn't have to give me a hard time . . . Way back in my head, I knew what the truth was, but the fib was at the head of the line. That's what everybody wants to hear, anyway. Randy doesn't want to hear that I'm talking to you—he wants to hear that you, you know . . ."

"Gave a guy a blow job," Briar said.

"Yeah. Okay?"

"Okay." Another helpless head bob.

"So let's go sit on that bench, across the street," Letty said, pointing at a bench in a riverfront park. "We can practice. I'll teach you how to lie to Randy. Like I lied to the cops. You can tell *me* about blow jobs."

She really did sort of want to know.

LUCAS, TALKING WITH the women at the hospitality committee, felt the ice going out: the break.

Lucy, the third woman, had said, "Raphael is dead."

Lucas and Dickens, the Secret Service agent, looked at each other, and another look passed between the three nervous women, and then Lucas said, "Who's Raphael?"

Cheryl Ann, the second woman, said, "Raphael Sabartes, this Latino guy . . ."

"Spanish," Fumaro said. "From Spain."

Lucy said, "He was part-time tech support back in the Washington office, and he died. In June. June twenty-first, midsummer's day. They said alcohol and pills. The cops did. The police."

Lucas's eyebrows went up: "You think different?"

"Well, it was a lot of pills," Lucy said. "A *lot* of pills. Couldn't hardly have been an accident."

"Police said it could have been an accident," Fumaro said. "You're drinking, you can't get to sleep, so you take a pill. The pill makes you confused, and you don't think you've taken the pill, so you take another one. And so on."

"Thirty pills?" Lucy said. "He took thirty pills by mistake?"

Cheryl Ann said, "Then there was his girlfriend."

Dickens: "What about the girlfriend?"

"Very pretty Latina, Mexican, I think, but older than Raphael," Cheryl Ann said. "Raphael was about twenty-five; this woman, I think, might have been in her thirties."

Lucy snorted. "She'd never see forty again, if you ask me. She took care of herself, but she was no spring chicken."

"Raphael liked her," Fumaro said.

"Raphael *loved* her," Lucy said. To Lucas: "I don't think Raphael was very sexually experienced."

"He was sort of odd-looking," Cheryl Ann confirmed.

"Like a Picasso," Fumaro said.

"So this good-looking older woman who shares his heritage . . . well, some of it, anyway, she can speak Spanish . . . she eats him up," Lucy said. She leaned toward Lucas: "Then he died, and *she never even came to the memorial service.*"

Lucas said, "He could have put together these rooms and names and organizations . . . ?"

Cheryl Ann snapped her fingers: "Like that. You know what? He was moody, that's what we told the police, he was moody, but we never saw him happier than after he hooked up with this woman. Why would he commit suicide?"

Lucy said, "What if she broke it off with him that night? That could be a reason . . ."

Dickens had taken a chair; now he leaned back and put his hands behind his head, stared up at the ceiling, thinking, then said, "You know what?"

Lucas: "What?"

"Just between you and me, the biggest street-money guy, I happen to know, is named Chuck Prince. He works for America-United Aerospace Association, which is a lobby group for all the big air-defense manufacturers. He probably has four times as much money with him as all these other guys . . . why didn't they hit him? I know he's in town."

Fumaro reached forward and called up a form. "He registered with us on twenty-nine June."

Cheryl Ann said, her voice hushed and conspiratorial, "They don't know about him. Because Raphael was dead. They killed him too soon. Holy shit. It's just like in *Clue*. Colonel Lesbo did it, with the poison in the drink at the hotel."

Dickens ventured a smile. "Lesbo?"

Cheryl Ann said, "The three of us saw them once—just once—at the Hamilton, in the bar, which is a weird place for Raphael, now that I think about it." The other two women nodded.

"They saw us and we saw them, and we stopped to say hello and look her over and I got a very definite lesbian radio wave from her," Cheryl Ann said. "Not that I'd really know."

"You'd recognize her again?" Lucas asked.

"Maybe—but you know what? There's a photograph of her," Cheryl Ann said. "He took a picture of her with his cell phone, sent it to himself at the office, and printed it out, and pinned it up on the wall of his cubicle. After he died, we took the stuff off the walls and put it in a box and gave it to the police, when they came around. They might still have it."

"What about the body?" Dickens asked.

"I think the Spanish embassy shipped it back to Spain," Fumaro said.

Lucas said, "Time to call the cops, I guess. Were these District cops, or are you over in Virginia, or what?"

"Right in the District," Fumaro said. "The guy who came to get the box was Detective Sams."

Lucas wrote it down and went home to confront Letty.

LETTY WAS STANDING in the living room with her arms crossed, one foot all but tapping, a pose that Lucas recognized from encounters with more women, over the years, than he cared to remember. Before he could say a single word, Letty said, "I'm trying to get to be what Jennifer calls a Real Fuckin' Reporter, and I do *not* want to hear about this story."

"What story?" Weather asked.

Lucas, fists on his hips, looking at Letty but talking sideways to Weather: "Your daughter here is running down hookers, in St. Paul, and I won't tell you what kind of questions she's asking them, because it embarrasses me."

Weather said, "Hookers?"

Lucas said to Letty, "I'm putting my foot down. I let you run all over me, but this time, by God, you are not going to go around this town looking for hookers. I mean, do you have any idea what those people could do to you? Of course not. You're a teenager and you don't have a single fucking idea what you're getting into . . ."

"I do have a fucking idea because I tracked down one of these girls—on my own—and she's no older than I am . . ."

"Watch your language," Lucas said, getting loud. He knew he was about to start waving his arms, so he put his hands in his pockets, afraid that he might frighten her.

"You started it," she said.

"Technically, you said 'fuck' first," Weather told Letty.

Ellen came in from the kitchen, carrying Sam. "What the heck is going on here?"

"Letty's interviewing hookers," Weather told her.

"Hookers?"

"Aw, for Christ's sakes," Lucas said. To Letty: "You, young lady, are grounded."

THAT WASN'T THE end of it, of course. Lucas had never grounded anyone before, so the term "grounded" had to be defined. He couldn't actually restrict her to the house, because she had to go to school the next week, and there was some slack there, and he actually approved of the idea of Letty working with Jennifer Carey. Besides, he wasn't a jailer.

When everything was hashed over, Letty had negotiated it down to one restriction: she was not allowed to go downtown on her own, and anytime she went out of the house, she had to tell somebody specifically where she was going. If she violated the deal, she'd be restricted to the house for the rest of the week, including the weekend.

"All right. It's not fair, it's not right, but you're the dictator," she said.

Lucas said, "What do you mean it's not right? You're going around . . ."

"I'm reporting the news," Letty snarled.

Weather jumped in: "Both of you shut up. A deal's a deal. All right? All right."

Ellen said, "Hookers? In St. Paul?"

"Aw, for Christ's sakes . . ."

LETTY STOMPED OFF to her bedroom to mope, but she didn't stomp as hard as she might: she had no intention of keeping the agreement.

LUCAS, ON THE way home, had called his secretary and told her to chase down the Washington cop, Sams, who'd looked into Raphael Sabartes's death.

"It's Sunday," Carol said. "I might not be able to get him."

"Try," Lucas said. "Have we heard anything at all about this Justice Shafer guy?"

"No . . ."

"Of course not," Lucas said. "If we had, you'd have called me instantly."

"Right."

"So find Sams."

As it turned out, Sams was working nights, and was due to come on at 11 P.M. Lucas called the number Carol got, and left a note with Sams's supervisor that he'd be calling right at eleven o'clock.

The rest of the evening was fairly tense, with Letty trudging up and down the stairs between her room and the refrigerator, stopping only once to say, "All my friends say it's unfair."

"All your friends are teenagers," Lucas said.

Letty said, "You told me one time that you had a beer in a hockey bar when you were fourteen."

"That was different," Lucas said.

"How was that different?"

"There were adults around," Lucas said.

"Huh, great. Adults giving a fourteen-year-old a beer," Letty said.

Weather said, "Shut up, shut up, shut up, both of you, shut up."

On her last trip down, she went to the refrigerator, got a bottle of water, and on the way back through the family room, where Weather and Lucas were watching the news, stopped and gave Lucas a kiss on the forehead, and went on her way.

"I think you're okay," Weather said.

AT TEN O'CLOCK, eleven Eastern, Lucas called Sams, got him, gave him the history, and told him about the interview with the women at the hospitality committee.

"Well, they might be right, but we couldn't prove it," Sams said. "No sign of violence, the kid was lying on his back on his bed, his shoes off, his hands crossed on his chest. Bottle of rum in the kitchen, glass by the bed."

"But no note."

"Nothing," Sams said. "We never did find the woman. We didn't know where to start, because nobody knew her name."

"Find any DNA in the apartment?"

"There might have been some semen stains, but we

didn't run it—I mean, it didn't come from the woman," Sams said. "We didn't do a full process, because . . . there didn't seem to be any reason to. Everything in the apartment was pretty neat and clean."

"No references to the woman . . . cell phone, date book . . . ?"

"Okay, here's one thing. The kid's cell phone had a lot of calls on it to one number, and the number was in the three-two-three area code. That's L.A. Pretty much downtown L.A. We ran the phone down, and it was a dead end—one of those over-the-counter pay-as-you-go phones. We called it, but it was out of service. It never came back, as long as we called it."

"So you don't even know that it's the woman's phone," Lucas said.

"Nope. We don't. But: I talked to his uncle, from Spain, because his folks don't speak English, and we figured out between us that he'd never been to California, and as far as anybody knew, he didn't know anybody from there. But he was calling the number six times a day for two months."

"So it's gotta be her," Lucas said. "He was in love."

"I think so. Now that you're asking, I'd have to say it was all a little odder than we thought at the time. She was just flat gone, and she shouldn't have been *that* gone."

"These committee women I talked to, they said you might have a picture of her," Lucas said.

"We do have that," Sams said. "When I got your note, I went and looked. The thing is, it was just odd enough that the ME didn't want to rule it as a suicide. He left the cause of death open. Means of death was a load of sleeping pills with alcohol. Anyway, we've still got all the evidence, what there was of it."

"Could you scan that photo and send it to me?" Lucas asked.

"Sure. Keeps me off the street—I'll do it tonight."

WHILE LUCAS WAS talking to Sams, Jesse Lane and Rosie Cruz were sitting at the back of Spor's, an upscale deli off West Seventh Street, two blocks from the convention center, watching Shelly Weimer finish a corned-beef sandwich with a mound of yellow sauerkraut.

"The guy is a pig," Cruz said.

"He ain't all that neat, is he?"

Weimer was sitting across the shop under a poster of Albert Einstein. He went after the sandwich like a starving man, hunched over it, eyes scanning the shop, pieces of bread and strands of sauerkraut falling like shrapnel on the tabletop and onto his jacket and shirt and lap.

Lane and Cruz worked slowly through their hot dogs and French fries, not much to talk about, until Lane asked, "You're from L.A., right?"

"We don't talk about where people are from," Cruz said. Her voice was soft and pleasant, her eyes amused.

"Well, everybody knows where everybody else is from . . . if Brute's from anywhere. Most of the time, he isn't, but he used to be from Birmingham."

"I like my privacy," Cruz said.

"Sure. But, I figure you're from L.A. You look California. You act California."

Now she was interested. "How do you *act* California?"

Lane checked Weimer, then turned back. "You know. Me 'n' Tate were talking. When we're done with a job, and you're heading out to the airport, you dress like California. Light and cheerful. Lacy. We don't dress like it in the middle of the country. Then, whenever we go to a restaurant, you pick at the food like you never seen it before. Like that hot dog. You ain't gonna finish it, are you?"

"It's not so good," she said.

"It's a good hot dog," Lane said. "I haven't had many better. But you guys, in California, you don't eat hot dogs. You eat . . . fruit. Fruit drinks. Yogurt. And *you* eat fruit, I've seen you do it. If you wanna get nasty, you eat a Fat Burger, or you go to In-and-Out. We all eat McDonald's out here. It's the food that makes me think California. You look big city, but in New York, they eat everything. In Dallas, they eat a lot of Mexican and a lot of ribs, and they don't really give a shit about anything else. You don't look like Chicago or Denver. You don't eat like Dallas or New York. You're L.A."

"You know a lot about L.A.?" she asked, implying that he didn't.

"A fair bit," Lane said, not taking the bait. He studied her for a minute, then said, "Marina del Rey. Or maybe you got more money than that. Laguna Beach."

"You're so full of shit, Jesse." She patted his hand. "But you're a nice guy."

Jesse leaned forward and said, "You didn't blink an eye when I said Marina del Rey, which means you know where it is. How'd you know that, if you weren't from L.A.?"

She shook her head and said, "Okay, Jesse, you got me. I'm from Marina del Rey."

He said, "Okay. So where in the fuck *are* you from?"

Cruz said, "He's moving." Weimer was up and brushing off his jacket and pants as he waddled between tables, headed for the door. Which was good for Cruz, because Weimer's move covered the shock of the conversation: she had a house more or less across the street from Marina del Rey, in Venice. Nobody had ever gotten close, and here this shitkicker from Alabama figured her out, because she ate *fruit*.

On her cell phone, she said, "He's coming."

WEIMER BEEPED THE rental car, an Audi A6, and punched himself lightly over the heart, where the sauerkraut was threatening to back up. He walked between the Audi and the minivan beside it, edged open the door—the van was parked too close and he didn't want to dent it. As he lifted a leg to pivot onto the front seat, he heard a metallic *slide* . . . and a heavy hand grabbed his coat collar and yanked him straight back inside the van, smashing his calves against the edge of the doorsill, one shoe popping off his foot, and then the door slammed.

The whole thing was so quick that he yelped, "Hey! Hey!" and then there was a gloved hand over his mouth, and a man said, "If you yell, if you make a fuss, I cut your fuckin' throat."

"Don't hurt me," Weimer said when the hand lifted back. "Don't hurt me. Take my wallet."

"Where's your room key?" Cohn asked.

A moment of silence, then Weimer said, "Oh, Jesus. You're them."

Cohn backhanded him across the face, hard. "Don't take the Lord's name in vain," he said. "Where's the card?"

"In my wallet," Weimer said. "My back pocket."

"Better be."

Cohn pulled a fabric shopping bag over Weimer's head, tied it with a string. Weimer said, "Don't choke me, don't choke me, I'm cooperating."

Cohn tied the knot, said, "Put your hands by your side," and when Weimer did it, he grabbed Weimer's feet and twisted them, which rolled Weimer onto his face. Weimer felt the wallet slip out of his pocket, and then, "Got the key. Let's go," and the van started to move.

WEIMER WAS AT the Embassy Suites, twenty blocks away. "Anybody else in your room?" Cohn asked.

"No."

"Better not be, because we don't want no one seeing our faces, you know? If you got a girlfriend, or something, and she sees our faces, well, too bad for her."

"There's nobody but me," Weimer said.

"Where's the money?"

Another moment of silence, then Cohn hit him again, hard, this time in the left kidney. The pain was excruciating, and Weimer groaned, and Cohn said, "You only got two kidneys."

"It's under the bed. But it's a platform, you gotta pull the headboard back a little."

There were cops all along the streets, but they made a wide circle to the hotel, no problem. They parked on the street, and McCall took the card: "See you in five."

Inside the hotel, he rode the elevator up to seven, put on his gloves when he saw the hallway was empty, entered the room, closed the door and turned on the light, wrenched the headboard off the bed, saw the briefcase, a square leather one, like a lawyer might carry, pulled it out, clicked it open—a third full, maybe, less than they'd gotten before. A lot less. Not so many hundreds and fifties, lots of twenties and tens.

He started to leave, then thought about what Weimer had said: *"You're them."*

He knew about them . . . He thought about it for a minute, then checked Weimer's other bags, found nothing but an expensive-looking camera. Started toward the door again, then stopped, went back, yanked the bed apart, pulled the whole platform away from the wall . . . and saw the backpack jammed against the foot of the platform. A cheap black nylon backpack. Weimer had been smart, having heard of the other robberies, and had set up a decoy bag . . .

McCall popped the backpack: here were the hundreds. Lots of them. McCall smiled and said aloud, "You da man."

Back out to the van, driving away, he said, "Weimer's a wiseass. There were two bags. I got both of them."

Weimer said, "I had to try."

"Shouldn't have," Cohn said, and he hit Weimer in the kidney again, and this time, Weimer screamed, and Cohn hit him once more.

McCall said, "Coming up." They took a one-way road between the back of St. John's Hospital and the freeway, a dark road, weeds on the freeway side, and halfway down, stopped, and Cohn rolled Weimer out into the street, the bag still over his head.

As they pulled away, Cohn slid the door shut and asked, "How'd we do?"

"Did good," McCall said. "Maybe more than the first guy."

"Damnit: it's like taking candy from kids. Put that with the hotel deal, and we can get anything we want. Anything."

"If it's what I think, we already got more than three million . . ."

"What're you going to buy in L.A. with three mil divided by five? Huh? Tate? You can't even buy a nice house with your share. We hit the hotel; if it's what Rosie says it'll be, you'll get maybe three for yourself. That'll buy a nice house. Live in Beverly Hills with that kind of money."

McCall thought about it, said, "Not in the best part of Beverly Hills," and Cohn started to laugh.

THE PAIN IN his back was brutal and Weimer stayed on the concrete, pulled the bag free, got oriented, and rolled to the gutter. All he saw of the van was two red taillights, disappearing around the corner. He had no idea what kind of van it was, or even what color it was.

The pain in his back was ferocious. He tried to stand, almost fell, then turned and vomited up most of the sandwich he'd eaten, along with all the sauerkraut. When it was all up, he remained hunched over, spitting, and he thought, A million-five. Jensen was going to shit.

He got to his feet, took a step and groaned again. He was hurt, and maybe bad. He didn't know which way to go, didn't know that the building he was looking at was the back of a hospital. He took a couple of steps, and the pain radiated through his back; he took another step and then headlights flared behind him.

He stepped to the side and started waving at the car. Hospital security, as it turned out. "I got robbed and beat up," he told the security guard, who'd stopped thirty feet away. "I gotta get to a hospital. I'm hurt bad. You know where a hospital is? We gotta call the cops."

12

THE NEWS ABOUT Weimer got to Lucas through the Secret Service. Dickens heard about it from a St. Paul cop on the security committee, and suggested that the cops call Lucas. A St. Paul lieutenant named Parker called at eight o'clock, and Ellen, the housekeeper, brought the phone to the bedroom and said, "St. Paul police. They say it's important."

Weather was already at work, and Ellen said that Letty was up and waiting for a ride to Channel Three.

"Tell her I'll be ready in fifteen minutes," Lucas said. He took the phone: "Yeah. Davenport."

"Don Parker at St. Paul. We had a robbery last night, and we've been told you're tracking them."

"Lobbyist guy?"

"That's what I'm told," Parker said. "He's not talking much, said they took his travel money, but said it was the same deal as two other ones he heard about. Anyway, he's at St. John's."

"Hurt?"

"Peeing blood. Probably get out tomorrow, depending. They rabbit-punched him a few times. Took him for a ride in a van, robbed his room. There's something going on there."

"I'll go talk to him," Lucas said.

"Dick Clay is working it for us, but he's back in the house already . . . if you need anything."

Lucas hung up and thought, *All right: the motherfucker's still in town.*

LUCAS GOT CLEANED up and headed out to the kitchen, where Letty was reading the newspaper and eating toast. They were a little reserved after the fight the night before, and Lucas had a quick microwave oatmeal with milk and a banana, then they loaded into the Porsche and headed north and west toward Minneapolis.

Letty said, finally, looking out the side window, "Can't wait until I get my license."

"You'll be lucky if you get a license at all, after a stunt like yesterday's," Lucas said.

She turned back to him and said, "You want to let it go, or do you want to argue? I mean, I'll argue if you still want to."

"Let it go," Lucas said.

"Okay. Like I said, I can't wait until I get my license." She reached out and ran a hand over the dashboard. "Take this thing out on the highway and blow the coon-farts out of it."

Lucas laughed and said, "You should live so long as to get your hands on this car, sweetie. I'm thinking Hyundai. Used."

"You should live so long as to see me driving a Hyundai," she said.

She got him laughing, and though he could feel the manipulation, it felt kinda good . . . because that's what daughters were supposed to do. Then they were across the bridge and into town and down to the station, and he waved and she was inside and he headed back to St. Paul.

SHELLY WEIMER WAS propped up in a bed, a fat man with a pencil-thin mustache in the St. John's Intensive Care Unit, a saline drip running into one arm. He was reading the *Wall Street Journal*, holding it up with one hand, while the other hand took the drip. He folded the paper when Lucas walked in, and asked, "Who're you?"

"I'm with the state Bureau of Criminal Apprehension," Lucas said. "Lucas Davenport."

"I'm really hurt," Weimer said, and the hand holding the newspaper trembled with the effort of speaking. He reached out, slowly, and dropped it on a service tray.

"I'm sorry," Lucas said.

"Kept hitting me in the back, in the kidneys. Hit me even after they had the money." He groaned, as if to emphasize *money*.

"You didn't see any faces?"

"No. The guy who was hitting me was wearing a mask," Weimer said. "The driver I couldn't see at all . . . You're Mitford's guy."

"Not exactly. We talk," Lucas said.

"But you know the score."

"More or less. You had a shitload of illegal money stashed in your room and a guy named Brutus Cohn and one of his gang members grabbed you in an alley and threw you in the back of a van, and put a bag on your head, got your room key and took the money. And beat you up."

Weimer nodded, shifted in bed, winced, and said: "That's it, in a nutshell. I didn't know his name was Brutus Cohn, and you might want to go easy on that 'illegal money' thing. Since you know all of that, why haven't you picked him up?"

"We're looking, we haven't found him," Lucas said. "He's ditched himself somewhere—could be headed out of town by now. But, we're looking. Got his face all over national TV."

"Won't get my money back," Weimer said.

"No, it won't, but it really wasn't your money, anyway," Lucas said. "So: what can you tell me?"

Weimer said, "I've been thinking about it, and I've got one thing."

"Yeah?"

"Yeah, I . . ." He groaned and arched his back and flailed at it with his good hand, groaned again, and then went slack and looked at Lucas. "It keeps twisting, like a muscle's turning back there . . . God bless me."

"The one thing," Lucas said.

"Ah . . . I was eating in this sandwich shop and I got up to go," Weimer said. "Left the money and the tip on the table, walked out the door, turned left, walked down this little short alley around the building to the parking lot to my car. I opened the door and bam! They got me. Just bam-bam! Like that." He had small, round hands and he slapped them twice. "So, I think they had to be watching me, to be all ready. The guys in the van couldn't see me, because you couldn't see into the back of the shop. I think somebody was inside the place."

"You saw somebody?"

Weimer shifted again, his face going pale, and he said, "Ahhh. God, I hate this shit . . . Okay: There was a tough-looking hillbilly guy and this cool-looking woman in a back booth. They didn't look like they should go together, but they were. I noticed her looking back at me two or three times—caught her looking. I am what I am, and my wife likes me okay, but I'm not exactly a chick magnet, okay? They don't look at me more than once."

"Okay."

"So she was checking me out," Weimer said, "Now I wonder if she was checking me out for this Cohn guy? Maybe she made a call when I got up to leave."

"You see her on a cell phone?" Lucas asked.

"No, but I didn't look."

Lucas asked, "There's no chance that she was a Latina-looking chick, was she?"

Weimer's eyebrows went up: "You know who she is?"

LUCAS CALLED CAROL, at the office, and had her check his e-mail. The photo from Washington was there. "Print it. I need it. Is there somebody who could run it over to St. John's? Lights and sirens?"

"I saw Jenkins down the hall, reading the paper—he could take one of our cars."

"Get him over here. Quick as he can make it," Lucas said.

He tried to pry more information out of Weimer, but the lobbyist didn't have much more: "The whole thing was quick. Professional. Bam-bam-bam. When the two of them were talking, they were totally calm and casual. Like a couple guys going out for a beer. Then, when the guy hit me for not telling about the hideout bag, he didn't seem angry. He hit me like he was punishing a kid. Just . . . hit me."

Lucas went down to the cafeteria while he waited for Jenkins, got a Diet Coke, read the *Star Tribune* about the convention: more marches, lots of people already arrested. Finished the story, glanced at his watch, took out his cell phone and discovered that he had no signal. He walked it up the stairs, and then outside, got a signal, and called Jenkins. "I'm two minutes away," Jenkins said. "I had to drive halfway around town to get here."

Lucas waited by the curb, saw Jenkins coming, waved him down. Jenkins passed a manila envelope out the window. "What a mess. You can't get anywhere. St. Paul's closing down the whole downtown area."

"Thanks for this. See you back at the office."

"I hope it's serious."

"It is." Lucas patted the truck on the door, and headed back into the hospital. In the elevator up to Weimer's room, he slipped the photo out of the envelope. The quality was bad—cell-phone quality—but the woman was recognizable, and, Lucas thought, somewhat hot.

Dark hair, dark eyes, caught unaware, he thought, as though she had just turned around. She seemed to be in a nightclub, or some kind of night place—there were sparkly lights in the background, the corner of a mirror, the shoulder of another woman in what might have been a cocktail dress. The woman wasn't looking at the camera, but off to the right; she might not have known about the picture, Lucas thought.

WEIMER WAS SITTING, unmoving, staring at the television that was attached to the ceiling. When Lucas came in, he turned his head: "Hurts when I move. This is awful, I'm like a baby. Could you take the top blanket off? My feet are getting hot."

Lucas stripped the cotton blanket off the bed, wadded it up, threw it on a chair and said, "Okay. I got a picture . . ." He should have had a bunch of pictures, a photo panel, and asked Weimer to pick one, but that, he thought, would be a pain in the ass. "I don't want you to say 'yes' or 'no' unless you're sure. Take a look."

He passed the photo over and Weimer looked at it for a second, or two, then nodded and said, "Hell yes. That's her. Who is she?"

Lucas took the photo back and said, "I don't know. But I will find out."

"Beat the shit out of her, for me," Weimer said. "Do that, and I'll get you a personalized autographed picture from the next president."

Lucas said, "You know who it's going to be?"

"Doesn't matter," Weimer said. "Either one. We're covered both ways."

AS SOON AS he could use his cell phone, on the way out of the hospital, he called Carol and said, "Jenkins is on the way back. Grab him, get Shrake, see if you can shake Del loose, he's wandering around town somewhere, doing his homeless act . . . Meet in the office in twenty minutes."

In the car, he called Mitford, the governor's man, and said, "We're meeting in my office in twenty minutes to talk about the people pulling these robberies. You might want to come by."

"The cop thing yesterday . . . is that going to break it open?" Mitford asked.

"Maybe, but maybe not," Lucas said. "The money is getting to be less important, in a way."

"All right. I'm over at the X. I can be there in twenty, if I can get through town at all."

"You're the guy who wanted to have the convention here," Lucas said.

"Hey, I think it's a great success and another sign that Minnesota is marching into a future that gets brighter and brighter minute by minute. See ya."

THEY GATHERED IN Lucas's office, and Lucas kicked Carol out, despite her curiosity, and said to the cops, "You all know Neil . . ."

Then he told them about it, about the money in briefcases and satchels, about the robberies, about the killing of the cop in Hudson, about Lily Rothenburg's story of the cop murders in New York, and about the Latina-looking woman and the dead kid in D.C.

"We're dealing with murder as a policy. They've killed at least four people and that's only the ones we know about," Lucas said. "They're a murder gang, and they're here, and we need to run them down."

"I didn't know," Mitford said.

"Nobody did—not really. We're coming in the back door on this," Lucas said. "Now, we've got to start pushing some buttons. I want to put this woman's face out there. One of those 'Do you know this woman?' deals on national TV. I can go back to Lily on that, and she can help: she's already plastering the place with Cohn's photo."

"What about me?" Del asked. "I've spent a lot of time getting tight with these protesters. I'm doing the sheriff's office some good, and the St. Paul cops."

"Stay with it until we get something we can use—and then I may have to pull you off," Lucas said. "My feeling is, the big convention trouble is about over, after the arrests yesterday. Maybe more on Thursday, the big McCain day, but . . . if we need you, we need you."

Del nodded. "Okay."

Shrake: "The question is, where are they? After the trouble in Hudson, they know we're papering the motels. So where are they staying? Out-state? Or have they taken off?"

"Condos," Jenkins said. "There are probably six hundred condos around town with nobody in them and the developers have been renting them out to the Republicans, to the media, to anyone who wants one. If they knew about that . . ."

"They would," Lucas said. "They've got good intelligence."

"Then that may be the answer," Jenkins said to Lucas. "Your pal Ralph Warren, you know, with all his connections everywhere . . . maybe they went through him. He had a couple hundred empty condos."

"Yeah, well. He's dead," Lucas said. Warren hadn't been a pal, and though Lucas had tried to keep him alive, he'd failed.

"Even if he's dead, there's still gotta be a business manager somewhere," Jenkins said. "Somebody's got to be running the company."

Lucas jabbed a finger at him. "I'll buy your idea. You and Shrake start running down condo managers, the ones with vacancies."

"Maybe we should hold off on the woman's picture for

a couple of days," Del said. "Maybe we can spot her without the TV. If we spook her, and she takes off . . . it's one thing we've got that they don't know about."

Lucas thought about it, then said, "Okay. A day. If we come up with anything, we can stretch it out. After that, we're going with the TV. I'll get Carol to print up photos of Cohn and this woman for you guys to take around town."

He turned to Mitford: "At night . . . they've been hitting these guys at night, because it's easier to locate them, and it's easier to operate without letting their faces be seen. We need the names of the four or five biggest money dealers that you still see out there, and we'll put somebody in their rooms. See if we can ambush them."

"I don't know if they'll go for that," Mitford said.

"They'll have to do their deals somewhere else. Maybe they can rent two rooms. But that's what we need, Neil. We got four dead."

Mitford nodded: "I'll make some calls."

LETTY HAD TWENTY dollars from Lucas when she walked in the door at Channel Three that morning. The receptionist buzzed her through the security gate and she walked back past the studios, where the *Bob & Jane* morning show was unwinding. She nodded to the weatherman, who walked by, on his way to do a thirty-second bit, shaking peanuts out of a cellophane bag, and said, "You've got something stuck to your cheek."

He said, "What is it?"

"Peanut skin?" She brushed it off. "Gone now."

"Thanks."

SHE WENT ON her way, turned into the greenroom, where people waited for their turn on *Bob & Jane*, got two sweet rolls, and ate them on the way back to Jennifer Carey's office. She'd had breakfast, but not much—she and

Lucas were both light eaters in the morning. She realized on the way over that since she planned to give the twenty dollars to Juliet, she'd better get a couple of sweet rolls when she could.

A coffee niche, for employees only, was located down the hall from Carey's office. She stopped there, looked around, stepped inside, and picked up the coffee donation can and peeled off the plastic lid. Three or four dollars. Not worth taking.

She needed eighty dollars more, although a hundred would be better, she thought—enough to convince Whitcomb that Juliet had been working.

Down the hall, she found Carey poking at her computer. Carey looked up and said, "Hi, good-lookin'," with just enough forced cheer that Letty instantly knew who'd ratted her out. It might have been Lois, but it had gone through Carey to Lucas.

"You ratted me out," she said.

Carey started to deny it, and then gave it up: "You're too young. You don't think so, but you are. When I was your age, I thought I was twenty-eight, too, but I wasn't."

"How old were you when you shot your first cop?" Letty asked.

"Letty, that's not fair." Carey was a hockey mom, and sometimes acted like one.

"How old were you when you first drove your drunk mother home from the bar?" Letty asked.

"Letty . . ." Carey was getting flustered.

"How old were you when you first stole money to get something to eat?" Letty was all over her now.

"For Christ's sakes, I gotta do what I think is best," Carey said. "You're fourteen."

Letty leaned into it: "I know how old I am. When it comes to trouble, I *am* twenty-eight. Try not to forget that the next time you turn me in."

Carey rolled her eyes: "I don't want to fight with you."

"I'm done," Letty said. "But I need a ride to St. Paul and

I need a camera in the park. I talked to some street kids—not prostitutes, just skaters from St. Paul—who are going to skate in one of the marches. It'll make a good snip of film."

"I'm going over in fifteen minutes," Carey said, eager to make peace. "The cameras are already over there, so . . . we'll hook you up."

Letty smiled: "I'm not really mad at you. Everybody thinks they're doing the right thing. You're not, but I appreciate it anyway."

CAREY HAD HER personal reporting rules that she'd been passing along to Letty. Like, before you go out on a job, always pee first. Even if you don't feel like you have to. A woman can never find a comfortable place to pee when she needs one. Check your makeup and your hair; there's never a place to do that when you need one—a little too much hairspray is better than too little.

Letty went out in the newsroom to chat with some of the producers, keeping one eye on Carey's office. When Carey came out and looked around, Letty waved at her, and Carey called, "I'll be right back," and she headed down toward the bathrooms. Letty ambled over to her office as she watched her go, and when she was sure that Carey was in the bathroom, she stepped into the office and pulled Carey's purse out from under her desk.

Carey never had any idea how much money she had or what she'd spent it on. She was one of those people who believed that if she had checks, she must have money. She made a good salary, and her husband was rich, so money, at least the kind you spend during the day, meant almost nothing to her: Letty popped the purse and took a peek into Carey's billfold. Must be a thousand dollars in fifties, Letty thought. She took two of them, decided that the thickness of the currency seemed not at all diminished and took two more. She put the billfold back in the purse, put the purse back as she'd found it, and ambled back out of the office and over to the people she'd been talking with earlier.

When Carey came back from the bathroom, she called, "Let's do it," and Letty went to join her.

THE SKATERS WERE gathering in Mears Park in St. Paul's Lowertown, an area of older brick warehouses converted to lofts and condos and small, marginal businesses. Letty pointed them out and Carey looked them over, from the front seat of her SUV, and then said, "You know, you do have a natural eye for this. I told your dad that last night."

"Maybe I'll be an economist," Letty said. "TV is starting to seem so superficial."

Carey made a rude noise and said, "Let's get a truck over here. You go get your friends lined up."

CAREY CALLED A Channel Three van, and let Letty out to talk to the skaters while she took her SUV to a parking garage up the block. Letty got her cell phone out and called Juliet Briar: "Where are you?"

"Still at home. Randy's sleeping," Briar said.

"Tell him that a guy called for a date, and that you'll walk down," Letty said. "I got some money."

After a moment's silence, Briar said, "Okay."

"Call me when you get out."

THE LEADER OF the skate gang was named Marv, a burly, cheerful busted-faced guy with a shaved head and jeans so old that they looked like paper. He was wearing a T-shirt that read, "Mathews Solocam, Catch Us If You Can," that was washed thinner than the jeans.

He held out a fist and they bumped knuckles and he said, "How are you, babe?"

"Don't call me babe," Letty said, but she said it with her happy face, and she asked, "So who's who?"

There were seven guys and one girl among the skaters, and all of them desperately wanted to be on television. As Marv introduced them, Letty kept looking at the girl, with her dry, underfed, feral face, thinking that she was the one; but she had to keep Marv and the others happy, too. A management problem.

After the introductions, she said, "Listen, we've got a van coming with a camera. I'll want to talk to Marv, and then to Jean, because she's a girl, and we don't have that many girl skaters, and then maybe whoever . . . but I'd like to see some runs, if you got anything that's good."

One of the kids, a too-tall teenager with a bandaged hand, said, "We were jumping barrels . . ."

"That's terrific, that's great," Letty said. "Why don't you guys get set up with the barrels and we'll get shots of you skating, and then I'll do a couple of quick interviews."

CAREY CAME BACK and Letty explained the situation to her, off to the side, and said, "Take a look at Jean's face. Isn't that a great face?"

Carey looked at her, then said, "You really *are* going to be good at this. That's a *great* face."

The van showed, and the kids gathered around the cameraman, whose name was Mike, not really believing that it was going to happen. So the kids did their tricks and Mike even lay on the ground behind a trash barrel that they were jumping and had a kid jump over him, which got everybody laughing.

Briar called and said, "I'm out, I'm walking down the hill."

Letty: "I'm doing an interview in Mears Park. You know where that is?"

"Yeah. I can come there."

Letty did a quick stand-up with Marv and a longer one with Jean, then they all bumped knuckles and the skaters took off. Letty did a couple of shots alone, putting up some background, and then she saw Briar standing on the sidewalk, watching.

Off-camera, she walked over to Carey and said, "I've got somebody you need to meet."

"Who?"

"Come on," and she grabbed the older woman's elbow and pulled her over toward Briar.

THEY GOT HOT dogs and talked for a half hour. Letty dug harder into Briar's passivity; to her way of thinking, if she could replace Randy Whitcomb as Briar's boss, she would be making progress.

Carey, on the other hand, was fascinated by Briar's story and her relationship with Whitcomb. "He can't possibly love you. He treats you like an animal," Carey said. "He loves himself, he doesn't love you. I mean, he *doesn't*, Juliet."

"You don't know him," Briar said defensively.

Letty pushed: "She's right. He doesn't love you. If you think he does—well, you're wrong."

Briar flinched, and put her head down, and said, "Okay," and Carey looked at Letty and said, "Get off her back, Letty. Jeez."

"I'm just backing you up," Letty said.

"I'm *discussing*," Carey said. "You're pushing her around."

"Letty's okay, she's a friend," Briar mumbled.

"Going home is out of the question?" Carey asked.

"As long as Don is around," Briar said. "He won't leave me alone, and Mom doesn't believe me when I tell her about him."

"You're sixteen?" Carey asked.

"Almost seventeen. Next month," Briar said.

"And Don's a mailman. So he's got to be quite a bit older."

"He's forty, I think," Briar said. "He's . . . an asshole."

"I DON'T WANT to embarrass you," Carey said, "but I've got to ask. What does he do?"

"Well, you know, he grabs me, he feels me up, he comes in the bathroom when I'm taking a shower—he's got a nail thing that he can push in the doorknob, and open it even when it's locked. He gets naked and he comes out and grabs me, and rubs himself on me. He's come into my bedroom naked and gotten in bed, and when I tried to get out, he's, you know, held me . . ."

"Hasn't raped you?"

"No, but he will, if I go back," Briar said. "He came into my bedroom naked and got in bed with me, when I was asleep, and when I woke up, he was all over me. He was trying to push my head down by his cock, and I bit him right here"—she touched her hip bone—"and he bled all over and was screaming at me . . . Mom pretended like she didn't hear."

"You've seen him naked," Carey said. "Does he have any identifying marks, you know, around his penis, or on his butt? You know, something you couldn't have seen if he wasn't naked?"

Briar thought for a minute and then said, "Well . . . he shaves. You know, he shaves his cock and his balls. He does have a big brown spot, like a football shape, where the hair should be."

"Great!"

"And when I bit him, I bit a piece out of him," Briar said, with satisfaction. She smiled with the memory. "That's why he was bleeding so much. I bit out a piece and spit it on the floor. Not a big piece, but you know, enough that he was really bleeding."

"So he'll have a scar," Letty said.

"Oh, yeah."

"How long ago was that?" Carey asked.

"Last spring. I ran away in June . . . and met Randy."

"Okay, then. We can handle Don," Carey said. "We can get rid of him. If we get rid of him, could you go back home?"

"Maybe," Briar said. She was twisting her hands, and then she said, "Maybe Randy doesn't love me. But you know what? He *needs* me. He needs me to take him around, and to rub his shoulders and his back, and clean him up. In my whole life, he's the only person who ever needed me. Who ever wanted me around. Except Don, I guess."

Letty leaned forward: "You want to be needed, become a *nurse*. Not a hooker. *God. Juliet*."

Briar looked doubtful, and Carey said, "Let's get rid of Don, for a start. When we get rid of Don, and Juliet has a place to stay, then maybe we can make some progress."

Carey got up, and Letty said to her, "I need to walk with Juliet for one minute. I swear to God it won't be any longer than that. I'll be right back."

"What don't you want me to hear?" Carey asked.

Letty said, "Come on, Juliet. I'll be right back, Jen."

DOWN THE SIDEWALK, Letty pressed seventy dollars into Juliet's hand. "Is that enough?"

"That should be," Briar said, and showed a little sparkle. "He hasn't caught me yet."

"He won't catch you," Letty said. "I can get some more money. We'll meet tomorrow—I'll call you. Remember what I said?"

"Yup." Briar showed a little grin. "Lie like a motherfucker."

CAREY HAD BEEN watching from a distance, and when Letty walked back to her, she said, "All right—that was interesting, but there's no story. I mean, nothing I would feel right about doing now. She's really too young to say 'yes' to it."

"I don't want to do a story, either," Letty said. "I wanted you to meet her because I need to tell somebody the rest of it. I can't tell Mom or Dad—Mom would freak out and she wouldn't know what to do. And Dad . . . well, that's the problem."

"What?" Carey asked.

"Juliet's pimp, this Randy. His name is Randy Whitcomb. Dad arrested him, and beat him up once—that's why he got kicked off the Minneapolis police that one time."

"That guy!" Carey said. "I remember that."

"Yeah. Then Randy got paralyzed and he blames Dad for what happened. So now he's trying to get back at Dad. By getting at me."

Carey's mouth dropped: *"What?"*

Letty filled in the rest of it, about Randy watching her in the park, tracking her to the McDonald's. "You know what Dad'll do if he finds out?"

Carey said, "He'll . . . oh, shit."

"He could get caught—they've had this long feud," Letty said.

"So what're you doing with Juliet?"

Letty shook her head: "First, tell me how we get rid of this mailman guy, Don."

"GET A CAMERA, you know, we've got guys who'll do it for me," Carey said. "We get a camera and ambush Don and ask him about rolling around with an underage girl, talk to him about the amount of jail time he'll get. When he denies it, we tell him that she described his physical characteristics . . . and then we tell him that we're more worried about her than about him doing jail time, so that if he moves out, and never comes back, there's no story. But the minute he comes back, or makes one single threat, or even a phone call, we make him into a movie star, off he goes to prison."

"Simple," Letty said.

"Not simple, but effective. There was this chick who used to work for a Lutheran social services group; she'd take underage hookers away from their pimps. I helped her out a couple of times this way. We could do it with Whitcomb, too. Back him off Juliet, back him off Lucas, tell him he goes back to prison . . ."

Letty was shaking her head. "I actually thought about that. He's on parole. I figured that we could send him back, because she's underage. Then Juliet told me about him being paralyzed, and . . . He can't do it. They don't have sex because he can't. He makes her work the street, and sometimes he makes her have sex with another guy, and he watches, and gets all worked up . . . but she could walk away if she wanted to. Just leave him. He can't drive, either. So, everything she's been doing . . . I mean, it looks voluntary. The other thing is . . . I'm not positive she'd testify against him."

"Ah, man."

"We need to get him," Letty said. She held Carey with an intense stare, and Carey felt almost unable to move out of it. "For *sure*. Randy is crazy. I've talked to Juliet a lot, about Randy, and he's crazy. If we don't get him, maybe he'll try to shoot Dad. Or me. Or Mom, or somebody. But he's crazy and he's getting crazier, so we've got to get him."

"How . . . ?"

"What I'm trying to do is . . ." Letty looked away from Carey, up into the tree branches, away from Carey's eyes.

"What?"

"I thought I might get Randy to . . . do something to her," Letty said.

"What?"

"When he gets mad, he makes her get down on her hands and knees, naked, and then he beats her with this stick," Letty said. "I've seen the stick—it has blood on it. He hasn't done it for a month and . . . I mean, I don't know how evidence works, fingerprints and all that. But if he finds out she's been lying to him, and he beats her with that stick, and she calls me, and we call the cops . . . He'll go back, right? Her blood will be on the stick, fresh, and her back will have the marks, and his fingerprints will be on the stick?"

Carey stared at her for a long fifteen seconds, then said, "Juliet is supposed to be your friend."

"My dad is my friend," Letty said.

"But Juliet . . ." Carey's jaw worked. "Letty, that's appalling. What you're thinking. That's the coldest thing I ever heard of."

"You do what you gotta do," Letty said, her eyes cutting back into Carey's.

Carey recoiled: "Not that."

"Look," Letty said. "She's gonna get beat, sooner or later. All we're doing is taking advantage."

"You're setting her up," Carey said.

"I'm taking care of Dad. Okay? That's what I'm doing. So let's take care of Don, and get Juliet a place to go if . . . this other thing happens."

"Letty! I can't do this. This is awful," Carey said.

"It's already going. There's nothing you can do to stop it that wouldn't help Randy, and hurt Juliet and Dad and me." Letty stepped back and said, "So make your pick. Who do you help?"

LUCAS, BORED, CALLED Jenkins and Shrake, and found them, bored, getting nowhere. He got some names from them and hit a dozen condo buildings himself, running down the presidents of the condo associations, getting head shakes and uh-uhs from each of them: nobody had seen anybody who looked like Cohn or the woman in the cell-phone photograph.

One of them said, "You might be on the right trail, though. We've only got twelve units here, and two of them are rented out. Bought on spec, can't be sold—might be foreclosed. Same thing all over town, so there's lots of space to hide out."

Lucas had stayed in touch with Mitford all afternoon, and on the last call, Mitford said, "I have six names for you. If they're going to hit again, there's a good chance it'll be one of these six guys. They've got the most money and they all got early reservations—before this Sabartes guy died in D.C."

"All six?"

"Well, I actually got eleven names, but five got reservations too late," Mitford said. "You shouldn't need those."

"All right. E-mail me the names: we'll set up with them this evening."

13

RANDY WHITCOMB SAT in the back of the van as they cruised Davenport's place, the sun going down across the Mississippi Valley. They went around and around the neighborhood looking for the girl, until Ranch said, "Man, she ain't here. We been doing this for hours." They'd been doing it for a half hour.

"Gotta be a better way," Whitcomb said. As he looked out the van window, he saw a woman who'd been digging in a garden stand up to look at them as they went by. They'd gone by her a half dozen times, and were starting to attract attention. "We need a plan."

Juliet Briar didn't say anything; she just drove.

"I thought you were gonna bullshit her over to the house," Ranch said.

"I don't think the bullshit was working," Whitcomb said. He'd read the distance in Letty's eyes during their few words at the McDonald's. Whitcomb wasn't the sharpest knife in the dishwasher, but he had an exquisite sense of class, and Letty was several class-steps above him. The chances that she'd fall for his bullshit were fairly thin, he'd decided. She was like one of the prom queens back in high school—they'd looked right through him. They couldn't even see him; they couldn't even *hear* his bullshit. He was like a mosquito buzzing around their heads.

He scratched his nose, breaking open a scab left by the Pollish twins, when they rolled him down the front steps onto the sidewalk. He looked at the blood on his fingertips, shook his head and wiped it on his pants leg.

Ranch said, "Maybe we just oughta do it."

"Do what?"

"Just grab her," Ranch said. "Me 'n Juliet. See her on the street, pick her ass up, throw her in the van."

"She'd scream and moan and piss and fight . . ."

"Whack her on the head," Ranch said. "Put a bunch of pennies in a sock, punch her out or whack her on the head. Throw her in the van."

"You ever done anything like that?"

"Used to whack fags down on Hennepin," Ranch said, a lie so transparent that his voice wavered halfway through it.

"You never whacked a fag in your life," Whitcomb said.

"Well—I heard about it," Ranch said. "Swat them with a sock full of pennies, you don't kill them, you knock them out. Hit them with a pipe, you kill them."

"You probably are a fag," Whitcomb said.

"I'm not a fuckin' fag, man, you seen me fuck Juliet."

"Yeah, well, when we get this chick, you're gonna have to fuck her."

Ranch nodded. "I can do that." Ranch would use any drug he could find, but methamphetamine was his drug of choice. He could no longer fuck on reefer or cocaine, but crank would still do it for him. Enough crank, and Ranch tipped over the edge into sexual insanity, and other kinds of insanity, for that matter: Whitcomb once saw him run full-tilt, face-on into a garage door, as a joke. He'd never flinched or slowed down. The impact had knocked him out, and somebody had to call an ambulance to come get him.

"What if we have Juliet call her up and pretend she's a friend whose car broke down . . ."

Whitcomb came up with a half dozen plans and Juliet and Ranch took turns punching holes in them: like, how would they find out the name of a friend of the girl?

Finally, Ranch rubbed his throat, then smacked his lips. "Wonder where George is?"

George sold crank outside the X Center, but his business had been displaced by the Republicans.

Randy's brain switched tracks. Formerly on the Letty track, now it was on the crank track. "Probably down by the park. When they get too many cops at the X, he walks over to the park."

"Maybe we could find him," Ranch said.

Randy pretended to consider the idea, to make it clear that it was his choice, but he was now far down the crank track and he said, "Okay. Let's go find George."

COHN AND CRUZ and McCall and Lane sat in the condo and argued about the next move: Cruz had worked a way to do the last hit with the three of them inside, and she wanted to stay down until it was time to make the final move.

Cohn was entranced by the money they were taking from the political guys.

"We've got three million dollars," he said, waving at a pile of cash in the middle of the condo floor. "No problem: not a word about it in the newspapers or on TV. And it's so easy. The money is there. We take it away."

"We know they're looking for us, for you," Cruz objected. "Somehow, they got onto us . . ."

"And two years from now, or five years from now, they pick me up down in South Africa or Australia or somewhere, how are they gonna be able to prove any of it?" Cohn asked. "They can't. These political guys can't even admit that I got the money. What are they going to charge me with? Random terrorism? They got nothing. Nothing. They don't even know about Tate or Jesse or you. They don't have a clue. Look at this money—it's like picking apples."

"But they're looking . . ."

Cohn said to McCall and Lane, "One more. You guys up for one more?"

Lane shrugged and McCall said, "Rosie's got a point. We could let it cool off for a day or two. Or we could say fuck it, cut up the money and go home."

"Three million just isn't gonna do it, boys," Cohn said.

"But we got the hotel," Cruz said. "God only knows how much that's worth, but if we pull it off, it could be four or five times what we've got."

"What if we hit one more guy, and that guy had *two* million?" Cohn asked. "Then we could be talking about retirement." Cohn got two shares, everybody else got one. They all did the numbers in their heads: if they got two million on the next score, one share would be worth a million dollars in cash, and Cohn would get two. Cohn continued: "This hotel deal is pretty complicated. I'd say if we could pick off two more of these political guys, maybe we could skip the hotel. Say fuck it, and go home."

"Not going to get two," Cruz said, shaking her head. "The guys are already passing out the money—some of them might not have any left."

"It's only the first day of the convention, I bet they're saving up until the big shots get here, make more of a splash," Cohn said.

Lindy was sitting on the floor next to the pile of cash, and she reached out and picked up a bundle of fifties. "You know what I think? I think we ought to go to New York and spend some of this. Like, right now."

They all looked at her for a moment and then McCall laughed and said, "That's one idea."

Cruz said, "Brute, let's go over the hotel. Let's work that through. We really need to be on it, if we're going to do it. These guys, the moneymen, they were supposed to be the cherry on the sundae; they weren't supposed to be the whole goddamned sundae. I've already got other stuff running on the hotel."

"One more," Cohn said. "Come on, Rosie, work it out for us. One more. Which one's got the most? I swear to God, whatever he's got, he'll be the last one."

Cruz looked at him for a long beat, then said, "It's a her, not a him. Goddamnit, Brute . . ."

LUCAS HAD SPRUNG five agents, including himself: Jenkins, Shrake, Jim Benson, Dave Tompkins. "Better if we had two guys in each room," he said, "but we just don't have the people. So: everybody has armor, everybody has a shotgun, you don't answer the door. After the knock, you wait: they can't stand there long, because of the masks. They'll walk away . . . that's when you pop the door."

Tompkins grinned. "Now I see why you picked all single guys."

"Hey. It's dangerous. No question about it. But we've got to do something."

They were all in place by eight o'clock.

ELEVEN O'CLOCK. LUCAS got up and stretched, yawned, looked at Buddy Snider and Sally Craig, sitting at the breakfast table playing gin rummy, then looked at his watch. From the hotel windows, he could see across the interstate all the way up to Capitol Hill. There'd been some semi-violent demonstrations during the afternoon, and a few more people had been taken off to jail, but nothing extreme. The downtown area was still loaded with cops, but everything below looked quiet.

Craig, a thin, fiftyish blond woman from Washington, without looking up, said, "You're pacing again."

"Yeah, well. You're playing gin rummy," Lucas said.

"Cards exercise the mind," she said.

Snider said to Lucas, "Maybe you should check your gun again. That was interesting."

"Gun's fine," Lucas said.

He'd been penned up for three hours; the first two hours in utter darkness, until Snider and Craig got back from the convention center, where, he suspected, they'd been passing out cash. Maybe lots of it. When they came through the door a few minutes before eleven o'clock, Craig had had a gorgeous soft deer-hide backpack slung over one shoulder, and it appeared to be empty. Lucas had carefully worked through the room while they were gone, and hadn't found any money. There was a safe in the closet, though, that might have held anything up to a half-million dollars. Since Craig presumably had a safe in her own room, that could be another half-million.

Lucas got on his cell phone and called Shrake: "Nothing here. Nothing at all," Shrake said.

Benson: "Nothing here." Voice dropped. "Whitehead's in the bathroom, she has some kind of a problem. The whole place stinks."

Jenkins: "Haven't heard or seen a thing. Sitting here watching West Coast baseball."

Tompkins: "Schott's gone to bed. Says he's too tired to stay up anymore. I'm lying here watching *Star Wars* with the sound turned off."

"Which *Star Wars*?" Lucas asked.

"*A New Hope*. Channel three-forty."

"That's the first one," Lucas said. "Where Princess Leia hints that she might go for a three-way with Han and Luke."

"Yup. That's the one."

Off the phone, he searched through the TV channels until he found *Star Wars*. "You mind if I watch this?"

"Better than this card game," Craig said. She tossed her cards on the table and said, "Go gin yourself," sprawled on the bed, and said, "Turn the sound up. They're about to jump down the garbage chute."

THE KNOCK ON the door came at eleven-fifteen, three raps with a key, like a hotel maid would do it, and Jim Benson rolled to his feet, slipped the vest over his head, and pulled the Glock 9mm from its holster. The shotgun was in the corner, and he stepped over to it. Janet Whitehead, who was lying on the bed, sniffed and said, "Oh my God," and then an envelope slipped under the door, and they could hear, faintly, somebody walking away. Benson, a short, square-shouldered blond with a dimpled chin and chiseled nose, did a quick peek at the peephole and saw nothing. Whitehead picked up the envelope, opened it, glanced at the paper inside and said, "Hey," and before Benson could slow her down, she turned the knob on the door.

The door latch-lock was engaged, as well as the safety chain; the chain allowed the door to open three or four inches. The doorjamb anchor was held in place by three Phillips screws. They were not sufficient. The instant Whitehead turned the knob, the door exploded, and Whitehead hurtled back into Benson, who staggered backward, off-balance, and then McCall was there in the doorway, Cohn behind him, a gun in his hand.

McCall looked with surprise at Benson and opened his mouth to say something but Benson, landing on his butt, while Whitehead bounced away, fired a single shot with his pistol, which hit McCall in the stomach. McCall staggered and shot Benson in the chest, in the vest, and Benson fired again, this time hitting McCall in the spine, and McCall dropped as though somebody had cut his puppet strings.

Cohn, still to the left of McCall, stepped farther to his left, the gun already up, and shot Benson in the face. Benson went down, dead, though Cohn didn't know it, and Cohn shot him again, in the head, and then stepped over McCall's body to Whitehead, who was crawling between the two beds, and shot her twice through the heart from the back.

McCall was on the floor, eyes wide, his mouth working, and Cohn, his hands covered with gloves as they had been in all the holdups, shot McCall in the forehead. Nothing more he could do.

Elapsed time, ten seconds? Cohn turned and ran down the hall.

OUTSIDE, HE SLOWED, made sure he was out of camera range, peeled off the mask and jacket and gloves and wadded them up into a small ball, which he carried under his arm, and walked a hundred feet to the street and saw Cruz coming in the Toyota, and flagged her and when she stopped, yanked open the door and climbed in.

"What happened?"

"Blew up. Fuckin' blew up." Cohn's voice was cold, uninflected, the way it got when there was trouble. "Tate's dead, woman's dead, cop in the room with her, he's dead, they're all fuckin' dead." He said it quietly enough, but she could tell that he was beaten up.

"Tate's dead? You're sure he's dead?" she asked.

"Yeah, he's dead, his brains are all over the hotel room, for Christ's sakes . . . Ah, Jesus, Tate, he walked right into the cop's gun. He kicked the door and the cop was right there and, boom, and he goes down, ah, McCall . . ."

"So now we're done," Cruz said bitterly. She was watching the speedometer. There was a tendency to drive fast after a hit, and she didn't want to do that. "Now we're done. Jesse's gonna be really screwed up about this, Tate was a good friend."

"Tate was a good friend of all of us," Cohn said.

"You're sure he's dead?"

"Yeah, I'm sure."

"If he's not dead, then the cops are going . . ."

"He's *dead*," Cohn said. "Ah, Christ . . ."

Cruz shut up and they drove along and Cohn thought, *Maybe I could have saved him.*

But he didn't really think so. McCall had been hit hard, right through the center of his body, he was dying on the floor, and Cohn didn't have time to wait for him to die, and no way to get him out of the hotel in a hurry. If Cohn abandoned him, and McCall *did* somehow survive, well, McCall might have been a little pissed.

Nobody was immune to extortion by the legal system. They would have given McCall a chance to get out, in fifteen, maybe, if he talked about Cohn and the other gang members. He'd done the right thing, but goddamn: it was *Tate*.

LUCAS HEARD ABOUT it from the duty officer at the BCA who called and shouted, "Benson's down. Benson got shot, Benson's dead, he's shot . . ."

Lucas ran out of the hotel room with Snider and Craig calling after him, "What? What?" and he shouted back, "Keep the door locked," and he ran down the stairs because the elevators were too slow, piled into the car and screamed across town and dumped the Porsche in a cluster of cop cars and a cop flagged him and he held up his ID and shouted back and then he plowed through a flower bed, through the lobby and into an elevator with another cop, a St. Paul uniform he didn't recognize, and he asked, "Is my guy dead?" and the cop nodded and said, "Yeah, fuckin' awful."

Lucas pounded the elevator doors, once, twice, with the heel of his hand, and then they came on out on twelve and two St. Paul detectives were standing in the hall outside an open door. Lucas headed for the door and one of the detectives, whose name was John Elleson, caught him around the waist and said, "Whoa, whoa, Lucas, slow down, slow down."

Lucas tried to push past him, but Elleson held on, jammed him into a wall. Elleson was a small guy, but strong. "I wanna . . ."

"We think that the shooter's on the loose, one of them,

anyway," Elleson said. "You can go in, but stay on the edges. We need to take everything we can get out of there."

Lucas nodded, took a breath, relaxed, and when Elleson let him go, went in past the busted door: Benson was there, with two other bodies. Benson was on his back, his head cranked backward, his forehead shattered, his bulletproof vest skewed around to his left, a pistol near his hand, a shotgun under his legs. A black man lay on the floor at Benson's feet, and a woman lay beside a bed, shot in the back.

Elleson said, "There's a couple in the room next door. They were in bed, heard the shots, the guy says he heard somebody running, so he thought it would be okay to look. They had to turn on the lights and he went to the door and looked, and the hallway was already clear. The shooter knew where he was going. There's no blood in the hallway or on the stairs, so if he was hit, he wasn't bleeding too bad."

"Benson shot the black guy?" Lucas asked.

"We don't know, but I think he probably did. We're gonna have to wait and look at the slugs, to see who shot who—it's too complicated."

"Ah, man . . ." Lucas put his hands to his temples, backed into the hallway.

"You okay?" Elleson asked.

"Fuck no." He wasn't; he was nauseous.

"We're gonna need a statement from everybody involved. We understand Benson was working as sort of a bodyguard."

"These are the same guys who did the robbery down behind St. John's last night," Lucas said. "The same guys who killed the Hudson cop. They're a murder gang hitting political money guys. I'll get you everything we know—we've got the main guy's picture out there . . ."

He gave Elleson a summary of what they knew, then said, "We think they've got a hideout somewhere around here—they either rented a house or a condo or something.

We've papered all the hotels and motels, and nobody's seen them."

"They got some balls," Elleson said. "There were two hundred cops within three blocks of here. They had to drive right through them to get in and out."

"Did we get them on video? Any chance?" Lucas asked. The feds had come up with a grant for surveillance cameras, and they were all over the streets.

"Depends on which street they were on," Elleson said. "We've got video on the front and the side, but not along the back."

"Got to look at it, man: if we could spot the car, that'd give us a big leg up. Can't hide the car."

"I'll get that going," Elleson said. "What's Benson's family situation?"

"He's single, divorced four or five years ago. No kids. Parents live up in St. Cloud, I think. I'll have our duty guy pull the file . . . We gotta look at the tapes."

"I'm sorry about this, man," Elleson said.

The elevator dinged and Del stepped out, looked both ways, spotted Lucas, and came on down the hall. "Is it true?" Looked at Lucas's face, and said, "It's true."

THE CONDO WAS only six blocks from the hotel, and after parking the car, Cohn and Cruz took the back stairs up. Cruz took a peek at the lobby before they walked into it, and then they were inside. Lindy was sitting on the couch reading a copy of *Women's Health* magazine, and Lane came out of the back room, a smile on his face, and he asked, "How'd it go?" And then, the smile slipping away, "Where's Tate?"

Cohn told him: "They ambushed us."

"Oh, no." Lindy, pale-faced, hand to her mouth.

"It's my fault," Cruz said. "I should have known. We couldn't do this many . . ."

"I thought they couldn't tell the cops," Lane said to her.

"That must have gone out the window when the cop was killed in Hudson," Cruz said.

Cohn said, "I'm so sick I can't even spit." He looked at Cruz. "It's not your fault, Rosie. I pushed for it, but there's a smart guy on the other side, and he punked us." He gave them a blow-by-blow account of the entry and the shooting, lied about McCall getting shot, said the cop shot him twice. "Never had a chance. Tate kicked the door and boom-boom, he goes down and I see the cop and I hit him, then I hit him again, and then this woman's on the floor and I hit her, and then I'm out of there. I got out clean, but . . ."

"I'm heading home," Lane said. He looked around the condo. "Clean this place up . . . get out of here."

"I'm with you," Cruz said. She looked at Brute. "You and Lindy ought to get out of here. You'd be safer as a couple. You can use your Visa card and driver's license for about two weeks yet, rent a car, head south. You've got enough money to last a long time in Belize or Costa Rica."

Lane said to him, "That's what you gotta do, man. You can have Tate's cut—they're not looking for me or Cruz, but you've got to get out of here, you need the money. With Tate's cut, you got almost a million and a half."

"Not enough," Cohn said. He ran his hands through his hair and said, "Fuck it, I'm gonna go get a drink."

Cruz said, "Brute, don't do it. The cops . . ."

Cohn said, "Fuck 'em."

"There are a million cops out there. If they spot you . . ."

"Fuck 'em," he said again. "I don't look anything like those pictures. Especially if I'm sitting down. I'm gonna get a drink." To Lindy: "You coming?"

"Brute, bad idea, I'm really scared." She looked scared.

"I'm going," he said. "That fuckin' McCall, man," and tears ran down his face and he went out the door.

The door opened behind him and Cruz came out with her purse and said, "If you're going, I'll go with you."

SHE'D SCOUTED THE town thoroughly, and steered him through the nearly empty skyways, for the best part of a half mile, then outside and across a street and into an outdoor mall, with bars and outdoor seating, to a place called Juicy's. They got a table in a corner back against a building where Cohn couldn't be seen head-on, and he ordered a cheeseburger and a double martini with four olives, and she got fries and a Diet Pepsi. He sat looking at the tabletop for five minutes, drinking the martini, then said, hollow-eyed, "What do I do, Rosie?"

"Can't do the hotel anymore," she said. "We really needed four people. Three was marginal. Now we've only got two, even if Jesse was willing. That won't work; too many people to control. So, we do what we did when there was trouble in the past—we get out. Jesse and I both have cars at the airport. We take the rentals back right now, clean out the apartment, get out of here late tonight, in my car. You and me and Lindy, maybe to Des Moines. Go out to the airport, you rent a car there, take it to Vegas, give the cash to Harry and move it to your investment account. What do you have left in there?"

"Maybe a quarter."

"So you'll have almost two. That'll kick off eighty thousand a year until you die. There are lots of nice places where you can live pretty well on eighty thousand."

"Pretty well—if you want to live like a retiree. You know, watching your dollars. Watching your budget," Cohn said. "Won't be any Social Security or Medicare or any of that . . . Goddamnit, I need at least four. Five would be better. On two hundred thousand a year, you know, I could live okay."

"Brute, you've got to deal with reality," Cruz said. "You get someplace safe, cool off, maybe I can put together one more big one. A good safe armored car, a credit union."

"Credit union won't do it. Most we ever took out of a credit union was a half," Cohn said.

"With no work and no risk," she said.

"So I need three more million, and my cut on a big credit union is maybe two hundred, so you're saying we ought to do fifteen credit unions?"

She leaned forward: "What I'm saying is, we need to get the hell out of St. Paul. We can worry about money some other time. There are more important things: like staying alive."

"But this hotel . . ."

"We don't have the personnel . . ."

They were talking about it, working through the original plan with Cohn on his second double martini, when a crippled man in a wheelchair, a dusty head-bent street kid, and an overweight woman took a table fifteen feet away. The cripple looked at Cohn without recognition, sneered and turned away and waved at a waitress and shouted, "Hey! Hey! Am I invisible or some fuckin' thing?"

Cohn leaned close to Cruz and said, "It's yon bugger—the one who ran over my feet at the airport." The *yon bugger* came off as an Alabama drawl—the British accent had vanished with four days in St. Paul.

"Ignore him," Cruz said.

"Right." Cohn gulped the last of the second martini and waved at the waitress.

Cruz said, "Better slow down on the martinis, you're gonna be on your ass."

"Ah . . ." He ordered the third one and said, "When I was living in York, I'd get up every morning and read the *Times*, the *Independent*, the *Guardian*, and the *Financial Times*. I'd have four cups of coffee, and by the time I was finished with all that, it'd be noon, and a friend would come around, and we'd have a lunchtime martini or two or three. The Brits drink like fish. So I'm in training."

"WAS THIS FRIEND male or female?" Cruz asked. Cohn cocked an eyebrow at her and grinned, and Cruz said,

"I hope Lindy doesn't find out. All we need is her throwing a fit."

"I ain't gonna tell her, but I don't think she'd be too upset. Probably guessed," Cohn said. The third martini arrived, and he took a sip. "My woman there . . . nice lady. Wish I could've said good-bye. Told her I'd be gone for three weeks and would see her then."

"That's life," Cruz said. She deeply didn't care.

"I'd read the *Financial Times* every morning," Cohn said. He was now drunk, Cruz realized. "You know what? All this stock market shit that's going on, they're all to blame for it . . ." He gestured around the patio. "The fuckin' politicians. People say I'm a criminal, look at these bastards. Fuck over ordinary folks, they're sitting here laughing and singing, suckin' up the money and power."

Cruz covered his free hand with hers and said, smiling, "You're not exactly ordinary folks, Brute. You're more like Jesse James."

"No, but my brothers and sisters are," he said. "Ordinary people."

"You don't like your brothers and sisters," she said. "And they don't like you."

"That's not the point . . ." He gulped down the last of the third drink, and fished out the last olive. "You know what I need . . ." He interrupted himself: "Look at this."

The cripple had the overweight woman by the neckline of her dress and was snarling something at her. Other patrons were looking away; nobody wanted to get involved in a fight between a woman and a cripple. A waitress eased away, looking for help.

WHITCOMB HAD BRIAR by the neckline of her dress and snarled, "Fuckin' bitch, you'll do what I tell you or I'll drag your fuckin' ass back . . ."

COHN, DRUNK AND angry at life, hissed at Cruz, "The bugger's a *pimp*. See that? That's one of his girls. Fuckin' nasty little pimp . . ."

WHITCOMB HEARD THE word, or enough of it, and turned and saw the tall dark-haired man staring at him from the corner table, and pushed Briar back and said, loudly, "You got a problem, fuckwad?"

The woman with the dark-haired man said something, an urgent twist to her face, and he said something back, and then the woman got up and walked rapidly toward the exit gate.

The dark-haired man threw money at the table, then stepped over to Whitcomb and said quietly, "If you don't take your hands off this young woman, you little fuckin' greasy pimp, or if you use that language on me again, I'm going to throw you in front of a fuckin' car."

The guy was drunk, Whitcomb realized. He realized it in a stupid, distant way, and the one thing he'd learned for sure as a cripple was that nobody fucked with cripples. Not deliberately. He flicked away Briar's neckline, and she rocked back and said, "Randy, maybe . . ."

Whitcomb snapped, "Shut the fuck up," and said to Cohn, "Listen, you fuckin' twat . . ."

Cohn yanked him out of the wheelchair so quickly that he might have been levitated by God.

COHN KNEW HE was drunk, knew this could be the end, but *McCall was dead,* and this *fuckin' cripple* . . . this *pimp* . . .

He snatched Whitcomb out of the chair with one powerful hand on Whitcomb's neck, and the other, as the cripple came up, on his belt. Two women screamed and he knocked a chair over with his leg and a table scraped across the brick patio with a metallic scream, and Cohn was blind now to everything but a hole in the air in front of him, leading out to the street.

He took six long strides to the fence that separated the bar patio from the sidewalk, yanking Whitcomb along, Whitcomb windmilling, another two steps through the patio gate and across the sidewalk to the curb, and then he heaved Whitcomb at the windshield of an oncoming minivan.

Whitcomb was unnaturally light, because of his withered legs, and he hit the hood of the car, flattened over the windshield, screaming, windmilling with his arms, then skidded off the far side and was hit by another car.

Cohn didn't slow down to watch, though he heard the satisfying *thump* of the second car. He turned back through the patio, walked into the bar, a woman's white face following him. Out of sight of the witnesses, he stripped off his black sport coat to show his white short-sleeved shirt, and quickly swerved out the side exit and down the street.

He could hear people shouting from the patio, but there was no pursuit as he turned the corner. He walked down the block and around, across the street, past a cluster of cops who were looking down at the screaming, talking on shoulder radios. Another half block, and he turned back into the same skyway they'd taken out of the condo.

Didn't feel good: there was still McCall back there, dead.

But he didn't feel as bad as he had, either.

LUCAS AND DEL sat on a bench in the hotel's lobby while the St. Paul cops worked the crime scene. Del said, "I got the notification going. He's got parents and a couple of sisters."

"Okay."

Neither one of them spoke for a minute, then Del said, "I feel kinda bad that I don't feel worse. I didn't much like the guy. He was a stiff."

"Still one of us," Lucas said.

"You know what I mean," Del said.

"Yeah. Freaks me out, though. Three cops killed, this year, and we were involved in all three of them. That Indian dude up north, on Virgil's case, the guy in Hudson, now Benson."

"Yeah. What can you say?"

"Lot of guys gone down over the years," Lucas said.

"Yeah."

Another minute, then Lucas looked at his watch.

"What're you going to do?" Del asked.

"First thing, right at the crack of dawn tomorrow, soon as the TV people wake up, I'm gonna have a big-mother press conference," Lucas said. "I'm gonna paper the country with pictures of Cohn and this chick. Then, we're gonna find them and kill them."

"Sounds like a plan," Del said.

14

LUCAS WOKE AT 5 A.M. after three hours of sleep. He came up feeling depressed, a mental cloud hanging overhead; a darkness. He shaved carefully, let a hot shower beat on his shoulders and back, getting in the mood to talk to the press. Thinking it over. And Benson . . . gone. If he'd been in the room, would he have done any better? Why had they opened the door? Benson hadn't been ready, his vest undone, the shotgun dropped . . .

Weather, who would have been up in a half hour anyway, had rolled out and was brushing her teeth when he got out of the shower. He toweled off and then wrapped his arms around her and squeezed and said, halfheartedly, "Naked man attacks helpless housewife."

She gave him an elbow and grumped, "Back off," and, "You better get going," and a moment later, "I still can't believe it." She'd known Benson, from another case.

"I . . . ah, never mind," Lucas said, and he went and got dressed, a somber suit for a somber day.

THE PRESS CONFERENCE was set for six, to catch the earliest news programs, especially locally and on the West Coast, where the unknown woman might have come from. That gave him time to eat breakfast before he headed out, time to again work through what he was going to say. Del and Shrake and Jenkins and Neil Mitford, the political operator, and Rose Marie Roux, the state public safety commissioner, would all be there, Rose Marie speaking for the governor, and both Mitford and Roux working the reporters off-camera.

Lucas ate Egg Beaters and bacon, with coffee, heard the paper hit the front porch and went and got it, glanced at the headlines. The killings had been too late to catch the paper, although they'd be all over the television broadcasts—one cop, one innocent woman, and one masked intruder, all dead in one of the most expensive hotels in the Cities, right in the middle of the convention.

The press conference, Lucas thought, on the way in, might not be entirely friendly. He took his truck instead of the Porsche, for the reduced flash, and wondered whether he'd screwed up. If they really believed that a murder gang was operating in town, maybe there *should* have been two cops in each room? And fewer rooms, if necessary? They simply hadn't had the manpower, with the convention in town—and maybe they hadn't had the faith that anything would really happen. Maybe he'd been a bit perfunctory in his briefing of Benson and the other guys.

But they were supposed to be pros—they were supposed to know how to handle a deal like this. They all knew that a cop had been killed in Hudson. Why had Benson unlocked the door? The killers had been able to kick the safety bolt, but wouldn't have been able to kick the cross lock, if the door hadn't been opened . . .

No answers yet: maybe he'd get some from the crime-scene people.

ROSE MARIE ROUX, his boss, was getting out of her Buick when he pulled into the BCA parking lot. She waited for him, squinting against the early morning sun, and when he caught up with her, said, "The governor's going to call Benson's folks this morning."

"All right."

"You good?" she asked.

"Aw . . . you know."

She nodded. She'd been a cop before she was a lawyer, and a politician. "Let a little of it out, when you're talking to the cameras. Get angry. Makes better tape—you'll get better distribution on the pictures."

He half-laughed—snorted—and said, "Pretty fucking pathetic when you have to pull that bullshit."

"Modern times," she said.

NELLY CASSESFORD FROM Channel Three was walking up the sidewalk from the Channel Three van, carrying a cable of some sort. She saw Lucas and Rose Marie and slowed down to wait for them.

"We need to get started right on time, because we're up to our necks in convention stuff," she said. She was a slight, dark-haired woman with warm brown eyes. "Lots of trouble last night, lots of tape."

"We're good," Lucas said. "Did you talk to your guys about getting this out to L.A.?"

"Yup. Larry Johnston called them last night. They like that L.A. connection with the woman, don't care so much about the convention, so you'll get some time. Did you talk to everybody?"

Lucas nodded. "Yeah. I just hope they don't kiss us off."

"They won't. This is great stuff—manhunt. Woman-hunt. Unknown killers. Good-looking femme fatale. Appeal to the public for help." She didn't say, "Dead cops," which was good.

THERE WERE FOUR cameras and a cooperative light setup in the BCA conference room. Del, Jenkins, and Shrake, all looking tired and ruffled, were clustered in the back of the room, and Mitford was talking to a St. Paul political reporter. He spotted Lucas and Lucas went that way, and Mitford asked, "You all set?"

"Yeah. You gonna say anything for the governor?"

"No. I'll leave it to you," Mitford said. "You know he'll be calling Benson's folks . . ."

"Rose Marie told me," Lucas said. He glanced at his watch. Three minutes to six. Time to do it.

ROSE MARIE WENT first, the usual political platitudes about tragedy and a life dedicated to government service. Then Lucas went on, and he did let it out, as Rose Marie had suggested, and though it felt a little calculated, he found it pretty easy to do.

"A murder gang is operating in the Twin Cities and they've killed two police officers and an innocent woman, and we need to take these people off the street *right now*," he said through his teeth. "We're distributing photos of two of the people involved. We don't know who the woman is, but we believe that she's in St. Paul and that she may have come from the Los Angeles area. If you see her, or if you know where or who she is, we need to find her. She may have been involved in the death of a young and innocent Spanish man whom she seduced and then possibly murdered in Washington, D.C. . . ."

Let it out. From the intent expressions of the reporters, he figured it was working; gonna be good tape.

When he was done, he bounced a few questions, and then said, "We'll keep you up on this. I understand that the governor will have a comment later. He personally knew and valued Agent Benson, and he'll be talking to Benson's folks this morning."

He saw Rose Marie nod and he was done.

WHEN THE REPORTERS were heading out, Del asked, "What next?"

Lucas said, "We've got about a million cops out there. Let's get some guys, and get these pictures to every one of the cops. Tell them, you know, if they're standing around, to talk to people—shop owners, bank tellers, whatever, ask if they've seen these guys. Maybe something will pop up. Maybe we'll get lucky."

"I hate it when we have to get lucky."

COHN AND THE other three had done some drinking over the night, a couple of bottles of blended whiskey, ginger ale, and ice cubes, an old-fashioned way to get hammered, and also to overfill the tank. Lane woke at seven o'clock, hungover, and had to pee so bad he was almost afraid to move. He first thought about McCall, and the dread of a close-by death hung on him. He coughed and stirred and pushed himself up and staggered off to the bathroom in his underwear.

The apartment had two bedrooms, with Cruz in one, and Cohn and Lindy in the other, with Lane bagged out on the floor of the living room. Now he hung over the toilet, letting it all run out, coughing, finally dried up, pulled up his underpants, and went back to the living room.

Needed a cigarette, but he'd quit smoking three years earlier. Still needed one, but he was used to the random flashes. He'd wait it out: turned on the TV and hit the mute, went in search of the local weather station.

Saw Cohn's face, and then, in a blink, Cruz's. "Holy shit."

He yelled, "Rosie. Rosie, get in here. Rosie . . ." He was

fumbling with the remote, finally brought up the sound, but Cruz's face was gone and he shouted, "Rosie," and caught, on the TV, the last part of a pitch for help: ". . . see her or Brutus Cohn, do not attempt to apprehend them, but call nine-one-one immediately. They are heavily armed and considered extremely dangerous."

The woman turned to another camera and said, "St. Paul police are braced for another day of trouble . . ."

Cruz stumbled into the living room, dressed in a cotton nightgown, took in Lane, looked at the TV, said, "What?" and then Cohn stuck his head out, and Lane said to Cruz, "They just had your picture on TV along with Brute's. They got a picture of you."

"Oh, shit . . ." She looked unbelieving, shaking her head, asked, "Are you sure?"

"Sure I'm sure," Lane said. He picked up the remote and started clicking through the channels. The apartment was a model, so they had only basic cable service, and after he'd run up to CNN, he ran back down, and at the bottom, on Channel Three, caught another shot of Cruz, a poor shot but identifiable enough, with the anchor in the background: ". . . Davenport said that the woman may come from the Los Angeles area, because the phone used to take the photo listed a large number of calls to a phone from the three-two-three area code in Los Angeles; that phone has not been found . . ."

"He took my picture with a cell phone," Cruz said, unbelieving. "He took my picture."

"Who?" Cohn asked.

Cruz ran into the bedroom and came back a moment later with another phone, flipped it open and pushed a speed dial, let it ring, hung up, pushed the speed dial again, and then, a third time, said, "It's only five o'clock out there . . ." and then somebody answered.

She said, "We're busted. Get out of there. Get the files and anything else you need, take them out to your car, move my car, and burn it. Burn it . . . I know, but they've busted us, and it's bad. Get out. They could be there anytime. We're seeing it now, on TV here, so you might have a couple hours. Get over to Ellen's . . . just don't let her see it. Don't let her see it and when everything slows down, get down south. I'll meet you at the beach. Yes. Yes. Maybe an hour. Don't push it any further than that . . . Go. Go."

She hung up and Lane said, "I was right—about where you were from."

She looked at him and shook her head, then said, "The fucker took my picture with a cell phone. I never saw it. He tried to take one once, and I told him I hated that, I made him stop before he took it. He took one anyway."

"Who?"

"The guy who gave me the names of the moneymen," she said.

"This changes everything," Cohn said. "Now we need to do the big one."

Cruz shook her head: "Are you nuts? We needed four guys with me outside, and then Spitzer went, and then McCall . . . we've got two guys and . . ." She flipped a hand at Lindy. "You."

"Fuck you, Rosie," Lindy said.

"Everything's changed," Cohn insisted. Lane was flipping through the channels. "I need to bury myself deep and I need more money to do that. And now, so do you, Rosie. They've got your picture. There are four cops dead, counting the ones in New York. They'll never give up. You need to go to Argentina or . . . India . . . or something. You can't stay here, babe."

Lane was looking at her, and he bobbed his head. "I don't know how much money you got, but . . ."

Cruz spoke slowly, as though they were stupid: "We—don't—have—enough—people. We don't have enough! Is that hard to understand?"

Cohn said, "We don't have enough if we have a mob scene."

She stared at him for a minute, then said, "What's the option?"

"We have to get on top of them. We kill one: we never give them a chance to resist. We pop one the minute we've got them, let them look at the body and think about being dead. I can hold them myself, that way. Even if we get twenty or thirty people. Jesse does the boxes, Lindy is the desk clerk, you're on the radios."

Cruz said, "No," and Lindy said, "I can't do that," but Cohn, ignoring Lindy, said, "Rosie, just think about it."

CRUZ WENT BACK to her bedroom, which had a tiny bathroom with a tight shower, and got cleaned up and let the water run over her head, and shampooed and conditioned and didn't think about it, until she was toweling off.

She'd killed three people in her life, after some long consideration, and with great care. Before this benighted trip to the Twin Cities, five others had been killed in the series of robberies she'd done with Cohn and his gang. None of the killings had been cold. All had been necessary, and in some way, self-defense, with the exception of the two cops killed in New York. Spitzer had simply gotten nervous and pulled his trigger, and Spitzer had paid.

Now the body count was out of control. Four dead in the Twin Cities, counting McCall. Another in the hotel would be five.

But the cops had her photo.

Laura was out of the Venice place, she thought, and the fire should already be cleaning up after them. She could change her face a bit, go blond . . . but she had to be *far* gone. Someplace like New Zealand, she thought. Some careful money, checks coming in from Ireland, a full-time straight job for a while . . .

Laura was still clean.

Five dead, best case. Hard to think about.

But Cohn had put his finger squarely on one critical fact: if they went in shooting, they could do it with three.

A COLD FRONT was headed down from Canada, and this might be the last day of summer: but it was another good one, a good day for shorts. Don Johnson, the perverted mailman, wearing shorts and a wrinkled blue shirt, climbed out of his truck with a bag on his shoulder and started up the suburban driveway, his second block of the morning.

Letty and Carey were in a Channel Three van driven by a tough nut named Andy Cramer, who Letty had thought was an Australian but turned out to be a South African. Cramer wedged the van into the curb in front of the postal truck and hopped out, slid back the side door and picked up his camera, and Carey took the microphone and they walked up the driveway behind Johnson, who looked back at them, and then at the house, wondering what was going on. Letty sat in the open door of the van and watched: Carey had said she wouldn't do it if Letty got involved.

"Mr. Johnson," Carey called. "Mr. Johnson."

Johnson was befuddled. "Me?"

Cramer said, for Johnson's benefit, "We're running," and Carey shoved the microphone at Johnson's face. "Mr. Johnson, we've been told by a sixteen-year-old girl that you have repeatedly forced yourself on her sexually."

"What-what-what?" Johnson held a handful of mail between his face and the camera lens. He was horrified and, Carey was pleased to see, frightened. Guilty-guilty-guilty.

Carey: "She tells us that she can identify your intimate areas by a variety of birthmarks and also by a bite mark she left on your hip, which left a scar, when you were forcing her to perform oral sex on you."

"Get away, get away . . ." Johnson tried to run around them and Cramer tracked him with the camera, stayed with him.

"Do you deny this, Mr. Johnson? Are you willing to speak to the police about these charges?"

"Get away, get away," Johnson shouted. "This is the mail, I'm delivering the U.S. mail here . . ." A few letters slipped out of his hand and he slapped at them, trying to catch them.

Carey bored in: "Did you force this girl to perform oral sex?"

"I did no such thing . . ."

"Did you force the bathroom door, naked, while she was in the shower and press your body against hers?"

"No-no-no . . ."

"Get into her bed naked after forcing the bedroom door?"

"No-no . . ." Johnson was trying to get back to his truck, but Cramer blocked him and growled, "Don't touch the camera, mate."

Carey put the knife in: "Are you going back to her house, Mr. Johnson? Are you going to continue seeing this girl's mother?"

"No-no-no . . ."

Carey turned to Cramer and said, "Turn off the camera."

He dropped the lens toward the ground and Carey put her face close to Johnson's, and he flinched away, a line of sweat on his upper lip, and she said, "We're friends of Juliet. And we're really from Channel Three. If you go back to see Juliet's mother, if you ever talk to Juliet again, we'll put this tape on the evening news, I swear to God."

Cramer said, in a working-class British accent, "You heard the phrase, tossing the salad?"

Johnson drew back from Carey. "Maybe."

"You're gonna be the designated salad-tosser at Stillwater state correctional institution if you go back on Juliet," Cramer said. "When you get out, *if* you get out, you're gonna have to walk up and down every neighborhood you'll ever live in, and knock on the doors and tell the people you're a registered pervert. Keep that in mind." He reached out with his free hand and pinched one of Johnson's nipples, hard.

Johnson squealed, "Ah," and jerked back.

"And I'll pinch your other nipple," Cramer said. "If you get out."

They retreated to the van. Cramer put the camera inside and they slid the doors shut, and left Johnson standing in the driveway, in a puddle of dropped political advertisements.

Letty said, "Harsh." But she was smiling.

"If the station ever finds out what we did, we might get fired," Carey said.

"You forgot to mention that," Cramer said, but he didn't seem worried.

"You would have come anyway," Carey said. To Letty: "So Juliet's good—she's got a place to stay."

Letty asked Cramer, "What was that thing about a salad?"

BUT WHEN LETTY called Briar, the other girl began sobbing. "I'm at the hospital. I've been at the hospital all night. Randy got hurt."

"How?"

"Some asshole threw him in front of a car," Briar said. "He got run over."

The image in Letty's mind almost made her laugh, but she pushed the impulse away and asked, "How bad? Are you okay?"

"I'm okay . . ." and Briar unraveled the whole story, starting with their failure to track down a methamphetamine salesman, on to the purchase of a pint of rum, Randy and Ranch getting loaded, the decision to stop at the café in St. Paul, still hoping to find George, the crank salesman, the argument, and the fight.

"So . . . this guy was sort of protecting you, right?" Letty asked. "Randy was threatening to beat you up, and this guy threw Randy in front of a car?"

"Well, I didn't need that, I didn't ask him for that, Randy

wasn't . . . Randy's really hurt, Letty. He's all bruised, you should see it, and his foot's broken. I can't go home now. Who'd take care of him? He can't even cook."

"Juliet—I've got to talk to you," Letty said. "Is there someplace to eat there, at the hospital?"

"The cafeteria . . ."

"Which hospital?"

"Regions. I can see the Capitol out the window."

"We're going to come there. I'll meet you in the cafeteria in a half hour," Letty said.

LETTY PERSUADED CAREY to drop her at the hospital; she'd catch the bus home. "She wants to talk to me alone. I'll tell her about Don."

Carey was skeptical: "This whole other thing that you were planning—that won't work if she just goes home."

"I've got another plan," Letty said. "Once she's home, and she's safe, and Don's not there, I'll get her to talk to the police about Randy," Letty said. "I asked Lorenzo at the station, he said that if she told the police about Randy, they wouldn't even have to have a trial. He's on parole, and they'd put him back inside, for drug use and prostitution and maybe assault. They might have a trial on some of those, but they'd put him away first."

Lorenzo the Lawyer covered legal affairs for the news department.

"That's enough for you?" Carey asked. "That he goes back to jail?"

"If that's what I can get, that's what I can get," Letty said. "It'll take care of the problem for a couple more years."

"I'll drop you," Carey said. "Don't forget to tell her about Don."

"I'll tell her," Letty said.

"Letty?"

"I'll tell her."

LETTY TOLD HER, but Briar, scared and sad and also, Letty thought, somewhat interested in Whitcomb's new disability, said she couldn't go home right away.

"I mean, I love it about that fucker Don," Briar said. "But Randy does love me somehow . . . I know, I know what you're going to say, but I can feel it . . ."

"He treats you like a goddamn dog," Letty shrilled.

"Not anymore; he *really* needs me now."

"What if he starts in again?" Letty asked. "What if he gets his stick out?"

"He won't. *He won't.*"

"Ah, God. Juliet, he'll put you out there again," Letty said. "You'll be trolling for old fat guys again."

"You just don't believe," Briar said, and then, "I gotta get back. He's really hurt."

WHEN BRIAR GOT back to Whitcomb's room, she found him scratching on a piece of printer paper with a ballpoint. "Where the hell you been?"

"I got your ice cream," she said, and passed the carton to him, with a plastic spoon. He took it, and she asked, looking at the paper, "What are you doing, honey?"

"Making a plan. I been fuckin' off, no help from you and Ranch, but we're going after that Davenport bitch when I get out of here. No more fuckin' off."

Briar looked at the plan: a list of words in handwriting so cramped, with letters so tiny, that they were illegible.

"You don't have to read. It's *my* plan. You do what you're told."

LUCAS JAMMED THE Porsche in a slot in the short-term parking lot, ran into the underground ramp, carrying his overnight bag, flashed his ID across the counter at the

Northwest Airlines ticket agent, said, "Plane leaves in twenty minutes, I gotta be on it . . ."

With his ticket in his pocket, he jumped the security line, and one of the TSA security guys got him a ride on a handicapped transporter, and the driver ran him out to the gate.

The gate attendant was standing at the door, the plane already loaded. She smiled at him as he hustled down the ramp and on board, and a flight attendant said, "Cut it close," and she smiled and shook her head, and he was in his seat.

Breathing hard.

He'd gotten the call no more than forty-five minutes earlier, that the Los Angeles cops thought they had a positive ID on the woman. Her name apparently was Elena Diaz, and she had an address in Venice, which the cop said was on the West Side, whatever that meant. More details coming; a couple of intelligence guys were going over to take a look, and a request for a search warrant was being considered.

"Have I got time to come out?"

"Nothing's going to happen for at least a couple of hours, maybe longer," the L.A. cop said. "Got to get our shit together, figure out what we're doing."

Lucas made a call, found out about the flight, called his housekeeper, got her to pack for him, and dashed across town and out to the airport.

Not until the plane turned down the runway did he remember how badly they frightened him, and here he was, strapped to a rocket, and then the plane blasted off and he was in the air, no books, no magazines, no pills.

Three and a half hours to LAX.

When he crawled off the plane at the other end, he turned on his cell phone and it lit up. He first returned the calls to Los Angeles, to the cop's cell phone. The cop answered, and Lucas identified himself, and the cop said, "There's been a fire . . ."

"Ah, shit."

15

THE LOS ANGELES cop said, "Get outside Northwest, over where the Hertz vans stop. I'm in a black-and-white Toyota FJ."

Lucas went outside, spotted the FJ and walked over. The cop, whose name was Lance Barr, and who looked like the third banana in a so-so cop film, poked the door open for him; they shook hands and Barr said, "Nice threads for a Minnesota cop."

Barr looked pretty good himself, in a tan suit and white shirt, with an ice-blue tie and high-shine brown oxfords. He was wearing skinny sunglasses under his gelled black hair. Lucas said, "We have a special suit for a guy traveling to the Coast. Gives us a chance to get out of the Pendletons."

"I suspected that—but I'm a detective," Barr said, and he pulled out and they headed east into a lot of blacktop.

"What about the fire?" Lucas asked.

"Well, sometime early this morning, about, mmm, six o'clock or so, this chick's house goes up in smoke. The bottom floor, anyway, and most of the top floor. That's before we were even looking at her. Her next-door neighbor was up and *heard* the place go—said it sounded like a gas explosion—and the silly asshole ran in there with a fire extinguisher and put some of it out. He said he was afraid the girls were in there."

Two women lived in the house, Barr said, but one was traveling, the neighbors said.

"Anyway, this guy slowed the fire down, and the fire guys got there and put the rest of it out. The Shell Avenue station is only a half mile away, right down Venice Boulevard, so they were there in three minutes . . . Somebody poured gasoline and touched it off. It's totally fucked, of course, but there are still some unburned pieces. One of the guys called and said they looked at a computer, but it had been cracked open and the hard drive was missing, so . . ."

"Probably cleaned the place out," Lucas said. "Anybody got any photos?"

"Not that we've found. Still looking."

"Got tags on their cars?" Lucas asked.

"No. Their names aren't in the database," Barr said. "I mean, their names are, but there are a number of people named Elena Diaz and Martha Knofler, and none of them live in Venice."

"Knofler. She's the roommate?"

"Yup. Rug-munchers. That's what their neighbors say. Long-term commitment," Barr said. "One of the neighbors, though, thought, for some reason, that Martha's name is Laura, or Lauren, and she's pretty sure about it, but she doesn't know why, since she only knew them to nod to at Whole Foods."

"So their names are probably phony, and they cleaned the place out and then burned it," Lucas said.

"Cleaned it out, but they didn't clean out the shower drain, so we got some hair. If you get some hair in Minnesota, then we can put our girl on your crime scene . . ."

"Don't have any hair yet," Lucas said. "And they don't have any in Washington. You gotta start processing it, because we *might* need it . . . but what we really need to do is chase down this Knofler, and break her ass."

"We're working on that," Barr said. "We're looking in garbage cans for hard drives, though they're probably in a canal or out in the ocean . . . or maybe she still has them, and when we catch her, we'll get them back."

"If the place burned at six, that'd be eight back home," Lucas said. "So Diaz, or whatever her name is, probably saw the TV broadcast at seven o'clock or so, and called out here. That'd be five o'clock . . . That'd give Knofler an hour to get out."

"Must have rehearsed it, though," Barr said. "She wouldn't have had much time. They maybe already had the gas in the garage. And, they leased the place, so they didn't lose anything but some furniture and their security deposit."

"These guys are no dummies," Lucas said. They were passing a cluster of small, hot-looking apartments off Lincoln Boulevard, and a woman with a dog on a leash and three small children in shorts and flip-flops. "Man, if we'd gotten this Knofler . . . Man."

DIAZ AND KNOFLER lived in a pink-stucco house on Carroll Canal Court, a blank-faced two-story cube with a forbidding incised-steel garage door and a canal in the backyard. The decoration on the garage door was of a sunflower, but that succeeded only in making it look more like a bank safe. A fire truck was still parked in the street, but the hoses had been reeled in and the firefighters were working in shirtsleeves.

Another cop, named Harvey Cason, was standing in the front door when they arrived, cleaning his teeth with a length of dental floss. He flicked the floss into the yard and said, "I'm gonna smell like a burned couch for the rest of the day."

"So, no change," Barr said. He introduced Lucas and Cason said, "Four cops?"

Lucas nodded: "Two in New York, one in Hudson, Wisconsin, and one of my guys last night. Plus they killed a civilian last night, and one of their own guys is dead with them—my guy got him."

"God bless him," Cason said, and he crossed himself.

"So whatcha got?" Barr asked Cason.

"Nothing since you left," Cason said. "There's some paper upstairs, but it's all wet and runny. We're looking for credit card receipts, official paper of any kind, you know. The crime-scene guys are looking for prints, hair, anything. We've got DNA, but no prints so far. We need prints . . ."

"Working the neighbors?" Lucas asked.

"Yeah. Looking for pictures, but they seem kind of camera-shy," Cason said. "They didn't go to block parties, they pretty much kept to themselves. Both of them did yoga; we're looking for a yoga place they might have gone."

"How do you know?"

"People would see them carrying yoga mats around," Cason said.

"What kind of cars?"

"Toyota and a Lexus. A minivan and an SC430 convertible."

There wasn't much more. Lucas stood in the doorway and looked in, but he wasn't going to find anything the crime-scene crew hadn't. He walked once around the house, and saw a tricycle in the canal, and wondered about it. A bicycle he'd have understood: you steal a bike, ride it, then throw it in the canal; that's the way of the world. Had somebody hijacked a trike?

WHEN HE GOT back around to the front, Barr and Cason had gone inside, and Lucas looked around, then wandered across the street, where a pretty woman, maybe forty or forty-five, was standing in the doorway, watching.

Lucas said, "Hi."

She nodded. "How's it going over there?"

"Not well," Lucas said. "Somebody asked you if you had photos, right?"

"Yes, but we don't."

"How about photos of the street in general?" Lucas asked. "You know, something that might have their cars in it?"

"I don't think so, but I'll check," she said. "They killed some police officers?"

The woman had a peculiar California look, a something-like-coral blouse and aqua slacks, which worked for her, and long blond slightly messy hair that she'd probably paid some guy two hundred dollars to mess up. Lucas took her in, and said, "Yeah, and they executed this woman. A political worker, you know, she worked for a community organizing group. Happened to be there, and bam! Killed her in cold blood."

That woke her up a little. "You got this from the Minneapolis police?"

"I'm from the Minnesota Bureau of Criminal Apprehension," Lucas said. "I was at the scene—my guy was the guy who was murdered. The woman . . ." He lifted his hands. ". . . I mean, why?"

"Ah, jeez, that's awful," she said, and she meant it. "Look, I'll go check my pictures, but I'm ninety-nine percent that we don't have any. We're not really picture people. I don't even know how to work my cell-phone cam."

"Thanks." Lucas turned and looked down the street. "Don't see cars. Are any of the other people home?"

"Dick and Carly live right there. I saw Dick a minute ago." She pointed sideways across the street.

"Thanks. Let me know," Lucas said.

He was halfway across the street when she called him, and she came down the ten-foot-long driveway, barefoot, and said, "You know, over on Venice Boulevard, there's a place about four blocks that way"—she pointed—"called David Something, Wedding and Portrait Photography. That guy is supposedly documenting contemporary life in Venice. He's always walking around in the evening taking pictures of the houses and the people . . ."

"Great," Lucas said. And, "You're a very attractive woman."

"I know," she said. "It makes me feel good."

"Are you in the movies?"

"No, no, but thank you for asking," and she twiddled her fingers at him and walked back up the driveway to her house.

Lucas found Barr and asked, "Could I get a ride?"

"Where?"

"A place called David Something's, a wedding and portrait photography place on Venice . . ."

DAVID HARELSON'S WEDDING and Portrait Photography, By Appt., was tucked in a corner of a strip shopping center three blocks down the street. Lucas spotted it, Barr did an illegal U-turn to get into the parking lot, and a patrol car lit up its lights and came after him.

"Ah, kiss my ass." Barr groaned. "Traffic school, here I come."

Lucas said, smiling at it, "I'll go talk to this guy, you talk to your guy."

DAVID HARELSON WAS in, but the door was locked. Lucas saw him moving through to the back of the place, and rapped on the door, and then rapped louder, and then banged on it, and finally Harelson came steaming out of the back, waving a finger like a windshield wiper, and he shouted, "We're closed."

"I'm a cop," Lucas shouted back. "Open up."

Harelson looked at him for a minute, then past him at Barr and the patrol cop, and the flashing lights on the patrol car, then turned a latch.

"What?" He was a short man, balding, running to fat, with a caterpillar-style brown mustache crawling across his upper lip, and a tiny soul patch on his round chin.

"A house burned down over by the canals—Carroll Court," Lucas said. "We hear you've been doing some documentary photography in the area."

Harelson looked astonished, stepped back to let Lucas inside. "A house on Carroll Court? Which one? Was it badly damaged?"

"Yeah, it's pretty messed up," Lucas said. "As you go in from Venice Boulevard, it's a left turn, about halfway down the block, a pink stucco. It's got a shiny steel garage door with a sunflower incised on it."

Harelson slapped himself on the forehead: "The Lu house."

"Lu?"

"He was the original owner . . . the builder . . . years and years ago. Oh, God. I've got to get over there."

"Wait a minute. We're really hurting. We've got dead cops, dead civilians . . ." He told Harelson the story, and Harelson said, halfway through, "I never knew. I don't watch TV."

Barr came in and said, "Beat it," meaning the ticket, and Lucas said, "Good," and Harelson said, "I keep my files in a Lightroom database and I sort them by block and some of them by address, but not the Lu house, it's not that . . . distinguished."

"We need a car, we need one of the women, we need anything."

Harelson nodded: "Come on. I'll show you."

HE HAD AN Apple computer in the back, a tall silver tower with handles on top and two screens, a really big one and a smaller one, and he called up the program, called up the block files into thumbnails, and they began looking up and down the block for cars. "How many pictures do you have?" Barr asked.

Harelson tapped a couple of keys: "On this block, four

hundred and twelve. Back in the film days, I would maybe have had six or ten. God bless digital."

"I've been shooting a little myself," Lucas said.

"Yeah? A cop would have some great opportunities . . ."

IN THE END, they found two photos of the Lexus sitting in the driveway, and one of the Toyota. The Toyota was taken side-on, and from some distance, late in the afternoon, and they couldn't make out anything special about it. In one of the photos of the Lexus, they could almost make out the license-tag number, in the thumbnail. "Hang on," Harelson said. He isolated the license, magnified it: "Got it."

"Amazing," Barr said, and he slapped the fat man on the back. "Print that."

THE CAR WAS registered to a Louise Janowitz, and Louise Janowitz had insurance through State Farm, and a driver's license with the state of California. "So it's Louise, not Lauren or Laura or Martha," Barr said.

Lucas was a little skeptical. "Who knows, at this point? Why would she give the right name to the DMV when she lies about everything else?"

Barr, operating from his cell phone, said, "We'll have her driver's license photo in two minutes, down at the office. They can e-mail it to me, and we can get it at a coffee shop Wi-Fi."

"Gotta find the car," Lucas said.

"We're looking," Barr said. "It's not a common car, even out here. So, if it's around, we'll get it."

THEY GOT THE photo at a Starbucks, of a dark-haired, sallow-faced woman with large plastic-rimmed glasses and

Three Stooges bangs. She peered out of the photo with a depressive frown, chin down. "Whoa. Gonna jump right on that," Barr said.

"Didn't think that was an option open to us," Lucas said.

"Hey, gay or straight, don't matter. Look at the vibration she gives out: you gonna jump on that, gay or straight?"

THEY DIDN'T FIND the car immediately, but they did get a break. One of the L.A. crime-scene people, checking the house phone, found an incoming call that morning, an hour and fifteen minutes before the fire erupted.

The call had come from an over-the-counter prepaid cell phone, with no real way to trace it—but after some rigmarole with the local prosecutor's office, they got a list of phone calls from that cell phone. There weren't many, but two of them, two days apart, went to a motel in Bloomington.

"Might be nothing, but might be something," Barr said.

They were standing in the driveway of the burned house, talking, and Lucas saw the garage door across the street go up, and the pretty woman walk around the back of a Mercedes SL500. He waved at her, shouted, "Hang on," and said to Barr, "Get your computer."

Barr got it from his truck, and they walked it across the street.

"Did David what's-his-face help out?" the woman asked.

"Yes, he did, and we're grateful," Lucas said. "Could you take a look at this . . ."

She peered at the photo of Louise Janowitz for several long seconds, shook her head and laughed ruefully, said, "Yeah, that's her . . . but that's not what she looks like. You'd never recognize her from that. She's actually quite attractive."

Lucas said to Barr, "That's not good."

THEY WERE SITTING in a Fatburger in Marina del Rey, three hours after Lucas arrived, and Lucas looked at his watch, and then at a list Carol, his secretary, had made. He could get on a plane at four o'clock—maybe—and be back in the Cities by 10 P.M. The Bloomington motel was five minutes from the airport . . .

"You think you could get me on a four-o'clock plane out of LAX?"

Barr looked at his watch. "We'd have to move right along. I could call a cop out there, have him push you through."

Lucas popped the last of the Fatburger. "I'm thinking this: I was hoping to get the house and maybe Knofler, and maybe see something you wouldn't see, because I've got some background. Now, with no house and no suspect, I'm not going to get anything you won't. The way I see it, they were ready for us: they had a whole exit plan all figured out. She's probably in Canada by now."

"Why Canada?"

"Well, Canada's full of criminals, so it's a good place to hide out," Lucas explained.

"I didn't know that," Barr said. "Anyway—there's that motel. In Bloomfield, or whatever it is."

"Yeah. Bloomington. Maybe I oughta get back."

Barr slurped up the last of his orange soda, looked at his watch, and said, "Let's go. You got a ticket?"

FROM BARR'S CAR Lucas called Carol, who called Northwest and got the ticket fixed; and he called Del, who said he'd get Shrake and Jenkins and they'd meet him at the motel.

At the airport, an airport cop was waiting at the ticket counter and pushed him through security, and got him a ride to the gate. The cabin attendant said, "Man, you were pushing it," and Lucas said, "Glad to be going home, though."

They pulled the door shut behind him, and as he settled into his seat his cell rang: the cabin attendant said, "Sir, you'll have to turn off your phone. We're ready to roll."

Lucas looked at the cell screen, saw that the call was from Los Angeles. He said, "I'm a police officer working a murder case. This will only take a minute and it could be important."

She nodded, curious, and Lucas opened the phone and said, "Yeah?" and Barr said, "We found that Lexus."

"Ah, jeez, I'm on the plane."

"Don't worry about it," Barr said. "It was illegally parked on a nice quiet street up in Pasadena, Ninita Parkway. Nice green oak trees over the street, nice houses, nice cars. They noticed it when it exploded and burned right down to the wheels."

"Man . . ."

"Some kind of bomb, probably on a timer," Barr said. "If a kid had messed with that car, or if a cop had checked it out, they might have been barbecued. So: take care."

"You, too. You ever need anything out of the Cities, let me know."

THE THREE AND a half hours going back wasn't as bad as the three and a half hours going out, because, to his own surprise, Lucas dozed off in the quiet cabin. He had a window seat, and declined the meal; dropped back, the seat softened by a pillow from the flight attendant, and closed his eyes. When he woke up, the guy in the next seat, who was poking at a laptop, said, "Wish I could sleep like that."

Lucas yawned and said, "How long was I out?"

"Close to three hours. Sleeping like a baby. We're coming up on Sioux Falls."

Lucas looked out the window, and there it was, lights

of the city twinkling in the distance, Minnesota ahead in the dark. He was on the ground in an hour, on his cell phone, walking down the concourse. Del said, about the motel, "It's pretty small and stinky. I don't know. It could be something."

"I'll be there in fifteen," Lucas said.

THE WAYFARER MOTEL was a crappy place, a long two-story rectangle with car parking on three sides and a chain-link fence and I-494 on the fourth side. Access was through two sets of hallways on each floor, up two sets of stairways. No elevators. The halls smelled of beer and cigarette smoke and disinfectant, with outdoor carpet hard underfoot.

Lucas hooked up with Del, Jenkins, and Shrake, and they did a stroll around the place, two-and-two, saw nothing of special interest, and met at the office. Two clerks were working the counter: a straw-headed kid, pale and thin, with Grand Theft Auto eyes; and a soft round Indian woman with a dot on her forehead.

They knew cops when they saw them, and the straw man said, "What's up?" and Del rolled out the pictures of Cohn and the woman-of-many-names. The clerks studied them for a minute, then the Indian woman, who wore a name tag that read, "Jane," shook her head and said, "No. They are not here."

"You're sure," Lucas said.

"I work here twelve hours a day," she said. "They're not here. Not only are they not here, they've never been here, not in the last eight months and twelve days, since I got here."

So they talked about the phone calls, and Jane explained that the phone number was the main number. If somebody called that number, one of the clerks answered it and then switched it to the room. There was no record of which room took which call.

"Nothing suspicious lately? Nothing out of the ordinary?" Del asked. "Nothing that caught your eye?"

Straw Man glanced at Jane, then said, "Curtis Ramp was here. Not with his wife."

Curtis Ramp was a Minnesota Vikings running back. Shrake said, "Jesus, I hope it wasn't *before* a game?"

Straw Man shook his head. "It was Wednesday. He paid cash. He didn't want us to know who he was."

"That doesn't help a lot," Lucas said.

"Sorry, dude."

"We may send a couple of guys over here to sit with you for a while, watch who comes and goes," Lucas said. "We'll call you."

"Call the manager," Jane said. "He'd have to set it up."

IN LUCAS'S ABSENCE, a cold front had come through, and the night was now chilly: the first night of the northern autumn, which sometimes started in August. Out in the parking lot, they looked up at the rows of windows, and Lucas said, "Well, shoot. I thought it might be something."

"Still might be," Del said. "Oughta get somebody here early tomorrow morning, watch people when they're moving around. Run some license tags . . ."

Shrake and Jenkins had come together in Jenkins's Crown Vic, and they broke away, and Lucas and Del ambled down to the end of the parking lot to Lucas's Porsche, talking babies. Del was saying, ". . . dilating, but then she got stuck. The doc said if she doesn't go by the end of the week, she wants to do a C-section. I worried about it, but . . ." He realized he'd lost Lucas, who'd stopped, staring back at the lot: "What?"

"Look at that old rattrap pickup," Lucas said.

"Uh . . ."

"It's got Oklahoma plates."

Del said, "Ah, jeez." He went and looked, and came back. "This can't be right, man. This can't be right." Down the lot, they could see Jenkins unlocking the door of his car, and Del whistled at them, and Jenkins looked up, and Del waved them back.

Lucas said, "It's got an NRA sticker; it's got a Bushmaster sticker." Bushmaster sold M-15 variants.

"Can't be right," Del said. "What'd the connection be?"

"Don't know," Lucas said. He scratched his head, mystified.

"Jenkins had some of the guy's pictures in his car," Del said.

Jenkins and Shrake came up and looked at the truck, and Jenkins said, "There're only two possibilities. Either it's a terrific coincidence and no big deal, or something is a lot more fucked-up than we know about."

"You got those pictures?" Lucas asked.

"Got one," Jenkins said.

"Let's go ask Jane," Lucas said. "She should know."

JANE SAID, "TWO-FOURTEEN. Been here almost a week."

Lucas said, "Let me get my gun. We'll take him right now."

16

DEL WAS WEARING jeans and a military-style olive drab shirt and yellow leather boots, and looked less like a cop than the rest of them, so they sent him ahead. He tiptoed up to Justice Shafer's motel room and stood with his ear to the door for a minute, and heard both the television and then a clunk from somebody moving around, and he tiptoed back down the hall and said, "He's there."

Shrake said, "How do we want to do this?"

"These guys have been rapping on the hotel doors with keys so they sound like a maid or something," Lucas said. He took a quarter out of his pocket and held it up.

Del said, "There's a peephole. He'll see us."

Lucas looked back down the stairway where they'd clustered, and said, "Go get Jane."

Jane had a well-developed sense of self-preservation, and didn't want to do it, but the four of them were several times larger than she, and they grouped around her and looked down at her until she caved and said she would.

"All you have to do is knock; as soon as you hear him start to open the door, you move away," Shrake said.

"What if he just shoots?"

"For a knock on the door?" Jenkins asked.

"It's almost eleven o'clock," she pointed out.

"Nothing's perfect," Shrake said.

"If it turns out nothing's perfect, I'm the one who gets shot," she said.

"Maybe . . . what if he had a package at the desk?" Jenkins suggested. "She calls him from the front desk, says, 'A woman just dropped a package for you . . .' "

"Sounds like bullshit," Shrake said.

"To you, but if his file's right, this guy ain't no mental lighthouse," Jenkins said.

"I could go with that," Lucas said. To Del, "What do you think?"

"The big thing is, we don't want him coming out of there behind a machine gun," Del said. "We don't want to spook him."

"We could call in an entry team," Shrake said.

Del: "You pussy." And to Jane, "No offense."

"Let's call him from the desk," Lucas said.

JENKINS WAS RIGHT: Shafer was not the Wizard of Oz.

Del was positioned at the end of the hallway, opposite the stairs that led down to the lobby, listening on his cell phone as Jane made the call from the front desk, with Lucas and his cell standing next to her.

Upstairs, Shafer snatched up the phone and said, "Yeah?"

"Mr. Shafer, a woman has left a package for you at the front desk. You can pick it up at your convenience," Jane said. "I get off in an hour."

"Thanks. Be right down."

Jane hung up and Lucas said into his cell phone, to Del, "He's coming out."

Lucas, Shrake, and Jenkins gathered at the bottom of the stairs, but in the cross-hall, out of sight from the stairs themselves. When Shafer unlocked his room door, Del started walking toward him, beer can in one hand, cell phone in the other. He said, "I'm on the way, darlin'."

Shafer glanced at him and turned away, headed down the hall, then down the stairs, Del moving fast now to catch up. At the very last second, as he stepped off the bottom stair, Shafer might have suspected that something was wrong. He turned and looked at Del, who was coming down on top of him in a linebacker's rush, and he flinched and then Jenkins kicked his legs out and Shrake landed on him.

Shafer started struggling and thrashing, but not too hard, grunting under the weight of Del and Shrake, because he knew cops when he saw them. He stopped thrashing after a few seconds and said, "What d'you want?" and Shrake put the cuffs on.

Lucas said to him, "Who're you gonna hit?"

"What are you talking about?" A little more thrashing against the cuffs.

"We know all about the .50-cal, Justice." Lucas squatted next to his head. "We found your little spot up on the hill. You gonna hit McCain? You gonna hit Palin? Who you gonna hit?"

"What hill? What?" His eyes were wild. "Hit McCain? Are you nuts?"

LUCAS CALLED DAN Jacobs at the security committee: "Listen, if you've got a couple of loose Secret Service guys rattling around, we nailed that Justice Shafer guy," Lucas said.

Jacobs shouted, "Lucas, goddamnit! That's great. That's wonderful. Where is he?"

"We're putting him in a car, taking him up to Ramsey County. Tell the Secret Service that they're welcome to sit in. Things might be a little more complicated than we thought. We've got a BCA crime-scene crew on the way to the motel where we grabbed him and we're staking the place out, looking for accomplices."

"Accomplices. What accomplices?" The joy was gone.

"Like I said," Lucas said, "it's complicated, and it's probably not good."

SIX SECRET SERVICE agents showed up to watch Del talk with Shafer. Lucas got the feeling that if there *were* an assassination plot against McCain, it wouldn't do a guy's career any harm to get in on the ground floor when it was broken up.

Del had brought the can of Budweiser with him, and it was sitting by his boot heel, unopened, where the video camera couldn't see it. Shafer was dressed like Del, in a khaki hunting shirt, jeans, and hunting boots, and was handcuffed to a metal table. He kept looking at the video camera in the corner, as though trying to see the crowd that gathered behind it.

One of the Secret Service guys, looking at the monitor, asked, "You sure about your interrogator?"

Lucas said, "Yes," and stopped.

Shrake, feeling a level of discomfort, added, "We're giving Shafer somebody he can get comfortable with. If we need somebody with a plutonium suit, we can put one of you guys in there. Later."

The Secret Service guy gave him a gentle poke to the gut with an elbow, and said, "You know I love you."

DEL SAID, PUSHING a picture of the woman-of-many-names across the table at Shafer, "You're sure that's her?"

"That's her. That's her, and she's Bill Hefner's girlfriend. The anarchists are coming in, and they're gonna tear you guys a new butthole. When you come looking for help, our guys'll be there, ready to go. We're coming in from all over the country, we're the final backstop. Hefner is tight with you guys. He's on your committee."

Del rubbed his forehead and said, "I hate to tell you this, Justice, but Hefner isn't on a committee, he's in jail in Oregon, and he never heard of you, and he doesn't have a girlfriend, he's got a wife, and this lady . . ." He tapped the photograph. "This ain't her."

"He's in jail?" Shafer suspected a lie.

"He sold a couple of modified ArmaLites to an ATF guy and he's in fuckin' jail," Del said.

"That's fuckin' crazy," Shafer said.

"Tell us about scouting out that bluff over town," Del suggested. "We know you were up there, because we found a couple of shells. They're your shells, Justice. They've got your prints on them."

"You're framing me," Shafer said. "You're trying to get me."

One of the Secret Service agents asked Lucas, "You read him his rights?"

"More or less," Lucas said.

The agent nodded. Lucas got the impression that he didn't much care; prosecution wasn't his problem.

DEL ASKED, PRESSING, "Then how'd they get up there? Answer me that."

"Somebody else put them there," Shafer said.

"Some other dude did it," Del said, the skepticism right out there. "The two-dude defense."

"It's the truth," Shafer said. Then, his eyes lifting, he said, "You answer me a question. Answer me this: How in the hell did I get wherever you said it was and let off a couple of rounds with that .50 cal and nobody noticed? You ever hear a .50-cal? How'd I do that?"

"Good question," one of the agents said. "How *did* he do that?"

Del said, "We don't know when you were up there. You

might have done it two weeks ago, and somebody thought they were backfires. The highway's right down the hill."

"Good answer," said another one of the agents.

"A .50-cal don't sound like no fuckin' backfire," Shafer said.

"Good point," the Secret Service guy said.

"And look at me," Shafer continued. "You got me swearin' like the devil. I don't talk like that, and now you got me talkin' like you."

Lucas turned to the head Secret Service guy and said, "Did Jacobs tell you about our murder gang?"

"I heard something about it," the guy said.

"So I got a story for you," Lucas said. He looked through the window, where Del was retracing his steps in the interrogation. "Let's find a place to sit down."

THE AGENTS ALL sat around straddling backward chairs, and Lucas laid out the details of the assaults on the convention moneymen, and the cop shootings, which the local Secret Service guys already knew about. "So we know who these guys are, more or less, and what they're doing. One of them is dead. Their usual practice, at this point, would be to get out—maybe they haven't gotten everything they wanted, but in the past, they've always been cautious."

"But now they're going crazy," one of the agents said.

"That's right," Lucas said. "And we don't know why. We do know that one of them is talking to Shafer and his .50-cal, and from what we understand, the woman with the gang actually financed the gun. Not only financed it, but gave him the list of stores to check out. She told him that the store guys were all connected to this Hefner guy, that the store might be bugged, so he should show up, talk about buying some ammo, and then get out. Then the store guys supposedly would pass the word that Shafer was still on the case."

"What a dumb shit," one of the agents said.

Lucas threw his hands up: "That's what we all get. *What a dumb shit.* But these other people aren't dumb shits. Why are they dragging Shafer under our noses? I mean, I guess the big question is, what're they up to? Something about the convention? Why haven't they gotten out of town? We're wondering, are they pointing at McCain's big night? Is there something in that?"

The lead agent nodded, and turned to his men: "Okay, you've heard it. We need to talk to the presidential details, we need to beef up the protection even more than it is. We need to work out new travel routes—we need to find new angles on everything. I want the goddamn X Center sterile. *Sterile.* McCain's here in two days, Palin will be here . . ."

"It's not Palin," Lucas said. "They were in town, all set to go, before she was even picked. If it's anybody, it's McCain—but we might be missing something completely obvious. What worries me most is that we have some ideas about Cohn, but we really don't know him. What if it's political?"

"You mean . . . what if they really make a run at McCain?"

"Yeah. Is that too weird?" Lucas asked.

"Nothing's too weird. You've got two dead cops." The agent brushed his hand through his neatly trimmed silver hair. "Man, this is serious. We need more guys. If they planned this out way ahead of time . . ."

Another agent said, "We got two days to figure it out."

DEL GAVE UP on the interrogation and gave one of the Secret Service guys a shot at it. "We can hold him, but there's not much—he had no idea about those .50-cal shells up on the hill. I got Nancy to run a quick comparo on the shells, and she says they came from the same gun, the extractor marks are right there. He says that when he was sighting the gun in, he always collected all his brass and keeps it in the back of the truck, in an army ammo can. I called Dick out at the motel, he looked in the can and says there were fourteen loose used shells, and Shafer says there should be twenty. He thinks this chick must have stolen them."

"Doesn't he keep his truck locked?" Lucas asked.

"Yeah, but with somebody like Shafer, dealing with somebody like this what's-her-name . . ."

"Elena Diaz."

"Yeah. I mean, she got the key, somewhere along the way," Del said. "That's all we could come up with."

"You're okay with that story?"

"Yup. Lucas—this kid is no planner. He's gonna wind up eating out of garbage cans, if he doesn't wind up face-down dead before that," Del said. "He's being set up. I keep thinking about that Kennedy assassination movie, Lee Harvey Oswald. Some people think *he* was set up."

"He wasn't; he did it."

"The point is, that idea could be floating around in some nutcake's head," Del said. "Like Cohn's. Shoot McCain, shoot somebody, and blame Shafer. I mean, Justice is defenseless. He's a goof."

WHEN LUCAS GOT home, the house was asleep—Weather always went to bed early on nights before she was operating, and she operated on most days. The baby and the housekeeper went to bed almost as early. But as he turned in the drive, he saw a glow from under the blind in Letty's room. A night owl like Lucas, she was sneaking a read.

Lucas went inside, checked all the doors, took his shoes off before he tiptoed upstairs, left his shoes on his bedroom floor, listened to Weather's even breathing for a couple of seconds, then tiptoed down to Letty's door and tapped a couple of times.

"Yes. Come in," she said.

She was finishing *To Kill a Mockingbird* in the light of a bedside lamp. He asked, "You almost done?"

"Almost; but I can sleep in tomorrow. I'm going back downtown with Jen."

"Your mom says you're getting some serious airtime," Lucas said. "I wish I'd been here to see it."

"Ah—it's kid stuff. They won't let me get near the better stories," Letty said. "Too young."

"Just . . . be patient." He perched on the end of the bed. "Beverly called this morning, before I caught the plane. I was going to call and tell you, but I got really busy. Anyway, we're set for Monday."

"Monday."

"Yup. We go see the judge on Monday afternoon, three-thirty. The last decision you've got to make is what to do about your name. You can be Letty Jean West, or Letty Jean West Davenport, or Letty Jean Davenport, or Letty West Davenport—however you want to do it."

"Huh." She made a moue. "The thing is, I never knew my father, hardly. He wasn't really my father, he ditched us, but Mom kept his name. Her maiden name was Martin. I wonder if they'd go for Letty Jean Martin Davenport. Or Letty Martin Davenport. I'd like to, you know, keep my first mom a little bit."

"We can do that," Lucas said. "You gotta let me know by tomorrow night, exactly, so they can fill out the paper. Then, we're done."

"That's . . ." She teared up a little and wiped her eyes with a corner of the sheet.

"You're still all right with it?" Lucas asked.

"I'm perfect with it," she said, with a choked-off laugh. "I can't wait."

Lucas patted her foot, under the light blanket, and said, "If I don't see you tomorrow before I leave, call me on my cell, let me know about the name."

"All right. Night, Dad."

WHEN LUCAS WAS out of the room, Letty dug her cell phone out from under her pillow, poked redial, and Briar picked up. "I'm back," Letty said. "So he gets out tomorrow—then what?"

"I don't know. He's really freaked out. Maybe it's the medicine they're giving him, it's something to stop blood clots in his legs. But it's making him crazy."

"Has he talked about my dad or me again?"

"Well . . . yeah, a couple of times. He was talking to Ranch, and they're going to try to do something, but Ranch is so crazy . . . I don't know. If you see the van coming, you should run."

"But you'll be driving it," Letty said.

"He makes me . . ."

"But you don't have to," Letty said.

"You don't know . . ."

"All right. All right. Stay calm," Letty said. "I'll think of something."

17

LUCAS WOKE UP tired but clear-eyed, and looked at the clock: 9 A.M. Perfect. He always felt better when he slept past 8:59. The eight o'clock hour was, in his opinion, when farmers got up, and God bless them, they were critical to the economy, and so on and so forth, but he was not a farmer.

Not only that, he had ideas when he slept late, and now he turned over on his stomach and got another fifteen minutes. When he popped open his left eye and looked at the clock, and then realized that he'd been sleeping on a crooked wrist and that his hand had fallen asleep, he straightened out on the bed and stretched and shook out the hand and yawned and picked up the bedside phone and dialed Del.

Del, panicked, snatched up the phone and said, "Jesus Christ, her water broke," and Lucas said, "Ah, shit. Well, talk to you in a couple of days, buddy."

So then he called up Jenkins, who asked, "You know what time it is?"

Lucas said, "Nine twenty-one. Get Shrake, meet me downtown in an hour. By the way, Del's old lady's water broke."

"That whole concept, Del having a child, is a little frightening," Jenkins said. "See you in an hour."

Lucas rolled out of bed, headed for the bathroom, turned around when the phone rang. The caller ID said it was Jenkins again. "Yeah?"

"You know, we gotta think about a baby present. Or a whole bunch of them, or whatever you do."

"I'll get Carol to organize it," Lucas said. "See you in fifty-nine minutes."

LUCAS MADE CALLS from his car, the first to the Minneapolis FBI office, the next to the Ramsey County attorney, and then to the Ramsey County public defender. He made a stop at the Ramsey County jail and spoke to Justice Shafer for one minute; got up and said, "You might be able to help us, Justice, and get your ass out of this crack. I'll get back to you. Talk to your lawyer. Do what she says."

"I didn't do nothing," Shafer said.

LUCAS'S OFFICE WAS on the second floor of the BCA building, which had cost a bit more than eighty million bucks and was only six years old, so even the government-gray carpet was still in good shape. He had one of the larger offices, overlooking a parking lot and the evidence collection garage on the ground floor. It had come with the standard new-building desk, but it was a desk that positioned him with his back to the door, which he disliked, with a conference table so stark in its design that it would have shocked a Scandinavian architect.

On the grounds that he had a bad back, he'd brought in a personal business chair, and then, the soil having been prepared, a simple dark-maple desk and conference table, with comfortable chairs, which allowed him to face the door; and an old, but not antique, coatrack, and a few metal file cabinets so he'd have a place to put his feet. He had pictures of Weather, Sam, and Letty on the wall, along with framed shots of the University of Minnesota hockey team, where he'd been a defenseman who wasn't quite good enough to turn pro. A hockey stick was mounted above the hockey photos. Also, stuck casually to the exposed side of one of the metal file cabinets, a shooting range target with five .45-caliber bullet holes in the ten-ring. Like he did it every day . . .

Carol was sitting at her desk outside the office.

"Del's wife has gone into labor and you're supposed to organize baby gifts," Lucas said. "I don't know if you take up a collection or what."

"Don't worry about it. Give me fifty dollars."

He gave her fifty dollars, said, "That seems like a lot," and she said, "You're rich, you can afford it," and then Shrake showed up and she said, "Give me twenty dollars."

Jenkins was a minute behind Shrake, and they scattered themselves around the chairs in Lucas's office.

"I just talked to Shafer again," Lucas said. "Diaz called him on his cell phone, which we didn't pay too much attention to because we already had the number. But. That means that Shafer can call her back. If we can get some FBI backup here, they've got choppers with location-finding equipment that can get pretty close to where she is, if Shafer calls her, and she answers."

"What if she tossed the phone?" Jenkins asked.

"Then we're out of luck. But, if she still has it, and answers, we can get it narrowed down to a couple of blocks. Then we can saturate the area, dig them out," Lucas said. "I talked to Shafer and he'll call her. Actually, he'll ask her for a meeting. Maybe we can suck them in."

"When?"

"The choppers are out at the airport, backup for the convention, so the feds have to 'retask,' whatever that means," Lucas said. "That's gonna take a couple hours, but the AIC says he'll push it and says he can get it. We'll know by noon, and we can be up in the air by one."

Jenkins looked at his watch: just ten-thirty. "We might want to jack up the SWAT guys," he said.

"Most of them are out in the city, working with the street teams," Lucas said. "I talked to Sandy, he's going to pull back whoever he can. We'll at least have a few."

"Like we were saying, Shafer ain't no wizard. You think he can do this?" Shrake asked.

"We're gonna drill him," Lucas said. "I could only talk to him a minute, because the public defender wasn't in the house. I talked to the PD this morning and he says a deal can be done. The prosecutor is willing to go along because, basically, you know, we don't have a case. And they got all those demonstration arrests in their hair and they'd just as soon get rid of Shafer if they can."

They all sat for a minute, then Jenkins said, "What do you think we ought to get for Del's kid? It's gonna be a boy, right? Something blue?"

"It's Del's kid; you gonna get him a blue gun?" Shrake asked.

"Let Carol do it," Lucas said. "But I like the blue gun idea."

"Now what?" Jenkins asked.

"Let's go over to the jail. Get Shafer going."

JENNIFER CAREY PICKED Letty up and asked, "How'd it go with Juliet?"

Letty shook her head. "She's not going to leave him. Says he's hurt, so she can't go. At least not until he gets better, which means never, because he'll get on top of her and make her do what he wants."

"Ah, boy. I don't know, Letty," Jennifer said. "Maybe we should talk to Lucas, explain the situation, tell him that our biggest worry is that he'll do something irrational."

"Let me ask you something," Letty said. "What would you do if suddenly, someday, in a couple of weeks, Randy just disappeared and was never heard from again? Or maybe, he's found in an alley with four bullet holes in his heart. Would you do anything about it? Ask any questions? Talk to Dad?"

Jennifer shook her head. "Couldn't tell you that until I got there. You know about Lucas and me; we almost got married, except that I knew I couldn't deal with him. He's too . . . harshly . . . smart. He's too intense. He's like Weather—he's like you. Not like me; I'm all over the place. But I don't think cops should kill people. I mean, murder people. People get trials, they get lawyers."

Letty sighed. "Let me think about it for a couple of days. I'm so confused." A little song and dance, she was thinking as she spoke: a little song and dance, because Jennifer Carey was no longer to be trusted. *I don't think cops should kill people.*

Bullshit, Letty thought.

A PUBLIC DEFENDER met Lucas, Jenkins, and Shrake at the jail, with an assistant from the county attorney's office, and they cut the deal: no harm, no foul. Nobody gets charged, nobody gets sued for false arrest. Shafer expresses his good citizenship by cooperating with the police.

Outside the jail, on the sidewalk, Shafer said, "She's a pretty good lawyer. Got me outa there, slicker'n snot on a doorknob."

"Yeah, right," Jenkins said. "You ride shotgun; that little lump in the back of your head is Shrake's pistol."

"Hey, I'm out," Shafer said.

"Yeah. One inch. You'll be back in just as fast, if we need you back in."

THEY GOT TOGETHER with the FBI team in a temporary office on Wabasha Street, six blocks from the convention center. The FBI's local agent-in-charge, Wilbur Rivers, told Lucas that the choppers were gassed and ready to go, and could be in the air over Minneapolis or St. Paul in twenty minutes. "The problem might be that she's out in Burnsville, or Stillwater, or somewhere. We won't be able to get close enough during a short phone call. We'd be able to identify the cell, but not where the signal's coming from—so we need some talk time."

"The call to L.A. came from a St. Paul cell, so there's a good chance she's here," Lucas said. "If we were willing to risk it, we might even want to bring both choppers here."

"Your call," Rivers said.

Lucas looked at Jenkins and Shrake, who shrugged, and so he said, "Screw it. We're already set, let's go with it. One each in Minneapolis and St. Paul."

They'd made Shafer sit in a corner while they talked, and Rivers looked at him and asked, "You think he can pull it off?"

"We talked to him on the way over. He keeps it simple. He says he got a call from his daddy, and his daddy says the sheriff has been asking about him, because the Secret Service says he's up here with a big gun. That the Secret Service thinks he's going to do something bad. So he's heading back down I-35, going home."

Shrake said, "I actually called him on his phone, in the car, and we pretended I was his daddy, and we . . . got him talking. I think it'll work, somewhat. Maybe not perfect."

"Well, even if it doesn't work, we'll get a shot at the phone, if she stays on long enough," Rivers said. "You want me to put the choppers up?"

"Let's do it," Lucas said.

COHN WAS HUNGOVER, lying on a couch with his forearm over his eyes. Cruz had found a police report about the fight in the bar, about a crippled man being thrown in front of a car. Randy Whitcomb had been hit by one car, and run over by another. He was listed in good condition at Regions Hospital.

"Dumbest thing I ever heard of," Lane had said. "Wish I'd been there to see it, though."

"Felt good, after McCall. Didn't do any harm, doesn't look like," Cohn said. "They don't know who did it."

But Lindy was scared, Cruz was worried, and Lane was talking about bailing out. "I'm not hurting that bad, financially," he explained to Cohn. "I got the farm, I got the business, they do okay. Nothing great, but I like it."

Cohn said, "Goddamnit, Jesse, the only reason you keep them running is because you got money packed away from the jobs. You put more goddamn money into those businesses than you ever get out—you keep saying you need this tool or that tool and that'll get you over the top, but it ain't the tools you need. You need customers, and you ain't got them. If you don't do these jobs, you ain't gonna have a business, either."

Lane sulked: "I always got the farm. That *does* make some money."

"Okay, it makes some money. But you're not a farmer, Jesse. You don't mind going out there and shoveling a little horse poop and tellin' Roy to plow the south forty, or whatever he does, but you don't want to do that every day. Sittin' up there on the John Deere in that hot sun, rolling up and down those rows every fuckin' day . . ."

"Air-conditioned," Lane said. "Got Sirius radio. Outlaw Country."

"Fuck Sirius radio," Cohn said.

CRUZ ASKED, "WHAT about Lindy?"

Lindy said, "I'm not doing it. I don't stick up places. I don't even know how to hold a gun. I'm gonna pee my pants just thinkin' about it. I'm not doing it."

"All you have to do is be a desk clerk. You've even *done* that," Cruz said.

"They'll wind up with a picture of me, and I'll be right out there in some fuckin' African jungle with you and Cohn." She started to cry. "I just wanna go back to B-B-Birmingham."

Lane jumped in on her side: "If you make her do it, I ain't going. She'll screw it up. No offense, Lindy, it's what you're saying your own self. If she screws it up, we could all go down. I'm telling you, this whole thing is running off the tracks."

Cohn asked lazily, "Does that mean you'll do it if she *doesn't* go?"

LANE NEVER GOT a chance to answer, because Cruz's cell phone rang. She had three cell phones in her purse, all with different rings, and she looked at her purse and then back at Cohn and said, "Uh-oh."

"What?"

"Nobody's got that number," she said.

She went to the purse and took the cell phone out, looked at the LCD screen and frowned.

"Who is it?"

"Says it's Shafer, but that can't be right." She clicked on the phone and said, "Hello?"

"You know who this is?" Shafer asked.

She did: "Yes. How did you get this number?"

"It's the only number on my phone, from when you called me before," Shafer said. "Listen, my daddy called me. He said the sheriff came around and they're looking for me. He said the Secret Service called the sheriff from St. Paul and they say that I'm up there with my .50-cal and they think I'm going to shoot McCain."

"Justice . . ."

"So I'm going home. I'm headin' out," Shafer said. "I got to get this straight with the sheriff."

"Justice, damnit, we might need you," Cruz said.

"I want to talk about it, face-to-face," Shafer said. "From what my daddy says, you've been lying to me. They say Bill is in jail somewhere."

"You sit right there," Cruz said. "I'm coming to talk to you. Give me an hour."

"Well, I don't know . . ." There was an odd pause, and then Shafer said, "My daddy said the sheriff was looking for me, and that the Secret Service, you know . . ."

"Sit right there," Cruz said, and she punched off the phone, turning it in her hand, staring at it.

COHN ASKED, "THAT was the gun guy?"

"Yeah." She told him what Shafer had said, and then, "There was something not right about it. He was talking in whole sentences, and loud. He usually mumbles around. Then there was this minute, there, when he ran out of things to say, and I could feel like something was going on, off the phone. You know? Then he repeated everything he said the first time, in the same words. And then . . ." She frowned.

Cohn asked, "What?"

"He said his daddy called to tell him that the sheriff was looking for him, down in Oklahoma . . . But when I was recruiting him, he told me his father had abandoned them years ago. That he hadn't seen him since he was a kid."

"You think the cops got him?" Cohn asked.

They all looked at one another, and then Lane said, "We need the guy, right?"

Cruz: "He's the cherry on the ice-cream sundae. People spot him down Seventh Street, and every cop in the area will be down there. Every one."

"And they'd spot him," Cohn said.

Cruz cracked a smile. "I can guarantee it. I was going to call nine-one-one every two minutes, to tell them where he was. But he didn't sound like himself."

Lane asked, "So . . . the cops got him?"

Cruz shook her head. "I don't know."

Cohn studied her for a minute, then rolled up from the couch he was lying on, carefully tied his shoes, and said, "I know how we can find out."

LUCAS LISTENED TO Wilbur Rivers talk on the telephone, then Rivers took the phone away from his ear and said, "The conversation was too short to narrow it down much, but the woman was calling from a St. Paul cell, and the tech thinks the signal was coming from south of Seventh Street, between St. Peter and Sibley. North of the river. That's as close as he could get it."

Shrake scratched his chin and said to Lucas, "That's probably thirty or forty blocks, total. Lot of condos in there. Apartments above some of the stores."

"But it's manageable," Lucas said. "We can handle that. We just grind it out. Talk to the guys at City Hall, the tax assessor's office, nail down the highest possibilities, work those first."

"Gonna need some more guys," Shrake said.

"That could be tough," Lucas said. "Everybody's on the streets. We need investigators. Not uniforms. I'll talk to Harrington, see if they can spring me a couple of guys."

"Harrington's up to his ass in alligators," the FBI agent said. Harrington was the St. Paul chief of police.

"We can handle it," Lucas said.

"You might not have to," Rivers said. He handed Lucas the phone. "Tell Mark to play the call for you."

Lucas listened to the replay, said, "Thanks," to the tech, handed the phone back to Rivers and said to Shrake and Jenkins: "She's on her way to the motel. She says she'll be there in an hour. We gotta run."

NEITHER CRUZ NOR Cohn had been in a hospital for years, and they talked about possible hospital security, about bullshitting their way in, about what to do if they were kicked out . . . but when they got to Regions, they found a reception desk, asked a volunteer lady, got a room number and directions.

"What if he starts screaming?" Cruz asked, as they went up in the elevator. She basically liked Cohn's idea; it appealed to her sense of humor.

"I'll strangle the little motherfucker," he said.

"Brute . . ."

"I'm going in money-first," Cohn said. He held up a pack of hundred-dollar bills. "Pimps are always willing to talk about money."

They found Whitcomb's room, a double, with Whitcomb on the window side. The near bed was empty, and the hooker they'd seen the night before was sitting at the end of Whitcomb's bed, reading a *Betty & Veronica* comic book. She looked up, saw them, then recognized Cohn and stood up, her hand to her mouth, and said, "Ohhh."

"Shut up," Cohn snapped, and her mouth snapped shut. He looked around the divider curtain as Whitcomb turned toward them. Whitcomb frowned, and Cohn held up the money and said, "Two thousand bucks."

"You fuck," Whitcomb said, finally recognizing him. Whitcomb looked clean and very white, in a hospital gown, tucked in with white blankets.

"Call me a fuck again and I'll throw you out the fuckin' window," Cohn said, and they both looked toward the window. Then Cohn held up the money again. "Two thousand bucks, hundreds, in cash."

Whitcomb said, "For trying to kill me?"

"No, asshole. I could have walked away from that," Cohn said. "But I felt bad, you being handicapped and all. I also need to borrow your woman for an hour."

They both looked at Briar. Then Whitcomb asked, "What has she got to do?"

"Entertain a pal of mine. He likes young pussy. A guy up here from Oklahoma. I don't know any entertainers locally. I saw you last night, looked you up in the paper, and here I am. Two thousand for my friend, and to keep your mouth shut if the cops catch up with me."

Briar said to Whitcomb, "Randy, I need to stay by you."

Whitcomb said to Cohn, looking at the money in Cohn's hand, "Just a quick one-time job?"

"Just a little . . . friendship," Cohn said, letting himself smile. "He'll think it's funny." He turned to Briar. "You'll like him. He's a nice guy. Clean."

Briar said, "Randy . . ."

Whitcomb said, "Shut up." To Cohn: "Where is this guy?"

"He's in a motel in Bloomington . . . but the thing is, he likes the schoolgirl look. You know, a ponytail." He turned to Briar. "Could you pull your hair back in a brown ponytail?"

Whitcomb took the money, then flipped the hospital blanket back and pushed himself up. To Briar, he said, "We're getting out of here. Unfold my chair and tell the nurse we're going."

"Randy, you can't—you're hurt."

"My foot's hurt. The rest of me is okay. Now shut the fuck up and get that fuckin' nurse in here."

WHITCOMB'S VAN ROLLED out of the parking garage and Cruz fell in behind them. "We're late," she said. "The checkout took too long."

Cohn said, "Worth the wait. She doesn't look that much like you, but with the ponytail, she's about the right height, the right coloring, the sunglasses . . ."

"She's about thirty pounds heavier than I am," Cruz said.

"That's disguised by her dress, at least some."

"I don't know."

Cruz grinned at her: "I don't know, either, but either some cops get a surprise, or Shafer does."

THEY GATHERED IN an empty motel room, eight of them, including four BCA SWAT guys in armor. Lucas said, "All right. We don't know exactly what she looks like, so wait until I call. As soon as she knocks on the door, we rush the stairs, both guys come up, put the guns on her, and then we pop the door and we've got her three ways. You gotta remember, maybe she's got a gun in her hand, planning to hit Shafer as soon as he opens up. So take care."

"If the other guys are with her?" one of the SWATs asked.

"You don't take any chances," Lucas said. "You order them on the ground and you keep your weapons on them. I don't think the whole bunch will come over—that'd be too conspicuous. But there might be one in the car, maybe another one comes up the stairs with her. Take care: they've already killed four cops, so a few more won't make any difference to them."

Lucas and Shrake would be in Shafer's original room. Shafer would wait in the motel room they were gathering in, and as a precaution, they'd handcuffed him to a bed rail, which pissed him off. "I'm like one of you guys."

"It's for your own safety," Lucas said. It wasn't, but they were like magic words and temporarily shut him up.

Jenkins and one of the SWAT guys would rush the front stairs, another of the SWAT guys would literally block the second stairway: they'd wedge an office chair between a down-railing and the door, so the door couldn't be opened. The SWAT guy was there just in case.

Two more SWAT guys were waiting in a minivan in the parking lot. They would block and then check the woman's car after she got out.

"If she comes in," one of the SWAT guys said.

"She's coming; she bought it," Lucas said.

AN HOUR AND twelve minutes after the phone call, another minivan rolled into the parking lot, and slowly down the line toward the office, and parked in a handicapped slot.

"Dark-haired woman in a minivan," one of the parking-lot SWAT guys called to Lucas. "But she parked in a handicapped slot. She's got a handicapped tag in the window."

"Watch her. That's a known behavior, and they grabbed Weimer from a van," Lucas said. "She might want to keep the van close so she can run."

"She's out," the SWAT guy called. "Dark hair, ponytail, sunglasses, she's got a scarf over her head . . . big purse. She's looking the place over. I mean, she's really looking the place over. She's going in . . ."

"That's her," Lucas said. "Everybody, set. Block the back door."

JULIET BRIAR, WHO thought Randy loved her, who thought she wouldn't do this anymore—she thought about Letty, who suggested that maybe she could become a nurse, and overnight, caring for Randy, she'd almost thought of herself as a nurse—and here she was, and she knew the guy was going to want a blow job, because that's what you gave guys for their birthdays. She felt the gorge rising at her throat, cast her head down, and walked toward the stairs.

Randy couldn't see any further than the two thousand dollars.

Randy couldn't see her at all, if there was money around.

AT THE TOP of the stairs, she lingered, just for a second, then walked down the carpeted hall, which smelled like smoke and beer and maybe a little pee. Found the number, took a breath, knocked.

A man appeared at the end of the hallway, wearing a helmet, carrying a gun, and he screamed at her, "On the floor. On the floor, on the floor . . ."

"What?" Her hands came up, in surrender.

"On the floor . . ."

And the door popped open and another man was there with a helmet and gun, pointed at her face. "On the floor . . ."

ACROSS THE ROAD, across a chain-link fence, behind a fast-food joint, Cohn and Cruz watched two guys in armor first block, and then rush, Briar's minivan.

"There you go, sugar bun," Cohn said.

"Cops," Cruz said. She put the car in gear. "Don't call me sugar bun."

The cops all stood around and looked at the weeping Briar, and Lucas said, "They were looking at us. They sent her in, and they were looking at us." He laughed, a sour sound. "Man, we took it right in the shorts."

18

THEY CUFFED THE woman, whose name was Juliet Briar, and took her down to the room where they were holding Justice Shafer, sat her down on a bed and told her that she was in a world of hurt.

"You don't even know what they'll do to you in that women's prison, they got wall-to-wall bull-dykes . . ." Shrake went on for a while, but stopped when Briar broke down again, weeping. Shafer said, "I could never be a cop, you know it? Doing this to a little kid. Why don't you pick on somebody a little older?"

"Because somebody a little older isn't part of a murder gang," Jenkins snarled at him.

"I'm not part of a murder gang," Briar wailed. "A guy gave me a hundred dollars to come over here and tell Justice that he was supposed to come to Half-Way Books and give him a ride . . ."

"He's got a truck," Lucas said.

"I didn't know that," she lied. She had them going, she could feel it. Mostly the truth, with a couple small variations, like Letty had taught her. "I just wanted a hundred dollars."

"What'd the guy look like?" Lucas asked. "The guy who gave you a hundred dollars?"

"Tall, thin, black hair, black mustache, blue eyes, really strong-looking. The woman was about as tall as I am. She had dark hair and . . ." She put her hand to her mouth, in sudden comprehension. "You thought I was *her*. They *tricked* you."

"How did you meet this guy?" Shrake asked. He was the bad cop. "Why would he give you a hundred dollars?"

"I didn't know why. He just said. I met him at Juicy's."

"You're too young for Juicy's," Shrake said.

"Not for a hamburger. I know a waitress there, but she wasn't working, but sometimes she gives me a hamburger for free. If I get hungry."

"So you were hustling a hamburger and this guy suddenly offers you a hundred bucks?" Jenkins was skeptical.

"I don't know," she said. "It sounded weird to me, too. I thought maybe . . . but he said I wouldn't have to do anything. Just pick Justice up and take him to Half-Way Books."

Half-Way Books was a comic and games store halfway between Minneapolis and St. Paul.

"Where'd you get the van?" Lucas asked.

"I borrowed it from a friend," she said.

"A crippled friend?" More skepticism.

"That's right. He gets a check from the government and sometimes he pays me to drive him around," she said. "I know how to run the power ramp out the side of the van and I push him up and down the ramps to his house."

"What's your friend's name?" Shrake asked.

She shook her head. "I don't want to get him in trouble."

Shafer grinned at her and gave her the thumbs-up. "Good for you. Take care of your friends."

"Shut up," Jenkins told him. To Briar: "Where do you go to school?"

"I dropped out. I'm working on my equivalent," she said. She let them see this lie, because she knew they expected it.

"Why'd you drop out?"

"I had to run away because my mom's boyfriend kept trying to fuck me," she said.

"You let him?" Shafer asked, suddenly serious.

"Of course not," she said to him. "That's why I ran away."

Jenkins looked at Shafer and shook his head, and then asked Briar, "You a hooker?"

"Why are you so mean to me?" she whimpered.

LUCAS SAID, "YOU sit on that bed and if you move your ass one inch, we will take you down and put you in jail." To Jenkins and Shrake: "Let's talk."

Out in the hall, Jenkins said, "She's a hook, and they picked up on that, and the fact that she looks like Diaz, and they sent her in here to see if anybody would jump. We did and they're gone."

Jenkins: "Now what?"

"We talk to the Secret Service, let them make the call," Shrake said.

"They don't want Shafer," Lucas said. "Why would they want the girl?"

INSIDE THE MOTEL room, Justice Shafer made his move; not having ever made one before, it was nervous and tentative. "Why's a good-looking woman like you running errands for assholes?" he asked.

"I wasn't sure he was an asshole," Briar said. She looked him over. "Are you a cowboy?"

He laughed, and she noticed that he had very white teeth. His best feature, maybe. "Yeah, I sat on top of some horses. Mostly, though, it was Gators."

She was puzzled. "Alligators?"

"No, a *Gator*. It's a John Deere four-wheeler. Or six-wheeler. Mostly use them instead of horses. Or I did. Mostly used for hauling shit around a ranch."

"I used to draw horses," she said.

"That's cool." He had a feeling that he was making progress, which was unprecedented. "I like the way you handled those cops. Those guys are jerks."

"I have a talent for finding assholes," she said, with the thinnest possibility of a smile. Then, "You really think I'm good-looking?"

"I think you're one of the most gorgeous things I ever saw," Shafer said, the sincerity shining through. "I wish you could come visit me sometime, down in Oklahoma."

LUCAS TALKED TO the lead Secret Service agent by phone, then he and Shrake and Jenkins went back into the room and found Shafer and Briar talking, and Lucas said, "Here's the deal. We're going to take you guys into St. Paul so you can talk to the Secret Service. They'll decide what we're gonna do."

"They owe me a truck and a bunch of gear," Shafer said. There was an assertive note in his voice that hadn't been there before.

"You'll get the truck," Lucas said. "I wouldn't push them on the gun."

"Hey, that gun is perfectly legal . . ."

Lucas held up a hand: "Justice, I'm just telling you. I wouldn't push them. A guy who's wandering around a national political convention with a .50-cal in his truck . . . he'd be best off not pushing too hard."

Shafer thought about that for a minute, then said, "I definitely want the truck. Then I'm going home to Oklahoma and I'm never coming back to this place. Minnesota sucks."

Jenkins said, "*Casse toi, pauvre con.*"

Shrake said to Lucas, "French lessons."

BACK AT THE apartment, Cruz told Lane and Lindy about the cops at the motel. "They're right on top of us," Lindy said. "We've got to get out of here."

Cohn was watching her: she was excited, pink-faced, scared, rattling around inside a thin cotton dress, and it was making him horny. Cruz, on the other hand, was pulling together, tighter and tighter.

"No. What they did was, after they found my place in L.A., they checked phone numbers and got the number from my phone," Cruz said. "That was the phone I used to call my friend, to get her out of the house. She did, and she's . . . safe. But they found the record and they traced that to the calls I made to Shafer. They're moving really fast. Really fast. I don't know how they dug Shafer out of the motel, but I've put enough word around about him, to wind them up, that they might have shaken down the whole motel and picked him up at random. So they get him, and they co-opt him, get him to call me. They still don't know where we are. They do know *who* we are. Brute and me, anyway. And Tate. They've digitized all the fingerprints and they'll nail Tate down in two minutes. If they find any connection to Jesse, they'll have him, too."

They all looked at Lane, who said, "I hung out with Tate a few years ago, in L.A., but never got busted with him. The only jobs I done with him I did with Brute."

"So you might still be clear," Cohn said. "Besides, they'll be looking for a guy with swastika tattoos. That little idea may save your bacon someday."

Cruz looked at her watch. "We're twelve hours away from hitting the hotel. If we can get through the twelve hours, we're good. I mean, we could have used Tate, but . . . we could still do this."

"We'll be in there for an hour," Lane said. "We'll be making noise. Christ . . ."

"We can do it," Cruz said. "If Lindy can make it as a desk clerk, we can pull it off."

Lindy shook her head, but she didn't say anything.

CRUZ HOOKED HER laptop to the television, took them through it, using PowerPoint, a series of photos and diagrams of the St. Andrews Hotel.

"We go in between three and four o'clock in the morning. Everything will be over for two hours, by then. Two cars here, in the parking ramp." She flashed the route with a laser pointer. "From the hotel, if we have to run, we have access to the ramp twenty-four hours a day, up the back stairs to the skyway, or down on the street, up through this stairway." She pointed out the access and escape routes on the photos. "We should walk it one last time, this evening. There'll be a night manager on duty, and a desk clerk, but all the restaurants and bars are closed. The safe-deposit room is right behind the reception desk. When I put my stuff in it, I got these photos . . . this is just a cell-phone cam, so excuse the quality."

The safe-deposit room was a six-by-eight-foot rectangle, with sixty steel-door boxes set into a concrete wall.

"What worries me is that whole 'one minute' business," Lane said. "Sixty boxes, sixty minutes. But if it's a minute and a half, then we're in for an hour and a half. If it's two minutes . . ."

"We get the point," Cohn said. "If we get pushed, we drop the tools and walk. But Don Walker said that he knows those boxes, and it won't take a minute. He says it'll take more like thirty to forty-five seconds . . . So now we're in for less than an hour."

"I would have liked to have drilled one myself," Lane said. "Just to *know*."

"I'M THINKING, IF we get in clean, I might want to talk to the desk clerk for a couple of minutes," Cohn said. "I'll take a rope along and strangle her a little, if I need to. Tell her we need the names of the boxes she put stuff in. The ones with the most jewelry, the most cash . . . She'll have an idea."

"That could work, if you're not herding other people

around," Cruz said, nodding. "If we get in clean, we move the manager and the clerk onto the floor in the safe-deposit room, put on the restraints. If they won't talk, maybe get rough with one of them . . ."

"That would cut the time down," Lane said. "If we knew which boxes to do first—or which ones were empty."

"We'll know which ones are empty, if there are any, because the desk will have both keys for them. For the ones being used, they'll only have one key. They keep their keys in a cupboard behind the front desk," Cruz said.

Cohn said, "The other thing is, I could take a look at what we're taking out. If we hit some certain point, we quit. Or, if nothing much is happening, if we're getting junk, if there's no cash, we wrap it up and take off."

Lindy asked, "Are you going to kill the clerk and the manager?"

Cohn said, "See when we get there. It's bad business, killing somebody when you don't have to. Tends to attract the eye." He didn't want her to know ahead of time.

Lindy was looking at the photograph of the safe-deposit room, and said, "Look at the wall plug-in. It looks like it's burnt."

They all looked and Cruz said, "Picture's not clear enough."

"I wonder if they had to drill a box, and it sucked down too many amps," Lane said. "If that outlet is burned out, we'd be fucked."

"That's a good catch, Lindy," Cruz said. "I didn't see that. There's another outlet on the wall behind me, behind where the camera is, but if there's a circuit problem . . . You know what, Jesse? You should stop at a hardware store and pick up one of those long heavy-duty extension cords. It's ninety-nine percent that we won't need one, but if we need one and don't have it . . ."

"I'll get one," Lane said.

WHEN THEY FINISHED working through it, they ordered out for pizza. Lindy met the pizza man at the door, overtipped him, and brought the pizza back into the living room and said, "What we need to do is ask, 'What if we didn't do this?' We know there are a bunch of cops on our asses. They know what Brute looks like, and Rosie. What if we walked away from it, and started planning another job somewhere else? We could get in the cars and be in Missouri by midnight. Jesse could be home by tomorrow morning . . ."

"Maybe not," Jesse said. "That's a long haul, south of St. Louis."

They all sat and chewed on the meat-eater's specials, with olives and mushrooms, and Cohn sighed and said, "The big money keeps getting harder. The trucks get better, the guards get better, there are more cops all the time. They got DNA now, and instant fingerprints . . . This money is right *there*. And Rosie and I gotta go deep this time. We've got to stay gone for *years*, maybe. If we pull this off tonight, we won't ever have to come back. I can move to India or New Zealand or South Africa and stay lost forever. If we have to come back for another job . . . I mean, the way fingerprints work now, if I get stopped coming across the border, and they print me, I could get busted right there."

"It'd still be safer," Lindy said. "I got a really bad feeling about this one, Brute. Really, really bad. We don't even know how the cops got onto this Shafer guy, we don't even know what they're doing."

Cohn sat chewing for a minute, then said, to Lane, "We can't do it without you. You in, or out?"

"If you make the call, I'm in," Lane said. "But Lindy has some points."

Cohn bobbed his head, smiled at Lindy. "You do have some points. You're smarter than I thought. Saw that thing on the outlet, too." He shook his head. "But fuck it: we're gonna do it. We're gonna do it, so let's get ready."

THEY FINISHED EATING and watched TV for a while, *Oprah*, and then Lane said, "I'm gonna go get that extension cord. Anybody want to come?"

Nobody did. Lindy was scared. "I'm afraid to go outside. This convention, I bet they got cameras everywhere. If they see me with you guys, I'm as bad off as you are, and I haven't even done anything."

Cohn nodded, stood up and stretched. "So you keep your head down," he said. "Once it gets dark, the cameras won't work so well." To Cruz: "Let's go walk to the hotel."

THE ST. ANDREWS was the modern counterpart to the aging St. Paul Hotel, as they stood side by side facing the CNBC TV platform set up in Rice Park, and conveniently outside the main security lines. The St. Paul was once the classiest place in town; now it was the second classiest, to the St. Andrews. Because they were only two blocks from the convention center, the richest Republican donors were stuffed into the two hotels, and the richest Republican nomination ball was set for that night in the St. Andrews ballroom, with John McCain himself scheduled to make a handshake tour and maybe dance with a couple of dowagers.

The main door of the St. Andrews faced Rice Park, but there were other entrances from the second-floor skyway, and out the back door onto St. Peter Street. Cohn and Cruz took their time, walking off the skyway escape route, with Cohn counting the steps. Cruz had already measured the distance, and, one afternoon in June, had put on jogging shorts and a T-shirt and jogged the route, timing herself, but she didn't disturb the count.

When they dropped down the stairs into the lobby, Cohn nodded at Cruz; he bought her timeline. Of course he did, because she wouldn't mess up anything that basic. At the same time, she appreciated the check. If anything went wrong, they needed to know their escape moves, and know them exactly.

Inside the hotel, they walked from the front desk to the bar, which was jammed with politicos and media, pouring it down as fast as it could be served. At the front desk, Cohn got a map from the desk clerk, consulting with her about the best route to the interstate entrance. And about the safe-deposit boxes: "I have a friend staying with me tonight, after the ball. If she needs one, would you have one available?"

The clerk shook her head. "As of now, we're all full. First time that's happened. Have you looked at your room safe?"

"She'll be wearing some fairly, mmm, important jewelry," Cohn said. "We thought that a real safe-deposit box might be more appropriate."

"If you can leave your name and room number, we can let you know about any availabilities," the woman offered.

Cohn shook his head: "Ah, it's six to eight hours. I guess we can do with the room safe. I thought I'd ask."

Back down the hall to Cruz: "They have no boxes available. They're all taken. I tried to impress her by telling her that we had some important jewelry coming in. She wasn't impressed. They must have goddamn Tiffany's in those boxes."

"Told you," Cruz said.

A guy went by with a broom and a dustpan, hurrying to clean up a mess somewhere. He was wearing a neat gray uniform, with his name in red script in a white oval. Cohn looked after him and asked, "How many janitors working overnight?"

"Couldn't find that out," Cruz said. "Probably a couple."

"Would have been nice to know."

THEY WALKED THROUGH the hotel for fifteen minutes, got a drink, watched the crowd, checked where the cops were. "The only really bad, serious, unpredictable factor would be if the protesters broke through the police lines and started trashing the area," Cruz said. "In that case, we walk away. There'd be cops every fifteen feet. Chaos. But from what I can tell, from walking it, they'll be kept well away, over to the north of the convention center. They're not going to allow anything down here. Lots of cops, but all out on the perimeters."

"The biggest problem won't be cops—the biggest problem is that we have to take down so many people that I can't control them," Cohn said. "Would have been easier with McCall. Goddamn McCall."

"You shoot him?" Cruz asked.

Cohn did a double take on the question. "What the fuck are you talking about?"

"Just . . . wondered," Cruz said. "If he was hurt, couldn't walk . . . I thought maybe you made sure."

"Jesus Christ," he said. The red-eyed anger was right there. "He was shot in the head and the heart by the cop. He was dead before he hit the ground. If I'd gone through first, it would've been me."

"Sorry," she said. But she wasn't; and she wasn't quite sure of Cohn's answer.

AN HOUR AND fifteen minutes after they left the apartment, they were back. They found Lane standing in the apartment, almost crouched, when they pushed the door open. He looked past them. Cohn asked, "What?"

"Is Lindy with you?"

"Ah, shit," Cohn said, looking around the apartment.

"She's not here," Lane said. "Her clothes are gone. So's the money. All of it."

AFTER A WHILE—a while—Cohn had to laugh. "She's fucked us, that's for sure. Now, there's no choice. Now, we have to do it. No calling it off."

"I should have thought of it," Cruz said. "It honest-to-God never occurred to me, because I didn't think anybody in the group would have the balls to do it to you."

"With good reason," Cohn said. "When I catch her, and I will, I'm going to kill her and anyone she's with. I'm gonna take my time with it, so she can see it coming."

Lane said, after a bit: "She has to know that."

Cohn looked at him.

Lane said, "She has to know that you'll kill her. So she has to believe that you won't be able to. She either figures the whole plan is fucked . . . or . . ."

"Or the bitch is gonna turn us in," Cohn said, erupting from the couch where he'd sat down. "Just to make sure . . ."

THEY PACKED UP, and wiped the apartment, in fifteen minutes. As they were stuffing what they could into their bags, Cohn said to Cruz, "You didn't say, 'I told you so.' You never wanted her here."

Cruz said, "I didn't have to say it. You knew it. No point in pouring salt in the wound. Wouldn't get us anywhere."

Then Cohn said, "You know what? She might turn us in—might get us raided. But she's not going to tell them about the hotel. She's not going to implicate herself. She's going to call in anonymously, and tell them that we're here. Call from a Target store. Like she's some citizen. Then, she's got to figure that whatever happens, she'll come out okay. If they get us, fine. If they get us at the hotel, that's fine. If they don't get us, and we get out with twenty million dollars, she figures that she can buy her way back in with us. Keep me from killing her. Tell us she panicked, and here's the money back . . ."

"Still can't take a chance," Cruz said. "Pack faster."

"But we're still good for the hotel," Cohn said.

"We can't do it, without Lindy as a desk clerk," Cruz said.

Cohn said, "You're the desk clerk." When Cruz opened her mouth to object, Cohn waved her down. "Yeah, yeah, you have to watch the radios. Well, watch them from the desk. Bring them with you. Anybody coming through the door will just think you're listening to the cops fighting the protesters."

Cruz said, "I've never been inside." That wasn't true. She'd just never been inside with Cohn.

"First time for everything," Cohn said. "We go with what we got, and you're what we got."

They were out of the building in fifteen minutes, and gone.

LUCAS LEFT SHAFER with the Secret Service. He'd be pushed around a little more, but nobody expected much: nobody mistook either Shafer or Briar for masterminds. Shafer was probably going to be locked up again, until after the convention and things had calmed down. After talking to Lucas, the Secret Service expressed little interest in Briar: her involvement was local, as far as they were concerned.

Lucas decided to take her back to the BCA, with Shrake trailing in her van. He took her up to the third floor, to the labs, where he sat her down with a guy who'd done the photo touch-ups. "When you're done with the pictures, you can take off," he told her. "Don't leave town. I'll need your address and phone number."

She gave him her mother's address and phone, and Lucas went down to his office, collected Shrake and Jenkins, and suggested that they go back to his house for an early dinner and to talk over the next move. He worked the phones as they drove along, trying to round up some help, and to warn the housekeeper that they were coming. He and Shrake and Jenkins trooped into the house together, and the housekeeper fixed them up with cold fried chicken, apple pie from the pie place on the corner, and milk and coffee.

"I want to suggest something," Lucas began, poking a drumstick at them. "That is, they must know the jig is up on these moneymen robberies. We ambushed them on the last one, and even if somebody got away, we killed one of them. They won't do another one."

Jenkins and Shrake both nodded.

"So, at this point, now that they know we have Shafer, there are really only two possibilities," Lucas continued. "First, they take off. They have a rep for being bold on strategy and careful on tactics. If they're gone, then there's nothing we can do about it. Put together what we've got, try to get as much publicity as we can, and let somebody else catch them."

"That's boring," Shrake said.

Lucas held up a finger: "The second option is, they go ahead with whatever they're planning. They know we're looking, they know we got to Shafer. But they also probably figured out how we got to Shafer—through Diaz's house in Venice. And they *still* were setting us up, taking a look at us. I think they were going ahead with whatever it is. They were checking on Shafer's status, and now they know."

"But what the hell is Shafer for?" Jenkins asked.

"I got one possibility," Lucas said. "It looks like they were lying to him from the start. He really doesn't have anything to do with the main job. But what if he's a diversion? Like this: they get him to come up here, go around to some quarries where he's sure to attract attention—he's shooting a .50-cal, for Christ's sake. They drag him through the gun stores, while *they* stay out of sight. They plant some shells, with his prints on them, up on the hillside . . ."

Jenkins picked it up: "So when they do whatever it is, they call nine-one-one and say they've seen Shafer with his gun. Cops rush in from all over."

"And the target is clear. Whatever it is. The commo guys start screaming about Shafer, and everybody starts running. There's panic . . ."

"What are they going to hit?" Shrake asked, as much to

himself as to the others, looking up at the ceiling. "They do banks and armored cars. God knows there's enough cash floating around."

"We need to scout some places. Armored-car warehouses. Someplace with . . . big money. Big money. We scout them, like we were going to hold them up—and then, if we find a couple of places that look particularly ripe, we set up ambushes."

They thought about it through their pie; halfway through, Shrake mumbled, "You know what? They're still here."

LETTY HAD BEEN lying on her bed, thinking about her next move, when they arrived, and she wandered into the kitchen as they were talking. Shrake said, "Hello, sweet thing," and Jenkins said, "The movie star."

Letty patted Shrake on his broad back and said, "If only you were forty years younger," which made Lucas laugh so hard that he choked. "A piece of chicken breading went up my nose," he said. Shrake pretended to sulk: "For Christ's sakes, I *am* only forty."

"And in good shape," Letty said. "For a guy that old."

"What're you up to?" Lucas asked.

"Not much going on tomorrow. I'm going to write the *Mockingbird* essay tonight, I guess."

"Better than messing around with hookers," Lucas said. He gave a short recap to Shrake and Jenkins.

"Sounds like a good story to me," Shrake said.

"You get better-looking by the minute," Letty said.

Jenkins squinted at her: "How old are you?"

"Fourteen."

Jenkins looked at Lucas and shook his head: "Jesus Christ, Lucas, you *attract* trouble. You're a fuuuhhh . . . trouble magnet."

"Was that a French trouble magnet?" Letty asked. "A freaky trouble magnet? A fancy trouble magnet? A . . ."

"Fuck off, kid," Jenkins said.

AFTER TRADING A few more insults with Jenkins and Shrake, Letty got a single-serving milk bottle and walked back up to her bedroom, sat on the bed and thought about it some more.

What if Randy killed Juliet? If he did, it'd be Letty's fault. The thought went round and round like a carousel, and always came back, no matter how she twisted it up.

What if Randy did something so *awful* . . .

And yet she had the feeling that Randy was too manipulative for that. He'd fly into a rage, he'd beat Juliet, maybe, but he wouldn't kill her. She was his sexual ATM. If she timed it just right, if she listened outside the house, she could have the police there within a couple of minutes.

And the original threat remained. If Lucas found out that Randy had been stalking Letty, he'd kill Randy. If he did it with his usual intelligence, it would be taken care of quietly enough; but now, because of Letty, Jennifer knew about it. What she would do, if Randy disappeared, Letty didn't know. She really *was* a goody-goody.

One way or another, Letty had to make the call. Had to make it.

19

THEY MET IN a BCA classroom as the sun was sliding down in the west, everyone that Lucas had managed to scrape up: two St. Paul detectives, six BCA agents who volunteered time because of the Benson shooting—more would have volunteered, but they were already on the street, working the convention—and two detectives from Minneapolis, along with Shrake and Jenkins. Two Secret Service agents sat in the back, but the Secret Service was so pressed by the night's political ceremonies that they couldn't free any men for the actual search.

Lucas unrolled oversized printouts from the county assessor's office, showing every building in downtown St. Paul. One of the assessor's men had gone over the maps and marked the buildings that had either rental apartments, or condos that somebody might rent out on their own.

"We didn't have time to write all this stuff on each individual map, so everybody take a contact sheet from Carol," Lucas said. Carol waved a stack of Xerox paper at them. "On it, you'll find the latest phone number we have for the condo association president or the apartment manager. Talk to them face-to-face."

They had too many buildings, but divided them up as well as they could, some of them getting a few large ones, some getting a bigger batch of smaller ones.

"Warn the president or the manager or the owner, or whoever you get, not to go nosing around on his own, or make any inquiries. We're pretty sure they're in there somewhere, and if we miss them, we'll either have to start over or figure something else out. Carol is passing out updated photos of the suspects, changing hair color and other stuff according to what we've found out about them."

There were the usual questions, and reiterations, and some confusion about geography on the part of the out-of-towners who didn't know the downtown area, but they got everybody oriented and ready to go by dark.

"Listen, people," Lucas concluded. "Do not—DO NOT—try to take these guys. They've already killed four cops, one of them our own guy, another one who was helping us out over in Hudson. If you get a line on them—anything at all—I can pull our BCA SWAT guys off the street and go in and take them down. These guys have a reputation for hitting armored cars and other hard targets, and they have access to any kind of firearms that they want. These are tough guys and we could be talking heavy weapons. Let SWAT do their thing. We don't need any more dead heroes."

THEY ALL WENT out in pairs, except for Lucas, who stuck with Shrake and Jenkins. The three of them took the two largest condos. Shrake said, "I bet they picked the biggest one they could get into. In a small one, somebody's always going to notice a stranger. Somebody'll try to make friends. In a big one, there are people coming and going all the time."

Lucas nodded: "I'll buy that."

"If that fuckin' Flowers was here, we could split up, two and two," Jenkins said.

"He's coming, but he was way the hell out in Bigelow," Lucas said.

"Where's that?"

"I don't know, but it's way the hell out."

THE TWO CONDOS were kitty-corner from each other in the same block, with a shopping area and offices in a mall between them. They parked underground and walked around the block to the larger of the two buildings. On the way, they ran into a walking train of people in formal wear, women with glittery icefalls of diamonds around their necks, down their breasts. They were heading up the skyways toward the convention hotels at the top of the hill.

Shrake: "She's got more money on her tits than I got on my house."

"Both our houses. Together," Jenkins said, looking after them.

Lucas's phone rang, and he looked at the screen. Del. Lucas punched him up and Del said, "It's a boy."

"You knew that," Lucas said, and "Congratulations. Jeez, whoever would have even believed it, Del." He passed the phone to the other two, who gave Del the raft of shit that he'd expect, and both congratulated him, and Lucas took the phone back and Del said, "I gotta get some sleep. I think I'm more beat up than my old lady."

"I doubt it," Lucas said.

"What're you doing?"

"House to house," Lucas said, deliberately discouraging him. "You wouldn't be interested."

"I'm going home," Del said.

AT THE APARTMENT, another jeweled train went by, and they gawked, and Jenkins said, "These aren't even the rich ones. The rich ones are *staying* up there. These ones have to *walk* in."

Lucas called the association president, whose name was Dan Eller, and Eller buzzed them up to his apartment on the twenty-fourth floor and met them at the door. He was bald, mustachioed, genially overweight, and retired.

After Lucas explained, Eller said, "The problem is, we have rentals here, too, and those people are coming and going all the time."

"How about the people on the floors? Who knows who?"

"I can help you with the condo levels, but I don't know about the rentals," Eller said. "I mean, I know a couple people, maybe they could chain you up with more."

"You haven't seen anybody who looks like these guys . . . ?"

"No, and I'm around the building a lot," Eller said. "Pretty much on every condo floor every day. We've been having roof and drainage problems, and it's gonna cost to fix, so I've been politicking."

"People have rented out their condos, though, right?"

"Yup. A few. People have cabins up north. They stay up there and make money down here on the convention."

Eller gave them a list of names—"most of them are older, they'll be home"—and also the name and phone number of his opposite number in the other apartment building. "That building's all rentals, but they set up an apartment association, and Ken runs it. More like a tenants' union than a condo association."

THEY DECIDED TO start at the top, and rode the elevator up, and when they got off, Jenkins stopped, and when Lucas and Shrake looked back, he said, "You know what? We look exactly like a bunch of flatfoots."

Lucas looked at them, and himself, and sighed and nodded. "All right. You two guys do this building. I'm gonna go talk to this Ken guy in the other building."

"This is feeling kind of weak," Shrake said, turning around to look at the empty hallways. "I got that empty-tank feeling."

"Maybe it'll go away when you do some actual work," Lucas said.

BUT IT WAS the worst kind of police work, Lucas thought, as he took the elevator back down. The kind of stuff done as a last resort, talking to people who you had no reason to suspect knew anything at all. Or maybe, he thought, like church bingo; sort of dull and hopeless, but *somebody* was going to win. Just not you.

On the street level again, another two glittery couples brushed past, aiming up the hill. Four cops went down the street on horses; horses seemed to be everywhere. The cops looked him over, but the last cop lifted a hand and said, "Davenport," and Lucas waved back, and pushed into the lobby of the apartment building.

Ken Jacobsen, who lived on the eighteenth floor of the second tower, looked at the photographs and shook his head. He'd been cooking liver and onions, and the apartment was fragrant with the gravy. "Let me give you some names, people to talk to."

"Are you around the building much?"

"Off and on," Jacobsen said. "But we're not directly responsible for the buildings. We're not owners, so it's not quite like it is in Dan's condo."

As Lucas was going out the door, Jacobsen said, "Hey, let me make a call, here. I'll see if the Hassans are still in the building."

The Hassans were two cell-phone-equipped Ethiopian janitors; their English wasn't good, but was good enough that Lucas was sure that they hadn't seen Cohn or Diaz.

"Terrorists?" one of the Hassans asked.

Lucas nodded. "If you see them, call nine-one-one."

"Nine-one-one," said the second Hassan. "We will do."

LUCAS TALKED TO two widows and a widower, and was growing depressed, looking into their tiny apartments, when a call came in from one of the Minneapolis detectives: "We got a hit. A good one."

"Good one?" Lucas asked, the evening suddenly brighter.

"Old lady in Park Vista says she saw a guy going through with a woman. Tall, thin, dark hair, mustache. She said the woman looked like a Filipino, but that seemed close enough—the picture you gave us does look sort of like something else. So I showed her the mug shots, and she's not sure on the woman, but she's fairly sure about Cohn. She said it's him."

"Terrific. This is terrific," Lucas said. "You said Park Vista? Where's that at?"

The cop told him, and Lucas said, "Hell, you're right down the street."

"It's Park Vista Two, exactly. It's the door on the left. This old lady was no dummy—I got a good feeling about it, man."

"Okay. I'm coming over, I'm bringing my guys, I'm cranking up the SWAT."

"Listen, I can watch the lobby and the door, but my partner thinks you should bring the SWAT in through the basement," the cop said. "They can bring their van right down the front ramp—it'll take a Sprinter van, the manager says, so the SWAT stuff should fit. From there, it's either up the elevators or up the stairs."

"I'll hook you up with the SWAT guy. His name is Able Peterson, you can talk him in. This is good work, man."

HE CALLED THE SWAT commander: "Able, we need you."

"Goddamnit, Lucas, you got them? Where?"

Lucas gave them the address off Mears Park. "It's the new ones, the ones with the colored panels. It's the one on the left as you look at them from the front. I've got the name of a guy who can let you into the basement level, the parking level."

"It'll take me twenty minutes to break off here, get my guys ready to go."

He gave Peterson the cop's phone number, and then called Shrake and Jenkins: "We've got a line on them."

"Where at?" Jenkins asked.

"Park Vista—those big twin buildings on Mears Park."

"That'd be about right. Half-full, big buildings . . ."

"Two minutes," Lucas said.

LETTY DECIDED THAT she had no choice—or rather, she had a choice, but both options were bad. One was bad for Briar, one was bad for Lucas, and that tipped the balance. You took care of your own.

She'd gotten Whitcomb's phone number the first day; now she rode her bike across town to the Capitol lawn as the evening came on. There were a couple thousand people floating around, after some kind of event, maybe a music thing. A Channel Three van was parked at the bottom of the hill, on the street. Among the crowd she spotted a group of frat boys from the University of Minnesota, who were towing some sorority girls around in little red wagons, tiny floats for Obama. She chained her bike to a tree and jogged over.

One of them, a tall young man with green soap-spiked hair that made him look a little like the Statue of Liberty, was wearing a homemade button that read "Greeks for Obama," and Letty grabbed him.

"You wanna be a TV star?" she asked him.

"Shit, yes."

"Try not to say 'shit' when you're on camera," she said. "I'll be right back."

She jogged down the hill to the van and knocked on the door.

Lois looked out at her: "Letty," she said. She seemed abashed, having ratted Letty out a couple days before. "Are you supposed to be here?"

Letty said, "Could we do a minute on some kids from the U? They're pretty funny . . . Frats for Obama . . ."

Lois said, "If they're coherent . . ."

Letty said, "Get a camera . . ." and she headed back up the hill to the frat boys. They did a minute, and then Letty told Lois that she better head home, but she wanted one last look around. Lois said, "Okay. And that frat boy stuff—not too bad."

"At least he didn't say 'shit' on TV," Letty said.

ALIBI.

Two minutes later, she was on her bike, the streets not so well-lit now, but she had her switchblade and the confidence that she could move quickly enough, and in the dark, that nobody could move on her. She was right.

From an outdoor phone at Metro U, six blocks from Whitcomb's house, she made the call: tried to put on an accent that she'd picked up from HBO specials on hookers. A male voice, and she said, "Randy, you know that bitch of yours is hanging out with the Davenport kid? Thought you'd like to know."

"What? What?"

"That bitch of yours is hanging out with the Davenport kid, told her what you were up to. You take care."

"This ain't Randy. Wait a minute."

Letty groaned. Wrong guy. Then Randy came up. "What?"

She did it all over again, then clicked off, got back on

her bike, headed up the hill toward Whitcomb's house, pumping as hard as she could.

ON THE WAY over to Park Vista, Lucas called Operations at the BCA and got an urgent warrant started: "I don't care who you call, but I need it in five minutes. If we don't get it, we might have to go anyway, because these guys are killers and they're going to kill again, and maybe tonight."

All recorded: building a case for a warrantless entry.

They walked over separately, keeping in mind that together, they looked like flatfoots. Lucas found the Minneapolis cop standing with a civilian, by the electronic gate on the parking ramp. Lucas said, "You're Doug Swanson."

"Swenson." The cop nodded and said, "My partner's Dan Long. We got a call from your SWAT guy, he's on the way." Swenson looked at his watch. "They're still ten or fifteen minutes out."

"What about the apartment?" Lucas asked.

Swenson flicked a finger at the civilian. "This is Carl Bishop, he's the manager. He gave us a key to an apartment down the hall. Dan's up there with the key in the lock, and if anything moves in their apartment, or anybody comes down the hall, he'll go on in, like they just caught him getting home . . ."

Jenkins: "We oughta get out of sight. If they're out and they come down that entry ramp and see us, it'll be the OK Corral."

THEY MOVED INSIDE, to the lobby, and then into the mail room, looking at the backside of three hundred mailboxes. Lucas called Able Peterson and asked, "How long?"

"We're staging, we're getting armored up. I sent Dick McGuire over there with some listening gear. He ought to be coming in the door with a carry-on suitcase. If you could get him into an adjacent apartment . . ."

Both of the adjacent apartments were occupied, but one of them was occupied by a retired cop who said he'd be happy to see them. About that time, McGuire came through the front door and they sent him up, after warning Dan Long that McGuire was a cop, and on the way.

Two minutes later, McGuire was at work, and two minutes after that, he called Lucas and said, "I can't hear a thing. If there's anybody there, I should be able to hear something. I should be able to hear them breathing—I think the place is empty."

"Gotta go in," Lucas said. "Could be somebody dead . . . maybe there's something about the walls that's defeating the listening gear."

"Wait four minutes for SWAT, send them right up," Shrake said. Thinking about the warrant. "That gives it at least the appearance of desperation."

LUCAS CALLED PETERSON again and passed on the word from McGuire, which Peterson had just gotten directly.

"Get here," Lucas said.

"We're loading. We're two blocks away. We'll be there in one minute."

THE SWAT TEAM came right down the ramp, unloaded, and Lucas briefed them on the situation, and the manager drew a sketch of the interior of the apartment. "No chances," Lucas told Peterson. "Blow the door down, flash-bangs, ready to rock." He got on the phone again, to McGuire: "Clear that apartment."

All but two of the SWAT team members started up and Lucas called the apartment on the other side, got no answer, and then the one across the hall, and outlined the situation:

"Some policemen are on the way up, they'll tell you where to go. Stay inside until your doorbell rings . . ."

The other two SWAT guys, both armed with automatic weapons, were stationed in the garage, watching the only entry. Lucas told Shrake and Jenkins to wait with the manager, in the mail room, where they could watch the lobby unseen through the glass fronts on the mailboxes.

"I'm going up," Lucas said.

"Oughta be up there by now," Jenkins said, looking at his watch.

A call from Operations, as he waited for the elevator: "You've got a warrant."

"Great."

He'd just stepped into the hall when he heard the door go down and then the flash-bang, and then the cops were inside: no gunfire, but a half dozen doors popped open up and down the hallways, and he heard somebody shout, "Police, please go back inside!"

Lucas hustled past a woman with her hair in curlers, and a copy of *Vanity Fair* in her hands, and said, "Best to go back inside," and she said, "No chance—this is too good," and he went on down the hall.

Peterson was waiting behind the door, which was broken around the knob, but still hung from its hinges. "Nothing. If they were here, they cleaned up."

"Ah . . ." Lucas said. "But—they might be coming back. We gotta have somebody wait for them. Close the door the best you can, settle down inside. Give me a guy who can watch things from the lobby, and keep those guys down in the garage."

"Oughta wait for the crime-scene crew," Peterson said. "We shouldn't wait inside."

Lucas shook his head: "I don't have time to lay it all out for you, but we decided that they're probably planning to go through with this job, whatever it is. There's reason to think that they're staying. This apartment"—he gestured around the empty rooms—"could mean anything. If they stayed, they've got to be close to pulling the trigger on whatever they're doing. They could be planning to stop here on the way out. As far as they know, it's still good."

Peterson shrugged. "On your head."

"Yup. It is. Have your guys check every inch of this place. We can't afford to miss anything."

"I'll stay in touch," Peterson said. "Been easier if we'd finished it here."

LUCAS RODE BACK down with the SWAT guy designated to hang in the mail room, left him there like Third-Class Mail, and collected Shrake and Jenkins.

"Dumpster dive," he said, on the way down to the garage.

"Man, I'm wearing some high-end threads," Shrake said. "Why don't you ever get me when I'm wearing jeans?"

"Maybe it'll be the first bag; maybe it'll take one minute," Lucas said.

"Fat chance. We're gonna smell like rotten bananas, rotten tomatoes, or rotten eggs," Shrake said. "It's always one of those."

"Not always," Jenkins said. "Sometimes there are baby diapers, and then you smell like baby shit."

"I don't believe they brought a baby with them," Lucas said. "You can sniff all the bags, and we can skip the baby-shit ones."

"Terrific . . ."

THE BAG WASN'T first, second, or third, but they thought it might be the fourth, a regular black-plastic garbage bag with a pull-tie, and filled with fast-food remnants and pizza boxes and an unused box of plastic garbage bags. Why would anyone throw away a perfectly good box of trash bags, unless they were cleaning out an apartment and had no further use for them? They took a closer look, and among other things, found a receipt for a wrench and a shovel and a box of garbage bags from a Home Depot in Hudson, Wisconsin.

"Sonofabitch. That's one block from the motel where the Hudson cop was shot," Lucas said. "I mean, one block. The store's right there."

"So this is them," Shrake said, emptying the last of the trash on the floor. "What else is in here?"

A few things: receipts in paper sacks. A receipt for two golf shirts at Macy's, size extra large, $69 each; a receipt from a sandwich shop on Wabasha Street a couple of blocks south of Macy's; a receipt for a box of bonbons from the St. Andrews Hotel. All paid in cash. A pizza box from Perruzi's, a higher-end Italian place down the street from the convention center. "It's all right here, right downtown, except for the stuff from Hudson," Shrake said.

"I gotta think the job is, too," Lucas said.

"Got some cash pickups at the bars, by the O'Meara armored cars. That's about the biggest cash deal downtown," Shrake said. "The O'Meara warehouse is pretty well protected . . ."

Jenkins shook his head. "Maybe they finally broke, and took off."

THEY LEFT THE SWAT team in place. "You have to plan to stay until daylight," Lucas told Able Peterson. "They may pull the job, whatever it is, and duck back here."

"Why?" Peterson asked.

"Get their shit together," Lucas said. "Maybe they've got a car stashed in the parking garage."

Peterson was skeptical, but agreed to stay—which was what Lucas wanted in the first place. Cohn wasn't coming back, but he might be around somewhere, and Lucas wanted the SWAT guys in his hip pocket, not out wandering around St. Paul.

He'd left Peterson, heading downstairs, when his phone

rang; took it out, saw that he'd missed three calls, all from Weather, while he was in the underground ramp—no reception there—and answered: "Weather?"

"Lucas, where have you been?" She sounded frightened.

"Working—out of range, in a parking ramp."

"Oh, God, I've been frantic. It's Letty."

20

RANDY WHITCOMB HAD checked himself out of the hospital against medical advice, and they drove across town to the house, the asshole guy and his girlfriend trailing behind. They got the asshole guy's cash at the house, and then Briar, leaking tears again—Whitcomb told Ranch that he'd beat it out of her eventually, dry her up—had gone off to the motel, with the assholes right behind her.

So Whitcomb had big money but no way to get downtown to spend it. Ranch woke up when Whitcomb came in with the money, and offered to walk downtown and find George, but there was no way that Whitcomb would trust Ranch with more than two dollars, and maybe not that.

So they waited, and stewed, and sweated, as *hours* crawled by, and Ranch even went down the hill where a pill seller sometimes set up, but the guy was not there, and he came back in a mood and he and Whitcomb had a screaming argument, because both of them were seeping back to a drugless world.

Ranch shouted, "You're a tit. You're gonna grab this cop's kid, and what do we do? Nothin.' Not a fuckin' thing, you tit."

"Gonna get her," Whitcomb shouted.

"Bullshit, because you're a tit," Ranch shouted back.

"Gonna get her. Gonna suck some smoke, then we're gonna get her. You're gonna fuck her. I'm gonna beat her with my stick until she's hamburger."

"Maybe I'll fuck her, if I say so," Ranch shouted. "I'm not gonna fuck her because you say so, because you're a tit."

"This is my house . . ."

Then Ranch tumbled facedown into a beanbag chair and didn't move anymore, though he snored every couple of minutes. Whitcomb rolled between the kitchen and living-room windows, looking out, looking out, looking out . . .

BRIAR GOT BACK after dark. Whitcomb had whipped himself into several furies, and had gone into a half dozen emotional slumps, looking at the two thousand dollars, *right there*, and not a fuckin' thing in the house, wouldn't you know it, and when the van finally turned into the driveway, he could hardly believe it.

He met Briar at the door. "You fuckin' moron, you, we *needed* that van. I'm fuckin' crippled . . ."

"I got arrested by the cops," Briar said.

RANCH WOKE IN the beanbag chair. He was used to the disappearance of large parts of his life. Sometimes, he passed out at ten o'clock in the morning, and when he woke up, it was nine o'clock in the morning—some other morning. At first, the time changes were disorienting, but over the course of a couple of years, he got used to it. He simply gave up on time—now life was daytime and nighttime, strung along like beads on a string, and the minute, hour, and date were irrelevant.

When he woke up in this darktime, he could hear Whitcomb screaming in the kitchen, which wasn't unusual, and wouldn't normally have shaken him out. He pushed up, and a string of drool drained away from his lip. He wiped it off, heard the noise that woke him. Telephone, right under his head.

WHITCOMB HAD BACKED Briar against the wall, extracting details of her arrest, when Ranch wandered in from the other room and handed Whitcomb a phone and said, "I got George, scrote."

"Who you callin' fuckin' *scrote*, you fuckin' douche bag?" Whitcomb shouted, and then stopped, as Ranch's words penetrated, and said, "George?"

Ten minutes later, Whitcomb was careening around the living room and kitchen in the wheelchair, waving his head-shop pearlescent-gold-twirl glass pipe over his head, shouting, "George is on the way." And he whirled in the chair and chanted it, waving the pipe as though directing an orchestra: "George is on the way; George is on the way; George is on the way."

He was rolling back toward Briar, pipe over his head, spasmodically jerking it back and forth, in time to the arrhythmic chant, and it slipped from his sweaty fingers in a long dangerous arc. Briar reached out to catch it, fumbled it, fumbled it again, and then it hit the side of the stove and shattered, and they all three stood looking at it, in all its pieces, scattered along the kitchen floor.

Whitcomb's mouth opened and closed, and, stunned, he said to Briar, "My fuckin' pipe. You broke my fuckin' pipe."

He looked around for his stick, saw it, looked back at her, hate in his eyes, but then Ranch said, "Fucked-up yuppie pipe anyway. You waste half the smoke; I can make a better pipe in eleven minutes, yo."

Whitcomb said, "Make a pipe?"

RANCH HAD SKILLS: there were a few ancient tools under the sink, left behind by a previous tenant. Included in the greasy, cobwebbed old green canvas bag was a pair of side-cutters and a rusty file. Ranch unscrewed a forty-watt GE Crystal Clear bulb from a sconce at the bottom of the stairs, and said, "A perfect bulb. Don't even have to wash the motherfucking white shit out."

"What white shit?" Whitcomb asked.

"Some bulbs got this white shit in them," Whitcomb said. "Tastes terrible."

They gathered at the kitchen table, and Ranch used the side-cutters to cut off the contact at the bottom of the bulb, and then carefully crack out the ceramic insulator that had held the contact in place. With the insulator gone, he broke the glass rod that held the light filament in place, and pulled the broken pieces of glass out of the bottom of the bulb by the wires that led to the filament. All that, he brushed onto the floor.

"This is the hard part," he said. "This is where you can fuck up if you don't know what you're doing."

Using the edge of the file, he scratched a line across the glass of the bulb, then went back into the scratch and drew the file across it again, and again, slowly, carefully. In two minutes, he'd opened a narrow hole to the inside.

"Really careful now, so's we don't break the glass . . ." He was breathing his words, holding the bulb, working the file with some delicacy. In another two minutes, he had a hole an inch long and an eighth of an inch wide. "That's where you load the shit," he said. And, "I need some tape."

They didn't have any tape, but Briar remembered that one of the seats in the van had a piece of duct tape on it, patching a rip, and she went out and peeled it off and brought it back inside, and Ranch pronounced it perfect. Using pliers, he made five small cuts in the aluminum screw-in base on the bulb, pushed the ragged tabs across the width of the bulb until they formed a small hole, and pushed a McDonald's straw into the hole and taped it in place.

"There you go," he said, holding up the bulb. "Best pipe in the world. You'll see."

Whitcomb took it, his hand shaking, looked at it, and said, "That's the greatest fuckin' thing I ever saw."

Even Briar was proud of Ranch.

Then George came.

George had the crank in little Ziploc baggies, and they bought three. Whitcomb, eyes narrowed, cracked one of the baggies, said, "Pretty fuckin' yellow."

"It's right out of the coffeepot," George said. He was a short fat man with short black curly hair, most of it sticking out of the neckline of a Vikings T-shirt; and he wore cargo shorts and Nike shoes. "Just come out that way, but I got no dissatisfied customers. It's good shit."

Whitcomb dampened a finger with his tongue, stuck the finger in the bag, picked up a schmear of the crank, tasted it and winced: the taste was bitter, cutting, perfect. No sugar, no salt, no baking soda.

"Okay." He passed over the money; George looked at each bill, then tucked it in his side pocket. "Call me."

"How's business?" Ranch asked, his eyes on the baggies in Whitcomb's hands.

"Shit. Republicans don't want nothing from me," George said. "They go for the high-end stuff, no fuckin' redneck drippin's."

"This shit's better than coke," Whitcomb said. "It's like somebody sticks a fuckin' knife in your brain."

George bobbed his head and said, "Party on, men," and he was gone. George was a teetotaler.

CRANK—ENOUGH OF it—affected Whitcomb the way a paddle affects a Ping-Pong ball. They loaded the GE crank pipe with a spoon of the stuff, melted it down with a Bic lighter, watched it bubble and then begin to smoke. Whitcomb took the first hit, closing his eyes, letting it scream into him . . . He and Ranch blew smoke at each other for a while, long snakes of black lung-leavings that held together in the air like dirigibles, and then, after a while, like the *Hindenburg*, fell apart. Then Ranch ripped off his shirt, backed against a wall and sat down, his eyes going goofy and red, into zombie mode, shaking with the intensity of it; but Whitcomb began crashing around in the chair, pumping with one arm, then the other, and then both, crashing into walls, chairs, the table, singing, "Oh, Black Betty, Bam-a-Lam," the words all screwed up, "Black Betty got fat lips, Bam-a-Lam," the "Bam-a-Lam" punctuated by a variety of impacts as he ricocheted around the two rooms and the bathroom that he could get at.

They went back to the pipe again, and again, and again . . .

THEN LETTY CALLED.

Ranch got the phone again, because, again, it was under his head, as he lay facedown on the beanbag chair; he had death in a corner, and was pushing on it, hard. Then the phone rang, and his life was saved.

"'Lo?"

Whitcomb, the comet, hurtled out of the kitchen and shouted, "Fuck you fuck you fuck you fuck you . . ."

Ranch listened for a moment, then said, ". . . this ain't Randy . . ."

He gave Briar a peculiar look and struggled to his feet, got in front of Whitcomb and caught the chair and when Whitcomb screamed at him, he put his face an inch from Whitcomb's and howled back, until Whitcomb stopped, and then he said, "Bitch needs to talk to you, and you needs to talk to her."

"Yeah?" Whitcomb took the phone and said, "This is me? Who's this?"

He listened, then looked at the phone, and then at Briar,

then tossed the phone in the corner and said to Briar, "Bitch says you been talking to Davenport."

"No," she said, but there was a lie in her eyes, somewhere, and Whitcomb saw it.

"Don't tell me 'no,' bitch, I can see you lyin'." Whitcomb's face was purple with rage and the crank. "Get down. Get down, bitch. Ranch, don't let this bitch out, she been talking to the cops . . ."

They shouted at her, made her confess, though the confession didn't make any sense, and Randy got his stick and made her get naked on her hands and knees like a dog and he beat her until she collapsed, her back red with blood, and then he said, "Ranch: fuck her in the ass, fuck her in the ass, fuck her in the ass . . ."

"Randy . . ." She was in a haze of pain and blood, and tried to crawl away and felt a foot on her back. Not Whitcomb; Whitcomb's feet didn't work.

"Fuck her fuck her fuck her . . ."

LETTY RODE UP the hill, saw lights at the house, ditched the bike, walked across the yard past the van, and listened; and heard the screaming: "Fuck her fuck her fuck her . . ." ran back to her bike, down the hill and to the pay phone and she called 911.

"I think somebody's being murdered," she said. "I can hear the woman screaming . . ."

RANCH PULLED UP his Jockey shorts and Briar crawled across the kitchen to her dress, and Whitcomb, exhausted, said, "We need to get George. Everybody in the van."

Ranch: "George," and he started toward the door, but missed the door and cracked his head on the doorjamb and fell down.

Whitcomb screamed, "Get up, you fuckin' turd," and Ranch got to his knees, and then his feet, and said, "You fuckin' scrote," and Whitcomb shouted at Briar, who was huddled in a corner, trying to cover herself with her dress, "Into the fuckin' van; we find George again, into the fuckin' van."

Ranch was all for it; $250 in crank all gone. He hovered over Briar, his insane face a half inch from hers, howling, no words, a dog howl, and she struggled into her dress, the blood on her back seeping through the thin cotton, and Randy marched them out the back door and down the ramp.

LETTY WAS THERE, bouncing her bike across the yard. They didn't see her immediately, and she climbed off and dropped the bike: Whitcomb, Briar, and Ranch looked like some kind of surrealist parade, something from a masked ball, a man in a wheelchair pumping a stick like a drum major, screaming unintelligibly, followed by Briar, hurt, staggering, bloody, and then Ranch, in his Jockey shorts, holding on to the ramp railing, barely able to walk, still howling like a dog.

Then Whitcomb saw Letty.

He hit the brakes, and Briar stumbled, and one of the chair's wheels went off the concrete at the bottom of the ramp. And the chair tilted and Whitcomb screamed at her, and she wrenched it upright.

Whitcomb jabbed the stick at Letty and screamed, "There she is. There she is. Get her! Get her! Ranch, get her!"

Letty crossed the yard and hit the button on the switchblade and the blade flicked out. "I'm going to cut your head off," she said to Whitcomb.

Whitcomb saw the knife and recoiled, then lifted his stick overhead with both hands and screamed at Briar, "Push me, push me," and at Ranch, "Get her, get her," and Ranch stumbled off the ramp and Letty turned the knife at him, and Ranch ran at her and she ducked away and he kept going in a straight line and then stumbled over his own feet and fell facedown.

Letty turned back to Whitcomb, who was screaming at Briar, "Push me, get her," and unsatisfied with the progress, turned and slashed at Briar with the butt of his punishment stick. The butt caught her on the end of the nose and she went down, bleeding from the nose, and he screamed at her, "Get up, you bitch; you fuckin' . . . gonna cut you a new goddamn nose . . ."

She got to her feet and Letty shouted, "Juliet, go back, go back in the house, the police are coming," but Briar pulled the wheelchair around in a circle and Whitcomb slashed at her again and screamed, "Not that way, you cunt, not that way . . ."

She'd aimed the chair at the back of the yard. The last renters had had a bad dog they had kept staked out at the back of the house, and the dog had worn the grass down to hard dirt; and behind that was the bluff that led down into Swede Hollow.

Briar said, "I loved you, Randy," and then she began pushing the chair toward the bluff, faster and faster, Letty calling, "Juliet, Juliet . . ." Ranch staggered to his feet and Letty turned toward him, pointing the knife at his chest, but he staggered around her, after Briar, as though he were trying to catch them—no chance of that; one of his legs was working harder than the other and he couldn't keep going in a straight line, but tended off in circles.

Whitcomb was still trying to thrash back at Briar with his stick, and tried to brake with one hand, but Briar was stronger than he was and at the end of the yard he grabbed both wheels and shouted, "Oh, shit," and she ran him right off the edge and Randy Whitcomb went screaming sixty miles an hour down a seventy-degree slope into a wall of trees.

He hit it with the impact of a small car driving into a brick wall.

Briar stood, looking down, stunned by what she'd done.

Letty came up and looked over the edge; then Ranch got there, well away from Letty, and he peered down the bluff and then said to Briar, "You fuck."

Letty heard a siren: still a way out, but not too far. She said to Briar: "Juliet, don't tell them I was here. Lie. Okay? Don't tell them."

Briar nodded dumbly, and Letty ran across the yard, folded the switchblade, climbed on her bike, bumped back across the yard, across the street, and headed down the hill. The cop car was a block over, on Seventh, as they passed, so she managed to get down the hill unseen, pedaling furiously, through the backstreets, to the Capitol. There, she stopped to turn her phone on, and found a dozen calls from home, and two more from Lucas's cell.

LUCAS HAD GOTTEN a fragmentary story from Carey, who'd been called by Weather when Letty hadn't gotten home on time. "I don't want her to think I'm betraying her, but I'm really worried," Carey said. Lucas had tracked down Whitcomb's address in a matter of a few minutes, and had broken off from the apartment surveillance.

Letty had always taken matters into her own hands, whatever the matters might be—she tended to believe that nobody could handle things quite as well as she could. Events had never proven her to be wrong. But messing with Whitcomb and one of Whitcomb's hookers, for whatever reason—and Carey had filled him in on the reason—could be an irretrievable error.

Whitcomb was a psychotic; people who got too close to him suffered because they did not—could not—understand the sheer uncontrolled malevolence of the man. Lucas believed that Whitcomb's condition was far beyond Whitcomb's own control. He'd been broken at some point, perhaps at birth, perhaps as a child, but he was simply wrong, a devil's child. There was really nothing to be done about it, other than to put him in jail forever, or kill him.

Lucas thought that one or the other of those things was inevitable, a matter of time.

Now, as he rushed through the night toward Whitcomb's place, banging down onto the interstate, then almost immediately off again at the Sixth Street exit, he saw the flashers on a St. Paul squad running parallel to him, a block over on Seventh, heading up the hill past the university. He ran the red light and turned the corner and accelerated down the block, turned onto Seventh and saw the squad make the turn over toward Whitcomb's and he knew with a cold certainty where the squad was going.

If Whitcomb had done anything to Letty . . .

Letty had been right about that. If he'd known Whitcomb was stalking her, or anyone else in the family, Whitcomb would have died, one way or another. The problem with a psychotic was, there is no way to deflect them, once they've fixed on a course. You can't talk to them, because they're nuts.

With fear gripping his heart like an icy hand, he went after the squad.

21

COHN, CRUZ, AND Lane spotted two bugout cars near the hotel, one in a skyway-level parking structure, another on the street. They all had keys in their pockets, and additional keys, in magnetic boxes, hung from under the bumpers of both vehicles. When they needed to move, they used the third vehicle, a rented Toyota Sienna minivan. Lane did most of the final scouting, because he was the unknown face, and what he said was what they wanted to hear: "You can't believe some of the stuff they're wearing. One woman, honest to God, she looks like she has a diamond Christmas tree hung on her. She was about a hundred years old, I could have taken it right off her neck."

"If only they're real," Cohn said. They were huddled in the back of the minivan in an underground parking ramp at a medical building near St. John's Hospital. They'd been moving since they abandoned the apartment, but the hospital turned out to be the best place to wait. People came and went at all times of the night, and sometimes sat in their cars, getting away from whatever it was that brought them to the hospital.

"There's gonna be some paste," Cruz told him. "But if

you got it, when are you going to wear it? Tonight, the Academy Awards, maybe the number-one inaugural ball. Maybe the first big ball of the season in Palm Beach. A couple of other times, but tonight, for sure."

"Surprised the insurance company lets them wear it," Cohn said. He was looking sleepy, yawning, like he always did before a job. "For a thousand bucks, they could make a replica that nobody could tell but a jeweler."

"If you got robbed, it'd be almost as big an embarrassment to admit that you were wearing fakes, as losing the real thing," Cruz said. "Some of these people—not so much the Republicans as the Democrats, really—have so much money that they really don't care. They've got so much money that if they lost a five-million-dollar stone, they'd say, 'So what? There's more where that came from.'"

"So why didn't we hold up the Democrats?" Lane asked.

"Because I didn't have the inside information on the Democrats," Cruz said. "When the moneymen would be there. And they didn't have a ball like this one, when all the big money was in one spot. They were more scattered around, movie stars in one place, hedge funds in another."

"I didn't know the Democrats had so much money," Lane said.

"An ocean of money," Cohn said. "Both of them, Republicans and Democrats. That's all that counts anymore."

"You think we'll elect a colored guy as president?" Lane asked Cruz.

"I hope so," she said. "I'm tired of all the racist bullshit that goes on. Maybe this will settle it."

"I don't know. I'm not sure that colored people are ready," Lane said.

"What are you talking about, Jesse?" Cruz asked with some heat. "Tate was a good friend of yours. You hung out even when you didn't have to."

"That was different," Lane said.

"Ah, phooey," Cruz said. "They're all different. Every

single black person is different, and when you get right down to it, none of them is what you rednecks made them out to be. You and Brute both probably got some black blood running through you, coming out of where you do."

"Some Indian, for sure," Lane said. "Cherokee."

"Lot of black blood in the Cherokee," Cohn said. "Your real God name is probably Willie Lee Thunder Cloud Crackeriferus Lane. Cracker, for short."

Lane said, "Now we hear from the fuckin' Hebrews."

Cohn laughed and said, "My great-granddaddy did all right by himself. My great-grandma was this good-looking blond southern belle. Her daddy was vice president at a steel mill down there, building guns for the Confederates. Bet her family hated that big-peckered Jew banging her brains loose every night. They had eight children before she gave it up and died in childbirth."

"How do you know he had a big pecker?" Lane asked. "They take a picture of it?"

"Well, if he didn't, where'd I get mine from?" Cohn asked.

"Ahhh, God. Men and their penises. If they didn't have them, we'd have to sew one on, just to give them something to talk about," Cruz said.

"You ever seen one?" Cohn asked casually.

"Brute . . ." She shook her head.

"I was just wondering, you being queer and all," he said. "If you haven't, I could show you mine. Something terrible could happen tonight. You wouldn't want to die without seeing one."

Made her laugh, which was one of the things Cohn was good at, in the last minutes before a job: taking the weight off. "I can get by without it."

"That's good, because, you know, sometimes I get that rascal out, and he don't want to go back in. I'm too goddamn tired for a big wrestling match."

A WHILE LATER, Lane said, "We never sat in a car like this, on the run, and still pointing at the job. Other jobs, we would've called it off a long time ago."

Cohn said, "Yeah."

"Would you be sitting here if Lindy hadn't taken off?"

Cohn nodded. "Yeah. Yeah. We gotta get out of this, Jesse. Our days are numbered. The cops got all this stuff now. You read about it on the Internet. You know, they can sometimes get DNA if you even just *grab* somebody; if you just *touch* something. You know, they can get DNA off a goddamn beer can. If you spend any time in a place at all, they can get DNA. It's always coming off you—hair and skin cells and blood and semen . . . if you sleep between two sheets, they just sure as shit can prove you did.

"Then in England, they put up these movie cameras everywhere," Cohn continued. "You see them on posts and street corners, watching you all the time. Big Brother. You're always watched. There were these Arab guys, they were up to something, they tracked them all the way across town on these cameras. Right from one camera to the next. You knock over an armored car there, or a bank, and the cops could get out the cameras and track you wherever you go. That'll be here, sooner or later. They'll watch every fuckin' thing you do, and people will be saying, well, if you don't do anything wrong, what's your problem? That's what they say in England."

"It's only going to get worse," Cruz agreed. "Look how quick they tracked me down—they're all talking to each other all the time now. They can do fingerprints in five minutes. Five minutes! Twenty years ago, it could take them weeks, even with a good set of prints. When I was scouting this thing, I read that Minnesota has a law that says everybody who's convicted of a crime has to give up some DNA. They put it on file, and when they get a crime, and they get some DNA, they can run it like that," and she snapped her fingers. "They were going to pass a law that said that whenever anybody was *arrested*, they had to give up DNA, even though they hadn't been proven guilty of anything. That got stopped, but it'll come back. Pretty soon, they'll start taking DNA from babies, to protect the babies, is what they'll say. In case your kid disappears, they can find him later. Identify him. They'll scare people into giving it up."

"There are still places you can go and get away from it—in our lifetimes, anyway," Cohn said. "Belize, maybe. Lots of Americans in Costa Rica. New Zealand, maybe."

"I'll just go back to the farm. Try to make that work," Lane said. "Get serious about it."

COHN SAID TO Cruz after a while, "Tell me the truth. Are you Mexican?"

She shook her head. "I was born and raised in L.A. My folks came across the border back in the fifties. Funny thing is, one of my grandfathers was an American who settled down there. Liked the women. Never did go back across to the States."

"You speak Spanish?"

"Pretty good," she said, nodding. "My mother learned to speak good English, but my father, not so much. So, we spoke Spanish in the house. I've lost some of it, though."

"Still, it gives you more options," Cohn said. "Me and Jesse, if we've got to run for it, it's gonna have to be an English-speaking place."

"Go to Israel," Lane suggested. "Lots of people speak English there."

"Ah, I don't count as a Jew," Cohn said. "They got something about how your mother has to be a Jew. We never did have a mother who was a Jew in our family. They were all Baptists."

"Well, fuckin' lie about it," Lane said. "You wouldn't be going there as Brutus Cohn anyway."

"Let me share something with you, Jesse. You get to be a Jew the same way you get to be a peckerwood," Cohn said. "You peckerwoods know all about stump-training a heifer, about using a corncob for toilet paper . . ."

". . . bullshit, that's fuckin' nuts. A corncob?"

". . . because you grow up with it. I didn't grow up being a Jew. I know as much about being a Jew as you do. End of story."

MORE TIME PASSED, the minutes dragging their feet.

Then, "If Lindy hadn't run, we'd have had enough money to go somewhere for a while," Cruz said. "We could have gotten ourselves back together."

"I would've wanted to do the hotel anyway," Cohn said.

"Yeah, but . . . I've got a story about a guy out in L.A. who's supposed to be the big money-mover man for a Russian gang. He moves cash around at a big discount, and the Russians get stocks and bonds and buy land and apartments and so on. The story is, this guy sometimes has ten or fifteen million dollars at his house. He's got some guys with guns around, but hell, if you feel fine about hitting an armored car, we'd have no trouble taking out a few guards."

"Have to kill them, probably, if they're Russians," Cohn said.

"Well, yeah," she said.

"I wouldn't do that unless it was just you, me, Jesse, and Tate," Cohn said. "You couldn't ever take the chance that somebody would talk about it. The Russians would track you down and cut you up an inch at a time."

"I was thinking about it as a last job. I never had the time to develop it, but if you went in shooting, you could probably do it with three people—just like tonight," she said. "But it would have taken a lot more research."

"If Lindy hadn't run," Cohn said. "I'm gonna kill her when I find her."

"You keep saying you were going to do this one anyway," Lane said.

"Yeah, but now I feel *pushed*," Cohn said. "I'm afraid it might be coloring the way I think. I need that money bad. I need to get out of this. I need to end it. If I'd had that money that Lindy took, and if we came up to the hotel tonight and I got a real bad feeling, maybe I'd just decide we should walk away. Now . . . I feel pushed. I can't explain it."

"I know exactly what you're saying," Cruz said.

"Wish Tate was here," Lane said. "He was a good ol' boy."

Cruz looked at her watch. "Goddamnit, time is really crawling."

22

LUCAS SAW THE cops standing at the back of the yard in the headlights of their own cars, the spinners on the car roof flicking scarlet light into the treetops at the back of the lot. A man and a woman stood with the cops, and they were all looking down into Swede Hollow, and then one of the cops started down.

Lucas parked and got out of the car and hurried toward the group, and the uniformed cop looked at him and held out a hand, and Lucas called, "Davenport, BCA."

The cop nodded and said, "Hey, Lucas," and Lucas recognized him but couldn't remember his name. Lucas looked at the woman standing next to the cop and recognized her as Juliet Briar, and he asked, "What the hell are you doing here?"

"I live here," she said.

"You live here?" Lucas looked from her to the cop, who asked, "What's going on?"

Briar asked, "Are you Lucas Davenport? Letty's dad?"

"What?" the cop asked.

Lucas said, "Where's Letty?"

Briar shook her head. "I haven't seen her. Is she coming?"

As they were talking, the cop below had skidded down the slope to the tree line and disappeared into the trees. Now he called back up, "Get an ambulance. Get an ambulance. Tell them to hurry."

The cop said to Lucas, "Keep an eye on them," and stepped away and called for an ambulance.

"What happened?" Lucas asked Briar.

"Randy was messing around and his chair went over the edge," she said, looking at the man with her, rather than at Lucas.

The guy nodded and then shrugged.

"Is that what happened?" Lucas asked him.

Ranch turned hollow yellow eyes to Lucas and opened his mouth, and then said, "I can't remember."

"You can't remember? It happened one minute ago," said the uniform cop, as he stepped back to them. Regions Hospital was just down the hill, and they heard a siren start.

"Uh, Randy and Ranch—this is Ranch—had been partying pretty hard," Briar said.

"On what?" Lucas asked.

"Maybe . . . a little amp," Briar said.

"A little? Or a lot?" the cop asked.

"Three zippies," she said.

Enough to kill the average pony, Lucas thought.

"What about you?" the cop asked her.

"They don't allow me. If I smoke, I can't work." She looked at Lucas. "Randy was going to take Letty and do stuff to her."

"Yeah? Did she know that?" Lucas asked.

"I think so," Briar said. "We mostly talked about my situation."

"Who's Letty?" the cop asked. "What's your situation?"

Lucas shook his head: "This is really screwed up. Letty's my daughter. I don't know where the hell she is . . ." He looked at Briar, then at Ranch. "If she's hurt . . ."

Briar stepped away from him.

THE AMBULANCE PULLED into the yard, its headlights sweeping across them, as the second cop, the one who'd gone down the hill, climbed back using his hands as well as his feet to keep his balance. Red-faced and out of breath, he said, "He's alive, but his head looks funny. He might have broken his neck."

One of the paramedics walked over from the ambulance and looked over the edge. "Holy cripes," she said. "Maybe we ought to come up from the bottom."

The second cop shook his head. "He's less than halfway down, and it's even steeper below him. Gotta hurry, guys, he's hurt."

The paramedics got a lightweight carry stretcher, a backboard, a cervical extrication collar, and safety straps, and went over the edge with the second cop.

The St. Paul cop with Lucas asked, "What are we doing here?"

Lucas shook his head: "Not my case. We picked up Briar earlier today . . ."

He told the cop about the scene at the motel, and the cop listened to it all, and then said, "What about your daughter?"

"I'm looking for her. She was down at the convention, but she was supposed to be home hours ago."

Lucas looked at Briar again, but Briar said, "We haven't seen her. Honest. Not since day before last."

"How do you know her?" the cop asked. "How's she involved?"

"She's not," Lucas and Briar said simultaneously.

Briar said, "She works for a TV station. She found me downtown. She wanted to interview me."

Lucas said to the cop, "She was trying to do a story on young . . . prostitutes. For Channel Three."

"Oh, yeah," the cop said. "I know her—the good-looking blond chick."

"She's fourteen," Lucas said.

The cop was unembarrassed: good-looking is good-looking. "You a young prostitute?" he asked Briar.

"I'm just a kid," she said.

Ranch, naked except for his Jockey shorts, dug his hand in his pants, scratched himself and said: "Some pretty good pussy, though."

Lucas and the cop both turned to him, and Lucas asked, "What'd you say?"

"Pretty . . . uh . . ."

"They raped me," Briar said. "Or, Ranch did. I think."

"You think?" the cop asked. "You're not sure?"

"Does it count if they do it in your butt?"

The cop rubbed his forehead and said, "Yeah, that counts." He said to Ranch, "Turn around." Ranch, head bobbing, turned around, and the cop cuffed him. "Hey, dude, that's pretty fuckin' . . . rude."

Briar said, "Randy made him do it."

LUCAS'S PHONE RANG, and he pulled it out of his pocket and checked the number: Letty.

"Where the fuck are you?" he snarled without preamble.

"I'm at the Capitol," she said. "I didn't realize how late it was. I'm sorry—I'm going home now."

"You're at the Capitol?" He wasn't sure he believed her.

"Yeah. I did some tape on some political kids here. For the weekend. Frat boys for Obama."

Lucas felt as though he were strangling: "You get home. Get home. Goddamnit, Letty . . ."

"I'm going," she said meekly.

Too meekly, Lucas thought, but she'd hung up, and he wouldn't call her back in the presence of the St. Paul cop.

"That was her?" Briar asked brightly.

"Yeah. She's at the Capitol," Lucas said.

"Glad she's okay," Briar said.

The cop shook his head, but didn't press. He had enough problems without picking at one that seemed to have solved itself. You could ruin a perfectly good evening, he believed, with one extra ill-placed question. He stepped away, got on his radio, and said, "We need another ambulance and we're gonna need a rape kit at Regions, better alert them . . ."

DOWN BELOW, THE paramedics were thrashing through the trees. The first cop, with Lucas, began talking to Briar about what had happened that evening, and Briar couldn't get through it—couldn't think of what to say, other than that they were partying and that Randy had been crazy in his wheelchair, and she told him about how Ranch had made the crank pipe. The cop asked, "Mind if we look inside?"

Briar said, "No, go ahead."

Lucas, who'd been looking down into the hollow, smiled to himself: *there* were a bunch of ill-considered words, he thought, though the cop could probably go in anyway. Now, there was no problem at all—he'd been invited.

"I heard that," he said to the cop, turning toward them, and the cop nodded to him. Lucas was looking right at Briar's back, and in the thin flickering lights from the house, saw what looked like stripes across her dress; but he recognized blood when he saw it.

"Hey . . ."

The cop picked up the tone and looked toward him.

"Check her back," Lucas said. "She's bleeding."

Briar started to weep, and sidled away from them. "He didn't mean nothing by it," she said. "He didn't mean nothing."

THE PARAMEDICS BROUGHT Whitcomb up out of the trees, strapped to the board, and hauled him to the ambulance and raced away toward the hospital. He moved not at all, though he appeared to be semiconscious.

The second cop watched them go, then turned to Lucas and said, "He's fucked. His neck is *not* right."

Lucas was about to comment when Ranch, who'd been standing, silently, a few feet away, fell over, unconscious. Because his hands were cuffed, he landed directly on his face. Lucas and the cop both flinched and glanced around, listening for a gunshot, then the cop crouched over Ranch and said, "He's breathing."

"Better call another meat wagon," Lucas said. He looked toward the house, where the first cop had taken Briar. He could hear Briar weeping again. "These people are messed up."

LUCAS LEFT THE St. Paul cops to straighten it all out, called Shrake and was told that nothing was happening at the apartment; and that the armored car companies were being monitored. "They might be gone."

"Maybe," Lucas said. "But they lingered. Why did they linger?"

"What about the SWAT?"

Lucas looked at his watch. "Leave them for a while. I'm coming back, but I've got to talk to Letty first. Something weird is going on."

WHEN HE GOT back to the house, he was determined to stay calm. He did, somewhat to his own surprise, because Letty was apparently as confused about events as he was.

"You arrested her at a motel? What for? How did you know her?" Letty asked. "Did you arrest Randy?"

"I didn't even know she was involved with Randy," Lucas said. "How do you know Randy?"

"I only saw Randy once, when I was in a McDonald's

with John and Jeff, the day they picked me up at the Capitol, when you gave me the twenty. I don't know what Randy wanted—I just thought Juliet would make a story."

"But you knew I'd been involved with Randy?"

"Yeah, later. I figured he might be coming after me to get back at you, but he was such a dummy, I decided that he really wasn't much of a threat."

"You were wrong about that," Lucas said. "He *was* a threat. People like that are always a threat, because they're nuts. But then . . . you kept going back, didn't you?"

"Only to Juliet," Letty said. "I didn't mess with Randy. Did Jennifer tell you about the perverted mailman? That whole thing?"

"What perverted mailman?" Lucas asked. He looked at Weather, who was draped over a couch, looking at both of them with great skepticism. "Do you know about a mailman?"

"First I've heard about a perverted mailman," Weather said.

"But what about the motel?" Letty asked. "You arrested a possible assassin who Juliet was supposed to . . . you know?"

"Let's go back to the mailman," Lucas said.

WHEN THEY WORKED through it all, none of it seemed to make too much sense. Lucas finally said, "All right, this is all done, okay? Randy's hurt, and it's pretty bad—he's broken his neck, maybe. But you're all done with Randy and Juliet, and I want a no-shit promise from you. I'm not pressuring you, I'm asking you: on our relationship, I'm asking you."

Letty stuck out a fist for a bump. "If I ever have one more thing to do with either of them, no matter how small, I'll tell you first," she said. She meant it this time: the Randy problem was gone.

They bumped fists and were done with it.

"Now," Lucas said, "if we could only find that fuckin' Cohn."

"You gotta watch your language a little more," Weather said to Lucas.

"Maybe they're holding up the Republican Party," Letty said.

"You can't hold up a party," Lucas said. "You gotta hold up a thing. There's gotta be one place, there's gotta be some money moving, we're watching all the armored car warehouses, they're all scrambling their routes . . . I can't get it."

"Sleep on it," Weather said.

BY THE TIME they were all done, it was after midnight. Weather and Letty went to bed, and Lucas checked again with Shrake, who said that nothing had changed. "I'm going to bag out on my couch for a while," Lucas said. "Maybe you and Jenkins should trade off. We need somebody there to keep an eye on the place until we're sure they're gone; but there's no point in both of you being there."

"What time will you be back?"

Lucas looked at his watch. "I'll set my alarm for three, see you about three-thirty. If you want to send Jenkins home, tell him to come back around seven to relieve me."

"Sounds like a deal," Shrake said. "What about the SWAT?"

"When were they due to quit?"

"Anytime."

"Ah . . . tell them to hang on until three o'clock. It's all overtime, anyway. But if it ain't happened by three, it probably won't—nobody working after that."

"See you at three-thirty," Shrake said.

Lucas got a pillow and an alarm clock from the bedroom—Weather was cutting in the morning, as she was most mornings, and he didn't want to disturb her in the middle of the night—kicked off his shoes and stretched out on the couch.

As he dozed off, he wondered what he had heard that night, pinging in the back of his head, that worried him so much.

23

THEY'D BEEN STUCK in the van so long that they were all a little groggy. Toward the end of the wait, Cohn looked at his watch every three minutes and finally said, "Fuck it: let's do it."

Cruz: "Twenty minutes yet. It's all right to be late, but it's not all right to be early."

"I'm going nuts in here," Cohn said.

"Then let's go for a walk," Cruz said. "There's nobody around right now, we can get out of here, down the stairs, take a hike around the block. And we'll feel better."

Lane said, "I could use a walk. I'm tired and I'm scared."

They piled out of the van, walked down the stairs. A nurse was just crossing the street from the hospital and she nodded at them and went into the parking structure. Lane said, "This way," and they followed him down the street, away from the lights of downtown. Around the corner, it was even darker, but they weren't worried, since they were the ones who were supposed to be lurking in the dark . . .

They turned another corner and suddenly there were lights on the street, and, in the distance, people—not many, but a few, outside the Xcel Center where John McCain had been nominated for the presidency.

"Still a little traffic," Lane said.

"This is why I had Shafer ready to go," Cruz said. "I was going to call the cops, tell them I'd seen him on a roof. Like he was hiding out in one of these old buildings, waiting for McCain to come in. Every cop in town would have been over here."

"Woulda worked," Cohn said. He windmilled his arms for a few steps, looked at his watch again. "Why'd you pick three-fifteen?"

"Because most of the overnight hotel employees get off at three," Cruz said. "There'll be a short-order cook and a busboy in the kitchen, but they stay down there—it's in the basement—because they're cleaning up. The rest of the people . . . You figure most people who get off at three might linger a few minutes, but not long. There's nothing to do. So, give them fifteen or twenty minutes to clear out. Then the day cooks and the rest of the kitchen staff start coming in at five o'clock. They never come in early—they're getting up on alarm clocks. Add it all up and the best time to get in will be around three-fifteen or three-thirty. That'll give us an hour without interference."

"Except maybe for a couple of night janitors."

"I explained that."

"I wish I could think of all that shit," Lane said. A moment of silence, and he added, "Little more than an hour from now, we'll know how it all came out."

Cohn laughed and said, "That's what I think when I'm going into the dentist's office. An hour from now, and you'll be walking out."

THEY AMBLED ALONG, taking the night air, looking for other street-walkers while forcing the minutes down the line: spotted some cops outside the X, but in twos, rather than in crowds. "Most of them have been sent home," Cruz said. "That's a bonus. If there was a riot somewhere, and they were all running around, that'd be another uncontrolled factor."

They turned another corner, walked down the street the hospital was on, and turned down toward the parking structure again. Cohn looked at his watch a last time. "If we drove out of the parking garage right now, we'd get to the hotel at three-fifteen," he said. "No point in slow-walking anymore."

BACK IN THE van, Lane took the wheel, Cohn sat in the passenger seat, and Cruz got in the back, popped her travel case, took out a gray pinstriped women's business suit, and changed over, aware that Cohn was paying attention to her ass.

"Thanks for caring," she said, as she buttoned the blouse.

"Hell, it'd be kinda insulting if I didn't," Cohn said.

She pulled on the jacket and snapped on a small red tie, and then an expensive long brown wig, looked at herself in the window, getting it all straight. Lane had had to make a loop away from the Xcel, circling, to get back through town to the parking ramp behind the St. Andrews. He pulled into the ramp, wound up three floors, and stopped behind one of the emergency cars. Cohn got out, popped the trunk on the parked car, and transferred the weapons bags, tool bags, gloves, and masks into the van, and slid the door shut. Lane took them back down the exit and out, and left, past the St. Paul Hotel, around the corner, down the street, and into the front turnout in front of the St. Andrews.

Cruz hopped out, shut the door, and walked inside, moving easily past the front desk, past the closed bar, past the gift shop, past the closed restaurant—and found two men sitting in the restaurant talking quietly, a liquor bottle and two glasses between them. Breath coming a little faster now, heartbeat picking up. She went back to the front desk where two young women smiled at her, and she asked, "Is anything open? Anyplace where I could just get a snack? I'm famished."

One of the women shook her head. "Everything's closed, I'm sorry. You could still get room service."

"Okay. Well, thanks."

Outside, Cohn popped the door on the van and she said, "We're good. Two women at the desk, two drunks in the restaurant, right inside the door, in the dark. That's it."

Cohn looked at Lane: "You good?"

Lane nodded and said, "I guess."

THEY ALL PULLED on latex gloves and Cohn rolled a mask up like a thin watch cap and then pulled a big baseball hat over it. The hat sat too high on his head, and looked a little goofy, but what the hell, there was a political convention going on, and goofier-looking people with goofier-looking hats were all over the place. Cruz pulled off the wig, put the end of a rolled-up nylon sock around the top of her head, and then pulled the wig back on. Cohn retrieved a silenced 9mm pistol from the weapons bag, and another, smaller, unsilenced weapon that he handed to Cruz. A silenced Uzi remained in the bag, with a big Cleveland drill and a bunch of spare drill bits—Lane's stuff. "All right?" Cohn asked.

"All right," Cruz said.

THEY POPPED OUT of the van, Cruz and Cohn together, and walked through the gilt front doors of the hotel, toward the two women still behind the desk. Except for the Muzak—playing an orchestral arrangement of "A Hard Day's Night," heavy on the strings—the hotel was utterly silent.

Cohn stepped up to the desk and said, "Good evening,

ladies," smiling, and they smiled back, and Cohn lifted the gun and said, "This is a robbery—if you don't do exactly what I tell you, I'll kill you. I'm not joking."

THEY MOVED THE two stunned, frightened women into the darkened nondenominational chapel, which featured a small group of pews looking at a stand with nothing on it. Cruz pulled down her mask—the stocking obscured her features, while still allowing her to see. They ordered the two women into one of the pews, and Cruz said, "If you make a sound, we will kill you. Do you understand that?"

They both nodded, and Cruz said, "I want you to say, 'Yes,' that you understand. We can't have any mistakes here."

"Yes," they both said.

"Okay. Now, I'm going to tell you what we're going to do . . ."

As she was talking, Cohn pulled the mask over his own face and walked over to the restaurant, where the two drunks were still talking. "Gentlemen, I have to ask you to come with me."

"Who're you?"

"I'm the robber who's sticking up the hotel," Cohn said. "If either one of you makes a single fucking noise, I'll kill you."

HE TOOK THE two men into the chapel and made them stand in the aisle, facing the two desk clerks, as though they were about to be married.

He pointed the gun at the younger man, a chubby, apple-cheeked blond who'd started to sweat: "What's your name, and what do you do for a living?" Cohn asked.

"My name is Rob Benedict, and I'm a consultant at Schumer and White."

"What's Schumer and White?" Cohn asked.

"We're a law firm . . . in Washington."

Cohn pointed at the older man, a heavyset, weather-beaten farmer-looking guy. "What about you?"

"I'm a farmer, from Nebraska."

"What're you doing here?" Cohn asked.

"I'm a delegate."

"How'd you two get together?" Cohn asked. "You queer?"

The farmer seemed about to object, but then said, "We were the last ones in the bar. They kicked us out. We were too cranked up to go to sleep."

"Okay," Cohn said. He considered for a moment, then shot the consultant in the forehead. As the consultant went down, the farmer jumped back, then half-turned away, waiting for the bullet, and the two women made soft screeching sounds in their throats until Cruz put a finger to her lips.

"Sit in the pew," Cohn said to the farmer.

The farmer sat in the pew. The dead man was stretched down the middle of the aisle, on his back.

"I don't actually like killing people, but I won't hesitate to do it," Cohn told the three of them. "I needed to make that point, and the consultant seemed like a more worthless piece of shit than a farmer. But, I got nothing against killing farmers or desk clerks or anyone else. That clear?"

They all nodded.

Cohn said, "Now, one of you girls is going with my friend. The other one will sit here with me. With me and the farmer. Which one of you two handles the safe-deposit boxes?"

One of the women glanced at the other, and Cruz picked it up. "Okay, Ann. You handle the boxes? You stay here. Karen, you come with me, like I told you."

CRUZ AND KAREN walked out to the front door, and Cruz waved at Lane, who shut down the van and got the tool-and-weapons bag from the back.

He followed them inside, and Cruz put Karen back behind the desk, and took up a station in the hallway, behind her.

"Remember, dear, if you try to run, or if somebody comes in here and you give us away, I'll kill both you and them. Do you understand, Karen?"

"Don't hurt me; I have a daughter," Karen whimpered.

"We won't hurt you if you do what we tell you," Cruz said. "We shot that other man to make the point—we don't want a massacre here, but we want you to believe us. We'll kill you if we have to."

WHILE SHE WAS giving the little lecture, Lane went back to the chapel, looked at Cohn, who nodded to Ann. Lane squatted in the aisle, his masked face a few inches from Ann's, and said, "Which are the biggest money boxes? Just judging what you think, from what people put in them."

"Oh, God," she said, her chin trembling. She glanced at the dead man. "Honest, I don't know many of them. I think—wait—sixty-six. And maybe, uh, forty-two. And one. I think one."

"Okay. I'm going to go open those," Lane said. "If they're empty, something bad might happen to you. If they're not empty, if they're good—well, you should try to think of more numbers before I get back."

"There might be something in two. An old man keeps stuff there, he keeps it in his hand in his pocket, so it's something, but I don't know what."

"Keep thinking," Lane said, and he touched her face with his gloved left hand, which made her flinch.

"Time's a-wastin'," Cohn said cheerfully. Lane picked up his bag, got the strong-room key from Cruz, who'd gotten it from Karen, and went inside.

The room was just as shown in Cruz's photos, with a wall of steel boxes set in a concrete wall. He put the bag down, picked up the oversized drill, plugged it in, and started on the lock on Box 2, the old man's box, just out of curiosity. He timed the cut.

Forty-eight seconds, and the lock cylinder was gone. "Excellent," Lane breathed. He could do all of them in an hour.

He flipped open the outer door, pulled the box—slowly, it was heavy, so heavy that he thought something was holding it in the slot. He stopped, and looked to see what was binding, saw nothing, and with some effort, pulled it the rest of the way out, and sagged with the weight of it. He put it on the floor, and popped the lid: and found, from front to back, a stack of small gold bars. Each was two inches wide, four or five inches long. They were laid three across, three down the length of the box. He dug them out: five deep. Forty-five bars that must weigh a couple of pounds each.

"Holy shit," he said. He put them in the tool bag, hefted the bag. He could carry it, he could even run with it, but not far. "Holy shit."

He went on to Box 1.

CRUZ PLAYED THE part of the late-night executive woman, a step up from an ordinary desk clerk; you saw them in all the better hotels. If she stayed back, lingering in the hall, nobody would pick up the mask. And she was close enough to control Karen. Karen was not holding up well, clutching at her hands, on the edge of weeping. Cruz was watching her closely, and the two men coming in from behind, down the stairwell, almost took her by surprise.

When she heard them, she instinctively stepped toward Karen, so the men wouldn't see the mask, walked behind the desk and then out the other side, and one of the men said to Karen, "Hey, is there anyplace we . . . are you all right?"

Cruz turned and saw them, two guys in ruffled shirts and tux pants, one still wearing a cummerbund, the other without, and she pointed her gun at them and said, "If you move or make any noise I will kill you. This is a robbery . . ." and before they could react, she half-shouted, *"Jim."*

Lane popped out of the strong room behind them, and they turned, scared now, and saw Lane with the heavy black mask and the Uzi, and one of them said, "Oh, my gosh," and the other one, "Oh, Jesus," and Lane said, "Into the chapel. Right there, across the hall, into the chapel. You won't be hurt if you pay attention . . ."

They moved into the chapel and Cohn took them: "Glad to see you fellas. Notice the dead man lying in the aisle . . ."

LANE WENT BACK to his drill, and Cruz, back in the hall, with one eye on the stairway now, looked at her watch. Twelve minutes. Seemed like an eternity.

Karen started shaking again, and there was a gust of odor from her direction, and Cruz said, "Did you . . ."

Karen started crying and nodded and said, "I peed my pants."

"Ah, Jesus," Cruz said. "Get in the chapel. Get in the chapel."

"Don't shoot me . . ."

KAREN WAS REPLACED by Ann, who seemed calmer.

"There's no reason to be afraid, as long as you do what we tell you," Cruz explained, with some asperity. "There was no reason for Karen to do that."

"She's scared," Ann said. She had a little accent, which made Cruz think she was from somewhere else, like Armenia or Russia. A peasant, like Cruz's own mother: peasants were tough, and needed watching.

"There's nothing to be scared about."

"Then why's there a dead man in there?" Ann asked. A

man and his wife, both in formal dress, pushed through the door.

Cruz said quietly, so only Ann could hear, "Good evening. Can we help you?"

Ann smiled at them and said, "Good evening," and Cruz moved back out of sight, and heard the man say, "Hi," and the two of them went on past the desk and down the hall to the elevators. A minute later, they were gone.

"See, that was easy," Cruz said. She looked at her watch. Eighteen minutes. She said to the desk clerk, "Come here. Just to the strong-room door."

The woman followed her back, not too close, and Cruz pushed the door open with a foot and asked, "How're we doing?"

"I'm working in a fuckin' gold mine in here," Lane said. He was sweating over the drill, had rolled the mask away from his face. "I can't believe it. A fuckin' gold mine."

And he hit the next box with the drill.

24

LUCAS WOKE IN the dark, disoriented, his neck twisted a little by the pillow propped against the arm of the couch. His pant legs and shirtsleeves were pulled up, and felt wrinkled and unclean, and his mouth tasted sour. He squinted through the dark at the red numbers of the alarm clock: 2:56. The alarm would go off in four minutes.

Not an easy sleep: he'd been disturbed by a sense of something undone, unrecognized, the running tail of a thought, but he couldn't quite catch it.

He sat up, in the light of a single lamp in the corner of the room, turned off the clock, picked up his shoes and then dropped them again, stretched and tiptoed down the hall through the master bedroom—Weather was breathing deeply, evenly, into her pillow—and into the bathroom. He shut the door, brushed his teeth by the light of a nightlight, splashed cold water in his face, and snuck back through the bedroom to the couch, and put on his shoes.

He stuck his face out the front door: the night was cool, almost cold. He relocked the door, got a light jacket from the front closet, and walked out to the car. The cool air felt good, fresh, and drove the sleep further back. He pulled out onto Mississippi River Boulevard, the lights of Minneapolis winking across the river valley, turned the corner and headed down to Cretin Avenue.

Mentally reviewed the evening before: the deployment of the troops, the search for Cohn, the discovery of the apartment. It was most likely, he thought, that Cohn had gone. At the moment, he could be rolling through Omaha, or Kansas City, or Chicago, on his way to a private plane ride to obscurity.

But why had he lingered as long as he had?

CRETIN AVENUE WAS essentially empty. In the mile or so out to I-94, he passed only a half dozen other cars. The highway itself was busier, but mostly with long-haul trucks, going about their nocturnal business. He let the car out a little, and was downtown in a couple of minutes. He parked in a no-parking area out front of the condos, and called Shrake on his cell phone: "I'm out front."

"Be right there," Shrake said.

Shrake pushed open the glass door to let Lucas inside, and asked, "Everything okay with Letty?"

"*She's* fine—*I* goddamned near had a heart attack," Lucas said; and again he felt the mental *bump*.

What the hell. He looked querulously at Shrake, who asked, "*What?*"

And then he got it.

"AH . . . AH." HE looked wildly around the condominium, turned back toward his car, said, "Ah . . ." and Shrake asked, again, "What?"

Letty had said something like, *Maybe they're holding up the Republican Party.*

Lucas said to Shrake, urgently, "Come on, come on . . . We need some guys . . ."

"What?"

"They're holding up the Republican party," Lucas said. "The party—the goddamn *ball.* The *dance.* All those people on the streets, we saw them all night walking up there, diamonds all over them . . ."

Shrake was the tiniest bit skeptical: "They're holding up the party?"

"C'mon," Lucas said. "Get in the car. Get on the phone. It's gotta be either the St. Paul or the St. Andrews. Hell, maybe it's both."

Shrake shook his head but got in the car and called the duty man at the BCA and said, "Get onto St. Paul, right now, get some guys over in Rice Park, over behind that TV stand, over by the Ordway, anybody you can get. If they got armor, it's better, don't let them be seen from the St. Paul Hotel or the St. Andrews. We think there could be a holdup going on . . . The Cohn gang, yeah, get some guys . . ."

Lucas let him talk and concentrated on the driving: in a straight line, six blocks or eight or ten blocks, something like that. But the streets were all blocked off, and he didn't know exactly where the barricades were. He headed up the hill at speed, running every stoplight they came to, and they were all red, and around the north side of the blockades. Shrake was clutching his phone: "Easy, man, easy, man, Jesus Christ, you're gonna kill us before we get there."

The Porsche held on like it had claws until he pumped to a stop behind the old federal building. "Let's go," he said.

Shrake was on the phone: "Gotta get some guys . . . I don't care, we gotta get some guys . . ."

There were two cops waiting, both from St. Paul. Lucas ran up, said, "I'm Davenport, with the BCA. This is Shrake. It's possible that either the St. Paul Hotel or the St. Andrews is being robbed exactly this minute—or maybe in a little while." He grinned at them. "Or maybe not at all. Shit, I don't know. But I think so. The thing is, if they're in there, we have to stop them. If they're still on the way in, we can't let them see us, because we need them to make their move. And maybe . . . we're wasting our time."

A squad car turned the corner and pulled to the curb. Shrake jogged over and talked quietly to the cops inside, and they both got out, unconsciously hitching up their gun belts.

"What're we going to do?" one of the cops asked Lucas.

"Shrake and I will take a peek at the hotels. We want one of you with us, for the uniform, and we want a couple more blocking the back exit. We need at least one guy to run around and take the stairway up into the skyway . . ."

The cops from the squad had a shotgun and an M16 in the trunk. Lucas put them back in the car: "Get around behind the hotels, fast as you can do it. I want you"—he pointed at the guy with the M16—"at the top of the stairway in the St. Paul. Don't let anybody through, but be careful with that thing, for Christ's sakes. Don't shoot any little old ladies."

The shotgun he wanted outside the back door.

Another cop car, directed by St. Paul communications, stopped behind Lucas's Porsche, and two more cops got out. Lucas kept talking to the first four:

"Talk to your guys, get some backup behind you, but get into place. If they're in there, they could be coming out any minute."

It took longer to get organized than Lucas had hoped, because it was, technically speaking, a cluster-fuck. But with everybody on their way, with more St. Paul cops moving in, he nodded at Shrake and said, "Let's look at it."

THE ST. PAUL Hotel was probably the oldest, and one of the two fanciest, in St. Paul. Lucas, Shrake, and the chosen St. Paul cop, a gray-haired sergeant whose name was Larkin, strolled down the sidewalk that ran past the side of the hotel, looking at the front entrance. The hotel cultivated a garden alongside the circular drive in front, and in the cold light from the street, the flowers looked pale and ghostly.

"Don't see anybody watching," Shrake said.

Lucas said, "Goddamnit. I fucked this up." He looked around him, in a circle, at the buildings surrounding the park: the central library, the old federal courthouse, the Ordway Music Theater. "We should have met somewhere else, but I didn't take the time. What if they're in the old courthouse? Or the library? That's where I'd be. I'd have a lookout up there with a radio . . . They might be looking right down at us, right now. C'mon."

Now he started jogging, down the street, up the driveway to the front of the hotel. He looked in. Two women behind the check-in counter, a guy in hotel livery with a lunchbox next to his hand, talking to them, leaning on the counter. He looked real, but the box might hold a gun.

Before they'd started over, he'd told Larkin to take off his cop hat and put it under his arm—it was too readily identifiable at a distance. Now he told him to put it back on: "Get your hand on your gun, but keep it out of sight," Lucas said to Shrake. "Through the doors all at once." He pushed through the revolving door, with Shrake and Larkin going through the swing doors beside it.

THE PEOPLE AT the desk looked down at them, and Lucas, one hand on the .45 under his jacket, held up his credentials. "Bureau of Criminal Apprehension and St. Paul Police. I'm a police officer, let me see your hands, please. Put your hands on the desk."

The guy said, "What?" but then put his hands on the desk. "What?"

Larkin asked, "Where's your safe?"

One of the women said, "Uh . . ." and looked to the side.

Nobody in the strong room, and Shrake checked their IDs. All Minnesota driver's licenses.

Lucas said to Larkin, "Call the guy on the back door. I want him here, behind the desk, in case they come in. Move the other guys around behind the St. Andrews. I think there's a skyway exit, too, out to the parking ramps; we need somebody in the skyway . . ."

As Larkin called, Shrake said, "St. Andrews?"

Lucas nodded. "Let's go."

"Starting to feel like an idiot yet?" Shrake asked.

"About forty percent," Lucas said. "It seemed like a really good concept. Christ, years ago, when I was first on the Minneapolis force, there was a hotel that got knocked over down in Miami, and they took millions out. Millions. That was more than twenty years ago . . . And there was no kind of thing like they had tonight . . ."

At the door, Lucas turned around and called to the women at the desk: "Did you guys have the big ball tonight? The Gold Key, or whatever they called it?"

One of them shook her head and said, "I don't know anything about that," but the other one said, "That was at the St. Andrews. I saw them all coming out when I was coming to work."

"What time was that?"

"One o'clock . . ."

LUCAS, SHRAKE, AND Larkin jogged toward the white limestone structure at the other end of the block, Larkin and Shrake chatting now, Lucas feeling that they just didn't believe, but he felt the impatience pushing him, a hand in his back, and halfway up the block he stepped up the pace. The St. Andrews was a new hotel, less than four years old, but modeled on the St. Paul, with a similar rose garden in the front. A Toyota Sienna was parked in the drive. Lucas detoured around the garden, leading the other two by fifteen feet as he came up to the double front doors.

The lights were down in the hotel lobby; he could see lots of marble, plush red carpet, wood paneling, and gold paint. To one side, a single woman stood behind the check-in desk, doing nothing, and Lucas felt a tingle.

Shrake and Larkin came up and Lucas said, "She looks like a fuckin' cigar store Indian. Get your hands on your guns . . . ready . . ."

They went in all at once, Lucas at the point, and six feet inside the doors, Lucas saw a second woman, this one in a gray suit with an odd face, something wrong here, and he dropped his gun hand to his side and suddenly the woman behind the desk dropped out of sight and the suit-woman lifted her hand and at the same time screamed, "Cops," and opened fire, flashes like firecrackers on the Fourth of July, and Lucas went down and rolled right and windows shattered and furniture exploded; he heard somebody screaming and he kept rolling and rolling and then somebody opened up with a machine gun . . .

25

CRUZ RECOGNIZED THE big dark-haired cop as soon as he came through the door—recognized him from the press conference. Didn't know how they'd broken it down, but here they were. She saw Ann hit the floor and she screamed, "Cops," and pulled the little pistol and opened fire. She wasn't a good shot, and hardly knew what she was doing, but bullets are bullets and she put as many as she had in the air, the cops scattered and then Lane was there, his mask still up his face, with the Uzi, and he burned through a clip and then Cohn was there, shouting at them, and they broke toward the back of the building, and Cruz registered the fact that Lane was carrying the tool bag: now the jewel bag.

They turned a corner in the hallway and at the far end of the hall, a cop was crouching in the doorway, and hesitated, and Lane fired a one-handed burst at him and the cop went backward—Cruz had the impression that he was scrambling, not hurt—into the street, and they ran down the hall and now Cohn was firing backward, back where the original cops were from, and they reached the stairway to the skyway.

LUCAS ROLLED AND rolled and the couches and the chairs in the big reception area were useless as cover and so he kept scrambling and the bullets coming in were way too high. Then stopped. In the sudden silence, he heard Shrake screaming at him, "They're moving, they're moving."

The only place they could move to would be down the hall behind them and Lucas had rolled far enough to the side that he was out of their line of fire, and he rolled to his feet and let his .45 lead him toward the hallway. From the mouth of the hallway he peeked down its length, saw nothing, and then Shrake was coming up from the side and Lucas shouted, "How bad are you hit?" and Shrake shouted, "I'm okay," and Lucas shouted, "You've got blood running down your face," and Shrake brushed at it and said, "I'm okay, it's glass, a glass cut." Lucas shouted, "What about Larkin?" and Shrake shouted back, "He's okay, he's got some glass cuts, he's okay, he's trying to get people into the skyway."

Lucas shouted, "I'm going down the hall," and Shrake shouted, "Go," and Lucas went, saw the stunned face of the clerk behind the reception desk, saw the shambles of the strong room through the door, passed it, did a peek at the corner and saw a tall man in a dark suit all the way at the end of a long hall, at the foot of a red-carpeted stairs, and the man saw him and fired three or four shots that zinged off the wall, and Lucas was about to peek again when a man called to him from a side room, "Help us, we've got a dead man here," and Lucas saw a dry country face close to the floor, a man on his hands and knees under a gold plaque that read "Nondenominational Chapel," and he said, "Help's coming," and he did another peek, saw a clear hallway, and launched himself into it.

Shrake came up and shouted, "Where'd they go?" and Lucas shouted back, "Up the stairs." He stepped into the hallway and there were two quick gunshots from the open ground-level door and two bullets smashed plaster off a pilaster next to his head and he went down and somebody from the doorway shouted, "Police!" and Shrake screamed, "Hey-hey-hey-hey, we're police, police here, for Christ's sakes," and then Larkin came up and waved his hat around the corner, and then out with his hands up, and they heard more shouting outside.

A uniformed cop came in, his face white and scared, clutching his gun like a hammer, and he shouted, "You got them?"

Lucas shouted back, "They went up, they're in the skyway," and they heard another gust of shots from up above, and Lucas and Shrake ran up the stairs, following their pistols.

COHN, CRUZ, AND Lane made the top of the stairs, breathing hard, paused in a niche of a wall. Lane slapped another magazine into his Uzi and Cohn asked Cruz, "Where'd they come from?" and she said, "I don't know—but it's the same guy we saw on television. The big dark-haired guy."

"Okay." Cohn looked both ways. "We got a fifty-yard run to the parking garage. If they're in the garage, we go down the side stairs and out the side and go for the street car."

"They won't let any cars out of the garage," Cruz said. "I think we gotta go for the street car. Right into the ramp, then down the stairs. That'll bring us out on . . ."

"We know. Let's go."

They ran then, sprinting, Lane still carrying the bag, but he heard clinking sounds as he went, and looked back and saw a trail of gold bars, like Hansel's bread crumbs . . .

They ran through the glass tunnel of the skyway, across a street; as they were coming to the entrance, a cop opened the door and stepped into the skyway, saw them, ducked back as Lane let loose another volley with the Uzi, and then they were at the entrance and they could hear the cop running down the stairs that led to the street—the stairs they were going to take.

"We go down the entrance ramp, the car ramp," Cruz gasped out.

They were at the ramp when the big dark-haired cop popped through the door behind them, fired a shot, and Cruz felt it hit her in the small of the back, felt a ripping wound at her stomach, and she went down and gurgled, "I'm hit . . ."

Lane fired a burst from the Uzi over her head, and then ran on down the ramp. Cohn was ahead of her, fifteen feet away and lower, already going down the ramp, and she saw him lift his gun, thought he was shooting at the cop. She never saw the muzzle flash.

Cohn shot her in the forehead and followed Lane down the ramp.

WHEREVER THEY WERE, they'd left the skyway—Lucas and Shrake could see sixty or seventy yards of it, and it was empty. "Parking garage," Lucas said. Shrake shouted at Larkin, who was coming up behind with his radio: "They're in the parking garage, the Clayton Ramp, get your guys outside . . ."

"There's gold bars." Larkin gasped. "There's little gold bars all over the place . . ."

Lucas ran toward the door, waited until Shrake caught him, then Shrake yanked the door and Lucas, ready to fire, saw the three of them just disappearing down the parking ramp and fired once, twice, and saw one of them go down. Another one opened with the Uzi and they both dodged back into the hall, behind the concrete blocks, and the slugs banged off the door and went God-knows-where, but neither one of them was hurt.

"I think I hit one." Lucas grunted. "They're running down the entrance ramp."

Shrake nodded and peeked around the door. "They're gone. You ready?"

"Let's go."

Using cars as cover, they made it to the mouth of the down-spiral as quickly as they could, found the woman lying on her back, dead, blank-eyed, a long brown wig lying beside her head, and a pistol lying by her hands. She'd been hit twice, once in the midsection, once in the forehead. "I only hit her once," Lucas said. "They're killing their own."

"Not leaving anybody behind to make a deal," Shrake said. "You ready?"

AT THE BOTTOM of the ramp, Cohn and Lane could see two exits—one read "Monthly Parking" and the other "Daily Parking," going in opposite directions. "Which way?" Lane asked.

"I don't know. We weren't supposed to come this way," Cohn said.

Lane said, "I'm down to my last clip. I'm going that way." He gestured at the monthly parking exit.

"I don't think that's right," Cohn said. "Ah, Jesus. I don't think that's right. I think it's out the other side."

"Well, I'm going this way," Lane said.

Cohn nodded. "I'm going the other way. If you make it, if I make it, I'll see you at the farm."

"See you there," Lane said, and he ran off toward the monthly parking with the jewel bag over his shoulder. The thought crossed Cohn's mind that he should shoot him, and take the bag; but he was too tired. Instead, he pushed himself up, shook his head, and headed toward the daily parking exit. There, he came up to a concrete pillar and looked out on the street; parked cars, but he didn't see the street car. Could he have been wrong? They'd come down the spiral . . .

He looked back, and heard footfalls coming down the ramp. Had to make a move.

He sprinted across the street, heard somebody shouting, saw two cops running after him, forty yards back, and he turned and fired two quick shots and broke out on the open street and looked around.

Wrong place. He was going the wrong way. Lane had been right. Almost made him laugh.

Instead of laughing, he sprinted hopelessly toward an ornate old building across the street that showed the mouth of an alley or intersecting street. One of the cops shot at him and he heard the round go by, close, but no cigar.

He turned down the street and up ahead, saw two more cops, fat guys, big fat guys. They were looking at him, bracing themselves, but didn't seem to have their guns out. He waved at them, shouted, "Help, help, gun, gun," and the cops looked past him for a moment and he closed to thirty feet and then one of them shouted, "Stop right there, stop . . ."

He realized then that they were not fat, they were armored. He lifted his gun and fired three times, fast, as he closed on them, the last from only a few feet, aiming low, at their exposed legs, and one of them screamed and went down and then he was past them.

The other cop fired at him and missed, and fired again and missed, and he was almost at the mouth of the street and a third shot missed and he turned the corner and forty feet away, two more cops, large guys, the guys from the hotel, he thought, and he said to them, "Shit!" and fired and the last thing he saw was the flash from the muzzle of one of their guns.

LUCAS CROUCHED OVER him. "He's gone. Was there another one?"

"I think so. I don't know where."

Shrake had fired the shot that killed Cohn; now he looked at the body and said, "Piece of shit."

"I better go back; you stay with this guy," Lucas said. An armored cop came around and shouted, "Police officer," and Lucas shouted back, "We're cops, we're police. You okay?"

"Got a guy hit bad, hit bad," the cop shouted. "He's hit bad . . ."

Lucas told Shrake, "Go see, get an ambulance started if this guy hasn't, I'm going back . . . You okay?"

"I'm good," Shrake said.

"Hang in there," Lucas said.

He turned and ran back the way they'd come, heading for the parking ramp. They'd come out on a diagonal street, and had gotten ahead of Cohn that way. Now he ran back on the same diagonal, into a cluster of cops spread around the ramp. They saw him coming, some turned toward him, but he could hear people shouting his name and he shouted back.

Larkin, the St. Paul sergeant, was there, and asked, "What happened?"

"We got two dead, the woman and Cohn," Lucas said; he reloaded. "We got one cop shot, I don't know who or what department, he was one of the control guys for the convention, got an ambulance started; what about here? Anybody hurt?"

Larkin's face was covered with blood from his facial and scalp cuts. "Not except for me getting nicked up. One guy got the shit scared out of him, he almost ran right into that fuckin' machine gun, but he made it out."

"That's the guy we're looking for. I'm not absolutely sure there were three, but I'm almost sure."

Larkin said, "There were. The clerk in the hotel says one guy held people in the chapel, as they came in. That was Cohn, I think. One guy drilled boxes and the woman watched the desk. They killed a guy in the hotel. Cold blood. Did it to prove that they'd do it."

"Ah, Jesus."

"Yeah."

"So what've we got around this garage?" Lucas asked.

"We're sealing it off now, for two blocks in every direction. Skyways, alleys, streets. We're checking everything that moves, getting ready for a sweep. We can have five hundred cops here in two hours. If we can make him hide, we'll get him."

"If he exists," Lucas said. "Let's start with the parking garage. Look under every car, don't let anybody out. Remember, the guy's got a machine gun."

LANE HAD GROWN up in the countryside, had followed twisted-up creeks for miles down to the river, had navigated mile-long cornfields with the corn so high that you couldn't see beyond your hands. He didn't get turned around easily, and he'd been pretty sure he was right about the exit; and hadn't been unhappy that Cohn had disagreed. If Cohn ran into the cops . . .

Lane made it out of the garage, looked around, and dashed up the street, beginning to hope, now, that he might again see his wife and daughters. He spotted the street car, groped and found the emergency key under the bumper, opened the car, threw the jewel bag in, slid into the seat, jabbed the key at the ignition a couple of times before getting it in, and he was rolling.

He turned at the first block, saw no cops, accelerated, turned again, saw a couple of cops standing on a street corner, cruised by them without looking, turned again, and was now on a major street.

In fact, he knew exactly where he was. He'd both walked and driven it, when he was scouting the hotel. He peeled off his gloves, let himself relax just a notch. If he went straight, he'd go down in a valley, then up a bridge above some railroad tracks, and if he made a right turn at the end of the bridge . . .

He wouldn't hit another streetlight until he got to Chicago.

That was almost halfway home.

26

ON SUNDAY, WEATHER slept in, until seven-thirty. Lucas usually got up with her, but this day, after the long week, he groaned and sat up, and Weather looked at him and patted him on the head and said, "Go back to sleep. You deserve it."

He dropped back on his pillow and was gone. When he finally did get up, a few minutes before nine o'clock, the house was unnaturally silent. He showered and shaved, put on fresh jeans—ironed, he thought, but not dry-cleaned—and wandered out to the kitchen in his stocking feet, carrying his shoes.

The place was empty, but a note dangled from the middle of the kitchen doorway, on the end of a strip of Scotch tapc.

8:45. Gone to bakery w/ Ellen+Sam. Letty still asleep. Back in hour—W.

HE YAWNED, STRETCHED, put a teaspoon of instant coffee in a cup, filled it with water and stuck it in the microwave, got a box of Honey Nut Cheerios from the cupboard and a bottle of milk from the refrigerator, carried it to the breakfast nook and went back to get the coffee when the microwave beeped.

As he took it out, Letty appeared, clutching her bathrobe, her hair a blond tangle, her eyes still sleepy; she was wearing bunny-rabbit slippers.

"Got more coffee?"

"This is instant."

"Okay . . ." She shuffled over to the counter and got down a cup, and repeated Lucas's ritual with the Folgers, complete with the yawn and stretch.

"Finish that *Mockingbird* essay?" Lucas asked.

"Yeah."

She carried the coffee over to the table.

"Is it any good?" he asked.

"I don't want to talk about that," she said. "I need to talk to you about something when Mom isn't here."

Lucas looked at her for a second, then said, "I don't keep much from your mom."

"You might keep this," she said. "It's for her own good."

"So . . . what?"

She took a sip of coffee and then said, "I didn't tell you the truth about the other night, with Juliet."

Lucas looked at her over his cup. "So what's the truth?"

"I was there—I just got there—when they came out of the house. Randy was yelling at Juliet and Ranch to 'get me.' Juliet didn't push him, and he slashed her with that stick, and then she took him over the edge. I heard the cop car coming, freaked out, and took off on my bike. I didn't want Mom to know, because it might scare her."

Lucas sighed. "Ah, jeez . . . But Briar said she hadn't seen you."

"I taught her how to lie," Letty said. "So she could deal with Randy."

"Letty . . ."

"That's not all . . ."

She told him about setting up Briar to get beaten. "I

knew it'd happen sooner or later—probably lots of times. I thought if I could get it to happen while I was there, I could call the cops, and they could get there, and Randy'd go back to prison. I didn't know they'd rape her."

Lucas looked at her for a bit, shook his head, poured some Cheerios.

Letty said, "I thought I better say something before, you know, tomorrow."

"Tomorrow?" He was confused.

"You know—the court thing."

"What does that have to do with this?"

She took another sip, then said, "You know—in case you wanted to change your mind."

"Aw, for Christ's sake, Letty. We're not going to change our minds. What're you thinking about?"

He actually saw her come unknotted: "I was a little worried," she said.

"I'm a little worried, too," he said. "If you called nine-one-one, that means your voice is on tape and there's no way to get it off. If Briar talks to somebody . . ."

"Why would anybody care?" she asked. "They know what happened. She got raped and beaten up, and she pushed Randy over the edge. You said they're not going to prosecute her, and besides, she's a juvenile."

"Ranch isn't," Lucas said. "If he brings you up . . ."

"You told me Ranch doesn't remember anything," Letty said.

"He doesn't—or says he doesn't. And he was so iced up, I believe him. But . . . there could be fallout. They could put him on trial, they could put Briar on the stand . . ." He shook his head. "There could be trouble."

"Nothing I can't handle," she said. "I'm a kid. I got scared and ran away after calling the cops, and never told you. What could they do to me?"

He looked at her for a moment, calculating, smiled, one of his smiles that tended to scare people—but not Letty—and said, "Nothing."

"And that's what we tell Mom, right?"

He thought for another moment and then said, "That would be best. We . . . let it go."

She stood up and said, "I've got to get dressed. I look like the witch in *The Wizard of Oz*."

As she was on her way out, carrying the cup of coffee, he said, "Hey."

She stopped.

Lucas said, "I'm not sure I'd have been smart enough to pull it off, when I was your age, but I would have tried. I would have tried the same goddamn thing. You take care of your family and you take care of your friends."

"Goddamn right," she said.

JESSE LANE WAS standing in the barn watching Max Gomez weld a broken tongue on the hay wagon, the place redolent with the burning metal, when his cell phone burped. He pulled it out of his pocket and looked at the face of it: "Caller Unknown."

He said, "Yeah?" half-expecting one of those robotic campaign recordings. Instead, he got Lindy.

"Jesse, you know who this is?"

"Where're you at?" he asked, stepping outside into the sunshine.

"That's for me to know and you to figure out . . . if you want to go to the trouble," she said. "I wanted to call and find out if you're going to hunt me down and kill me."

"I thought about it. Brute would have. He said so," Lane said.

"Yeah, well, if you're gonna try to get me, I'll have to try to get you first. I got the money to do it," Lindy said.

Lane laughed and said, "Hey, Lindy. Don't do that."

"We gonna let it go?" she asked.

"Fine with me," he agreed.

"You heard about what the cops say—that Brute shot Tate and Rosie."

"Don't surprise me none," Lane said. "He'd think that was the efficient thing to do."

"Efficiency isn't everything," she said.

"Nope, it ain't. It ain't even most things."

"I was right about the hotel. If I'd gone in there, I'd be dead, too."

"Yes, you were. Right," he said. A butterfly flittered by, and in the barn, Gomez killed his torch.

In the silence, she said, "I owe you some money."

"I got some money."

"I guess," she said. "I've been reading about it. Should be enough to prop up that fuckin' farm, and any other farms you know about."

"I did all right," he agreed.

"But I still owe you," Lindy said. "You know that little bridge over Cross Creek?"

"Yeah." The bridge was three miles down the gravel road. Kids would park there, walk a half mile upstream to a broken-down dam, and swim in the summer.

"If you park, and then go under the bridge, and walk down, away from the dam, to that big oak tree where they used to have that tire swing?"

"Yeah?"

"If you look behind the tree, you'll see a rock, right on the top. There's six hundred thousand dollars under the rock," she said. "Your share. I'm keeping the other shares."

Lane laughed with the joy of life and said, "You're a nice girl, Lindy."

"Brute used to say, 'You're not very nice, but you are pretty good.'"

Lane said, "Yeah. He did say that."

"So we're okay?"

"We're okay—and listen. You take care of yourself, hear?"

JUSTICE SHAFER WAS released by the Secret Service, without the .50-cal, and took off for Oklahoma. He thought about Juliet Briar occasionally, on the way back, but by the time he got home, she'd pretty much slipped his mind.

JULIET BRIAR WAS arrested for assault, but nobody much intended to prosecute, not after the rape charges were substantiated, and the beating wounds were photographed by the public defender's office. She was released to her mother, and when school started, went back. She thought about Justice Shafer, off and on for the first week or so, but then he slipped away.

The second week of school, she walked over to a McDonald's on University Avenue and was there, sipping on a strawberry shake, when Dubuque and Moline came in the door, and she took in the low-slung pants and the brass billfold chains, and felt a little thrum in her heart. The two men ordered and Dubuque was looking around when their eyes touched, and Dubuque's face lit up and he said to his brother, "Look what we got here."

Briar smiled at him, and Dubuque came over and said, "How you doin', Mama?"

"I'm doing okay," she said.

They chatted for a minute, then Moline came over, and they sat across from her in the booth, and talked about Randy. Randy had broken his neck and was paralyzed from head to foot.

"That motherfucker is a talking head, that's all he is," Moline said.

"He's a fuckin' paperweight," Dubuque said. "Ain't no good to a woman like you."

"I was gonna take care of him," Briar said, "but everybody said that I can't. He's too hurt. They're gonna put him in a home."

"A little shit falls on everybody's head," Moline said,

waxing philosophical. He took a fry, popped it in his mouth, let his eyes sink into hers. "Me 'n Dubuque—we been out riding around. That's our truck out there."

She looked out in the parking lot: a black Toyota 4Runner with chrome spinners on the wheels. "So what do you say, Mama?" Dubuque asked. "Wanna go for a ride?"

She laughed. "It's a fuckin' Toyota," she said.

They left without her.

A DOCTOR CALLED Weather on Monday evening, and Weather gave the phone to Lucas, and Lucas took it and listened, and said, "All right. When? All right. I can do that."

He hung up and Weather asked, "What was that about?"

"Randy Whitcomb wants to see me," Lucas said.

"I didn't think he . . . I thought he's pretty messed up."

"He is," Lucas said. "I don't know what he wants." He stood up. "I'm gonna run over there. Back in an hour."

He took the Porsche, idling through the evening light, thinking about the past week. Lots of problems out of the way.

The whole business of the moneymen never made it into the papers, because the deaths of the cops rode over it all, and the deaths of Cohn and Cruz seemed to settle it. Mitford, the governor's man, went away happy.

Unless they uncovered a man with two watch-like swastika tattoos, they wouldn't find the third robber, Lucas thought. As for DNA in the apartment, there were so many human traces—the place had been a model apartment, and hundreds of people had been inside, shedding hair and skin cells—that any results would be functionally and legally meaningless, as well as enormously expensive. So they didn't process for DNA.

The county attorney would decide later in the week whether to prosecute Whitcomb for assault and rape. Lucas expected a deal, an arranged guilty plea, which would allow Whitcomb to be remanded to a state hospital. No fuss, no muss, and little paperwork.

Ranch was another problem: the shrinks were having a close look at him. The public defender was claiming that Ranch couldn't assist with his own defense, because of drug-induced brain damage. Ranch, in fact, didn't seem to remember anything after a Fourth of July fireworks display in Stillwater, Minnesota, in 2006.

A lot of problems: gone.

AT REGIONS HOSPITAL, Lucas got the room number from a nurse, and at the nursing station asked for Dr. Grigor Papirian. Papirian came out and they shook hands and Papirian asked, "How's Weather?"

"Good, she's fine. Working all the time," Lucas said.

"Surgeons," Papirian said. Then, "You know about Mr. Whitcomb's accident?"

"Yes. I was actually there that night, after he'd been hurt," Lucas said.

Papirian nodded. "A tragedy. We knew as soon as we saw the film—the spinal cord was crushed. We took the pressure off, but the nerve was like mush."

Lucas nodded. "You know, he and I—we've had some trouble. He blamed me for his paraplegia, even though I didn't do the shooting. I can't think why he'd want to see me."

Papirian shook his head. "I know nothing about that. He said he wanted to see you, but he wouldn't say why. His vocal cords aren't functional, by the way—he can only communicate in a whisper. You may have to lean close."

"What's the prognosis? I mean, I know he's quadriplegic, but will he have any residual movement at all?"

Papirian was shaking his head, sadly. "Doubtful. There was too much damage. He'll probably die in a year or two.

That's what happens in these cases. They tend to go more quickly when they don't have family support."

They'd been walking along and now Papirian indicated a room, and said, "In here."

Lucas led the way in. Whitcomb was lying flat on a hospital bed, staring wide-eyed at the ceiling. He appeared to be dead, until he blinked, and Lucas said, "Randy."

Whitcomb's eyes shifted toward Lucas, and then widened a bit more. He whispered something, his lips barely quivering.

"You'll have to lean close," Papirian said.

Lucas leaned over him, one ear toward Whitcomb's face, smelling the sweat on him. "Randy?"

Whitcomb's whisper was soft, but clear enough. "Davenport . . ." Breath. "Davenport." Another breath. Finally, his eyes pleading, sweat shining from his immobile face:

"Davenport . . . Killlll meee . . ."

THE NEXT DAY, Tuesday, in third hour, her gym class, Letty sat on a metal folding chair as the gym teacher handed out fitness books, and held one up and called, "Letty West?"

Letty held up a hand. "My name is changed now. It's Letty Davenport."

A girl named Susan snickered. "What happened, you get married?"

Letty turned and looked at her, held her eyes for a second, showed some teeth, in a thin smile, and the other girl froze. Letty held her for another second, then turned back to the teacher.

"Letty Davenport," she said again.